TIES THAT BIND

After a bomb destroys Esme's London home and kills her son, she moves to Woodicombe, her old country house in Devon, to begin the impossible task of recuperating. Soon she is drawn back into the world of espionage, and as her marriage to Richard starts to crumble, a local airman pulls her closer.

Meanwhile, Lou awaits confirmation that she can relocate to Canada to be with her husband Douglas. Biding her time back home, she notices her father behaving strangely and disappearing at odd hours to wander the nearby cliffs. With rumours of spies afoot, she needs to learn the truth before anyone else does.

Lou and Esme still have battles to overcome as the war continues. Will Esme betray her wedding vows, or can she find her way back to Richard?

ROSIE MEDDON

—————————◆—————————

TIES THAT BIND

Complete and Unabridged

MAGNA
Leicester

First published in Great Britain in 2022

First Ulverscroft Edition
published 2022

*A catalogue record for this book is available
from the British Library.*

ISBN 978–0–7505–4932–5

Published by
Ulverscroft Limited
Anstey, Leicestershire

Printed and bound in Great Britain by
TJ Books Ltd., Padstow, Cornwall

This book is printed on acid-free paper

The Russell Family Tree

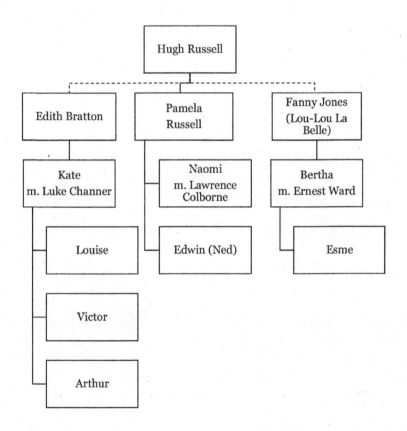

London, August 1943

1

In the Blink of an Eye

'I'm sorry, darling, but would you repeat that?'

Fearing she had misheard amid the hum of conversation and the clinking of cutlery, Esme Trevannion held her breath. Then, for good measure, she crossed her fingers.

'I *said*,' Richard replied, his voice held low as he leant across the table towards her, 'I've been to see the solicitor about buying the house in Teddington.'

So she hadn't misheard at all: her husband really did mean for them to buy that lovely Edwardian villa, in that smart tree-lined avenue just a minute's walk from the river.

'Goodness, Richard, that's wonderful! But why didn't you tell me? This past week you've let me ramble on about how perfect I thought the place was, without giving any hint whatsoever that you shared my enthusiasm, and yet all the time you were planning to go and —'

'Darling, please,' Richard leant further across to urge. 'No need to let the entire restaurant know our business.'

Flushing pink, Esme glanced to the adjacent tables. Had it not been for the Luftwaffe destroying every decent alternative within walking distance of Richard's office, then The Walsingham Hotel, with its nineteen-twenties Palm Court Dining Room, wouldn't even have made it onto her shortlist of venues for today's luncheon — and with good reason. Not only were their fellow diners predominantly Whitehall types sporting permanent frowns and complexions that were grey with the pallor of war but, with its glass-domed ceiling now boarded over to protect against flying glass from air raids, the mood was even more funereal than her mother had warned her it would be. However, since there was, as the popular saying went, still a ruddy war on, the choice had come down to The Walsingham or nothing.

To be fair, Esme thought as she withdrew her attention from the grey mass of Whitehall officialdom, their meals had been surprisingly good. Despite being restricted to three courses from the regulation five shillings menu, the food had been tasty, the chinaware Staffordshire, and the crystal, Royal Brierley — no mean feat when almost every other establishment on this particular street now stood in ruins.

'Sorry,' she said, her voice lowered. 'I'm just miffed that you chose not to tell me what you were up to.'

When Richard's expression changed to a grin, she realised how rare it had become to see him looking anything other than serious. By nature a man who abhorred spontaneity, the prospect of leaving anything to chance brought him out in a cold sweat. He simply *had* to plan for all possible outcomes. It was, to her surprise, a trait she had grown to find reassuring: through the air raids and the bombings, the terror and the uncertainty, he'd remained solid, constant, unshakeable — her lighthouse in a storm. Which was why for him to have sprung news of this magnitude upon her was nothing short of astonishing.

'To be truthful,' he said, 'I wasn't sure I could pull it off. Knowing how you'd fallen in love with the place, I didn't want to risk getting your hopes up before being absolutely certain I could actually buy it.'

Proof, if proof were needed, she thought, of how lucky she was to have married him. Not many men would show such consideration for a woman's feelings.

'Well, that's very thoughtful of you —'

'And then I thought, why not wait until today and tell you over lunch? Two celebrations for the price of one.'

Despite struggling to conceal her delight, Esme affected despair. 'And there was I, thinking you'd forgotten all about it.'

'Forgotten about turning thirty? Hardly.'

'No, silly.' Reaching between their empty glasses, she took hold of his hand. 'Not your birthday, the house. When you made no further mention of it, I thought you'd gone off the idea. I assumed you thought it either too far from town or else beyond you financially — beyond the means of your grandfather's trust.'

His grin softening to a smile, Richard squeezed her fingers. 'I happen to think the asking price perfectly reasonable. And I've known for some time how Grandfather's trust stands because I've had access to it since we got married.'

'And you really don't think Teddington is too far out? You're sure it won't make for an arduous commute every day? Only, you've always said that six stops on the tube and a short walk to the office is quite the luxury.' What she didn't want, was for the practicalities of moving so far from town to hit home later on and give him cause for second thoughts. If he changed his mind, her disappointment would be unbearable.

'Actually,' he said, his tone drawing her eyes to the sudden seriousness of his expression, 'I've been thinking I might hold onto the flat — at least until after the war. With the hours I'm expected to put in at the moment, and the state of the trains, it could turn out to be a useful bolthole.'

'And you can afford to do that?' she asked. While the attraction of keeping somewhere close to White-hall was obvious, running *two* homes — especially in wartime — did seem a touch profligate. Besides, if that *was* his intention, would there be enough money to pay for both Nanny White and a daily woman? She might have fallen in love with the Teddington house, but she didn't fancy having to run it all on her own.

'I won't lie,' Richard said. 'From a financial stand-point it will be tight . . . it will certainly swallow up every penny from my promotion. But I've weighed it carefully and believe it would be worth the scrimping.'

Scrimping? There was a word she'd rather not hear! 'Well, it's your money.'

'I prefer to think of it as *our* money.'

'I know you do. And that's incredibly generous of you,' she said, her mind already on the matter of how to redecorate that lovely drawing room. With its high ceilings and easterly aspect, it cried out for something light and airy. Perhaps a pale lemon colour for the walls. Or even *eau-de-nil*. 'But it's not *our* money. Not really.'

'Anyway,' he said, and with which she noticed how tightly he was suddenly grasping her hand, 'when we do eventually sell Anstruther, I was thinking it might not be a bad idea to set aside the proceeds for school fees . . .'

At the thought of their son, Esme's free hand went to her locket — the one Richard had given her the day they'd brought their darling Kit home from the hospital. Just last week she'd put a new photograph in it — one she'd snapped in the park on his second birthday. Hard to grasp just how quickly he was growing up, harder still to believe that they should be sat there discussing schools.

'That *would* make sense.'

'After all, who knows how much that sort of thing will cost after the war.'

'Mm.' Richard was right; making provision for Kit's school fees might seem dull now, but in a couple of years' time, they would probably congratulate themselves for their foresight.

'Especially since it won't just be Kit to pay for.'

'And especially if we want him to —' Wait. *What? Not just Kit?* Reluctant to trust her ears a second time, she stared back at him. 'Richard, are you saying —?'

'That once we're settled in the new house, we should have a second child?'

He'd *changed his mind?* He was no longer adamant they should wait for the end of the war?

'Oh, darling, yes! That would be perfect! After all, we did say we wanted four . . . and I am twenty-eight.'

'A *stunning* twenty-eight.'

'Seriously, Richard . . .' Good heavens. The day just kept getting better! '. . . you do mean it? About us having another child?'

'I do. I know we said we'd wait . . . but I've come to find life in this perpetual state of postponement depressing. So, Hitler be damned! The time has come to get on with it.'

'Well you'll get no argument from me.'

With Kit having been born just nine months after their wedding, and with daily life in the aftermath of the Blitz still a struggle, they'd agreed not to even think about having a second: London was no place to be raising a family, they'd said. But, for all their subsequent happiness, just lately, she *had* begun to feel as though they were only half living, that, like everyone, everywhere, they were just going through the motions, their ambitions and their dreams on permanent hold. What she *hadn't* realised was that Richard had been feeling the same way. For a man who didn't like surprises, that was twice this afternoon he'd taken the wind out of her sails!

Feeling him release her hand, she looked up to see him steal a glance to his wristwatch.

'Well, delightful though it is to be having lunch with my wife in the middle of the week —'

'It's not every day you turn thirty.'

'— I'm afraid I really must be getting back to the office.'

'And I suppose *I* should be getting back to Nanny White. You know what a stickler she is for punctuality.'

Moving to assist her to her feet, Richard smiled. 'I'll see you later then.'

'Not *too* much later, I hope.' Leaning across to kiss his cheek, she went on to whisper, 'Only, apparently, we've another baby to make.'

His burst of laughter brought about the raising of eyebrows at the adjacent table. 'Unfortunately,' he whispered back, taking her arm and leading her smartly away, 'the only chance *I* have of being home sensibly in the foreseeable future, is if you can somehow achieve what even our best brains have so far failed to . . . and bring about an end to this war.'

'If I thought it would get you home at a decent hour,' she said, the heels of her shoes clicking on the tiles as they crossed the hotel lobby, 'I'd hotfoot it to Berlin this very second and put an end to Hitler myself.'

Still laughing when they emerged onto the street, Richard shielded his eyes against the late summer sunshine and scanned for a cab. 'I half think you would, too.'

'Only *half*?' As she leant closer and lowered her voice, her lips took on a mischievous curl. 'Then you clearly don't appreciate quite how badly I want you home while I'm still awake tonight, Mr Trevannion.'

* * *

Two surprises in the same afternoon. Two *wonderful* surprises in the same afternoon!

In the taxi back to St John's Wood, Esme couldn't stop smiling. The moment they'd set eyes on the house in Teddington, she'd known that Richard was as taken with it as she was. But never, in her wildest dreams, had she expected him to just go ahead and buy it. Not that it would be theirs any time soon: as he'd said to her only moments ago, these things took time. She shouldn't get her hopes up. But was it too much to hope to be living there by Christmas? After a cosy little festive lunch *en famille*, they could take a stroll along the Thames. And what if it snowed! Imagine being able to take Kit out into that lovely long back garden to build a snowman.

Kit. Gosh, *he* was going to love it. Now that he was so curious about everything, a lawn for him to run

9

around on would be perfect. Perhaps they should get a swing and put it down near the apple trees at the bottom — better still, a pair of swings for when he had a brother or sister. What a surprise *that* had been, too — Richard suggesting they should have a second! She'd been thinking for a while that she didn't want the gap between Kit and the next one to become too great. But now, assuming she didn't have any problems falling pregnant again, he would have just turned three.

Glancing out through the window of the cab and recognising from the bombed-out parade of shops that they were on the high street, she gave a contented sigh. Kit could have the larger of the two bedrooms at the back, and the new baby could start in that little one next to it. Goodness, whoever would have thought that *she*, of all people, would become the sort of woman to get excited by the prospect of a new house and another child? Even after she and Richard had married, and she'd finally extricated herself from SOE, she hadn't exactly rushed to embrace domesticity. But now, here she was, a wife and a mother, her one-time activities for the war effort seeming like a different lifetime. Three short years and how life had changed. How she had changed!

'Beggin' your pardon, ma'am.'

Brought back from her thoughts to see the cab driver looking over his shoulder at her, she frowned. 'Yes? What is it?'

'Circus Road's blocked off. Should I take you the long way round?'

She craned to see. Bother. Now what was going on? 'No, it's all right. I'll walk from here. It will be just as quick.'

10

Her cab fare settled, she picked her way through the line of stationary vehicles to the corner of Circus Road, where a man wearing an ARP armband was preventing anyone from passing beyond a hastily put-together barrier.

'Sorry, love,' he said as she approached. 'Road's closed.'

'Yes. I can see that. But *why* is it? What's happened?'

'Gas main went up. Most likely damaged by that last bomb.'

Peering beyond him along the street, Esme frowned with displeasure. The bomb a few nights ago had certainly been a near miss. Even so, what a nuisance. Now she would be late getting home.

'So, which roads *are* open?' she asked. 'Only, I have to get to Anstruther Court before my little boy's nanny goes home at three.' As little as two minutes late and Nanny White got twitchy. Besides, she was bursting to tell Kit about the new house and its wonderful garden.

'Anstruther Court? 'Fraid you won't be going *there*, miss. That's the one what's been brought down. Nothing left *there* now save a pile of rubble —'

Seemingly of its own accord, Esme's hand shot to the barrier. *Anstruther Court? Brought down?*

'Wait. No. You can't mean . . .'

'Come on, now, folks, move along. Nothing to see here.'

Nothing left there now save a pile of rubble? What — their home was . . . gone? But what about Kit? And Nanny White. Oh, dear God, Kit!

Pushing her way beyond the barrier, Esme broke into a run. 'Kit! *Kit!*'

'Miss? Oi, Miss!' Above the pounding of her heart

she could hear the warden calling after her. 'You can't go down there! It's not safe . . .'

Not safe? What did safe matter? Her son was down there. And she had to get to him. She had to get to him . . .

2

Darkness

'You didn't come home.'

With the weariness of someone who'd been up all night, Richard Trevannion loosened his necktie, tugged it from beneath his collar, and started to unbutton his shirt. 'Not for want of trying, I assure you. But there's a real frenzy over this latest operation Churchill's come up with.'

Having heard it all before, Esme scoffed. 'There would be.'

'Truly. It's the single matter consuming all of us at the moment. I did think about telephoning you to say there was a possibility I might not make it back . . . but if there was any chance that you'd already gone to sleep, then I didn't want to wake you. I've only been able to get away now because the last of the uniforms finally cleared off.'

'But it's . . .' Turning to look, Esme squinted through the gloom to the bedside clock. '. . . seven in the morning.'

'Trust me, darling, I know. And I'm afraid I'm only here now for a shave and a clean shirt — if there's one to be had.'

With no recollection of whether Richard's shirts had come back from the laundry — let alone whether she'd sent them in the first place — Esme hauled herself up from the bed, pushed back the covers, and swung her feet down to the rug. 'Sorry. I couldn't say.'

13

She supposed that at some point during the night she must have slept; between those little pills she took every morning — supposedly to numb the pain of her grief — and the sleeping tablets she took each night, it was becoming steadily more difficult to distinguish between the two states of oblivion in which they kept her. They were certainly making it hard for her to remember to do things, the fact that she had clearly forgotten to secure the blackout — again — being a case in point.

As she sat staring down at her toes, the sound of the rain becoming heavier, she could tell that at the wardrobe, Richard had abandoned his search for a shirt and was stood regarding her. Clearly, he had something on his mind. And it didn't take a genius to work out what it was.

'Listen, darling, I've been thinking.'

She didn't look up. 'Oh?'

Coming to sit alongside her on the edge of the bed, he reached for her hand. 'I don't think we can go on like this. Either of us.'

Her response was wooden and stiff. 'Like what? Like parents without a child? Like two empty husks of human beings?'

'I meant —'

'Or did you mean like this?' With her free hand, she gestured generally about the dimly lit bedroom. 'The two of us coming and going in a couple of rooms of my parents' shut-up house, barely even seeing one another . . . let alone talking?'

His hand, when he wrapped it more tightly about her cold one, felt large and warm and ought to have been a source of comfort. But this morning it wasn't. In fact, the only feeling it generated within her was

14

one of guilt.

'All of those,' Richard said softly. 'But specifically, I meant you being here on your own all day. It's not your fault — far from it. I should be here with you, supporting you, I'm well aware of that. And if it wasn't for my work . . . and if it wasn't for me being utterly lost to know how to go about it, then I might be of more help in that regard. I know Mrs Colborne said we can stay here as long as we want — and don't get me wrong, I shall be forever grateful for the roof over our heads — but it's not good for you to spend all day alone in an empty house.'

When he paused and looked directly at her, she knew it was in the hope of seeing that she agreed. But, while everything he'd just said might be true, what was he expecting her to say? That since he had no choice but to be elsewhere, she would make more of an effort — that today, she would get up, dress, and go out and do something? For heaven's sake, barely two months ago they'd still had a home and a son.

'Richard —'

'You won't reconsider my suggestion of going to Windsor, I suppose?'

In her despair, she sighed. Not Windsor again.

'No, I won't. If it was just Great Aunt Diana there then I might think about it, but I couldn't tolerate being cooped up there with Mummy and Grand-mamma Pamela as well. Not all three of them. Not in that mausoleum. I'd rather be alone *here* than that.'

'Then I'm afraid it's settled. You're going to Wood-icombe —'

'*I am not.*'

'Yes, Esme, you are. Louise is more than happy to have you. She's said so countless times. Besides, it's

15

already arranged. I telephoned her yesterday.' When he squeezed her hand, presumably to elicit a response, she purposely kept quiet. 'Seriously, darling, you *can't* stay here like this. If you had work to go to each day . . . or had friends nearby . . . If I was able to be back here by a sensible hour each evening —'

'If, if, if. *If* that bomb hadn't dropped. *If* that gas main hadn't exploded. *If* I'd taken Kit to the park that afternoon instead of dallying with you over lunch . . . Besides, what about you? Why is it all right for *you* to be alone here but not me?' Her point made, she stared back at him.

'Because I'm *not* alone here, am I? Because *I* have no choice but to spend my every waking hour in Whitehall. Because from the moment I walk into my office, I have to give my mind fully to my work. And if Churchill's proposed operation gets the go-ahead, then it's only going to get worse — there will be even fewer chances to keep normal hours — which is why I want you to go to Louise. Either that, or you go to Aunt Diana's and make the best of it. Not only do you need the company, but you'll be safer out of town. Clarence Square has had several near-misses over the years . . . and I know for a fact you haven't been going down to the basement when the siren sounds.'

There was no use denying it. 'What's the point?' she said instead. 'If this is what living is like, then what does it matter whether —'

'The point, Esme,' Richard said shortly, 'is that Hitler might already have taken my son but there's no need to make it easy for him to take my wife as well.'

Slowly, she turned to regard him. 'But it's all right for you to stay here and let him take *you*?'

16

His grasp on her hand tightened.

'Of course not. Once you're gone, I shall stop coming here. Two floors beneath Whitehall there's a dormitory with bunks, bathrooms and a canteen. I've put in a request for a place there and fully expect it to be granted. If I find myself desperate for a change of surroundings, I can always go to Father's club. And your Uncle Ned has said he's more than happy to sign me in as a guest at his place, as well.'

Men and their clubs. It was all right for them. But where was the equivalent for women? Where did *they* go for company and respite? To be fair, going to Woodicombe did make sense. It *would* be better than being here, where she rarely ventured beyond this bedroom and its adjacent bathroom. It would also be better than Aunt Diana's. As company went, Cousin Lou — or *Louise* as she liked to be called since she'd married Lieutenant Douglas Ross RCN — was all right. More than all right really.

'Well, if I must.'

'You'll go? To Louise?'

Feeling her shoulders slump under the weight of her resignation, Esme exhaled heavily. 'If it gives you one less thing to worry about, then yes,' she said, 'I'll go.'

Finally, Richard released her hand. 'Thank you. It doesn't have to be for months on end — just until this push at the office is over . . . until we both feel able to start looking to the future and . . . planning what we're going to do. And I shall pop down and see you whenever I can. I shall put in for some leave. If necessary, I shall say that for the benefit of my own health, I need a few days of sea air with my wife.'

'Yes.'

17

'Who knows, it might even be nice to spend Christmas there . . .'

Christmas. Kit's third — or it should have been. Everyone said Christmas with a two-year-old was the most magical one of all.

With a slow shake of her head, she fought back tears. 'Perhaps.'

'Well then, before I head back to the office, I'll telephone Louise to confirm . . . unless *you* would rather do that?'

She could see that he wanted her to. Right this minute, though, she couldn't face talking to anyone, her cousin included. 'No, you do it.'

'Very well. And I'll get you a train ticket for Saturday.'

'If you wish.'

'Now, do you think there will be a suitcase here somewhere?'

She nodded. There was bound to be something up in the trunk room. 'I should imagine so.'

'And you have enough clothes to take? You wouldn't like to make a trip to . . . oh, I don't know . . . Bourne & Hollingsworth? Or one of the other places you like? We still have some of those emergency clothing coupons they gave us.'

Ordinarily, the prospect of going shopping for new outfits — even in blitz-damaged Oxford Street, and even with the newly reduced coupon allowance — would put a spring in her step. But, having lost everything except Richard himself, clothes had come to feel like little more than a necessity — and only then when a nightdress wouldn't suffice. Some slacks might be a good idea, though. And perhaps a pair of boots if there were any to be had. Woodicombe

18

usually meant mud — even if it *hadn't* been raining for weeks on end.

'I'll think about it. I'll ring the laundry and get a couple of things cleaned and pressed. And your shirts done.'

When Richard bent to plant a kiss on her forehead, she thought he looked fractionally less wrought. How awful of her to have become so selfish. How awful to be unable to console him in his own grief, to have simply become another of his worries.

Well, if, in the short term, her decamping to Woodicombe eased his burden, then she would do as he asked and go. In truth, what did it matter where she was? Whether she went to Devon or remained in London, it wouldn't bring Kit back. Nothing would. Wherever she was, and whatever she did while she was there, it was clear that her life was never going to be the same again.

3

In the Bosom of Family

'You all right, there, love?'

Fingering the locket at her throat, Esme looked up from the remains of her supper. Fried liver never had been a favourite of hers but, served with mashed potato, a thick gravy and plenty of crisply fried onions, her aunt's presentation of it was more palatable than some she'd had to force down. It also made a change from the sandwiches of either corned beef or tinned ham she'd taken to surviving on while in Clarence Square.

'Oh, yes, thank you, Aunt. I'm fine. I think the warmth in here was just making me drowsy.'

It was now a little over a week since Esme had arrived at Woodicombe but, so far, the enforced change of scenery had done nothing to lift her mood, nor to stop her from dwelling on her loss. It was no one's fault; everyone had been immensely kind and wonderfully welcoming. But whether she woke up in London or Devon each morning changed nothing: Kit was still dead.

'It *is* a trifle warm,' Kate Channer agreed, getting up from the table with its jolly checked cloth to stack their plates. 'Better that than chilly, though, I always say.'

Returning her aunt's smile, Esme nodded. 'Much better, yes.' Carrying the serving dishes, she followed her aunt through to the scullery.

'Lou tell you about my little sideline?' Kate asked, her tone conversational as the two of them stood waiting for the sink to fill with water. 'My little . . . business, if you will?'

Watching the painstakingly slow trickle from the tap, Esme tried to recall what Louise had told her of family matters. While she might not have been the most attentive of listeners these last few days, she was fairly certain she would remember her cousin mentioning Aunt Kate going into business. 'No,' she said. 'I don't believe she did.'

'Ain't nothing to get excited about,' Kate went on, reaching to the shelf for the box of soda and sprinkling a handful into the sink. 'Though I rather grandly call it my guesthouse business, in truth it's nothing of the sort.'

A guesthouse that wasn't a guesthouse? Esme was intrigued. 'Do tell.'

'Well, see, a few weeks back, I had a visit from some air force chappie who said he was looking for billets for personnel — not long-term ones, just the odd night here and there. 'In need of somewhere quiet,' he said to me. Wanted somewhere folk could have a day or two of fresh air and rest before moving on.'

Watching as her aunt took her dishmop to a dinner plate, Esme frowned. 'Moving on where?'

'You can leave them plates in the rack to drain, love. Just dry the cutlery and whatnot. As to the whys and the wherefores of what these folk get up to, well, I didn't think it my place to ask. Anyhow, I told this fellow it wasn't down to me alone, and that he'd have to ask permission from the owner. So, I wrote down your Grandpa Hugh's details for him and thought n'more of it. Blow me down, barely a week later, he's back. 'First two chaps arrive at the weekend,' he says. 'They'll be no trouble, keep themselves to themselves'. And then he hands me a list of what I'm to provide for them, along with two ration books to use as I see fit, no questions asked. Oh, and the particulars of some feller who would telephone each time beforehand — you know, to say when to go to the station and collect them.'

'Goodness.' Was she just being overly suspicious, Esme wondered, or did something about this arrangement sound a bit . . . well, a bit off?

'Oh, and he gave me an envelope with ten guineas in it,' her aunt went on, 'to help with the cost of anything I needed to get set up. Couple of days after that, he delivered a motorcar and explained that when the time came, these chaps were to be taken to an RAF base.'

'And have you had many of these . . . guests?' Esme asked. For her aunt's sake, she hoped sincerely that everything was all above board.

'Just the two so far. But see, I'm minded it could be a nice little earner, 'specially with being able to get the extra rations . . . you know, regardless. And that's before reckoning on the handiness of having the motor.'

'Well, good for you,' Esme said. And she meant it, too. It was heartening to come across a woman actually benefitting from doing her bit. In her experience, the contributions of women to this war were being shamefully overlooked.

'And what about you, love?' Kate asked, feeling about in the sink for the plug and then pulling it out. 'How are you faring now? If you don't mind my saying, you still look terrible drawn.'

22

Watching the dirty water eddying down the drain, Esme gave a lengthy sigh. 'To be truthful with you, Aunt Kate, I'm not doing all that well. I'd like to tell you otherwise, but there's really no point in me saying I'm all right when it's plain to everyone that I'm not.'

'No, love.'

'I seem all adrift. I feel nothing and yet I feel everything. I feel . . . well, what I suppose I'm trying to say is that while I no longer seem capable of appreciating anything good, everything that's bad seems magnified several times over. For much of the day, I can't seem to put my mind to anything, and time seems to stand still. And yet, perversely, when I do have something to do, I don't seem able to concentrate long enough to do it. I don't seem to have the stamina for anything but the simplest of tasks, sometimes not even those.' Having started to speak openly, Esme felt drawn to keep going. 'Mornings are the worst. For a few fleeting seconds when I first open my eyes, everything seems normal. But then, with an almighty crash, I remember. I remember that my son is dead. And back comes the ache in my chest . . . and the twisting blade in my stomach.'

'I remember feeling like that. Cruel, ain't it?'

Oh, dear God, of course! How could she have forgotten the Channers had lost a son? 'Forgive me,' she said quickly. 'I'd forgotten about Arthur.'

Seemingly unperturbed, Kate continued. 'Three years he's been gone now. And were you to ask me how I got through it, I'd have to say I haven't the least idea. What I can say, though, when I look back on those early weeks and months, is that suffering so sudden a loss seems to bring on more than just grief.'

Uncertain what her aunt meant, Esme put down

the tea towel and turned to regard her. 'I'm afraid I don't understand.'

'Looking back now, it seems to me that before you can grapple with the grief, you got to first overcome the shock of the thing. Let's face it, any death — but 'specially one so unexpected and in one so young — has to be the biggest shock there is.'

Perhaps her aunt was right. Perhaps, by waking every morning to recall afresh what had happened — even after all these weeks — it was a sign that she had yet to even accept her loss, let alone learn how to live with it. Grief or shock, though, what did it matter? Kit was still dead. 'Worst of all,' she said, 'is not being able to see how I will ever feel any differently.'

Putting down the frying pan she'd been rinsing, Kate sighed. 'Love, I should like to be able to tell you that the pain goes away — that the leaden ache in your chest ceases to be. But it doesn't, not entirely. It does fade sufficient for you to get on with the business of everyday life though. Eventually, you do lose the feeling that you can't even think straight. I won't pretend you go back to being the person you were before, because from what I've experienced of it, you don't. But you do at least find a way to go on. And though no one can make it better, nor tell you how to feel, and though each of us has to find our own path through it all, you got to hold onto the fact that it will get better. Something else I know for certain is that while nothing I say will seem of any help to you this very minute, you got to cling to the knowledge that you won't *always* feel as lost as you do right now.'

'No?' How dearly she wished she could believe that!

'And don't forget either that you're not alone. Whatever you need, whether that be to talk . . . or not to talk, we're all of us here to help you.'

Feeling tears welling, Esme nodded. 'Thank you,' she said. 'Sometimes, I *do* want to talk about him — Kit, I mean. But it's plain that even just my being in your home has left you all feeling obliged to tiptoe around so as not to upset me . . . and so, the last thing I want to do is to make matters worse by keeping talking about him.'

Bringing her hands to rest upon the edge of the sink, Kate turned towards her. 'Death comes hard to everyone, love — even to those folk one step removed from the loss. But, while it's only natural for everyone to fear saying something to upset you, that doesn't mean you can't talk about him.'

Although her aunt's words were filled with kindness, for Esme, they did nothing to ease the unrelenting ache in her heart.

'It's true what you say — about people being afraid to upset me. It's even true of Richard. And Mummy, too. Richard, it would seem, *can't* bring himself to talk about Kit, and Mummy, I think, is simply terrified of saying the wrong thing. Do you know, at his funeral, the only person to talk about Kit as though he was an actual person was Great Aunt Diana. She reminded me about Christmas morning, when he wouldn't let anyone help him to open his present. Those few words from her were the most comforting thing anyone said to me that whole day. As for Grandmamma Pamela, well, do you know what *she* said?'

Pressing her lips together as though she had a pretty good idea, Kate smiled. 'Knowing Pamela Russell, I doubt I'd be far out.'

' 'Don't worry,' she said to me. 'You're young. You'll have others.' You'll have others! As though I'd

25

accidentally killed off a prize clematis or lost a necklace. I mean, yes, obviously, Richard and I sincerely hope that we *do* have more children. But they won't ever be a replacement for Kit. How could they be? He was unique. Each *person* is unique. If it had been *my* funeral, would she have gone up to Richard and said 'Don't worry, you'll have others'? Would she? I don't think so. So why is it any different simply because Kit was so young?'

'It isn't,' Kate said softly. 'It isn't at all. And although unlike your Aunt Diana I don't have memories of Kit to share with you, if there's things you'd like to tell me about him, then I should always be happy to sit and listen.'

Feeling the warmth of Kate's damp hand on the back of her own, Esme raised a smile. 'Thank you,' she said. 'You're all being so very kind to me. And if I don't tell you how much I appreciate you having me here, and the boundlessness of your patience with me, then please know that I'm deeply grateful.'

'Like I said, love, we'll be of whatsoever help we can —'

'Esme . . .' Hearing her name, Esme turned to see her uncle standing in the doorway. '. . .forgive me butting in but Richard's on the telephone.'

Desperate not to waste precious seconds of his call, Esme dropped the tea towel onto the drainer and dashed along the passage and up the stairs. Panting for breath, she grabbed the receiver. 'Hullo? Richard? Are you still there?'

'Darling, hello. Yes, I'm still here.'

'Sorry . . .' she said, trying to slow her breathing, 'but I was down in the scullery . . . with Aunt Kate.'

'In the scullery, eh?'

26

'Yes . . .'

'And how are you?'

Unsure how to reply, Esme hesitated. 'Perhaps . . . a tiny bit better.' Her dishonesty made her wince. Why tell a lie? Why do that? *You do it*, she reminded herself, *to spare him worrying more greatly than he already does.* Besides, she hadn't been completely untruthful: at least here, she was getting up in the morning, which, given that for the seven or eight weeks they'd been in Clarence Square she'd rarely got out of bed, had to count for something. *A step in the right direction*, as her mother would say.

'That's good to hear.'

'Yes.'

'And what have you been up to these last few days?'

Time, perhaps, to be more open with him. 'If I'm brutally honest, not that much.' True so far. 'Everyone here is unbelievably busy. They volunteer for everything. Most days, Louise and I do manage a walk together — usually a rather wild and blowy one.'

'That's good. And is all that sea air helping you to sleep any better?'

Another line to tread carefully. 'Since I'm still taking the pills, I couldn't really say. What about you? Are you home?' *Home.* Huh. 'In Clarence Square, I mean.'

'At this precise moment, yes. I managed to get away from the office decently for once. But only so that I might pop in to get my things.'

'You've managed to get a bed in the hostel then?'

'I have. I'm going back there after this. But I'll duck out during the evenings to call and see how you are. I say, I suppose it's all right for me to leave your odds and ends here — the stuff you didn't take with you?'

27

Unable to picture the 'stuff' to which her husband was referring, Esme nodded. 'Of course. No one will mind.' In truth, there was no one to mind. 'Richard?'

'Yes, darling?'

'I'm sorry.'

'For what?'

'For . . . everything. For not being there for you. For putting you under so much strain when you've already so much else to worry about . . .'

'Heavens, Esme, there's no need to apologise. I hate that we're apart. It's ghastly. But we agreed that you should have company . . . that it would be for the best.'

It wasn't quite what she'd meant. Not that it mattered. 'I know.'

'And you do sound a little brighter.'

'Do I? That's good.'

'Well, look, darling, believe it or not that's our three minutes up, so I'd better say goodbye. But I'll telephone again in a few days.'

'Yes.'

'Take good care then.'

'You too.'

'And keep it up.'

'Yes.'

'Goodnight, darling.'

'Goodnight, Richard.'

The receiver back on its cradle, Esme wiped at the corners of her eyes. Why was it that, no matter how badly she wanted to speak to him, the moment he telephoned she couldn't bring herself to be honest with him? Why lead him to believe she was recovering when, in truth, she didn't feel the slightest bit different? To spare him the pain of knowing that she was

28

still no better? To try and convince herself that she was healing? Why? Why lie?

Shivering in the chilliness of the vast hallway, Esme wondered what to do with herself. Louise wouldn't be back from her shift until gone midnight. Uncle Luke was about to go on duty with his Home Guard detachment again, and Aunt Kate had said something about needing to finish running up a pair of curtains for the accommodation above the stables — for one of the rooms to be used by these new guests of hers. So much for Woodicombe providing her with some company, then.

With no better idea, she went up to her room, switched on the lamp and sat on the edge of the bed. By any normal measure it was far too early to think about retiring for the night. Trying to sleep at this hour would only make the hours of darkness seem to last even longer. But what else was she going to do? She supposed she *could* write to her mother. She really *ought* to. She could even telephone her at Aunt Diana's for a chat. But to what end? To be fed yet more platitudes about time being the best healer? To be told yet again that fresh air and exercise were balm for a tortured mind? No, thank you very much. She'd had her fill of all that at the funeral. Drivel of that nature would be of no more help now than it had been then.

Glancing about the room, her eyes came to rest upon the copy of *Candleford Green* that Richard had bought for her on Waterloo station. *To help pass the time on the train*, he'd said as he'd tucked the little book into the top of her bag. But she hadn't even opened the cover, let alone tried to summon the concentration necessary to read the words, no matter how charming the story was supposed to be. And she felt no more inclined to do so now, either.

In the end, feeling utterly lost, she sat at the little dressing table and proceeded to unpin her hair. That done, she went to the bathroom, wiped away the last traces of her make-up and brushed her teeth. Returning with a glass of water, she put on her nightdress and reached to remove her locket. As she had done every night since his death, she opened the clasp and stared down at the tiny little face of Kit beaming back at her. Then she brought it to her lips, kissed him goodnight and placed it gently on the bedside table. Having swallowed her sleeping pill with a mouthful of water, she got into bed, where the chill of the starched sheets forced her to curl tightly into a ball. Tomorrow, she must remember to ask for a hot water bottle. Tomorrow, she must hope to feel less numb. Or, perhaps, to feel more numb. Just lately, it was becoming difficult to decide which of those two states felt least awful.

★ ★ ★

'Hello there, love. How did you sleep?'

'Quite well, thank you, Aunt Kate.'

'Morning, Esme. Sleep well last night, did you?'

'Yes, fine, Uncle Luke. Thank you for asking.'

It was the following morning and as usual, Esme arrived in the kitchen to face the same round of well-meant enquiries as on each of the previous days, and to which, by turns, she responded with precisely the same answers. That she should awake each morning to find everything precisely the same as the day before had ceased to surprise her. Even the tone of

30

the news being broadcast by the BBC Home Service never seemed to be any different.

'...*in the Mediterranean, the German army has now conquered the island of Kos. By contrast, in France, the liberation of Corsica by Free French forces has begun, while in Italy, the British 78th Infantry Division's 11th Brigade has* —'

'Tell you what,' Luke said, pausing between taking bites from a slice of toast spread with margarine and gooseberry jam, 'if you've need of a few breaths of air later on, then once I've cycled down with the wireless accumulators to be charged, you could come up the rectory with me. I've a cartload of logs for the orphanage. Nice change of scenery for you ... if you fancy it.'

With no little effort, Esme fixed what she hoped was a grateful smile. 'Thank you for the suggestion, Uncle. But perhaps I'll wait and see how the weather looks.'

'Or,' Aunt Kate chipped in, bustling across with the kettle to top up the teapot, 'if you've no mind to go muddying your shoes, I'm due down at the WVS for a couple of hours this morning. It's the weekly knitting party and we're doing gloves for sailors. You'd be surprised how many pairs we can get done in two hours, especially when there's someone to keep us plied with tea.'

Sit and knit? With a group of middle-aged women? To Esme, it sounded the very definition of torture. 'Thank you, Aunt,' she said carefully, 'but I'm not sure even the most desperate of sailors would want a pair of gloves that *I'd* knitted.'

Returning the kettle to the range, Kate brought her hands to her hips, her expression one of mild determination. 'Nonsense. There's plenty of help at hand if you go wrong. Besides, there's nothing like having to concentrate on counting stitches for taking your mind off things. And we're not *all* old fogeys. Some of the women bring their daughters, granddaughters even . . .'

Given the kindliness of her aunt's smile, Esme felt mean declining. But women knitting — and, no doubt, gossiping — was something she just couldn't face. 'Maybe next time.'

'Well, I shan't force you,' her aunt replied matter-of-factly. 'Nothing worse than being coerced into doing something you've taken against.'

Now she felt even more guilty. 'It's not that. It's just —'

'Truly, love, you've no need to apologise. Just promise me you won't stay cooped up indoors all day. At least say you'll go for a walk for an hour or so. Maybe even wait and go with Lou once she's up. It's not a bad day out there, least, not for the time of year, it idn't.'

Time to relent, Esme supposed. 'All right. I promise you I'll go outside.'

The trouble was, while she might have fended off this current round of invitations, she knew that her reprieve would only be temporary; as had become the pattern this last week, once Louise got up from sleeping in after her night shift, the agony of ducking out of doing things would start all over again.

Indeed, when, much later, Esme returned to the kitchen to lend a hand preparing lunch, it was to find her cousin smiling broadly as she finished reading a letter.

'From Douglas,' Louise explained, pushing the

sheet of paper back into its envelope. To Esme, the brightness of her expression made her appear girlish and gay, the shorter length of her newly cut hair making her look stylish and modern.

'Is he able to write to you very often?'

Louise continued to smile. 'Never misses a week. But it's not unheard of for two envelopes to arrive together . . . or even in the wrong order!'

'At least he's able to write,' Esme observed.

'Yes. So, what did you find to do with yourself this morning?'

Steeling herself to decline whatever invitation her cousin was about to extend, Esme shrugged. 'Not much. I started a letter to Mummy . . .' It wasn't a lie; she'd penned at least three lines on a sheet of notepaper before giving up. 'Started reading a book.' Now, though, she *was* in the realms of exaggeration since all she'd done was pick up the little tome, flick disinterestedly through the closely printed pages and put it back down again.

'In that case,' Louise said, 'I think I'll do as Dad suggested and take you with me when I go on shift up at the beacon tonight. When he first suggested it, I said I didn't think you'd want to stand about getting frozen to the bone . . .'

Frozen to the bone? Her cousin wasn't wrong about that. But how to get out of it without sounding ungrateful?

'You know, I never really have understood what it is you do,' she ventured. Rather damningly, it was true: although her cousin must have explained a dozen or more times over the last couple of years, she'd always been rather too wrapped up in affairs of her own to pay much attention.

33

'I'm a member of the Royal Observer Corps.'

'Yes,' she said with a smile, 'I know *that*.'

'I've been doing it since they first let women in, about two years ago.'

'All right. But what do you actually *do*?'

Louise drew a breath. 'Officially, we detect, identify, track and report aircraft.'

Heavens. She hadn't been expecting anything *that* complicated. Rather unkindly, she'd always assumed that her cousin filed reports or made tea. 'And where is this post thing you go to?' she asked, still half expecting it to be the case.

'Well, do you recall, summers past, the two of us going up on the headland — can you picture what it's like up there?'

Unexpectedly, Esme found she could see it clearly: an exposed clifftop covered with springy turf, mounds of prickly gorse, and very little else. 'I can, yes,' she said. 'Walking through the heather up there one August I got stung on the wrist by a bee.'

Louise gave a surprised laugh. 'Goodness, that's right. You did. And when we came back, Aunt Naomi gave us a proper scolding for being up there in the first place.'

Recalling both the pain of the bee sting and the smarting from the humiliation of being reprimanded in front of the whole family, Esme gave a dismayed shake of her head. 'She did, yes. And I don't think we ever went back up there again.'

'Well, anyway,' Louise resumed, 'up there is our lookout — or, more properly, our *observation post*. It's a little bunker from where we scan the sky with binoculars for enemy aircraft and then, if we happen to spot one, use a device to work out its location and

34

altitude . . . and estimate its speed. There's something of a knack to it. Anyway, once we've calculated the details, we telephone them through to Control Centre, where they plot the sightings from all the posts in the southwest of England onto a single map.'

'To what end?' Esme asked.

'To alert the RAF to German aircraft.'

'Oh, yes, of course.' Suddenly, it was obvious. 'You know, I quite envy you.'

'Envy me?'

'Yes. Because while you could have curled up and moaned about the lousy hand this war has dealt you, you don't. You show stoicism . . . and . . . and fortitude. Despite having barely seen Douglas since the day you married him, you continue to throw yourself into helping others. At the same time, here am I, without even one half of your hardships, and yet the only thing of any value I've done since getting married is have Kit. And now even that turns out to have been for nothing. Sometimes, when I compare myself to you, I feel utterly worthless.'

'I wouldn't compare yourself to me,' Louise replied, a note of alarm in her tone. 'The only reason I do any of these things is to fill the enormous hole in my life . . . and because *I* envy *you*. Three years I've been married and yet I know nothing of being a wife, let alone a mother. Nor can I see, with the way things are going, when I ever will. So, yes, I do try to help others, but trust me, it has nothing to do with selflessness. I do it purely to keep my mind from dwelling upon things over which I have no control — all the things I'm missing out on by being an ocean apart from my husband. Without something to fill my days and to force me to consider others, I'd be lost. I don't

35

particularly want to do Mrs Harding's bidding up at the church hall. She can be quite the old battleaxe when it suits her.' With a grin, Louise went on, 'Mum reckons she never got over being turned down for evacuees and chooses to direct all her pent-up energies into the WVS instead. Anyway, neither do I especially *want* to spend four nights a week in a little concrete bunker on a wild clifftop. But feeling useful is what helps me to get up each morning and spend another day without Douglas. And I think, if you found something similar to fill *your* days, you might find that your . . . situation becomes a little more bearable, too.'

Reflecting upon her cousin's words, Esme exhaled a long sigh. Louise wasn't entirely wrong — not at the most fundamental of levels, she wasn't. But how on earth, feeling as she did, was she supposed to apply her mind to anything more than the essentials?

'I don't doubt you're right about the benefits of being useful,' she said. 'But you seem to have rather more talents than I. I mean, this observation thing . . . I couldn't do that. I couldn't take on that sort of responsibility.'

Apparently considering her point, Louise pressed her lips together. 'I don't deny there's a responsibility to it. But that's the point. The long hours of observing — and the calculating and reporting in particular — take concentration and stamina. But those are the very things that stop me fretting about Douglas. Not only that, but it gets me out of the house to see other people too. There's a little team of us. Mr Aldridge from up near the rectory does it full-time, and me and four other women are part-time, which amounts to us giving up twenty-four hours a week of what the corps rather quaintly calls our 'leisure' in order to 'help out'.'

Esme gave an ironic smile. War or no war, attitudes towards women everywhere were still slow to change. 'And are you paid for forgoing your 'leisure' to 'help out'? Or are you a volunteer in the truest sense?'

'I get 10d. an hour, which is a bit rich when Mr Aldridge gets a shilling and thruppence for doing the same thing.'

To Esme, the difference came as no surprise. 'And do you ever see any aircraft?'

'You'd be astonished by just how many. Though mainly they're ours. You get to learn pretty quickly which is which.'

Unable to help it, Esme laughed. 'I should hope you do.' With that, she spotted a reason to decline her cousin's invitation, because, despite understanding why Louise wanted her to go, she knew in her heart that it wouldn't do any good.

'So, given the nature of what goes on up there, I wouldn't even be allowed in, would I? Surely what you do is top secret. And the last thing you need would be to get into trouble on my account.'

When Louise paused to think for a moment, Esme felt a twinge of meanness.

'It's true we're not allowed to talk about the equipment we use . . . nor about the sightings we report. Or about Ops Room. But, since I'm certain you once told me you'd signed the Official Secrets Act, I really don't think that would be a problem.'

Bother. She hadn't expected her cousin to remember that. So, now what did she do? Seemingly, the only way she was going to get out of this was to wait until teatime and then say she felt unwell. But could she really do that when Louise was only trying to help? Could she keep on lying to the very people showing her sympathy and putting themselves out for her — even if her deceit was only intended to spare their feelings?

'Though I feel feeble to even be admitting it,' she said carefully, 'I really don't fare very well in the cold . . .'

'All right. Don't come then. I thought that's what you'd say anyway. But, if you're not coming on duty with me tonight, then this afternoon, you're coming up the church hall. A couple of days back I promised Mrs Harding I'd go and help her set up for the clothing exchange. And *you*,' Louise said, wagging a finger at Esme, 'are coming with me whether you like it or not.'

'The clothing exchange?' Realising she had somehow let herself become cornered, Esme thought frantically. If she wasn't careful, this could be a case of 'out of the fat and into the fire'.

Leaning against the edge of the sink, Louise frowned. 'You haven't heard of clothing exchanges?'

'I haven't.'

'Saints alive, Esme. Not even after going through the Blitz?'

'Not even after that, apparently. Although, from your tone, I feel as though I should be ashamed to admit it.'

'Well, since emergency clothing coupons only go so far, and take a long old time to even get, the WVS collects clothing to give to families bombed out of their homes . . .' Apparently realising what she'd just said, Louise looked sharply down. 'Christ, Essie. I'm so sorry. I forgot. You of all people know first-hand what that's like.'

Moving nearer, Esme reached to touch her cousin's hand. 'I'm not sure I do, not really. What I mean is, I can't say with any honesty that I know what it's like for most people. When we lost Anstruther Court, we were extraordinarily fortunate to have families with empty homes in town. And not only did Mummy let me go through her wardrobe and take whatever I needed, but Richard had sufficient income to enable us to make use of the coupons we were given. So, at no stage were we destitute.'

'Be that as it may,' Louise said softly, 'I should have thought before opening my mouth.'

'It's all right. Besides, I want to hear about this clothing exchange.'

Louise looked as though she somehow doubted it. 'Well,' she said nevertheless, 'while we might not have refugees — and we're fortunate in that round here, we don't have bombed-out families either — we do have evacuees and we do have ordinary folk struggling to make ends meet, especially women — widows in particular — with growing children. I mean, let's face it, clothing coupons are only any good if you've got the money to make use of them. So, once a fortnight, mothers can come to the church hall and swap an old garment for something they need more. Like trousers their boy's grown out of. Or a pair of shoes for their little girl to go to school. We'll take anything they donate just so long as it's clean and wearable. And if they come in one day and can't find what they need, then they leave their old stuff with us, and we enter it into a book so they can come back and have another look next time. We do the same with women's and men's clothing as well, but adults are limited to coming once a month.'

Listening to her cousin explaining, Esme had to concede that the idea was a clever one. 'That's actually quite ingenious.'

'It's actually quite awful,' Louise said flatly. 'That's what it is.'

Louise's response made Esme prickle. 'Well, yes. Of course it is. I'm not making light of families' hardship, truly, I'm not. Rather, I meant that when presented with a problem, it's amazing how inventive women can be, given the chance.'

'Mm. Anyway,' Louise went on, 'it's up to you which of the two things you choose to do but you're going to do one of them. If nothing else, you need to get out of the house. You need to be doing something. So, either you come up the church hall and lend a hand there, or, later, I take you up the beacon. And before you decide which it's to be, you should know that saying you don't want to do either won't wash.'

Esme had to admit Louise was right: she did need to get out of the house. And at least the church hall ought to be warmer than a windy clifftop. Moreover, seeing the plight of some of the local women and their families might take her mind from her own situation for a while — might even help her on her road to recovery. So, yes, she would force herself to go.

'In that case,' she said, concealing her reluctance behind a smile, 'church hall it is.'

4

False Dawn

Esme had been wrong about the church hall. As became quickly apparent the following afternoon, the little building was only marginally less draughty than the clifftop would have been. Situated across the road from the church at Woodicombe Cross, it had thick stone walls and tiny windows that allowed in precious little light, let alone warmth. And, although to protect the entrance from the elements there was a porch — the lintel above which, she noticed with a certain gloom, was inscribed '1845 AD' — it didn't stop the wind from whistling under the badly fitting doors to quickly cut off all feeling below the knees.

Her spirits dropping at the recognition of what she'd let herself in for, Esme followed her cousin into the main hall, where standing at a trestle heaped with clothing was a stout middle-aged woman in a bottle-green overcoat.

'Aha, Mrs Ross,' the woman looked up to say. 'And you bring us another pair of hands! Excellent.'

'Good afternoon, Mrs Harding,' Louise called across. Gesturing to Esme, she went on, 'This is my cousin, Mrs Trevannion. She's stopping with us at Woodicombe for a while. Esme, this is Mrs Harding. She runs the clothing and food sections of our WVS Centre.'

Mrs Harding, Esme decided, taking in the woman's upright stance and no-nonsense outfit as she stopped

41

what she was doing and came towards them, had to be the wife of either the rector, or else the headmaster of the adjacent school.

'How do you do, Mrs Harding.'

'Mrs Trevannion, how awfully good of you to join us. I'm pleased to say that charity has been kind this last fortnight and we have a considerable mound of donations to sort through before tomorrow morning's exchange. So, let me show you what needs to be done.'

The task turned out to be simple enough: examine the donated garments for damage and then sort the acceptable items first into boys' or girls', and then by size. On an adjacent table was a row of cardboard boxes labelled 'Boys' Infants', Girls' Juniors', and so on. And on the wall above them was a handwritten sign.

Westward Quay & Woodicombe Cross
Clothing Exchange
Garments for donation must be clean
and serviceable
Exchanges are permitted only on
a like-for-like basis

'If it's not in tip-top condition,' Louise explained when Mrs Harding had moved away, 'put it on that trestle over there. We have a Make Do And Mend working party who'll see if there's anything to be done for it. If it's truly beyond repair, it'll go into the rag bag to be used for patching up something else. Waste not, want not.'

Having put her handbag beside Louise's on a nearby chair, Esme pulled a garment from the pile: a tweed

42

jacket for a boy of about ten or twelve, it had patched elbows but appeared otherwise fine — assuming its new owner didn't mind reeking of mothballs. Reaching across, she put it in the box marked 'Boys' Juniors'.

The next item she picked up was a cotton nightshirt. Judging from its size and smell, it had belonged to the same child as the jacket. Having examined it for holes and found none, she put it into the box.

'So,' she said, picking up the next piece of clothing, 'you do this once a fortnight?'

Examining the hemline of a girl's brown corduroy shift, Louise nodded. 'I do. See, most of the members of our WVS centre live down in the village and can't get all the way up here to help out. On top of which, there's something like four hundred evacuee children down in Westward Quay now, and so the members already have their hands full with seeing to them.'

'And do you also come every time for the . . . the exchange . . . or whatever it's called?'

Alongside her, partnering pairs of girls' ankle socks, Louise nodded. 'I can't have it on my conscience not to. See, for the women hereabouts, there's precious little help and no means for them to get into Westward Quay — not since the daily bus service was stopped. No, it's hard enough for them to get clothing for their children at the best of times, and so the exchange is a proper lifesaver. Women walk in from all over the place in the hope of getting what they need.'

Continuing to sort through the clothing, Esme nodded. 'It must be a hard life, stuck out here.'

'Real hard.'

'And you manage to fit in doing this alongside your shifts for the corps.'

'Uh-huh. As the rector says, God might have put

43

seven days in a week, but when it comes to resting, He considered the Sabbath alone quite enough.'

'Hm. What do you think?' Esme asked, holding up a plain woollen vest. 'Boy's or girl's?'

'Don't suppose it much matters. I'd put it in 'Boys'. They certainly seem to wear through their clothes quicker than girls.'

'Can we count on seeing you back here tomorrow, dears?' Mrs Harding came across to ask, when, about a half an hour later, they had sorted the clothes and placed the boxes in the storeroom for safe keeping. Turning to Esme, she said, 'I simply don't know what we'd do without Mrs Ross. A real treasure. Terribly good with the children.' Locking the door to the cupboard, she added, 'And at keeping the Day Book up to date.'

Louise sent Esme a wink. 'Don't worry, Mrs Harding. We'll be here. Ten o'clock sharp.'

'She's very good at keeping order in the queue, too,' Mrs Harding went on as she walked with them to the door. 'Righty-ho, then, dears. I'm off to cycle over and see Mrs Cox at Gooden's Farm. She's supposed to be lying in but . . . well, you can imagine how it is for her with that lardy lump of a husband and those four little ones. Cheerio, then.'

Moments later, as the two women were making their way back along the lane towards the house, with the debris of leaves and twigs brought down by last night's gales crunching beneath their boots, Esme felt Louise take her arm.

'Nice to see some sunshine again.'

Having been lost in her thoughts, Esme looked absently through the trees towards the sky. 'Lovely, yes.'

44

'Nothing like a burst of autumn colour to brighten up a dull day.'

Colour? Oh, Louise meant on the trees. 'Yes,' she agreed. 'Nothing quite like it.'

'I hope it's dry tomorrow — at least until lunch-time. You can get a real drowning coming along here in the wet. Not to mention how the mud clags your boots.'

'Will it be busy?' Esme asked, surprised to find that she genuinely wanted to know.

'There's really no telling. There'll be a queue, that's for sure. The women who come often know that if you want first pickings, you've got to be there early. Mind you, what isn't that true of, these days?'

'You know,' Esme decided to admit, 'being there this afternoon made the time fly past.'

'It does that when you're busy. Like I said to you before, it's why I do these things. Well, not *only* why. I do also like the fact that I'm helping others.'

'Did you know that our mothers volunteered in the *last* war?' Esme said, recalling her mother once mentioning the fact.

Beside her, Louise nodded. 'At a women's centre, yes. Can't for the life of me remember the name of it, though.'

'St Ursula's. In Paddington.'

'That's right!'

'Mummy said Aunt Kate didn't stand still once in the whole war. She said she never had an idle moment, that she used to spend three or four days a week helping the widows and orphans and then come home and run the house. Mummy said that at times, Aunt Kate's stamina made her feel woefully inadequate.'

'Yes, but your mum had *you* to look after.'

'I think the two of them did that together,' Esme observed. 'Aunt Kate certainly figures as prominently in my early memories as Mummy does.'

'Mm. Anyway,' Louise said, 'I'm glad you've decided to come again tomorrow. Mrs Harding will be pleased. And I shan't mind the help, either.'

In fact, the following morning when she awoke, Esme was relieved to find she didn't need to dream up an excuse not to go because she was genuinely looking forward to it. And, despite it still being well before ten o'clock when they arrived back at the village hall, when she saw the half a dozen mothers already standing quietly in line, their expressions heavy with resignation, she felt a stab of sympathy for them. Although none of them seemed exactly destitute, they did look grey and weary — in need of both a good meal and a decent night's sleep. While it wasn't unusual to see women in London looking ashen and exhausted, she had never supposed that out here, in the countryside, away from the bombings and the danger and the general despair, four years of war would have exacted the same sort of toll. It was a realisation that made her feel a twinge of guilt; here was Louise — *and* Aunt Kate and Uncle Luke — all playing their parts, and here *she* was, a fit and able woman, who, since leaving SOE, hadn't so much as lifted a finger to help anyone else — certainly not people like this, people in genuine need. Granted, being a wife with a young child had exempted her from being drafted into compulsory war work but what was her excuse now? The government might not have resorted to calling up married women but most of them had taken it upon themselves to do something useful all the same. So, perhaps, when she went back to London, she should

46

make enquiries — find the nearest WVS centre and see if there was a way she could help. She might not want to take on a responsibility like driving an ambulance — as she suddenly remembered her mother saying she had once done — but something like this clothing exchange ought surely to be within her abilities. In the meantime, while she was here in Devon, and since at this precise moment Mrs Harding was opening the doors to the line of waiting women, she would try to be of as much help as she could.

'Short trousers,' the first women who approached her said, fishing about in her shopping bag. 'Bit bigger than them ones, if you've got any.'

Accepting the dark grey garment the woman withdrew from her bag, Esme looked them over. 'These look hardly worn,' she said, checking the pockets and finding in one of them a glossy conker.

'They shouldn't. Only put him in them back in the summer but already the waist don't do up no more.'

'Then let me see if we've got anything to suit.'

'You all right there?' Louise enquired when, a while after that, they were both searching the same box for sweaters.

Without even pausing to think, Esme nodded. 'Actually, yes, I am.'

'Good. Well, keep it up. We don't close the doors until twelve.'

By the time they'd dealt with what Louise called *the initial surge*, it was almost eleven o'clock and Mrs Harding called them through to a small room at the back that had been set up as a tiny kitchen.

'Bovril, Mrs Trevannion?' she asked, holding up a jar and waving it in Esme's direction. 'Rather a poor choice I'm afraid but it's all there is at the moment.'

47

'No, thank you, it's all right,' Esme replied. 'Save it for someone else.' Hearing footsteps, she moved to peer out of the door; looking about the main hall was a young woman with a small child. 'You two have your drink and I'll go and see if I can help this lady.'

As Esme drew near to what was clearly mother and son, she had a sense that it was the young woman's first visit.

'I'm sorry but is this where you get clothes for children? Only . . . I've not done this before.'

Making her smile a warm one, Esme nodded. 'That's right. What is it you need?'

Dressed in an olive-coloured gaberdine, the belt of which was pulled tightly about her waist — presumably to disguise the fact that it was several sizes too large for her — and with no hat or headscarf over her auburn hair, the woman struck Esme as being no more than eighteen or nineteen years old. She was also startlingly pale and frighteningly thin.

'He needs a warm sweater. I know I should try an' knit him one before coming begging to you but . . . well, see, I've not the first clue how to go about it. Woman up the road gave me one of them pattern things . . . but I couldn't make head nor tail of it.'

'It's all right,' Esme said, careful to keep her tone kindly; the poor thing looked like a young rabbit who might at any minute bolt. 'I can't knit either. Have you brought anything to swap for it?' Seeing the girl's confusion, she hurried on, 'An old jumper that he's outgrown perhaps?'

Flushing scarlet, the girl bit her lip. 'He's only got the one he's wearing. And he's worn it to holes. It's why I've come.'

Glancing across to the door to the little kitchen,

48

Esme hesitated. 'Like for like', Mrs Harding had said this morning. 'One in, one out. It's only fair.' But it wasn't really, was it? What about this unfortunate woman, whose little boy only had the sweater he was already wearing?

'Tell you what,' she said, 'come and sit him up here and we'll see what we've got.' At the farthest trestle, the boxes upon which contained the clothes for toddlers and infants, Esme delved about. But when the girl lifted the boy onto the table, and Esme got her first proper look at the child's face, she struggled to withhold a gasp: his mischievous brown eyes were identical to Kit's. Flustered, she turned sharply back to the box. 'How . . . old is he?'

'Going on three.'

Going on three. A few months older than Kit. A few months older than Kit *would have been.*

Unable to risk looking back, Esme continued to rummage. 'He . . . has lovely eyes.'

'I was hoping he'd come out with blue ones like mine. Now all I see when I look at him is the feller who said he loved me and then cleared off, leaving me with nothing but an address for some place that don't even exist. Oh, and this one.'

Keep looking in the box, Esme told herself. *You can't start crying in front of the poor girl.* 'Here,' she said, coming across a hand-knitted arran sweater. 'This looks about right. Shall we try it on him?'

When the girl pulled the boy's ragged jumper over his head to leave him sitting in a thin little vest, Esme once again turned away. *Do NOT start crying. This woman has had to swallow her pride to come here. She needs help, not tears.* Fixing her attention back on the box, she rummaged deeper.

'It's perfect,' she heard the girl whisper. 'Nice and warm, bit of growing room. Are you sure it's all right for me to just have it?' Not trusting herself to speak, Esme confined herself to nodding. 'Well, I'm sure I don't know what to say. Maybe you should have his old one in its place?'

'No, please,' Esme whispered, refusing the shapeless woollen garment. 'Why not keep it for him to play in?' *You have the greater need of it.* 'Our little secret.'

Seemingly unable to believe her good fortune, the woman lifted the child from the table and sat him on her hip.

'Say thank you to the nice lady then, Christopher.'

Christopher? Oh, dear God. *Kit . . .*

'Fank you, lady.'

With her mouth held in an unnatural smile, Esme returned the little boy's wave. But only when mother and son had disappeared through the door did she allow her expression to crumble under her pain: in her chest, the same old weight was once again dragging relentlessly towards the floor; in her stomach, the familiar hollow ache demanded that she wrap her arms about her midriff. But these were not agonies that could be soothed by warmth or touch. In their deepest grip, nothing brought respite.

Abruptly unable to see for tears, she stumbled away from the trestle for the support of the wall. How ridiculous to think she could help other people when she couldn't even help herself. No matter the kindly perseverance of her family — their well-meant occupying of her hours with chatter and company and chores — her distress at the loss of Kit wasn't to be overcome. Unlike the young woman with the red hair, her own Christopher had been snatched cruelly away:

never again would she know what it was to hoist him onto her hip; never again would she wrestle his wriggling limbs into a warm sweater; never again would she have to remind him to say thank you.

Finally, the enormity hit home. Her dearest Kit was gone — and he was never coming back.

★ ★ ★

'Oh, sorry. Did I wake you?'

'No, it's all right, I've been awake for hours.'

It was the morning after Esme's visit to the clothing exchange; a morning when, despite having barely even dozed, she had awoken at the same ungodly hour as usual, her mind still weighed with such a heavy grief that she'd stood absolutely no chance of getting back to sleep.

Now, hearing the chink of china as her cousin negotiated the door, she raised herself up to see Louise carrying a tray towards the little table under the window.

'Then I wish I'd thought to look in on you sooner,' Louise said, setting down the tray and bringing a cup and saucer to place on the bedside table. 'No doubt you could have done with this a while back. But I didn't want to risk waking you.'

The irony of her cousin's comment made Esme scoff. 'Huh. You could have brought it to me at four o'clock and you wouldn't have woken me.'

Slowly, Louise lowered herself onto the side of the bed. 'You didn't have a good night then?'

Raising herself higher, Esme pushed aside her hair. 'I didn't, no.' Louise, she noticed, was studying her with concern. 'And yes, I *have* been crying again.'

51

The sympathy in Louise's expression deepened. 'Oh, Essie, I'm so sorry to hear that.'

Unsurprisingly, her cousin's kindly tone brought on fresh tears. 'No, *I'm* the one who should be sorry, coming here . . . putting everyone out . . . making you all miserable with my moaning and my weeping —'

'No, no,' Louise rushed to reassure her, reaching for her hand and grasping it tightly.

'You go to all the bother of thinking of things to occupy me, and yet here I am this morning, back to square one.'

'Well, I really don't think you're back to —'

'No. I am. It's hopeless.'

Louise, though, wasn't about to give up. 'What happened yesterday was *my* fault. The clothing exchange seemed such a good idea . . . but I hadn't stopped to think that it would involve children. And I can't tell you how sorry I am for not seeing that. But we mustn't stop trying. You already told me that waking up each morning is the hardest part of the day for you. So, let's not look upon this morning as too great a setback. Let's not be too quick to lose heart . . . rather, let's just regard how you feel right now as understandable. Hang on to the idea that it will pass. Instead of giving in to it, let's look forward. Let's say that we'll —'

'No,' Esme said, the familiar leaden sensation once again dragging at her chest. 'I know you mean well, truly, I do. But you don't understand. I realise this morning that in thinking I was ready to go out and help others, I was only fooling myself. I got caught up in the moment. I latched onto a false dawn. I'm not ready to go volunteering . . . I'm not ready to do anything. And I fail to see how I ever will be.'

Briefly, Louise looked away. But when she looked back again it was to say, 'Dearest Essie, though you might feel that way right this moment, it's not true. When we were helping those women, I saw a change in you. You looked . . . lighter. Brighter, like you'd turned a corner.'

To avoid her cousin's searching gaze, Esme lowered her head. For a moment, she'd thought the same thing. Having applied her mind to something other than her sorrow, she'd felt as though perhaps there was an end to the tunnel of her grief. Now, though, she could see that it had been nothing more than a trick of the light. 'I'm sorry,' she said. 'Truly I am. It's just that —'

'Tell you what,' Louise interrupted, her tone calm and encouraging, 'how about tonight, you come up the beacon with me? I'll show you how we scan for aircraft and how we use the plotter. Not because I want to recruit you into volunteering,' she hastened to clarify, 'but because I think you would be surprised at what we do. And interested, too.'

It would be an act of ingratitude to decline her cousin's well-meant offer, Esme knew that. But she also knew that she would struggle to summon the interest to do anything, let alone trek all the way up a cliff to stand about in the cold and the dark. 'No, it's kind of you to offer but I don't think so.'

Her cousin's disappointment was plain. 'Well, I shan't push you against your will. I'm just trying to think of things you might find interesting —'

'And I appreciate that.'

'Who knows, perhaps being out later of a night would even help you to sleep.'

'I doubt it. But thank you again for offering. And

53

I'm sorry.'

'No need to be sorry. The last thing I want is to upset you even more —'

'You won't . . .'

'— but how about you at least get dressed then? Mum's lit a fire in the drawing room. We could play cards. There's nothing Nanny Edith likes more than to thrash someone at gin rummy. Remember when we were little, how she would never let us win? Not even at a game of snap? Well she hasn't changed. Rather than mellow as she's got older, I do believe she's got worse. I suppose I should be grateful Mum didn't inherit that meanness . . .'

Listening to Louise rambling on, Esme knew she would struggle to find the energy to get dressed, let alone concentrate on a daft card game. But, unable to summon the stamina to refuse, she was left with no option but to give in. 'All right. I'll get dressed and come downstairs.'

In a way, Esme reflected once Louise had left the room and she was stood pulling a sweater over her head, it would be so much easier if everyone wasn't so incessantly nice to her — if they just left her alone to succumb to her pain. At least that way, she wouldn't seem so doggedly ungrateful. As everyone kept pointing out, she wasn't to blame for her agony. It was just the way it was — just the way it was going to be from now on. And, although she knew it would be hard for any of them to accept, the sooner they all just left her alone to shut herself away and surrender to it, the sooner she would stop being so much trouble for all of them.

★ ★ ★

54

'You on duty tonight, love?'

It was later that same day and, having reluctantly made the effort not to withdraw to her room, Esme had passed most of it listlessly, much as she had just spent supper with the family.

'Six 'til midnight,' Louise answered her father's enquiry.

'Taking Esme with you?'

Having exchanged a brief glance, neither woman answered. Then they both spoke at once.

'Not tonight.'

Seated opposite her uncle, Esme watched as he used the crust from his slice of bread to mop up every remaining trace of gravy.

'So, who's up there with you then?' he asked.

'Connie tonight. Polly tomorrow.'

His plate gleaming, Luke sat back in his chair. 'I still say it idn't right, two girls being up there on their own like it.'

Louise shot Esme a pained look. 'We're none of us girls, Dad. For a start, me an' Polly are both married.'

'Neither here nor there. Upshot's the same.'

'Besides,' Louise somewhat wearily picked up again, and with which Esme felt genuine sympathy for her, 'you know as well as I do how the rules state there's to be no rostering of a female member alone on a nightshift with a man —'

'I'd far rather you be up there alone with old Clive Aldridge than with young Polly . . . or that flighty Connie.'

'— even if there was a man to take a shift anyway,' Louise finished saying. 'If there was, then the five of us women wouldn't be put down to take quite so many turns at it. Without us *girls* as you insist upon calling

55

us, this part of the coast wouldn't have an observation post at all. I never have understood what it is you fret about anyway.'

'Your Dad worries what would happen if the Germans were to invade,' Kate said. Catching Esme's eye, she sent her a wink. 'He worries that . . . well, we've all heard the tales of what's gone on when they've gone marching into other places.'

Watching to see how Louise would react, Esme saw her give a despairing shake of her head. To be fair, Uncle Luke's concern did seem unfounded: surely, an isolated stretch of the North Devon coast was an unlikely place for a German invasion, even if, as Richard was forever pointing out, Hitler didn't exactly play by the rules.

And Louise was clearly of the same mind.

'Dad! As I keep telling you, and as any sane person would rightly agree, Hitler is highly unlikely to come rowing up into Woodicombe Cove, let alone go to the effort of scrambling up the cliff path just to make hostages of two women.'

'Unlikely, yes,' Luke conceded, his lips forming into a grin. 'But there's a rule against two women being alone together up there for a reason.'

'Mind you,' Kate chipped in, getting to her feet and starting to gather up their empty plates, 'Gerry would get more of a walloping from young Polly Webb than old Mr Aldridge. While Clive Aldridge was clutching his chest with one hand and surrendering with the other, Polly would be kneeing them all in the groin.'

'And so would I,' Louise remarked.

Across the table, Luke threw back his head and laughed. 'I taught you well!'

'Anyway,' Louise said, 'what about you, Dad? You

on duty tonight?'

'I am.'

'Again?' Kate asked. 'That'll be the fourth time in as many nights. You know something the rest of us don't?'

With a glance to the kitchen clock, Luke scraped back his chair and got to his feet. 'Such as?'

'Such as somebody somewhere thinking we're going to be invaded after all.'

'No, just doing my bit.'

'You did your bit last time around,' Kate grumbled. 'And nearly lost your leg for your troubles.'

'For heaven's sake, woman,' Luke said, crossing the room to give his wife a hug. 'How many times have we been through this? It's precisely because of last time that I can't sit about and leave it to others. It's not in my nature to. I need to play my part. Besides, wouldn't you rather there was a band of us at the ready, should the need arise?'

'Well, of course,' Kate conceded. 'But just lately you're never home.'

'Can't be helped. Anyway, quick look at my back tyre and then I'll be off to the drill hall. So, Lou, just you take good care.'

'Yes Dad.'

'And I'll see you all in the morning.'

The moment her father's back was turned, Louise sent Esme a grin. 'Are you sure you don't want to come with me?'

Slowly but purposefully Esme nodded. 'Truly. I'd be miserable company. No, you'd be better off without me to get in the way of your duties.'

'You'd be no trouble to me,' Louise ventured, getting to her feet and turning towards the door.

57

'Be careful then,' Esme said, feeling mean-spirited at willing her cousin to just leave. After all, the poor girl was only trying to help. But this way was for the best: the less she did, the less she was courting disappointment, not only for herself but for Louise and the family, too.

Barely fifteen minutes later, though, dressed in a uniform that made her look as though she was a member of the WAAF, Louise appeared in the drawing room.

'Quick, Essie. Richard's on the telephone.'

From the armchair by the fireplace where she had gone to sit with one of Aunt Kate's old copies of *Woman's Own*, Esme tensed. Richard? On the telephone? But he'd only rung the day before yesterday.

Resting the magazine on the arm of the chair, she pushed her feet back into her shoes and stood up. 'Really? I didn't hear it ring.'

'Well it did,' Louise said briskly. 'So, come on. You're wasting valuable time when you could be talking to him.'

Crossing the room, Esme continued to frown. Why did something about this feel off? Was Richard calling to try to corral her into doing something? Had he, behind her back, been talking to Louise? She'd thought for a few days now that the two of them might be in cahoots. Well, she wasn't going to be herded into anything against her will, no matter how noble everyone's aims.

Arriving at the telephone, she lifted the receiver from the table.

'Richard. Hello.'

'Darling, there you are.'

'This is a surprise. We only spoke the day before

yesterday.'

'Call me soft but I just wanted to hear your voice.'

Unexpectedly, Esme felt the tension in her neck and shoulders beginning to soften. 'That's nice.'

'Louise told me you went to a WVS centre yesterday. And that she invited you to go on duty with her tonight.'

The tension returned. Clearly, her suspicions hadn't been without foundation.

'You've been speaking to Louise?'

'Only for a moment when she picked up the telephone. She says you were a natural with the women at the WVS. Must have felt good to be useful again.'

Good. Useful. Now he was even starting to *sound* like Louise. Not that he was wrong. Briefly, it *had* felt good. Sadly, as she had since come to realise, that was the very reason she felt such guilt today: *because it had felt good.*

'I won't deny it,' she said evenly. 'For a while I forgot about . . . everything . . . which is why I shan't go again.'

Briefly, at the other end of the line there was only silence.

'Not sure I understand, darling. If it did you some good, then why won't you —'

'Because it's wrong.'

'Wrong?'

In her imagined picture of him, he was frowning so deeply that his dark eyebrows were almost meeting in the middle of his forehead. 'It would be wrong to go again,' she said, 'because I would only be doing so to ease the pain . . . when the pain is there for a reason. I'm meant to feel it. I'm not supposed to get over it. Don't you see? It's there to remind me of what

59

I've lost.' In her desperation to make him understand, she gestured impatiently. 'The minute I stop feeling the pain, it will mean that I've forgotten . . . that I've moved on —'

'Darling, that's not true —'

'— that Kit doesn't matter anymore —'

'Esme, trust me when I say that's not how it works —'

'And no matter what you or Louise maintain, or try to get me to do, I'm not going to let that happen.' Forming in the back of her throat was the familiar lump that meant she was about to cry. 'I must never forget all that Kit meant to me . . . to us. I must keep the memory of him alive. I must strive to keep him in my thoughts —'

'And you will,' Richard said. 'Just because you —'

'— because if I don't, it will be as though he never existed in the first place —'

'Oh, no, my darling girl, that's not true. Getting past your grief doesn't mean forgetting. It's not the same thing at all.'

No longer really listening, Esme started to sob. 'His short . . . little life . . . will have been for nothing. And I can't . . . I can't be . . . that disloyal . . . to him. I just can't.'

'Darling, you're being far too hard on yourself. Look, is Louise there?'

'. . . Louise?'

'Yes. I think I should speak to her about coming down.'

The thought of Richard coming all the way to Woodicombe only made Esme cry even harder. 'I don't think you —' But, before she could finish her sentence, at the other end of the line there was a click

60

followed by the steady brrr of the dialling tone. They had been cut off. 'No-o . . .' she wailed between sobs.

Cradling the receiver to her chest with one hand while clasping her locket in the fingers of her other, she sank down onto the stool, failing to notice as she did so that someone was dashing towards her.

'There, there,' she heard Aunt Kate whisper, and felt two arms close around her heaving shoulders. 'It's all right, love. It's all right.'

'No-o-o-o,' Esme sobbed into her aunt's sweater. 'It's not . . . all right. It's not. And it won't ever . . . be all right . . . again.'

5

Obsidian

'That uniform really makes you look the part.'

'It does?'

'I meant to tell you the other day. Very smart indeed.'

It was now several days since the WVS clothing exchange but, despite continuing encouragement from Louise, and the gentle but dogged persistence of Aunt Kate and Uncle Luke, Esme really didn't feel any better: the black cloud that followed her everywhere still refused to lift, and each morning she awoke feeling utterly wretched and convinced that, no matter how well-meaning everyone was, nothing and no one could make it otherwise. How could any of them possibly understand when none of *them* had lost their infant son?

That said, she was trying to make more of an effort. She dressed promptly each morning. She forced herself to take an interest in what everyone else was up to. And she tried desperately hard only to cry when she was alone, her bouts of tears coming fractionally less often — but only fractionally.

And now, having earlier declined a further invitation from Louise to accompany her on her shift up at the observation post, coming across her cousin adjusting her beret in front of the hall mirror, she had purposely shown an interest in her appearance. To be fair, she really did look rather striking.

'Took me more than a year of haranguing to get

this uniform,' Louise said, gesturing with one hand to her steel-blue jacket while, with her other, swinging a canvas satchel over her shoulder. 'But that's a story for another day, since if I don't leave this very minute, I shall be late relieving Connie. And I can't really complain about her not showing up on time if I do the same to her, can I?'

'I suppose not, no.'

'Are you're sure you won't come?' Louise said, her grin betraying that she had absolutely no expectation of Esme changing her mind.

'No thanks. I'm quite happy to stop in the warm and make a start on reading this.' For Louise's benefit, Esme held up her copy of *Candleford Green*. 'By all accounts, it's rather good.'

'Then tomorrow, you can tell me whether or not it is.'

'All right. Well, at the risk of sounding like your mother, please take care —'

'Always do.'

'And I'll see you in the morning.'

With Louise heading away, Esme turned towards the drawing room. She would poke some life into the fire, curl up in one of the armchairs and see whether this book really was any good.

But no sooner had she got comfortable than Luke put his head around the door. 'Thought I might find you in here,' he said, skirting the furniture swathed in dustsheets on his way towards her. 'Once the fire's proper ablaze, this is the warmest room in the house. Always has been.'

'Uncle Luke,' she greeted him, lowering her feet and slipping them back into her shoes.

'Don't disturb yourself, love.' Rounding the end of

the sofa, he came to perch on the edge of the chair opposite. 'How are you?'

As had become her habit when someone enquired, Esme withheld a sigh. 'A little better, thank you for asking.'

'Good to hear.'

It was tempting to ask what was on his mind — because something clearly was — but, instead, she waited.

Growing up, she'd had something of a soft spot for Uncle Luke — a soft spot that, in her adolescent years, had gone on to develop into something of a crush. She had certainly envied Louise her warm and gentle father, a father who, no matter how often you broke something, seemed able — as if by magic — to put it back together. She remembered marvelling at how his hair curled — his blonde mop being so different from the ebony and brown heads of her own family. And, whereas Louise and Victor and Arthur always groaned every time he began a story with the words During the war, she had never tired of hearing how he'd escaped capture by hiding in a tiny village and then, when the Germans had started shelling it, had helped everyone to safety. Even the limp he'd been left with after being shot in the thigh, in her eyes made him a hero.

'Not on duty with the Home Guard tonight?' she eventually felt obliged to break the silence and ask.

'Though it mightn't seem like it, maid, I don't go every night. Just Tuesdays for drill and a couple of turns on patrol.'

'That's still quite a lot —'

'Shortage of trained men. Look, love,' he said, and with which she realised he was finally ready to share

64

with her what was on his mind, 'I won't beat about the bush. I'm after a favour. I've a bit of nerve, I'll own to that, but, well, you're likely the only person who can get me out of a fix.'

Noticing a new earnestness in his expression, Esme frowned. 'A fix? Goodness, Uncle. Now you do have my attention.'

'Your aunt's told you about her 'guests', as she calls them.'

Esme nodded. 'She mentioned them. But that's all.'

'Well, when the chap first approached us about getting involved, the request was for us to provide the billets *and* the transport. So, since we were keen to help out, your aunt said she didn't mind readying the rooms and providing the meals if I'd do the driving. Didn't bother me, not with it meaning the loan of a motorcar. You'll no doubt recall how engines and motors are a thing of mine.'

With no idea where her uncle's story was going, nor what it had to do with her, Esme nevertheless nodded. 'I do. I seem to recall you once telling how it was your knack with engines that first got you talking to my father. And subsequently into the army.'

That she should remember clearly surprised him. 'That's right. It was. You've a good memory to recall that. Well, anyway, what happens is that these chaps have to be collected from the railway station, brought here for the night, and then, usually the next day, driven to an RAF base over Chilverleigh way. Now, though we've only had the one set of them so far — something of a dummy run for all concerned we were told afterwards — straight away I could see how me doing the ferrying back and forth was going to prove tricky. See, no one told us we'd have to deliver these folk to the RAF camp *at night* . . . nor that their arrangements would be prone to changing with the wind. And since in the Home Guard I'm a sergeant, I can't just choose when I turn up — can't just chop and change to suit. Don't get me wrong, the driving part is straightforward enough but, since it now seems their habit will be to depart from here when I need to go on duty, I can't see how I can keep on with it. That said, your aunt's real keen to have these folk staying here . . . a nice little sideline. So, it occurred to me that you might like to take it on — the driving, I mean.'

'Me?' She hadn't been expecting that! 'You want me to take these people about the countryside?'

'Why not? You know how to drive. And unlike the rest of us you would seem to have the time . . .'

What a peculiar thing for him to suggest. Although . . . was it? What if . . . ?

'Once a week, you say?'

Luke nodded. 'That's how it was put to us, aye.'

'Collected from the railway station —'

'From Barnstaple.'

'And brought back here.'

'That's it, love. Then you'd take them over the stables, see them settled. Or your aunt could do that, if you'd prefer. Next morning, you get a telephone call —'

'From?'

'From some chap called Mulberry. When you confirm to him you have his people, he tells you what time they have to be at the camp.'

'So, these guests are RAF personnel?'

Still perched on the edge of the chair, Luke shrugged. 'With them being in civvies, it's hard to say. But what

66

else would they be, going to an RAF place?'

Fair point. 'Men or women?'

'First lot was two men. Youngish. Carried a small bag each.'

'And once you've dropped them off, you just drive back here?'

'When you get there, they tell you if they need you to wait, just in case.'

'In case of what?' To Esme, what had initially sounded straightforward was now beginning to sound more involved.

Luke scratched his head. 'Can't rightly say as they told me. Nice motorcar, though. Austin Fourteen. Not very old and nicely kept up together. Green it is. Footrests for the passengers. Little heater. All the comforts. Comes with its own book of petrol coupons. Obviously.'

What was it, Esme wondered, that made her feel inclined to get involved with this peculiar little set-up? The fact that it appeared to have an element of intrigue attached? The fact that it would give her something to do that didn't involve draughty church halls or windswept clifftops? Or was it simply a wish to help her dear Uncle Luke out of his supposed fix?

'I should probably tell you,' she said, reminding herself not to jump into anything willy-nilly, 'that it's rather a while since I've driven anything. In town, we have no need of a motor.'

'Wouldn't worry about that, love,' Luke replied. 'I can take you out to get your hand back in, see you get on all right, give you some tips if needs be.'

'And how far away is the place to which I would have to drive them?'

'Roughly twenty-five minutes. The place you'd be

going is different to where I had to take the first lot. Apparently, there's a new camp been set up but, at the time I made that first run, it wasn't ready. Behind schedule, was what they said.'

To her surprise, Esme found herself drawn to saying yes. But not this very minute. 'May I sleep on it?' she asked. No sense committing on the spur of the moment and then feeling obligated to stick with it even if she had a change of heart.

''Course, girl. Tell you what, tomorrow morning, I'll take you round the stables and show you the motor.'

Watching her uncle get to his feet, Esme laughed. 'Why do I get the feeling you'll be able to tell me more about the motorcar than about anything else to do with this?'

His grin was a wry one. 'You know me — mechanical things I can fathom. People not so much.'

'By the way,' she called after him as he started across the room. 'Did Louise put you up to this?'

Coming to a halt in the doorway, he turned to look back at her. 'No, love. I've come to you so as you might make up your mind for yourself.'

Left alone to reflect, Esme stared into the fire. Collect a couple of people from the station and then deliver them to an RAF base. As her uncle had said, hardly onerous — certainly nothing anyone could object to on the grounds of risk or danger. So, where was the harm? Might she not enjoy meeting these people? In fact, might this not be the very distraction everyone kept telling her she so desperately needed?

★ ★ ★

68

Uncle Luke was right. The Austin Fourteen was surprisingly roomy. It was also pleasingly quiet and particularly comfortable for its passengers. The trouble was, once in motion, it seemed to take on a life of its own. It wasn't especially difficult to handle but, after several years without having to control anything larger than a perambulator, Esme quickly realised that she seemed to have forgotten how to drive. And while most of her uncle's enthusing about its horsepower and straight-6 cylinders — whatever they were — went over her head, the tips he'd given her when she'd proved rusty at double-declutching into first gear were a Godsend.

'It'll come,' he'd said when she'd repeatedly crashed the poor gearbox on her first run out.

Thankfully, he'd been right about that, too. After numerous trips up and down the drive, her uncle calmly offering observations and advice from the passenger seat, she'd soon remastered the basic techniques, including the execution of a three-point turn — a manoeuvre that had always brought her out in a cold sweat.

Just as it had been a sensible idea to practise, deciding to make a reconnaissance run had also been wise. Driving to the airfield while there was still some light in the day was enabling her to note down the approximate distances between the turnings she needed to take, as well as one or two of the more deceptive hazards: the unexpectedly tight bend by the church; the ford with the treacherous gravel bank on the far side; the narrow stone bridge with the surprisingly pronounced hump.

Earlier, before leaving Woodicombe, she had told Uncle Luke that all she was going to do was drive to her destination and then turn back. But, as she was now so close, she was minded to go in and make herself known to whomever might be there. When she had to make the trip for real, being recognised at the gate would make her appear more professional in front of her charges. And that was another thing: what was she supposed to call these people? 'Passengers' felt mildly insulting, the terms 'operatives' or 'agents' — which she had a suspicion better described them — seeming rather on the nose. Anyway, having secreted in her handbag her identity card from her days with SOE — or Joint Technical Board as it had been outwardly known— she would see whether she might be allowed in to talk to someone and piece together what she wanted to know. After all, who were these people really? Why did they come here, of all places? And why specifically at night? While she already had a pretty shrewd idea, it would be helpful to have her suspicions confirmed.

Edging the nose of the Austin carefully down what she hoped was the final stretch of narrow lane, she spied a stone pillar in the hedgerow, nailed to it a sign upon which was painted the name 'Pond Farm'. Beyond it she could see a guard post. This, then, had to be it.

Turning to pull up alongside the latter, she wound down her window.

The young man who stepped forward and peered in at her looked confused. 'Your business here . . . miss?'

Reaching across to the passenger seat, she retrieved her handbag and pulled from the pocket in the lining her identity card, the photograph upon which had been taken on one of her visits to Croydon more than three years back. In it, she looked rather glamorous, which was largely why she'd hung onto it all this time. She certainly hadn't been expecting to use it again.

'To be honest,' she said, handing the guard her card and smiling warmly, 'my trip this afternoon is purely for my own benefit. I'm reconnoitring. You see, I shall be coming here quite often and wanted to make certain of the location.'

Looking back and forth between her face and the photograph, the guard frowned. 'Wait there please, Miss . . . Ward.'

Ward. There was a name she hadn't heard in a while!

Letting out a little sigh, she peered out into the fading afternoon light. Perhaps this hadn't been such a good idea. After all, she was trying to gain access to what was probably a top-secret RAF camp using an identity card she shouldn't really still have . . .

With that, from the nearest hut came a tall chap, the sleeve of his uniform displaying four rings. Christ. Who had she thought she was going to fool? Now they probably thought her a spy!

'Miss Ward,' he called towards the Austin as he came striding along the row of duckboards laid over the mud. 'Group Captain Hall. Was I expecting you?'

Taking in his relaxed demeanour, she shook her head. Perhaps she wasn't in trouble then. Even if she was, a bit of simpering ought to get her out of it.

'I shouldn't think so, no. I'm the driver charged with bringing your personnel and I've just been reconnoitring the route — looking for landmarks to make it easier in the dark.' Realising none of that explained why she wanted access into the airfield itself, and hardly able to say that she was curious as to the nature of the operation that went on there, she added, 'And now I'm here, I thought I should take the chance to

71

introduce myself.'

'Right-ho.' Seemingly unconcerned, Hall handed her back her identity card. She *knew* it had been a good idea to hang onto it! 'Well, as you can see, it's still a bit of mud bath. But drive on in. I've just finished a briefing and so I have a moment or two before I leave. There's a couple of faces you can meet.'

Heavens. This was proving easier than she'd anticipated. Clearly, it was still the case that few men suspected a woman of duplicitous intentions, even those sufficiently senior to know better.

'Thank you,' she said, her look deliberately demure.

From what she could see as she got out of the car and stood looking around, Pond Farm was a desolate spot. In almost all directions stretched open pasture, the only real shelter from the elements provided by a small copse behind the group of Nissen huts.

'Come on in,' Group Captain Hall said, pushing open the door to the nearest of them. 'Welcome to Operation Obsidian.' Stepping inside, Esme looked about. From where they had been examining two oversized maps on the far wall — one appearing to be of the south-west of England, the other of the coastline of northern France — three young men in pilots' uniforms turned to regard her. 'Flying officers Grant, Haxby and Timmins. Chaps, this is Miss Ward, the courier who'll be responsible for getting your cargoes this far.'

One by one, the three pilots stepped forward and shook her hand. None of them looked to be more than twenty-five years old.

'How do you do,' she greeted each of them in turn. Continuing to glance about, she took in the sparse furnishings — long table, a dozen or so folding wooden chairs, a filing cabinet and a soot-stained stove. At least the place was warm, she thought, watching as Group Captain Hall pulled two chairs from beneath the table.

'May I?' Indicating the stove, and without waiting for him to answer, she went towards it, held out her hands and rubbed them warm. What on earth did she do now? Having never expected to get this far, she felt a bit of a fraud. Remain calm, she told herself and, turning about, went to sit down.

'You know, not so long ago,' Group Captain Hall began, smoothing his fingers over his moustache, 'I would have been tickled pink to discover that someone so attractive could be from Joint Technical. But nowadays your lot seem to come in all shapes and sizes. And why not?'

Rather than groan, Esme treated him to what she hoped was a fetching smile. If charm was all it took to find out what she wanted to know . . .

'Why not indeed.'

'Anyway, inside just two weeks,' he picked up again, 'we've turned an absolute quagmire of a pasture into an airfield, complete with tarmacadam runway, hangar, this ops room . . . the whole shooting match. But all *you* really need to know is that when you arrive at the gate over there, you'll announce yourself and the code names of your passengers to the guard, drive in, show them in here, check the status of their departure with the pilot, and then either head off home or hang around as instructed. Nothing to cause you any headaches. Nothing *too* taxing.'

What, Esme thought, *even for a woman?*

'Excellent,' she said. 'Well, my apologies for arriving unannounced. You said you were about to depart and so I mustn't detain you.'

'Before you do,' the group captain said, 'come and take a gander at the runway. Only one of its kind in the southwest.'

Stepping outside, she followed him cautiously along the side of the building. Apart from a further couple of heavily camouflaged Nissen huts away to her right, the runway was the only feature to break up the otherwise endless expanse of pasture. Raising her hand to shield her eyes against the last few rays of sunshine, she squinted into the distance. 'Goodness.'

'Fifteen hundred yards. Far more than is required for the aircraft *this* squadron is ever likely to operate out of here. Designed to allow for a Halifax, should future operations require heavy equipment drops.'

'And that's it?' she said. 'The entire set up is nothing more than a strip of tarmacadam and a few huts?'

'In this game, Miss Ward, the order of the day is stealth and so we keep the whole thing as low-key as possible. This close to the coast, we can't afford to draw attention. Hence, no lights, no control tower to stand out. Just an ops room, hangar and workshop. Oh, and a fence to keep out the sheep.'

Stealth? Would she be pushing her luck to ask in what respect? Probably.

'Not even any aircraft yet,' she said instead, glancing about to make sure of the fact.

'There's a Lockheed Hudson in the hangar,' he replied, moving to stand closer and point out where he meant. 'The chaps you just met came down in it last night to see what's what. If an operation requires it, they can carry up to ten passengers as opposed to the two — three, at a push — the Lysanders have been converted to take. Initially, this squadron will

74

comprise two of the latter — one that's been making reconnaissance trips from a nearby airfield, and one that's coming down tonight from Bedfordshire with our new pilot. He'll be one of those flying your operatives.'

Operatives. Just as she had thought! Amazing what you could piece together from just the odd word.

'Well, thank you for your time, Group Captain Hall. I'm glad I came.'

'The pleasure was entirely mine, Miss Ward.'

Choosing to ignore the length of time he held onto her hand after shaking it, she hoped her expression was as inscrutable as she intended.

'You've been tremendously helpful.' *Far, far more than you could know!*

When they arrived back at the Austin, Group Captain Hall leant beyond her to open her door and then assist her in.

'Goodbye, Miss Ward. I look forward to seeing you again, hopefully before too long.'

Smarmy devil! Not even an ounce of subtlety.

'Goodbye, Group Captain. And thank you again.'

Starting the engine and switching on the headlights, Esme edged the Austin out into the lane, a glance in her mirror telling her that he was making no effort to conceal the fact that he was watching her leave. Definitely someone to keep her eye on.

But how worthwhile had this little trip turned out to be! Not only would she now be better prepared for when she had to bring her first passengers here, but she also knew rather more about what she was getting involved with: the map of France; the low-key nature of the airfield; the flights under cover of darkness. And then there was his use of the word *operatives*. Even the name Obsidian hinted at obscure goings-on. Yes, unless two and two made five, this isolated little place was a covert base for taking SOE agents into France. It had to be. But it was a deduction she would have to keep to herself: if what she had stumbled upon really was a top-secret operation, then she couldn't tell anyone — not even Louise, nor her aunt and uncle, no matter their indirect involvement.

Who would have thought it, she reflected, slowing the Austin to make a right turn at Sheepstone Cross: quite by chance, she'd found something that would not only keep her usefully occupied, but that also hinted at a touch of excitement. Possibly even the odd whiff of danger. Which was something else she might want to keep quiet about, too.

★ ★ ★

'There's no need to worry about anyone prying. I assure you, you won't be disturbed.'

It was Monday afternoon and, less than an hour beforehand, Esme had stood on the platform at Barnstaple railway station waiting to meet the four fifteen from Exeter. Scanning the alighting passengers, she'd had no difficulty identifying the two she was there to meet: a Mr Salmon and a Miss Steel. When she'd learned their code names, she'd smiled; clearly, SOE had run out of the more ordinary names of colours to use for their agents' aliases!

Having brought her two charges to Woodicombe, she was now showing them around the newly tidied-up rooms above the stables. Miss Steel had removed her beret and was stood unbuttoning her raincoat — a rather more stylish design than anything available on this side of the Channel, Esme noted with a touch of envy. And, although the woman's highly arched eyebrows gave her the appearance of being in a permanent state of surprise, she looked otherwise relaxed. Mr Salmon, on the other hand, appeared uneasy, his eyes flitting about the small sitting-room-cum-kitchen. If the two of them were supposed to be a married couple, they weren't particularly convincing. But then perhaps that *wasn't* their cover. Perhaps they weren't even supposed to know one another.

'It's very cosy,' Miss Steel remarked of the little room, Aunt Kate's newly made checked curtains giving no indication that, until a few days ago, they had been a tablecloth given a reprieve from languishing, unused, in the linen cupboard.

'You'll be left quite alone,' Esme went on, trying to remember all of the things they would need to know and surprised by how nervous she felt. 'In here,' she said, reaching to a small cupboard, 'you will find things for breakfast . . . porridge, jam, tea, coffee, marge. First thing in the morning, on the doorstep you'll find a jug of milk and a loaf. Tonight, around six o'clock, and tomorrow evening the same, Mrs Channer will bring you a hot supper. And tomorrow morning, she'll bring across a Thermos of soup for your lunch. Her food's good, so you won't go hungry.'

Smoothing a hand down the front of her slacks, Miss Steel smiled. 'Thank you.'

'And do feel free to wander about the grounds, find your way down to the cove . . . whatever takes your fancy. Or, if the weather's no good for walking, there's a chess set, the wireless, a pack of cards —'

'I'm sure we'll be fine,' the woman said.

Esme blushed. 'Yes, yes of course you will. Well,

then, the only other thing you need to know is that tomorrow night, we'll set off from here at half past— at twenty-one thirty hours. In the dark, we need to allow a good thirty minutes.'

Finally, Mr Salmon spoke. 'You'll be our driver?'

'I will.'

By way of response, he nodded.

'Thank you, Lavender,' said Miss Steel. 'You've been very helpful.'

Trying not to giggle at being addressed by the code-name newly assigned to her by Mr Mulberry, Esme drew a breath. 'Well, then. I'll say goodnight and leave you to it.'

Opening the door to be hit by a blast of salt-laden air, Esme picked her way carefully down the narrow wooden staircase to the yard and, plunging her hands into the pockets of her jacket, made her way back to the house. What two odd people! To be fair, they must be terribly nervous: here they were, on the eve of being dropped into enemy-occupied France, where she could only guess at the nature of their mission. They might be required to remain completely hidden. Or they might be expected to blend in with the locals. The woman, Miss Steel, had definitely seemed less anxious than the chap. But perhaps ordinarily he was the quiet type. Somehow, seeing them this close to their departure made her fear far more for their fates than she ever had for the operatives she'd met in Brighton. There, the last time she'd seen any of them was at the end of an evening of drinks and small talk or dinner and dancing at The Aurelian. Golly, what a long time ago that all now seemed! Better not to wonder how many of those men she had passed as fit for duty were still alive today.

'Everything all right over yonder?' Aunt Kate wanted to know when Esme arrived in the kitchen and stood unwinding the scarf from about her neck.

'Seems to be, yes,' she said as she unbuttoned her jacket.

'And they're all right with six o'clock for supper?'

'They didn't indicate otherwise.'

'Man and a woman I seen, was it?'

Esme nodded. 'That's right.'

'Last lot was two fellers.'

'Mm.'

'Well, since your Uncle Luke's down at the Home Guard again tonight, and Lou's got a shift starting at six, we'll sit down for our own supper at five, if that's all right with you, love?'

'Of course. And in which case, I'll just go and freshen up,' Esme said, congratulating herself on having successfully completed the first part of this, her inaugural mission. Not that she could afford to relax her guard, nor grow too confident. After all, the hardest part of this new role was beginning to look as though it might actually be concealing from the Channers what she now knew about the people they were accommodating in their stable block — deceiving the very people who had so kindly taken her into their home and their lives.

That being the case, later, as the family was finishing supper, she decided to check that the Channers really were, as she supposed, in the dark. Handily, when her uncle asked her how her first run had gone, she saw the perfect opportunity.

'So, what do you know, Aunt Kate, of these people I'm ferrying about? I mean, who are they? What are they doing here? Those two I've just collected look very smart . . . but were so quiet on the way here I thought they'd fallen asleep.'

Sitting back in her chair, Kate exhaled heavily. 'From what that first RAF chappie told *me*,' she said, 'it would seem they're RAF personnel with a couple of days' leave between postings. Can't get all the way home to their folks I suppose. More than that, I didn't think it my place to ask.'

'Mm. And this Mulberry fellow,' she said, turning to her uncle. 'He gave you no clue either?'

'Not a word. As far as I'm concerned, as long as they keep themselves to themselves while they're here and don't cause trouble, I'm happy to have them — and to take the government's money for doing so.'

'Well, yes,' Esme agreed swiftly. From their manner, neither her aunt nor her uncle appeared to know more than they were letting on, in which case she would stop asking questions. No sense her putting ideas into their heads. 'You never know,' she picked up again, 'perhaps, one day, one of them will be more talkative and I'll be able to fill in the blanks for all of us.'

'Happen you will, love,' Kate said, glancing across to the kitchen clock and then getting slowly to her feet. 'But now, I suppose I'd best take them their suppers.'

'Yes,' Esme agreed. 'One would imagine they must be quite hungry.'

When her aunt went across to see to a pan on the stove, Esme went to the dresser, collected the tray, and then, returning to the table, started to clear the debris of their meal. Seemingly, when it came to the true identities of the people they were billeting in their stables, the Channers really were in the dark, which, for the safety of all parties concerned, was how it should be. And it fell to her to keep it that way. Moreover, unless she wanted Richard to insist she give up the job before she had even properly started, it might be wise to spare him the finer details as well.

★ ★ ★

She'd checked the headlights. She'd inspected the tyres. And she'd read the fuel gauge. Just as Uncle Luke had shown her, Esme had checked that the Austin was ready to go. And now, here she was, her two passengers in the back, their equipment stowed in the boot, heading in the direction of Chilverleigh, from where she would turn towards the airfield at Pond Farm.

At first, with the grills on the headlights making it impossible for her to see more than two or three yards beyond the end of the long bonnet, she was utterly terrified, negotiating the first few miles of narrow lanes only by craning towards the windscreen, her hands gripping the steering wheel so tightly that the tops of her arms had started to ache. She had tried to calm her nerves by telling herself that at least it was neither raining nor icy. And at least she didn't have to fear looking like a novice by continually crashing the gears. On the other hand, when all she could see in front of her was a narrow band of tarmac and, out of the corners of her eyes, the towering hedge banks looming up in the darkness, the drive was hardly relaxing. Why, she belatedly wondered, hadn't she thought to also make a dummy run in the dark?

Once out in more open countryside, though, her progress became more confident. She even relaxed

81

sufficiently to pick up a little speed. Ahead, her route was almost a straight line up a gentle rise to Sheepstone Cross, where she would turn left, skirt the village of Chilverleigh and arrive at her destination.

As it turned out, on the final stretch of lane, she missed the entrance, only noticing as the narrow beam of her headlights picked out the sign on the gatepost. Pressing rather heavily on the brake pedal, she brought the Austin to a halt.

'My apologies,' she said over her shoulder before reversing a few lengths. 'The entrance is rather well concealed.'

When she then pointed the nose of the Austin gingerly between the gate posts, a beam of light appeared to her right and seemingly from out of nowhere came the guard. Bringing the vehicle to a halt at his outstretched arm, she wound down the window.

'Your business, please, sir.' Directing the beam of his torch at her face, he stepped back. 'Apologies, *ma'am.*'

While she blinked to steady her eyes, he shone his torch into the rear.

'Lavender,' she said, remembering the instructions she'd been given that morning by Mr Mulberry. 'With Salmon and Steel for Sage.' It could only be nervousness, she decided — for why else would she have the urge to giggle?

With that, further into the field, a dim lightbulb came on. Beneath it was illuminated the door to the ops room.

'Ahead to the right, please, ma'am, and come to a halt beneath the light.'

Pulling up in the same spot as the other day, she switched off the engine. Goodness. Somehow, she had made it unscathed.

Hearing her passengers alighting, and the sound of the boot latch being unfastened, she opened her door and got out. Hopefully, given a moment or two, she would stop trembling quite so much.

'In here, if you would, sir, ma'am,' the voice from earlier addressed her passengers.

Away to her right, she saw them step inside the Nissen hut. Pushing back the sleeve of her jacket to see her wristwatch, she angled her arm towards the meagre light; five past ten. She was a few minutes late. In future, she would allow longer — an extra ten minutes at least, more if the weather was poor.

Recalling that she was to await instructions before leaving, she wrapped her coat about her body and went to the back of the Austin, where she closed the boot and secured the latch. With that, the young man from the gate stepped out from the hut and closed the door behind him. She could see now that, rather than being in uniform, he was wearing dark trousers with a dark jacket and plain cap.

'Should I wait?' she asked as he took in her own appearance.

He shook his head. 'No. You're done. Watch out going back. Goodnight.'

'Yes. Thank you. Goodnight.'

Getting back into the Austin, Esme let out a sigh of disappointment. While it seemed faintly ridiculous now, she had thought she might see her charges board the aircraft and take off. She'd thought they might thank her and that she might wish them bon voyage. As it was, they hadn't even said goodbye. Still, if *she* had been nervous, she could only imagine how *they* must be feeling — trained and briefed for this

83

moment or not.

Switching on the engine, she turned the vehicle in a wide circle and proceeded towards the gate where she paused for a moment, wound down her window, and drew a deep breath of the night air. No matter the lack of ceremony, she'd done it. She'd played a minor part in a secret operation. How she'd missed the feeling of satisfaction that came from being a part of something — especially something covert like this!

Winding up her window and edging the motorcar out into the lane, she smiled into the darkness. Now all she had to do was work out what, precisely, she was going to tell Richard about her new role — always assuming, of course, that he didn't already know, and that he hadn't been in league with Uncle Luke — or even with SOE — in the first place . . .

★ ★ ★

'So, darling, how are you getting on in the hostel?'

'Pretty much as you might imagine, I suppose. Naturally, one misses one's privacy. But, on the upside, there's no need to drag oneself out of one's bunk for an air raid.'

'Small mercies.'

'Indeed.'

It was early the following evening and Esme was standing in the hallway, speaking on the telephone with Richard.

'And what about you?' he asked. 'Dare I risk remarking that you sound a little brighter?'

Hm, did she tell him why? Or did she say nothing? Perhaps first, she should sound him out — see if he'd had any part in her becoming involved with the oper-

84

ation to start with. She wouldn't put it past him.

'I am a little brighter, yes.'

'That's good to hear.'

'Richard, have you been speaking to Uncle Luke?'

'Your uncle? No. Not in ages. Why do you ask?'

'Have you spoken to *anyone* about me?'

'*About* you? No, the only person I've discussed you with is Louise. And that was more than a week ago now. Why? What's happened?'

'Oh, well, nothing, really.' *Here goes.* 'It's just that I've got a little . . . job. Not a job in the sense you might think . . . just something I'm doing to help Uncle Luke out of a fix.'

When, from the other end of the line there came no reply, she decided to wait, the tone of his response informing what she went on to say next.

'Have you, indeed.'

'Yes, and I wondered whether it was as a result of the two of you discussing my needing something to do.'

'No. As I say, the only person I've spoken to is Louise. But she certainly didn't mention anything about a job.'

'You don't mind, though, do you?'

'Of course not. As long as you're not in harm's way. What is it that he's got you doing?'

'It's barely anything.' At least he didn't sound cross. 'But a nearby RAF base needed a chauffeur —'

'Did you say *chauffeur*?'

'— just for little runs between here and one of the neighbouring villages.'

'A chauffeur.'

There really was no need for him to sound so derisive. 'That's what I said.'

'For the RAF.'

'Yes. Now and again, a local airfield billets people here. Aunt Kate puts them up in the rooms above the stables. And while they're here they need —'

'Chauffeuring. Yes, I get the picture.'

'You're not cross, are you?' Having thought just now that he wasn't, suddenly she wasn't quite so sure. His tone did seem to have shortened somewhat. Although that could be down to him considering the role of a driver unfitting for a married woman.

'Should I be?'

'No, of course not. I wanted to tell you sooner but until I'd been to see the . . .' Best to remain vague, she thought, even though he did work with top-secret plans every day. After all, you never knew who might be listening in. Besides, she was pretty certain it was a treasonable offence to discuss any sort of operation over the telephone. '. . . until I'd been to see the person in charge, there wasn't anything to tell you.'

'All right, well, look, if you've found a little something to keep you occupied, then I'm pleased. All I would ask is that you don't take on too much. I wouldn't want to think you were involved with anything that risked . . . well, you know . . . anything that might put you under any sort of strain. And it goes without saying that I would put my foot down immediately if I thought it involved any sort of danger.'

'Oh, goodness, no,' she said quickly. 'There will be absolutely no danger. It's all exceedingly pedestrian. You really needn't worry on that score.'

'All right. Well, our three minutes must be just about up.'

'Yes, I suppose they must.'

'So, I'll wish you goodnight. And *well done, you.*'

'Yes. And thank you for calling, Richard. It was lovely to speak to you.'

'You too, darling. Take care.'

'Always. Goodnight.'

Replacing the receiver, Esme caught sight of her reflection in the hall mirror. She hadn't lied to him; she'd just been circumspect with the truth — and only then because she really didn't want him needlessly concerned. Unlike the work she'd done for SOE in Brighton, this little venture was devoid of any and all danger — merely required just enough involvement on her part to necessitate getting out of bed in the morning. In fact, she already had the suspicion that once the novelty had worn off, the whole thing might turn out to be exceedingly dull indeed.

6

In the Dead of the Night

'*Barely a month after fighting against Britain and her allies, Italy has declared war on Germany. The announcement, made yesterday, Wednesday the thirteenth of October, at three p.m. local time, was made by Italian Prime Minister, Pietro Badoglio. In his statement, the Prime Minister said —*'

Sitting at the breakfast table a few mornings later, listening to the news from the Home Service, Luke blew out a long stream of breath. 'Well I never. Italy's changed sides. There's a turn-up for the books. That'll knock the Germans back, an' no mistake.'

Across from him, scraping a spoon around the inside of a jar to get at the last of the gooseberry jam, Kate looked up. 'So, does that mean we're closer to winning?'

It was something Esme had found herself wondering, too.

'Could be,' Luke said. 'Switched sides or not, the allies will still have to drive the Germans out of Italy . . . and I can't for a minute think they'll go without a fight. Italy herself won't be of much help, they've been in a hopeless state for months. But it's certainly a step in our favour. To my way of looking at it —'

Spotting Louise coming along the passage, Esme turned away from her uncle's explanation. '*Two* letters from Douglas?' she said, gesturing to her cousin's hand.

Louise shook her head. 'No, one of these is for you.'

'Oh. Thank you.' Recognising the handwriting on the envelope as her mother's, Esme put it beside her plate. Presumably, if Mummy had bad news to impart, she would have telephoned rather than written, and in which case her missive could wait until after breakfast.

By contrast, Louise was already sliding a butter knife under the flap of hers. And as Esme watched her cousin's eyes working their way down the page, she felt a rush of sympathy. How awful to be parted from Douglas for so long — let alone under such trying circumstances.

'He says his sister's had her baby. A girl. Lorna May. Seven pounds two ounces.'

'Lorna May,' Kate repeated. 'That's pretty.'

Continuing to read, Louise's mouth curled into a warm smile. 'He says he's going to put in for two days' leave to go and see her.'

'Good of him.'

'And he'll try to send a picture.'

'That'll be nice.'

'Any other news?' Esme asked.

Louise shook her head. 'Just the usual about there always being too much to do. Not opening yours?' she asked, nodding to Esme's envelope.

'After breakfast. It won't be important.'

'Well, can't sit about here, clucking with you mother hens,' Luke observed as, on the radio, the news broadcast came to an end. Getting to his feet and leaning over to switch off the wireless set, he sent Esme a wink. 'Not when my wife tells me the porch door hinge needs fixing again and the drain in the scullery needs unblocking.'

89

'Cheek of the man!' Kate said good-naturedly as her husband ambled from the room. 'Clucking, indeed.'

But before any of them had even moved from the table, Luke was back. 'Telephone for you, Esme. Mr Mulberry.'

Raising an eyebrow, Esme got to her feet and made her way up to the hall. Presumably, this would be instructions for another mission.

'Hullo? Lavender speaking.'

'Ah. Good. Got you. Mulberry here.' The voice at the other end of the line wasn't, Esme realised, the usual one. 'Damson and Plum. Ready to collect at twenty-one fifteen. Sorry it's short notice. Rush job. Sage will be waiting.'

Esme frowned. 'Waiting when?'

'Tonight. As I say, bit of rush job. No overnight storage required. Straight to the usual address. Got that?'

'Twenty-one fifteen. Got it.'

'Good show. Cheerio, then.'

The receiver replaced, Esme shrugged. What did it matter that this next lot of operatives wouldn't be staying overnight? Aunt Kate would be disappointed to miss out on some earnings but, from her own point, it was easier to drive them straight to the airfield than make a separate trip. Better still, she now had something to look forward to again — short notice or not!

* * *

'Here we are, then. This is it.' Drawing the Austin to a halt alongside the Nissen hut just after ten o'clock that same night, Esme turned to see one of her pas-

90

sengers wipe the condensation from the window and peer out into the darkness.

'Thanks, Lavender.'

It was only then she realised that she didn't even know which of them was Damson and which was Plum. Not that it mattered: already her brief part in the operation was complete; in a moment or two, her passengers would be gone. In a couple of hours, they would be in France.

Hearing the rear doors opening, she buttoned her coat and got out into the frosty air. How thoughtful of Richard to have sent her those clothing coupons. How fortunate that old-fashioned little clothing shop in Westward Quay should have had a wool blend trench coat in her size. With winter just around the corner, it was going to be a Godsend.

'In here,' she addressed her charges, switching on her torch and gesturing towards the hut. 'Your pilot should be waiting.'

'Thanks,' the second of her passengers replied, hoisting his haversack onto his shoulder.

Inside the hut, they found two men seated at the table, playing cards, the shorter of the two clad in overalls, the other in pilot's uniform. In unison, they rose to their feet.

'Lavender, I take it.'

Esme gulped. To borrow an expression from Aunt Kate, *well there was a sight for sore eyes*. And yes, as a married woman, she really shouldn't be thinking that about another man!

'That's . . . right. Yes. Delivering Damson and Plum for Sage.'

The pilot grinned. 'Sage. That would be me.' Feeling unexpectedly warm, Esme stepped aside and watched

91

as he moved to address her two operatives. 'Put your kit in the corner and then come over and have a seat. The Lysander's fuelled and ready but we've another twenty minutes to kill before we can take off.'

'We can't leave now?' the taller of her two passengers asked. The moment she'd seen them alighting from their train, she'd known he would be the more nervous of the two.

The pilot shook his head. ''Fraid not. We're forecast to pick up a tail wind over the Channel. Depart now and we'll be early to the rendezvous. And since we can't risk arriving before they're ready for us, we have to wait.'

To Esme, the discovery that they weren't about to depart came as a disappointment; she'd been hoping that this time around she would be there to see them take off. But then . . . perhaps she still could be. 'Mind if I stop for a moment and warm up?' she asked, her question posed as casually as she could manage.

Having dragged two more chairs across to the table, the pilot shrugged. 'Be my guest. There's a pan of cocoa over there if you fancy some. Clean mugs on the shelf.'

What luck — a mug of cocoa would give her genuine reason to dally; having failed to glean much last time she was here, she'd been hoping to learn a bit more about what happened next.

To that end, she went to where the contents of a steel saucepan were being kept warm on a small spirit stove. Reaching for one of the enamel mugs, she poured sufficient of the thin brown liquid to fill it halfway. Then, rather than go and sit at the table, she perched on the edge of one of the chairs against the wall, from where she could take it all in.

The first thing to capture her interest was a black-board — a new addition since the day Group Captain Hall had shown her around. Upon it was painted a grid, the columns of which were empty apart from the topmost row. Beneath the heading that read 'Captain' had been chalked 'F/L Carey, J', beneath 'Take Off' was written '2220', and underneath 'Remarks' had been scribbled what appeared to be '2 pax.' Above the board was a clock with a large 'Z' printed across the face, the minute hand of which chose that moment to advance with a click to show ten past ten.

From the card game at the table came laughter followed by a groan. Looking across, she saw the air-craftsman shake his head and throw down his hand. 'How the devil . . .'

'Here,' the pilot said, pushing half the pile of cop-pers back towards him, 'keep it. And for Christ's sake work on that twitch of yours. If you can't get that under control, you might as well just show me your hand and be done with.'

'Yes, sir. Thank you, sir.'

'And no need for the 'sir' when it's just the two of us and a pack of cards.'

'No, sir.'

Watching as the aircraftsman gathered up the play-ing cards and slipped them back into their sleeve, she wondered whether they were the only two personnel on duty. There was the guard at the gate, of course, but if this was all it took then Group Captain Hall hadn't been joking when he'd described the operation here as low-key.

With that, the flight lieutenant got to his feet. 'Right then. Jump to it, Leading Aircraftsman Pugh. Time to get underway. Chaps,' he said, turning towards the operatives at the stove, 'give us five minutes and then come on out.'

While she didn't know what she'd been expecting, when she accompanied the two operatives outside several minutes later, and the beams from their torches enabled her to pick out the shape of the aircraft, she was shocked to see how small it was; the dinky little thing looked barely large enough to take one passenger, let alone two. *Flying by the seat of their trousers*, she imagined Uncle Ned — a pilot in the last war — remarking fondly of it. *Proper flying.*

In the flickering of their torches, she was able to make out the first of her passengers climbing into the opening behind the pilot before turning to help his colleague follow suit. The canopy secured above them, she saw the aircraftsman jump to the ground and dart around to the nose. Then, after a series of explosive splutters, she heard the propeller clatter to life and was quickly engulfed in an evil-smelling cloud of exhaust.

'Wind's from the southwest,' Aircraftsman Pugh came jogging back towards her to explain. 'So, he'll taxi up the runway as far as that torch, turn back and take off towards us.'

'It's a very small aeroplane,' she said.

'But ideal for this type of sortie.'

With no idea why that should be, she decided not to show her ignorance by asking. But, with nothing save the glow of the flare in the distance and just the sound of the engine to betray its whereabouts as the aircraft headed away into the darkness, she spotted an opportunity to satisfy her curiosity on another matter. 'Has the pilot been flying these operations long?'

'No. But when I came here, I was told that Flight

94

Lieutenant Carey is one of the best. If not the *best* of the best. Handpicked for these missions by someone high up. Word is he was offered a promotion to Squadron Leader to come here but wouldn't take it.'

'Wouldn't take a promotion? Why not?'

'Beats me, miss. *Ma'am.* I overheard Group Captain Hall saying Jack could even have had *his* job if he'd wanted it, could even have been on his way to wing commander by now.'

Jack. So that was what the 'J' stood for. 'Goodness.'

'Before he came here, he used to fly Hurricanes . . . and you've got to be red-hot to handle one of those. Don't get me wrong, this sort of flying still needs nerves of steel.'

With that, the note of the plane's engine changed, and Esme guessed that having made its turn, it was gathering speed as it came back towards them.

'How far before they leave the ground?' she raised her voice to ask.

'Any moment now,' Pugh raised his own to reply. 'She goes up surprisingly quick. Two hundred yards tops. Though Jack can get her up in one-fifty.' In the darkness, Esme smiled. Leading Aircraftsman Pugh was clearly in awe of the flight lieutenant. 'There. She's up.'

Realising she'd been holding her breath, Esme listened as the little craft climbed away into the night. How must it feel, she wondered, to be literally heading into the darkness? For her, getting the operatives safely underway marked the end of her involvement; she could go home to her bed. But their parts in this mission were only just beginning. And no matter their training for this moment, surely even the bravest of them had to be anxious about what lay in wait for

95

them at the other end?

'Well, goodnight, then,' she said to the aircraftsman.

''Night, miss.'

'See you next time.'

'Yes, miss. See you next time.'

Settling into the freezing cold Austin and hurrying to start the engine, Esme let out a sigh. Two missions successfully under her belt. And yes, compared to the parts those brave operatives and their pilot were about to play, her contribution was insignificant — less than insignificant if such a thing were possible. Nevertheless, she felt proud of what she was doing, not only for the war but for her own recovery, too. She was glad she'd allowed Uncle Luke to talk her into it, the fact that she'd now gone several days without feeling *quite* so debilitated by grief only reinforcing her opinion that agreeing to take this on had been the right thing to do.

And it was just as well because, a few days later, having received further instructions from Mr Mulberry that she was to collect two more agents, Esme once again found herself back at Pond Farm.

'Busy tonight,' she remarked to Aircraftsman Pugh as she arrived in the ops room and glanced about. Pulling off her driving gloves, she set them down on the end of the table and then turned her attention to the group of three men studying the wall map of France.

'Practice run for a Hudson crew,' Pugh explained. *Hudson.* She'd heard that name before. 'Must be a big drop coming up if they're involved.'

'What time do my two depart?' she asked, shaking the droplets of rain from her mac. There was, she noted, no sign of Flight Lieutenant Carey.

'Ten minutes. There's a depression barrelling in from the Atlantic and so the pilot's keen to get out and back sharpish. He's just making his final checks. I'll let him know you've arrived.'

Removing her beret and giving it a shake, she repositioned it on her head and ran her fingers over the front of her hair. The beret was only one she'd borrowed from Louise, but she thought it leant her a certain modishness. 'Thank you,' she called after Pugh's departing back.

The pilot who came through the door moments later, though, wasn't who she'd been expecting. Fair-haired, and incredibly young-looking, he gave her the merest of nods before turning stiffly to her two operatives.

'Fit, chaps?'

As the agents shouldered their kit bags, she scanned the operations board. *F/L Pashley, A. 2240. 2 pax.* A different pilot. Well, that was a shame.

'Thank you, Lavender.'

Drawing her attention smartly back to the operatives, she sent them a smile. 'The pleasure was mine. Godspeed.'

'Goodnight,' said the second.

Once they had left the room, Esme scanned the blackboard: the name Carey was nowhere upon it. Perhaps he had a night off. Heading for the door, she giggled at her foolishness: did pilots get a night off from war? Unlikely. Never mind. Her part of the mission accomplished, she could head home. Besides, she thought, dashing through the continuing downpour and ducking back into the Austin, why the sudden fascination with Flight Lieutenant Carey? Momentarily deafened by the drumming of rain thundering

97

down on the motorcar's roof, she grinned. She had a crush! She had a *thing* for a pilot. How ridiculous! How corny. Mind you, if she was ever to be infatuated with a man she shouldn't be, she would be hard pressed to do better. Tall. Dark. Apparently fearless. And probably married, she decided with a rueful grin; too much of a catch not to be.

Impatient to be back at home and out of her wet mac, she was dismayed by how quickly the lashing rain made driving tedious. Falling so heavily at times that it overwhelmed the wipers and obliterated her view of the way ahead, she had no choice but to nose the Austin along at a crawl. With the inside of the windscreen continually misting up and making it even harder to see out, she wasn't even sure how far she still had to go. With a despairing sigh, she reached for the chamois leather and gave the screen another good wipe. 'Keep this where you can get hold of it in a hurry', Uncle Luke had said the day he'd tucked it at the back of the dashboard for her. 'All motorcars mist up when it's damp.' Dear Uncle Luke. He did look out for her. There, she thought, her side of the windscreen wiped clear yet again. That was better.

The chamois replaced, she sat back in her seat. Finally, the rain seemed to be letting up; not much longer and she would be filling her hot water bottle, getting out of these damp clothes and settling into bed with a warm drink. Since it was still reasonably early, she might read for a while; now that she was a couple of chapters in, Candleford Green was more captivating than it had seemed from the first few pages. And then, tomorrow morning, she'd agreed to go and do something with Louise — some sort of training at the church hall. Quite what, precisely, she

98

couldn't remember. But, if Louise was involved, then it was probably— *Thud!*

Quick! Brake! Brace!

Silence.

Heart thundering, Esme eased herself back into her seat. Then, slowly opening her eyes, she peeled her fingers away from the steering wheel and stared out through the windscreen. What the devil had just happened? Had she hit something? A badger? No, something larger than that. A deer? Oh, merciful God, please don't let it be a deer!

With that, beyond the nearside wing, she caught a flicker of movement. Whatever it was, she hadn't killed it. No, but what if it was badly injured? What if it was a ghastly bloody mess? What then? She couldn't just leave it to die; it might be in pain. But something as large as a deer? How would she even drag it out of the way?

The dizzying rate of her heartbeat not letting up, she fumbled in the darkness for the handle, opened the door and tentatively extended a leg towards the ground; from beneath the sole of her boot came the squelch of mud. Really, she would rather not do this. Really, she would rather just try to stop shaking and drive on home. But she had to see what she'd hit. Swivelling her bottom on the seat, she lowered her other foot to the road only to have it skid away from her in the wet. *Just take a quick look*, she told herself. *Then you can decide what to do.* Pulling her collar up to her ears and lowering her head against the stabbing of icy raindrops, she edged along the side of the car. But at the sound of groaning, she froze. What sort of animal groaned? Wishing she could just get back into the car and drive home, she forced herself forwards.

She had to see what it was.

At the end of the bonnet, she peered around. Wait. Was that . . . a man? She'd hit *a man*? Dear God, she'd hit a man! She cast about. What to do? *Go for help.* Yes, but where? Out here, in the back of beyond, there might not be a house for miles.

When the man moved again, she bent low. 'Forgive me,' she ventured, 'but are you all right?' When all she got was a grunt, she tried again. 'Are you hurt?'

In the paltry light from the Austin's shuttered headlamps, she made out heavy clothing, and that the man was clutching his arm. The most important thing, she reminded herself, was that he was alive. But since he also seemed to be injured, she had to get him to a doctor. *A doctor? Out here?* How was she going to do that? Again, she glanced about. *Think*, she urged herself. *Where is this place? How much further to Woodicombe?* Surely, it couldn't be far. If the pungent smell of decaying leaves and general dankness was anything to go by, this had to be the narrow stretch of lane that twisted its way through the woods about a mile before Woodicombe Cross. If so, then in a few minutes she could be home and telephoning for help.

Doubled over in the road, the man gave another groan. 'Christ . . . almighty.'

She ventured closer. 'Here, let me help you.'

Raising his uninjured arm, he waved her away. 'Leave me be.'

At least he wasn't a German spy, she thought, marking down his accent as that of a local. *A German spy? In the wilds of Devon?* To even be considering such a ridiculous thing she had to be in shock. Shivering with such severity that her entire body convulsed, she forced herself to concentrate. She hadn't passed any other vehicles. Nor had she seen any sign of a bicycle. So, he had to have come here on foot. And in which case, she should offer to drive him home.

'Do you live around here?' she asked. 'Only, if you do, I can —'

'No.' Again, he waved her away.

'I'd really rather not leave you. You might be suffering from concussion.'

'I said no.'

In the dim beam from her headlights, Esme found herself looking at his boots. Heavy-soled, they were the type a soldier would wear, his trousers, khaki and muddied, likewise. Pulled down low over his brow was a woollen hat, concealing his chin, a scarf. Could he be a deserter? Unlikely. Around here, he was more likely to be a poacher and in which case, given that he'd repeatedly refused her help, perhaps she should just leave him to his own devices. On the other hand, what if he was properly hurt but just didn't realise it yet?

When he let out another groan, she decided to make one last try. 'It really wouldn't be any trouble for me to —'

'For the love of God, girl.' His voice this time was an urgent hiss. 'Just go on home.'

Aghast, she reeled backwards.

'*Uncle Luke?*' In an instant, she was crouched back down beside him. 'Uncle Luke, here, let me help you.' But when she reached towards him, he shook her away.

'*I told you. Go home.*'

'What . . . and leave you here? I don't think so. Aunt Kate would kill me —'

'Look, maid, if you care for me at all, go home. Say

101

nothing of this to no one.'

'But —'

'For Christ's sake, Esme, just get in the car and go home.'

Struggling to understand what was going on, Esme got to her feet and stood looking down at her uncle's hunched form. Then, feeling rain trickling down the back of her neck, she swivelled about, made her way along the side of the car and climbed back in. With her hands numb from cold, she fumbled the gearstick into neutral, started the engine, and then paused to peer out into the darkness. No. This was madness. What was she thinking? No matter her uncle's reason for not wanting to come home with her, she would have to insist. He could shout at her all he liked, she couldn't drive off and leave him there. If anything happened to him, she would never live with herself. Whatever he'd been doing out here, it didn't matter. She didn't care. She had to get him home.

Throwing open the door and getting back out, she once again edged her way along the side of the car. But . . . where had he gone? Dumbfounded, she cast about, flicking her torch up the steep banks to either side of the lane. How on earth could he have just disappeared? Where was there even for him to go? Unless he'd somehow scrambled up one of the banks, there was nowhere for him to go.

With rain running down her cheeks and dripping from her chin, she returned along the side of the Austin and climbed back in. Trying to look for him was pointless; she had no idea which way he'd gone and only the light of her torch to see by. Grabbing the chamois leather, she rubbed it ferociously across the inside of the misted-up windscreen and craned for a

102

final look. No. He was gone. He was nowhere to be seen. In those few moments while she'd been dithering, he'd given her the slip. But why, for heaven's sake? Why hadn't he let her take him home? What was he hiding? What didn't he want her to know?

Shivering so hard that her teeth rattled, she gave a defeated shake of her head. Whatever Uncle Luke was up to, he clearly didn't want her involved, which meant that she had little choice but to do as he'd said — to go home and say nothing. If she was going to do that, though, she would have to tell herself that he was just on patrol with the Home Guard and then somehow ignore all the evidence that indicated otherwise. She would have to trust that he knew what he was doing. In reality, by disappearing like that, he'd left her with no other choice.

Rubbing her hands to bring some life back to her fingers, she started the engine, released the handbrake, and pulled slowly away. But even doing as he'd said felt wholly wrong. What if he'd hit his head and, although believing he was all right, actually did have concussion? Or what if he was in trouble of another sort and had played down his injuries in order to escape from someone? So much about this didn't make sense! How was it possible to not be there one moment and almost under her wheels the next? He couldn't simply have dropped from above. The only comfort in all of this was that he hadn't seemed seriously hurt. Nor, from what she'd been able to make out, was there any damage to the Austin. Tomorrow morning, in daylight, she would have to check that nearside wing.

Moments later, recognising she had reached Woodicombe Cross, Esme brought the Austin to a halt at the junction and sat staring ahead. What *was* Uncle Luke involved in? And what would he do now? Would he explain? Make excuses? Say nothing? Presumably, tomorrow, she would find out. Until then, she would do her best to put the whole thing out of her mind and try to get some sleep. And she would do so purely because some of the explanations for her uncle's behaviour were just too alarming to even contemplate.

★ ★ ★

The sky was barely light. So gloomy was the morning that, when Esme crept down two flights of stairs, stole along the kitchen corridor, and let herself out of the back door, she wished she'd waited until later. But, at least this way, she told herself as she tried to cross the yard without making a noise on the gravel, she could check the Austin for damage before anyone else was about. And then, if it was dented or scratched, she would have time to work out what she was going to do about it — in particular, how she was going to explain it away.

Drawing alongside, she went towards the front of it and, holding her breath, rounded the wing. No damage. In her relief she exhaled. What luck. No need to invent a story about what had happened or try to work out how to get it repaired.

'Playing you up, is she?'

She shot upright. *Uncle Luke.*

Turning about, she found him staring at the nearside headlamp. At least he'd come home.

'Um . . . no, not at all,' she said. What was he doing out here? Had he, too, come to inspect the Austin? Or was he here to see whether, despite her tacit agreement last night to say nothing of what had happened, she would do so anyway? And now what did she do? Concoct a story and he would know she was lying. Confront him and he might get cross. Neither option was without peril. 'It's just that last night,' she began, unexpectedly spotting a middle ground, 'when I was coming back from the airfield, I thought I collided with something in the lane. Not far from here — around Farracott Wood, possibly?'

With the onus now on him to respond, she waited. But, rather than reply, he stood staring fixedly down at the wing until, after a moment's consideration, he stooped to run his hand along the line of it. 'See what you hit, did you?'

So that's how he was going to play this: force her to show her hand first — the very ploy she'd planned on using.

'Initially,' she said, 'I thought I must have hit a deer. But if I did, then by the time I'd come to my senses and got out to look, it had run off.'

'Big creatures, deer,' Luke replied matter-of-factly. 'Make an almighty thud, that would. Must have frightened the life out of you.'

'It . . . did.'

'Must have given you quite the shock.'

'Quite . . . yes.'

'And then, when you got out and couldn't find no trace of it, well, you must have wondered whether it really happened at all . . . or whether perhaps, for a split of a second there, you'd failed to notice it was no more than a fallen branch. Especially what with there being no sign of damage to the car.'

So, his plan was to suggest that their coming together

105

never happened? Unsure what to make of that, Esme found herself looking to where the unbuttoned cuff of his shirtsleeve was hanging open to display a patch of purple and maroon bruising extending upwards from his wrist. Aghast at the extent of it, she winced. How on earth hadn't she broken his wrist?

Wishing he would simply tell her what was going on, but concerned not to make life difficult for him, she could see no option but to accept his version of events — even if it did make her appear scatty.

'I did begin to doubt —'

'If it *was* a deer,' he continued evenly, 'it can't have been harmed. Not for it to have disappeared so quick like that.'

Ordinarily, concealing something wouldn't trouble her — after all, she'd been expertly trained to do just that — but this was Uncle Luke. Family.

Her unease colouring her cheeks, she cleared her throat. 'It can't have been, no.'

'If you *had* hit something, there would be damage to the wing here . . . or the grill, wouldn't there?'

Uneasily, she nodded. 'One would think so, yes.'

'At worst, you can only have caught something with a glancing blow.'

'That's what must have happened, yes,' she said. That he was deliberately avoiding meeting her look told her that he was as uneasy about all of this as she was. 'A glancing blow to a deer that . . . ran off unharmed.'

'Got to be careful round them lanes,' he said. ''Specially with next to no lights. Perfect menace, deer can be.'

'So it would seem.'

'Wouldn't want to bring one down and then have

to eat the evidence, would we?'

Catching sight of the fact that he was now grinning, she laughed. 'We would not.'

'Though . . . should it prove necessary . . .' Finally, he met her eye. 'I won't tell if you won't.'

'Uncle Luke,' she said plainly, 'if there's one thing you can rely on, it's that I never betray a secret.'

'Nor me, girl. Nor me.'

'And on that note,' she said, anxious to bring this extraordinary conversation to a close, 'I had better get back indoors. I said I would accompany Louise to the church hall this morning for ARP training. And she won't want to be late.'

'Well, mind you have a care with that, too.'

'Yes. Of course.'

Remaining for long enough to watch him saunter away to his workshop, Esme fought to make sense of what had just happened. *I won't tell if you won't.* Clearly, whatever he had been up to, he trusted her not to say anything. And nor would she. Whatever her uncle had chosen to involve himself with was none of her business. A regrettable upshot of this protracted war was that sometimes, all sorts of otherwise distasteful activities became unavoidable, the line between right and wrong having of late become uncomfortably blurred. So, whatever Uncle Luke was doing, she would assume it was with good reason. After all, she didn't really have any other choice.

7

No Smoke Without Fire

'Had I known there was going to be so much water, I would have worn wellingtons.'

'Had I remembered there was going to be so much water,' Louise countered Esme's observation, 'I would have warned you beforehand.'

It was later that same morning, and the two women were now stood behind the church hall, where Louise had been roped into assisting Mr Aldridge with what he called *refresh-your-memory fire training* for ARP wardens.

'One of the downsides to being so far from all the action,' he had said to them when they arrived, 'is that without the chance to put one's skills into action, one quickly forgets what one's been taught.'

'Preferable to the alternative,' Esme had whispered to Louise.

And so, the motley crew of volunteers, who only last week had been tested upon their first aid abilities and put through bandaging practice, were now awaiting their turn to put out a fire as might be occasioned by an incendiary bomb. In this instance, the conflagrations in question were actually wire containers, about the size of an armchair, stuffed with wastepaper and bracken. Once ablaze, it was down to a team of three — in this case, half of those present — to man the stirrup pump and extinguish the flames in as short a time as possible.

'Now, let's see what you remember,' Mr Aldridge said as he stood, newspaper wick and box of matches at the ready. 'On a standard stirrup pump, how long is the hose?'

When the others stood shifting their weight, it was Louise who replied. 'Thirty feet.'

'Well done, Mrs Ross. Thirty feet. And how far will the jet of water carry beyond that?'

In the silence, it again fell to Louise to answer. 'Thirty feet.'

'Correct. And so how far from the fire should No. 1 operator position him or herself?'

'As far as bloody possible,' one of the other women mumbled.

'Correct, Mrs Groves! As far as possible. Although not so far that the water falls short of dousing the flames. Now, an incendiary bomb, as you will doubtless all remember, ignites on impact, where it then proceeds to burn very bright and very hot for about one minute. While it is unlikely you would be on hand to tackle the fire so quickly, you must nevertheless wait for that initial blaze to die down before getting stuck in. Now, when you do, where must you aim the water?'

Again, it was Louise who answered. 'At the base of the fire.'

'Correct. Keep low to attack the fire because at ground level there will be less heat. You want the nozzle turned to 'spray' for the incendiary itself and to 'jet' for the rest of any fire. And how do we set ourselves up?'

'Position number one mans the hose, position number two works the pump, position number three keeps bringing the buckets of water.'

'Spot on. And how quickly will this stirrup pump get through a bucket of water?'

Depends how big the bucket is, Esme felt tempted to reply.

'At a rate of sixty-five double strokes, the jet draws one-and-a-quarter gallons a minute.'

Clive Aldridge looked impressed. 'Very good, Mrs Ross. Right then, Team A, prepare to deploy.'

Once alight, the bin produced rather more smoke than flame. Even so, it was, Esme realised, the first time she'd seen anyone other than the fire brigade attempt to put out a fire.

'Well done,' she said afterwards to Louise, who, not surprisingly, had volunteered for position number one.

'Though I don't let on to Mr Aldridge,' Louise whispered, 'and despite the almost non-existent risk of us ever being bombed, Dad made sure all of us knew how to do this years ago.'

Esme nodded. 'I noticed the pumps about the house. And there's one in the stables, isn't there?'

'There is. Anyway, look, while I wind up the hose, would you go and refill the bucket — you know, from the standpipe around the back — and then we can go on home and get warmed up.'

'Of course.'

Walking back to the house a while later, her thoughts never far from Uncle Luke, Esme turned to study her cousin's expression. Was it just her own heightened senses or did Louise look to have something on her mind? If so, was it her father? Had she somehow found out what had happened?

'What?' Louise looked up to ask.

'Nothing. It's just that since we left the church hall,

110

you haven't said a word. And it's unusual for you to be quiet.'

As they continued walking, it was some time before Louise eventually said, 'Actually, there is something.'

Please don't let it be about your father.

'And that is?'

'Probably nothing . . .'

'But . . . ?' *I won't tell if you won't.*

'Well, see, the other night, Connie told me she'd seen Dad with Frank Hodge —'

'Frank Hodge . . . ?' Whoever he was, heaven be praised.

'— who's the sort of fellow,' Louise went on, 'to rob you blind as soon as look at you.'

Careful now. 'Doesn't sound to me like someone Uncle Luke would be mixed up with.'

'That's what *I* said. But Connie was adamant. Said she saw the two of them coming out of The Black Sheep, thick as thieves.'

Esme relaxed a little. 'So? Perhaps he just bumped into him and was being cordial.'

'Happen he was. But when I told Connie she couldn't have seen him because the night in question was one of Dad's Home Guard nights, she said I was wrong. She said that her Uncle Robert's in the same platoon, and that they go two or three times a week, Tuesdays for drill and then a night or two out on patrol.'

Struggling to follow her cousin's reasoning, Esme frowned. 'And so...?'

'And so, as even *you* can't have failed to notice, Dad goes out at least five nights a week — sometimes six. Occasionally he's even been every single night — and he always saying he's going to Home Guard.'

Seeing her cousin's point, Esme tensed; unfortunately, this Frank Hodge character sounded just the sort to prowl about in woodland. 'All right. But isn't your father a sergeant? And so might he not have to go more often than the ordinary members?'

'Ye-es,' Louise conceded, 'but six or seven nights a week? After all, around here, it's not like down in Plymouth, where the Home Guard goes out every night on fire watch . . . and to man pillboxes against invasion. Round here, there's a lot less to worry about. By Dad's own admission, pretty much all they train for these days is what to do in the event a German aircraft comes down. Which is why, when Connie said what she did, it set me to wondering.'

Her unease increasing, Esme sighed. 'Set you to wondering whether he really does go to the Home Guard as often as he says? Or whether, really —'

'He *is* somehow tangled up with Frank Hodge and . . .' With that, Louise glanced over her shoulder. '. . . and black marketeering or some such.'

It ought to sound so unlikely, Esme realised, that under any other circumstances she would be laughing. As it was, all she could manage was a sort of strangled chuckle. 'Sorry,' she said, making an exaggerated show of bringing her hand to her mouth, 'but I really don't think you should worry about that! Uncle Luke must be one of the most honest men on earth. He's not like that fellow . . . oh, what was his name — that dodgy chap you were dating when you worked in Plymouth?'

'Harry.'

'Truly, Louise, you mustn't let the experience of one bad sort colour your judgement.'

'Why would I?' Louise said shortly. 'That was three

112

years ago. It's all forgotten.'

'However,' Esme continued, seeing a way that might lead her cousin to drop the matter, 'if you genuinely think your father is up to something, why not just ask him?'

'What? Accuse him of lying about where he goes? I can't do that!'

'I'm not suggesting you accuse him of anything,' Esme said carefully, sensing she was almost there. 'More that you casually mention how Connie claims to have seen him coming out of The Black Horse —'

'Sheep. The Black Sheep. It's the pub in Farracott.'

At the mention of Farracott, Esme stiffened.

'And . . . that you told her she was wrong. How he responds to your observation will tell you all you need to know.'

'I can't,' Louise said.

And thank goodness for that, Esme thought. Disaster narrowly averted. At least, for now it was.

'Then don't,' she replied. 'But if you're *not* going to, then I strongly suggest you put the whole business out of your mind. Don't give doubt the chance to eat away at you.'

Louise gave a heavy sigh. 'If only Douglas was here.'

'Douglas?'

'Then I could ask him to talk to Dad for me. Man to man, as they're so fond of saying. Dad would listen to him — wouldn't brush it off as nothing.'

'Poor you,' Esme said, reaching for her cousin's hand and giving it a squeeze. 'You must miss him terribly.'

Louise's eyes filled with tears. 'I miss him so much it hurts.'

'I'm sure it must do. But just try to think that it

won't be for ever.' It was a feeble thing to say, she knew that. But what other comfort could she offer? What could anyone say that would possibly help? 'And with this other thing,' she said, still holding onto Louise's hand, 'I really do think you should try putting it out of your mind. Truly, I don't believe you have any reason to worry.'

Putting it out of her mind was advice she would do well to heed herself. Unfortunately, despite what she'd let Uncle Luke believe, she knew she couldn't do that. One way or another, she had to establish what he was up to — and preferably before Louise stumbled across it for herself.

✷ ✷ ✷

Re-reading the letter made Esme laugh. Great Aunt Diana wrote precisely as she spoke — directly and without a care for whom she might offend. Some members of the family considered her opinionated, others found her terrifying. But, to Esme, she was a breath of fresh air in an otherwise stuffy family, with a habit of hitting the nail on the head. *Feeling as though you have lost everything*, Diana Lloyd had written, *can make you question who you are, lead you to ask where do I go from here? Dear girl, please bear in mind that while such questions are normal, they're best not answered in haste, nor from a state of raw grief. Trust me, I know.* Yes, what Great Aunt Diana said — or, in this case, wrote — showed insight and understanding, which was why, to pass the time until she had to go to the airfield, Esme was now stood in the hallway, waiting for her mother, in Windsor, to arrive at the other end of the telephone. *Talk to your mother*, Great Aunt

Diana had gone on to write, *if not for the words of comfort she might have to offer, then simply to do so on your own terms.*

'Darling! So sorry. I was upstairs.'

'Hello Mummy,' Esme returned her mother's breathless greeting. 'Don't worry. The fault's mine for calling so late.'

'No, it's fine, darling. Luckily, we still have a couple of minutes.'

'We do. So, how are you?'

'Being driven slowly round the bend by the combination of Aunt Diana and your Grandmamma Pamela . . . but otherwise well enough, thank you. You know, I do wish you had come here instead of going all the way down there to Woodicombe.'

'Because it would have deflected some of the old girls' attention from you? Would have diluted the torture?' It was precisely the reason, Esme reflected, why she'd rejected the idea almost before Richard had even suggested it!

'Careful, darling, you're in danger of becoming as outspoken as they are. Anyway, more importantly than all of that, how are you getting on?'

Having rehearsed for her mother's questions beforehand, Esme reminded herself not to get rattled. 'Better of late. I have my ups and downs, of course, to which Louise would no doubt bear testament. But I've come to see that Richard was right and that what I needed was some company and something to do.'

'I'm so glad.'

'How's Daddy?' The less Esme had to talk about herself, the better.

'From what little I can gather when he telephones, he's fine. Doing far too much, of course —'

115

'Along with everyone else in Whitehall, it would seem.'

'Well, you know your father — only ever truly content when he's up to his neck in policy.'

'And Uncle Ned?'

'Drowning in government contracts, apparently. Another one who's as happy as Larry.'

'As so many men are in this war.'

'And you're managing to speak to Richard?'

'A couple of times a week. He's another who's frantically busy. By the way, thank you for your letter. I was going to write back but then I thought it would be nicer to speak to you over the telephone.'

'And it absolutely is, isn't it?'

'Yes. Lovely. Although, our time must almost be up. Three minutes flies.'

'Well, take care darling. And thank you so much for telephoning. My turn next time.'

'Perhaps in a week or so,' Esme suggested. Nice though it was to talk to her mother, she didn't want to fall into a habit — *it's Sunday, I must speak to Mummy.* And she *definitely* didn't want to let slip about her driving. No sense courting an argument!

'A week or so. Yes. All right.'

'Please give my love to Grandmamma and Aunt Diana.'

'Will do. Goodbye then, darling.'

'Goodbye, Mummy.'

Fingering her locket, Esme replaced the receiver and turned to check the hall clock. As far as telephone calls with her mother were concerned, that one hadn't gone too badly. By not giving her mother the chance to ask difficult questions, neither of them had become cross or upset. Better still, she hadn't needed to lie; she *did* have ups and downs, and she *did* feel as though she had turned a corner, the number of good days she had now outnumbering those when she succumbed to grief. In fact, her recovery felt not unlike trying to make a giant snowball: having finally got it started, the effort demanded of her to keep it going was far less; she just had to do more of the same.

But now, she really must go and get ready. Having only yesterday received yet another last-minute notification that she was required to 'collect a delivery of Moss and Fern', and 'store them overnight', she was going to have to wrap up warmly against another bitterly cold and windy drive to the airfield. Not that she was complaining. In fact, she'd spent the whole afternoon looking forward to it immensely.

* * *

'Tell me your name's not really Lavender.'

Having hoped on the drive over that the pilot for tonight's mission would turn out to be the very man now standing next to her — the intriguing Flight Lieutenant Jack Carey — Esme was surprised at how difficult it was proving to look him in the eye.

'Why?' she responded to his enquiry. 'Does it not suit me?'

'Let's just say,' he replied, reaching for one of the mugs and handing it to her, 'that whenever I catch a whiff of the stuff, I'm reminded of my grandmother.'

'*My* grandmother,' she said, picturing Pamela Russell holding court from her favourite sofa, 'invariably wafts in on a cloud of Guerlain's Shalimar.'

'Then we must have very different grandmothers.'

'Mine *is* rather one of a kind.' Waiting while he

117

poured her some cocoa, she went on to ask, 'Will you be away on time tonight?'

From where he was leaning against the end of the trestle, Jack Carey nodded. 'Visibility's good, wind's light.'

When he then took to staring across the room, she studied his appearance. Unusually — given the current fashion among pilots — his chestnut brown hair had been left unoiled, giving him the appearance of having only just got out of bed. His moustache was neat, his stubble light, his eyes a sincere brown. Viewed in profile, the lines of his nose and jaw were clean and pleasing. Classic. *Masculine*. And if her mother were here, she would point out that the way he held himself betrayed breeding. These days, it was a compliment she rarely bestowed. *Does no one stand up straight anymore?*

'Where did you fly from prior to this?'

'*Immediately* prior to this, Bedfordshire. Before that, I did a spell on the Sussex coast. Before *that*, I was at Biggin.'

She nodded slowly. 'And your family? Where are they?'

'Suffolk.'

'And —'

'And now,' he said, the way he angled his head suggesting she was prying, 'it's time to get your chaps safely stowed.' With that, downing the dregs of his cocoa and then pushing himself away from the trestle, he reached to the back of the chair for his jacket and beckoned to Aircraftsman Pugh to accompany him out.

Ruing her bluntness, Esme glanced to the clock. Almost eleven. 'Yes. Of course.'

'But I'll see you next time.'

'Yes,' she said, determining that *next time* she would be more subtle with her enquiries. In fact, if there was a next time, she could do worse than employ some of the techniques she had used to such good effect in Brighton because, suddenly, she found herself gripped by an urge to find out more — in fact, rather a lot more — about Flight Lieutenant Jack Carey.

★ ★ ★

'Well, there's no mistaking you seem brighter, love.'

It was an evening later that same week and, with an apparent lull in SOE operations, and both Luke and Louise gone to do their respective shifts, Esme found herself helping Aunt Kate to bottle mincemeat — or at least, to bottle what her aunt called *an approximation of it*.

'Yes,' she replied to her aunt's observation. 'I suppose I am a little brighter.'

Wiping her hands on the corner of her apron, Kate stood back to survey their efforts. 'I should have liked an orange or a lemon, you know, for the zest. Having to make do with marmalade instead won't lift the taste nowhere near as much. Still, managing to scrape together sufficient suet by itself was a triumph. And though the cinnamon and nutmeg must have been going on three years old by now, at least I found some.'

'Worse where there's none,' Esme said, sending her aunt a grin. 'And with the amount of that Pedro Ximenez you poured in, I'm not sure anyone will notice anyway.'

'Truth to tell,' Kate said, 'that had seen better days, too. One of your mother's old bottles, that must have been.'

Esme smiled. 'Too sweet for Mummy's tooth. More like Grandmamma Pamela. Anyway, I'm sure people will be grateful for a mince pie of any description.'

'They'd better be. So, what have we ended up with then — four jars?'

'And this little bit left over,' Esme replied, staring down at the half a dozen spoonfuls left in the mixing bowl.

'Tell you what, since the WVS late autumn fayre's not far off, how about I find the smallest jar in the cupboard and we use what's left to make a donation. Tie a scrap of pretty fabric round the top and no one will notice it's barely half full.'

'Good idea,' Esme agreed. 'Someone will be glad of it.'

The modest jar covered and labelled, the two women carried the washing-up through to the scullery. And while her aunt stood swirling the water to dissolve the soda, Esme regarded her expression; seemingly, she had something on her mind.

'So,' Kate duly remarked as she plunged the mixing bowl into the sink, 'you've turned a bit of a corner then.'

Lifting the tea towel from the hook, Esme thought for a moment before answering. 'I suppose I have. Obviously I still have my moments — usually at night or when I first wake up. But you and Louise were right when you said that having something to do would help.'

'Anything that occupies your mind can't really fail to,' Kate replied, 'no matter how trivial or mundane the task. Not that I'm saying your little bit of driving doesn't count for anything. Far from it.'

'Funny how things happen sometimes, isn't it?' she said, reflecting on that very point. 'What I mean is, without you providing these billets, I would never have got talked into driving people about the countryside.'

'I'll tell you what strikes *me* as funny,' Kate said as she rinsed the mixing bowl under the tap. 'That's how these folk you drive about only ever seem to leave here in the dead of night.'

For a moment, Esme wondered whether her aunt's observation was as casual as she'd made it sound, or whether she was becoming suspicious. Either way, she knew to be guarded with her answer. 'I thought the same thing. But I don't mind. It's not as though I have to get up early the next morning.'

'Is it far — this place you have to take them? Your uncle said you go someplace different from where he went that first time.'

'Not too far, no.'

'Still an RAF place, though?'

No sense hiding the fact; every time Mr Mulberry telephoned with the details, he made no secret that he was from the RAF. She was fairly certain, though, that he was nothing of the sort — that more likely he was SOE.

'RAF, yes,' she settled for saying.

She wasn't surprised that Aunt Kate should be curious. After all, she put these people up in her stable block with no clue as to where they came from, why they were there, or what they went on to do afterwards. But, since it was always better to appear to satisfy someone's inquisitiveness rather than heighten it, she would divulge just enough to appease her while at the same time making it all sound so dull that, with

121

any luck, she would lose interest.

'Get to meet many other folk? Anyone else like you?'

'Not that I've come across,' Esme replied. 'But usually there are some people to talk to.' Into her mind came a picture of Jack Carey. 'Some of whom are more chatty than others.'

'Well, good for you, love. Like I said to Lou when she came back after her wedding and was pining for Douglas, best way, always, is to keep busy. Nothing makes the days pass quicker than busy hands and a busy mind.'

'Well, all three of *you* are certainly testament to that,' Esme said, seeing the opportunity to move the topic of conversation away from Obsidian. 'You, Louise, Uncle Luke . . . all three of you are forever on the go.'

If she'd hoped her aunt might comment about Uncle Luke and the Home Guard, she was wrong.

'You can say that again. Never a still moment for any of us. Right, well, then, thanks for your help, love. And now, since I've been on my feet all day, I'm going up to soak the poor things in a bowl of Epsom salts. And truly,' Kate went on, turning towards Esme and patting her arm, 'it pleases me greatly to see you with a bit of colour back in your cheeks.'

Did she look brighter? Esme wondered as she went up the stairs and along to the drawing room to retrieve her book. In front of the fireplace, she paused to examine her reflection in the mirror. She did look less pale, but that could be down to any number of factors. For a start, she was getting lots more fresh air. Then there was the excitement attaching to all things covert, and how she felt energised to once more be a part — albeit a tiny part — of something vital.

122

There was also, she was forced to acknowledge as she turned away, something else putting colour into her cheeks: the frisson of excitement she felt when she pictured Flight Lieutenant Carey, and the dizzying rush of recklessness that had sent her reeling off balance when she had spoken to him. Schoolgirlish, really. But also entirely harmless, she told herself as she reached to the lamp table to pick up her book.

Bending to check that Aunt Kate had thoroughly damped down the fire, she switched off the lamp and turned to leave the room. Yes, enjoying a fling with a handsome pilot — as long as it never went beyond the bounds of her imagination — posed no danger to anyone, did it?

Imaginary or not, as she was about to discover, the weight on her conscience was surprisingly real; when the telephone in the hallway began to ring, and she picked it up to hear her husband's voice at the other end, the prospect of entertaining even a pretend fling made her prickle with discomfort.

'Esme, darling, how are you?'

'Um . . . not too bad, actually.'

'Sorry it's a bit late but I've only just finished for the night.'

'That's all right. It's good of you to think to call. How are you?' *Come on*, she urged herself. *For heaven's sake put Jack out of your mind!*

'Oh, you know, much the same, I suppose.'

'And London?'

'Going along as usual. Although, no, to be fair, it's been quieter of late. The Germans have their hands too full on the Eastern Front to bother much with us here. Moscow reckons thirty thousand Germans were killed there last week alone, and that the troops

123

still there are abandoning everything in their haste to flee — stores, ammunition, cattle, you name it.'

'Is there light at the end of the tunnel, then? Dare we hope this war is finally coming to an end?'

For a moment, Richard didn't reply.

'Bit too soon to say *that*, perhaps. German losses this year might be vast, but by our chaps' calculations, Hitler still has at least four hundred divisions at his command.'

Despite being grateful for news that offered even a glimmer of reassurance, Esme glanced over her shoulder to check that she was alone before whispering into the mouthpiece, 'Should you be telling me any of this?'

'Nothing that's not common knowledge. Anyway, I'm more interested in hearing all about you. What are you— Blast, hold on, I just need to wave at— There, that's better. The dear girl has given us a few more minutes. So, how are you getting along with this thing you got roped into doing?'

A picture of Jack back in her mind, Esme winced. 'Very well, actually. It's only a couple of times a week. And while it's really nothing much, I'm glad to be doing it. Without wishing to sound too self-important, I feel proud to be a part of something again. Makes me appreciate how fortunate we are to have so many good people working to defeat evil.' *There. That was more like it.*

'No harm feeling proud to be doing your bit, darling. I can hear from your voice that it's doing you good.'

'You can?'

'Definitely.'

'Aunt Kate says I have more colour, too.'

'You couldn't really fail to have — not after having been shut up here for so long . . . and especially not with you being so close to the sea.'

'I suppose not. How are your parents?'

'Much the same. Mother and Sophia are still with Aunt Helena in Bath. And yesterday I had lunch with Father, who seemed well enough.'

'Good.'

'Right, well then,' Richard said. 'I might have found a way to get more than our regulation three minutes, but I mustn't abuse the privilege.'

'Sweet-talking Cynthia on Switchboard?'

'I don't know what you mean!'

'Hm. Anyway, tell her thanks from me. And thank you for telephoning.'

'All right. Well, take care, darling. And goodbye.'

'Goodbye, Richard.'

Replacing the receiver onto the cradle, Esme smiled. Her husband thought she sounded brighter. And it was true, she was, especially now that they'd had a nice chat. How foolish to be fantasising about a fling with a pilot, even if she did find something about the man in question fascinating; she had Richard, who thought the world of her — just as she did of him.

8
Unexpected Developments

'Aha. The fragrant Miss Ward.'

'Good evening to you, too, Flight Lieutenant Carey.'

It was now early November and, after a spell of soggy weather during which everything had been continually begrimed in mud, and every moment spent outside meant battling against salt-laden gales, the countryside of North Devon was once again serene, the hours of daylight a dazzling assault on the senses, the nights either breathtakingly starry or else shrouded in cold dense fog. Thankfully, Esme reflected, closing the door to the Nissen hut behind her as she stepped inside, tonight was the former.

'Chaps,' the flight lieutenant greeted her two operatives as he moved to shake hands with each of them. 'Put your kit down in the corner and get comfortable. I'm afraid our departure is delayed.'

Unbuttoning her driving gloves and peeling them off, Esme frowned. 'Do you know by how long?' On the one hand, she now had genuine reason to stay a while. On the other, it was already late.

''Fraid not. Storms over northwest France have left our rendezvous site too wet to land. So, we're awaiting new coordinates. If we get them in the next two hours, we can still head off. Any later than that, and we'll have to abort.'

Esme glanced to the clock. Already it was showing quarter to midnight. 'So, if you're not away by zero-

126

two-hundred . . .'

'You take them back to their billet and we try again tomorrow.'

Making a quick assessment of the practical considerations, Esme nodded. 'All right. Then I suppose we'd better get comfortable. And if it's called off, we'll await new arrangements.'

'Pugh will make some cocoa,' Jack said, 'and I'll poke some life into the stove.'

Rueing that she would now have to remain sufficiently alert to drive back to Woodicombe — with or without her passengers — at two o'clock in the morning, Esme unbuttoned her coat.

'So, in France, do you just land in a field?' she asked Jack, when, later, they were sat sipping mugs of cocoa.

'Usually, yes. Although my preference would always be a decent clearing in woodland. You see, while the single most important factor for landing and take-off is clean lines, with this sort of operation you also want surrounding cover. Too exposed, and one will be spotted. In addition, as tonight has shown, the site has to be firm and dry.'

'I see.'

'One needs to be able to get straight in and straight out again, no hindrances. Especially if things on the ground aren't in order.'

She frowned. 'I'm not sure I follow you.'

Swilling the dregs of the cocoa in his mug, he angled his head. 'Until you're actually on the ground, you can never be entirely sure whether the people signalling to you are friend or foe — whether they're Resistance or Gestapo. If it turns out to be the latter, you want to be up and away again before they can do any real damage to the aircraft.'

127

'Golly.' Until now, she'd only ever considered the risks awaiting the operatives; she'd never thought about the dangers faced by the pilot trying to get them down on the ground to start with — let alone the practicalities of getting away again afterwards. 'So, what you said about tonight's site being too wet to land —'

'When we train operatives how to lay on an operation, the thing we ram home to them is that while a pilot can *land* in a bog, he *can't* take off from one.'

'No,' she said, seeing his point.

'In this game, you're entirely reliant upon the person at the other end picking the right place for the drop, which is why, after a couple of disasters early last year when pilots had to abandon their aircraft and then spend valuable weeks evading capture, we now only use agents we've trained ourselves, here, in England.'

'But they're local French people?' she asked. Since he seemed happy to talk, she would let him. This was all helpful stuff to know, and information she wished she'd had back in Brighton.

'One or two of them are. But the best agents are usually those who've been pilots themselves. They're naturals at looking out for hazards like telegraph wires, and they know what a six-hundred-yard stretch of ground looks like without the need to measure it.'

Suddenly, talk of evading capture put the job this man did in a different light: SOE agents *expected* to have to evade detection, were highly trained to that end; a pilot, on the other hand, would surely be less well equipped to survive in enemy territory.

Her cocoa finished, she reached to put her mug on the table. 'I have a feeling not many men could do

128

what you do.'

'Fair to say they're not sorties for run-of-the-mill pilots. In fact, next to nothing of what I learned flying Hurricanes out of Biggin to go after German bomber formations has been of any use for this caper. Don't get me wrong, fighter command was hairy stuff. If you came up against a Messerschmitt, it was you or them. But the month of training I underwent for this squadron was far more intense than anything I'd done before. And all to operate what is, essentially, a glorified bus service.'

'I hardly think —'

'I'm not joking,' he said, looking directly at her. 'Essentially, I navigate a tin can, albeit by moonlight and often in weather conditions that would keep most squadrons on the ground, to an unmarked strip of grass in enemy-occupied France. Then I drop off my passengers and head home . . . all the time on the lookout for flak. And, since not even our own people know this squadron exists, when I say flak, I mean theirs *and ours.*'

At the sight of him sat there, recounting it all so calmly, she felt nothing but admiration. 'Did you know how dangerous it was going to be when you volunteered?'

'I didn't volunteer — although had I known the squadron existed, I would have done so in an instant. No, I was picked. We all were — picked for our ability to think on our feet. As our training officer was quick to tell us, this is one of only two squadrons in the whole of the RAF that doesn't operate by a set of rules — and that's because the sheer number of variables in this game renders rules of engagement impossible. Hence the need to think on one's feet.

129

Say,' he went on, pushing back his chair as though about to get up, 'ever seen inside an aircraft?'

Her eyes widened. Was he proposing to show her? 'Never.'

'Come on, then, put on your coat and I'll give you the tour.'

Uncertainly, she got to her feet. 'You're allowed to do that?'

'It's only an aeroplane I'm proposing to show you, not details of tonight's mission.'

With a laugh, she lifted her coat from the back of her chair and, when he took it from her to help her into it, she let him. 'Then yes, please. I'd love to see it.'

'You know,' he said, reaching to open the door and then gesturing to her to go ahead of him, 'we're going to have to come up with a different name for you.'

Sensing that the earnestness of his expression was put on, she laughed. 'Because?'

'Because I refuse point blank to call you Lavender.'

'And for some reason you've also taken against calling me Miss Ward?'

Closing the door, he pulled up his collar. 'I have. Makes you sound like someone's secretary. *Take a letter, Miss Ward.*'

'But it's all right for *me* to call *you* Flight Lieutenant Carey?'

Switching on his torch, he directed the yellowy beam to the ground. 'Not in the least. You should call me Jack.'

'All right . . . *Jack* it is.'

'And next time you come through that door,' he said, nodding back to the ops room, 'you had better have come up with something else for *me* to call *you.*

Otherwise, I'll land you with something of my own invention.'

What a nerve this man had! She could only suppose it went with the territory — flying covert missions into occupied France was hardly a task for a shrinking violet. Either way, she could see that she was going to have to be on her guard. 'Perhaps you should do that anyway,' she said, immediately ignoring her own advice.

'Very well. But just remember, if you don't like it, you'll only have yourself to blame.'

As they moved further away from the hut and she felt the chill wind about her legs, she began to wonder whether she would have been better declining the offer to see the aircraft — at least until a night when the weather wasn't so brutally cold.

Clearly unbothered by the bitterness of the conditions, Jack directed the dim light from his torch immediately ahead of them.

'Wait there,' he said, and with which she made out the dark mass of an aircraft, 'and I'll move this last board so that you don't have to step in the mud.'

'All right. Thank you.'

With her eyes slowly growing accustomed to the darkness, she peered up to see what looked to be struts supporting a wing. This close to, the aircraft looked larger than it had on the night she'd stood watching it taxiing away from her.

The length of board repositioned, Jack reached out a hand. 'Here. Be careful.' Edging towards him, she felt him grasp under her elbow. 'Good. Now, down here,' he went on, directing his torch under the body of the craft, 'is the fuel tank. An extra one-hundred-and-fifty gallons to extend her range from six hundred miles to

131

about a thousand. Now, see this bit here?' Again, he indicated with his torch. 'You're going to put one foot right there, then follow it with your other. You won't be able to climb inside — not dressed like that — but you *will* be able to look over and see the controls.'

Her first thought was that she would never be able to get a foot up to the height of what looked to be a small step or platform; her second was that it was so dark, she wouldn't be able to see anything of the inside anyway.

'I don't think I'm going to be able to —'

'In retrospect, probably not, no. So —' Feeling a hand land either side of her waist, she inhaled sharply. 'Ready?'

'For wh —'

Lifted smartly from the ground, her feet came to rest on a surface that flexed under her weight. Feeling herself wobble, she grasped the first thing she could.

'Good. Here, take the torch. But for heaven's sake don't drop it inside or I'll have to send Pugh in to retrieve it.'

Wrapping her fingers tightly around the steel shaft of the torch, and still breathing rather rapidly, she directed the pale beam of light into the cockpit. What she saw, wasn't what she'd been expecting.

'It's so . . . cramped,' she said over her shoulder, shocked by conditions inside. Down at floor level, she could make out two pedals, not dissimilar to those in a car, and a mass of what she assumed were pulley cables. Directly in front of the well-worn seat were upwards of a dozen dials and, on an arm above them, what she guessed was a compass. 'How on earth do you make sense of all this?'

'With difficulty at first, if I'm honest. But, with

132

decent instruction and sufficient practice, you soon go by instinct — just as a bird knows to make use of thermals or how to counter the wind, flying an aeroplane becomes second nature. Once you get the hang of it, you just know what she wants.'

'Really?' For her part, she still hadn't entirely got the knack of double-declutching the Austin. And that was on firm ground.

'Want to see in the rear?' he asked. 'See where we put your Joes?'

'Joes?' she raised her voice above a sudden gust of bitterly cold wind to ask.

'Passengers on covert flights are called Joes. And before you ask, no, I haven't the least idea why. It's just a term one picks up in training. So, do you want to see?'

She definitely did. 'Yes please.'

Lifted back down to the ground, she was grateful that it was too dark for him to notice how her cheeks were burning: when she'd accepted his invitation to come and see the thing, she hadn't expected to find his hands about her waist as he hoisted her halfway up the side of it! That said, she was genuinely fascinated.

'This ladder is a relatively new addition,' Jack remarked, flashing the beam of the torch to show where he meant. 'Having it permanently fixed to the fuselage means that your chaps can climb down and disembark without me having to come to a complete stop, saving the amount of time they're out in the open and I'm down on the ground.'

'Clever,' she said, staring at the flimsy looking rungs. 'But isn't it dangerous to alight from a moving aircraft?'

From the tone of his voice, she sensed he was trying

133

not to laugh.

'My dear Miss Ward, just about every aspect of these missions is dangerous. They're one enormous bloody hazard from start to finish.'

In the darkness she flushed even deeper. 'Yes. Of course. It's just that to someone like me, it seems merely another peril waiting to cause a disaster.'

'As concerns go, yours isn't entirely misplaced, but, so far, we've only had the odd mishap.' Reaching over her shoulder, he slid back the rear canopy. 'Go on, then, up you go. Or are you waiting for me to *lift* you up there?'

Without turning towards him, she curled her fingers around the top of the ladder and climbed the first three metal rungs. 'You fit two people in *there*?' she said, peering over into the oddly shaped void behind the pilot. To her mind, a couple of ten-year-olds would have trouble getting comfortable in that confined space, the only thing resembling a seat being a rear-facing bench with what looked to be a storage locker beneath.

'Yup. Two adults. *And* their equipment. Once, when we really should have run a double but for operational reasons that wasn't possible, we crammed in three.'

'Well it looks jolly uncomfortable,' she said, trying to imagine a couple of hours, wedged in, unable to see anything and already terrified of the operation to which one was headed.

'That's because this particular aircraft was originally designed to carry a rear gunner. By stripping out the armaments and adding the sliding canopy, it's been converted to carry passengers.'

'I prefer to travel in a little more comfort,' she said.

'Who doesn't? But don't underestimate the old girl.

134

She might not be comfortable but she's perfect for the job. That cockpit gives the pilot a better view than anything I've ever flown. The engine's powerful but perfectly safe for a slow approach — critical for covert drops. And, though *you* might think it's cramped back there, few other aircraft of this size could take three passengers and their kit.'

Carefully, Esme edged her way back down the rungs of the ladder to the ground.

'Thank you,' she said breathlessly.

'Eve,' he said.

Staring back at him, she frowned. 'I'm sorry?'

'I've decided you look like an Eve.'

With a jolt, she realised what he meant and started to laugh. How uncanny that he should choose a name so close to her real one. And what a shame she couldn't tell him. 'I look like an Eve,' she said drily.

'Either that . . . or Clover.'

'*Clover*?' Now he was just being daft.

'You have to admit, it sounds a lot less stuffy than Lavender.'

'It also sounds like a cow.'

'Does it?'

'I'll settle for Eve.'

'Come on, then,' he said, taking back the torch and flicking the beam of light along the duckboards. 'Let's get out of this perishing cold.'

Back in the operations room, Aircraftsman Pugh was on the telephone. 'It's the butcher about his order,' he said, holding the receiver towards the flight lieutenant.

'About time,' Jack replied, moving to take the call and then proceeding to note down and repeat back a series of numbers. Hanging up the phone, he looked across at the operatives. 'New co-ordinates. And less than a mile from the old ones.'

Soon, then, Esme thought, they would be off. Soon, she could go home and get warmed up. Not that she would sleep — not after the way this evening had turned out. Not only had the object of her curiosity provided her with some intriguing insights, but he'd also chosen a name for her. And to have done that — especially with such uncanny accuracy — could only mean he'd been thinking about her. And *that*, she supposed, had to be why she had suddenly gone from completely frozen to uncomfortably warm!

★ ★ ★

'They kept *you* out late last night, didn't they?'

It was early the following afternoon, and, after a few hours' sleep and then a bowl of vegetable soup for lunch, Esme found herself walking up the lane to the church hall with Aunt Kate and Louise, dismayed to have been reminded of her promise to help them pack Christmas parcels for servicemen. On the day they'd invited her, she had been in the 'wanting to occupy her mind and feel useful' stage of her grief — that, and the fact that it had sounded like a festive thing to do. But now, grumpy through lack of sleep, she would have given anything to get out of the task.

'It was terribly late, yes. There was a delay and I had to wait with the— What I mean is,' she said, remembering just in time not to use the word *operatives*, 'I had to wait.' Sensing that her cousin had turned to regard her, and recalling the feel of Jack's hands around her waist, Esme kept her eyes on the lane. 'I don't have any say in the matter. Those are my instructions.'

'Well, we're real glad of your help this afternoon,' Kate said. 'We've just short of sixty parcels to wrap — the whole lot of which should have been sent last month. Westward Quay got theirs off on time. But up here, dear old Mrs Harding insisted there was no rush. *They don't have to be ready until the end of November*, she kept saying. And when she gets something into her head, there's no budging her. 'Course, now she's found out they were supposed to be gone by the end of October, she's in a real tizzy.'

'Where is it you send them?' Esme asked from politeness rather than genuine interest.

'All over. HQ sends us a list of the names and addresses. Previous years, we've sent cards to POW, too, but apparently, this year, the GPO has decreed we're not to.'

'That seems a shame.'

Kate agreed. 'Mean-spirited, if you ask me.'

When they arrived at the church hall, Mrs Harding came hurrying towards them.

'Come in, dears, come in. Mrs Channer, Mrs Ross. Mrs Trevannion, how lovely to see you again. So good of you to come. Now, without further ado, what I usually find works best is a straightforward division of labour. Mrs Channer, if you wouldn't mind . . .'

The tasks doled out, Esme found herself seated at the far end of a trestle, where her job was to address the boxes that Aunt Kate packed, and Louise wrapped in brown paper and secured with string and a blob of sealing wax. By watching what her aunt was doing, she discovered that into each parcel went four randomly selected items, ranging from socks and gloves, through cigarettes and sweets, to soap and playing cards.

'So,' she heard Mrs Harding say at one point, 'fancy the milk ration going down again.'

'Mm,' Kate and Louise absently agreed.

'Two pints a week? And only one tin of dried? Whatever next?'

'I dread to think,' Kate replied good-humouredly.

Another of the parcels addressed, Esme looked along the table. If Mrs Harding was in *such a tizzy*, then why didn't she take her hands off her hips for a moment and lend a hand?

'*Some* good news, though,' Mrs Harding went on, 'Mrs Keith has heard there's to be a sale of parachute silk.'

'Is that so?' Kate responded equally absently.

Conspiratorially, Mrs Harding lowered her voice. 'Village hall, Westward Quay, Saturday morning. White silk. Marvellous for underthings. Best of all, it's going on sale for reduced coupons. And reject stockings, apparently, too.'

Lifting the nib of her pen to avoid smudging the address she was writing, Esme giggled. Reject stockings? Rejected why — because they came already laddered? Or because there was only one of them?

'My son-in-law, who I think I might have told you commands a naval base in Canada,' Kate said, and with which Esme saw her shoot Louise a grin, 'has promised to send us some first-rate ones for Christmas.'

'Ooh, hark at you, not having to make do with rejects!'

Sometime later, with all the boxes packed and addressed and daylight fading, the three women headed back along the lane.

138

'Well, that's that good deed done,' Kate remarked, tying her headscarf tighter under her chin.

'Yes. Nice to think of someone receiving something they weren't expecting on Christmas day,' Louise agreed.

'Hard to think about it yet, though, ain't it?' Kate continued. 'In just over two weeks it'll be Stir-Up Sunday. But scrimp and hoard though I do, I still can't see there being much of a puddin' again this year. And this'll be the second Christmas running without a cake.'

Christmas. What on earth would that be like this year, Esme wondered? Where would she even spend it? Last year, they'd gone to Windsor on Christmas Eve and had stayed until the day after Boxing Day. The year before that, Richard's parents had hosted them in Cornwall for an entire week. But that was before Vyvyan Trevannion, MP, had come over all magnanimous and handed his Cornish estate to the War Office to use as some sort of training centre for top brass. In her opinion, his family were well shot of it. The house might indeed be *of unique historical interest and architecturally significant* — as Richard's brother, Hedley, had seemed compelled to keep pointing out to her — but it had been so bitterly cold and so dismally draughty that she had actually feared for Kit's health. At barely seven months old, he had only just recovered from a lengthy bout of croup.

And now that it was coming up to Christmas *again*, Aunt Kate was right: it *was* hard to think about. Presumably, very soon now, Richard would ask what she wanted to do in that regard, a question that, in itself, would raise the wider issue of what she was going to do more generally, neither of those matters being a discussion for which she felt anywhere near ready yet. If nothing else, standing in the way of her return to London was the small matter of where they would live; at the very least, her return would necessitate Richard removing from the dormitory in Whitehall, which, given the strain of his work, would surely only add to his burden.

And yet, if she *didn't* return, how would they ever go back to being husband and wife? If they continued to live apart solely for the ease of it, what did that say about their marriage? If she put off returning, how would she ever know whether she was ready to ... well, to move on? At Woodicombe, she faced few reminders of Kit. In town, she would only have to look at Richard and a picture of their son would come to mind — the physical similarity of Kit to his father had been remarkable — and for all the grief to come flooding back. And what good would she be to Richard in that state? What good would she even be to herself?

Realising with a sudden jolt that she had no idea what her aunt and her cousin had taken to discussing, she turned towards them.

'I suppose we could always do without a Christmas pudding altogether this year — not even go to the bother of attempting to rustle up a feeble substitute of a thing.'

Alongside her mother, Louise gave a resigned sigh. 'We won't be the only family going without. And we'll fare better than most when it comes to everything else.'

Listening to them talking, Esme was struck by a thought. 'What is it you're most struggling to find?' she asked. 'For the pudding, I mean.'

140

As though surprised that she was still there, both women turned to regard her.

'Truth be told, love,' Kate replied, 'pretty much everything this year — from the flour to the suet to the fruit. Just about all I'd be able to lay hands on at the moment is the eggs and the brandy. Oh, and the little bits of spices we didn't need for the mincemeat.'

'We'll be all right to make eggnog then,' Louise quipped.

'Maybe don't be too quick to rule out a pudding altogether,' Esme said, wary of making a promise she might not be able to keep. 'Like you said, it's not Stir-Up Sunday for a while yet . . . and who knows what might turn up between now and then?'

Yes, she thought, ignoring the look of puzzlement Louise was giving her, especially if she were to telephone Uncle Ned: explain to him how helpful and kind Aunt Kate and Louise were being to her and, just maybe, he would find his way to procuring the things they were short of. She was pretty sure he wouldn't mind her asking. After all, wasn't granting favours what godfathers were for?

* * *

'So, what will you do with your week's break? Catch up on some sleep?'

It was several days later that same week and, having just brought two more operatives to the airfield, Esme was seated with Jack at the table in the operations room while he waited to depart.

Glancing up to see him grinning, she frowned. 'Week's break?'

'A dark moon next week means no missions for

141

Obsidian and, therefore, one presumes, no driving for you.'

Struggling to contain her disappointment at the discovery, Esme affected to have merely overlooked the fact. 'Right. Yes, of course.' *Bother*. She'd forgotten that his operations needed moonlight.

'So, what will you find to do with yourself?'

It was a good question. Without operatives to collect from the railway station, keep an eye on, and then bring to the airfield, she would have time on her hands. Time that might find her backsliding into grief. Not that she was going to admit any of that to Jack.

'I fear I shall grow dreadfully bored. Either that or I shall get roped into the latest WVS working party . . . which, to be fair, isn't always *entirely* awful.'

When he didn't come back with a witty remark, she glanced towards him. His expression suggested he was mulling the wisdom of something.

'Then have supper with me.' Without giving her the chance to reply, he went on, 'Nothing fancy. I'm billeted at The Fleece in Chilverleigh . . . and the landlady's cooking is what I'd call homely. But in this weather it's just the ticket.'

'Well —' Was she seriously considering the offer? *Truly*?

'If it suits you to get there a bit earlier, we could have a drink or two beforehand.'

'All right.'

The speed with which she agreed appeared to take him as much by surprise as it had her. Pulling himself swiftly upright, he looked directly at her. 'You could get away? What I mean is, I know nothing of your circumstances.'

'I can get away.' *I can, but I probably shouldn't.*

142

'Then shall we say . . .' Clearly, he was still thrown by the ease with which she had accepted. 'Next Wednesday? Nineteen hundred? Sorry. What I mean is, how does seven o'clock Wednesday sound?'

Unexpectedly hot all of a sudden, Esme forced herself to swallow. 'Seven o'clock Wednesday sounds perfect.'

'Well . . . good.' He shot a glance to the clock. 'But now . . .'

'You have to go.'

'I do. but I'll see you Wednesday . . . unless we're back here before.'

Signalling first to Aircraftsman Pugh, Flight Lieutenant Carey got to his feet, pulled on his jacket, reached for his helmet and goggles and, appearing as though he was trying not to grin, crossed to the door and stepped outside.

Watching him go, Esme thrust her hands under the table and clasped them tightly in a bid to stop them trembling. Had she been wrong to accept his invitation? Almost certainly. Although why? Where was the harm? It was only supper at his billet: he hadn't proposed whisking her away for a weekend in a country hotel to begin an illicit affair. No, were she to be challenged, she could genuinely say that Flight Lieutenant Jack Carey was a colleague, who, knowing that she was going to be at a loose end for a few days, had simply proposed that they dine together. Entirely reasonable. All above board. Utterly beyond reproach.

So, if that was the case, she thought, getting carefully to her feet, then why did she feel like a dizzy debutante who'd just received her first request for a date? More importantly, how was she going to conceal her giddiness from everyone else, Richard included . . . ?

143

'So, darling, how are you getting on, zipping about the wilds of North Devon in your little motorcar?'

In the chilly hallway of Woodicombe the following evening, where she was on the telephone with Richard, Esme tried to relax the irritation wrinkling her forehead. *Zipping about in her little motorcar?* Did he have any clue how insulting that sounded? Still, it was her own fault, since to save him needless worry she had decided to play down her role, what had she expected? With no idea what she really did, it was no wonder he thought she just *zipped about the place*. And given how things were turning out, it was even more important it stayed that way: let slip words like 'covert' and 'operative' and he'd pretty quickly insist she gave it up. And there were so many reasons why she couldn't do that. And no, this wasn't just her guilt talking; tonight, his tone was genuinely patronising.

'I'm getting along fine,' she said, fighting the urge to set him straight. 'As you might imagine, there's really not much to it.'

'Well, I'm glad you've found a little something to do. The main thing is to be sensible about it — not to take on too much, not to get drawn into doing anything too onerous.'

'Too onerous?'

'Nothing too taxing. I shouldn't like to think you were doing the same sort of thing as you did in . . . well, as you did previously.'

'Goodness, no.' Yes, she definitely couldn't afford to let on.

'I would hate to find that in a bid to push aside your grief, you'd thrown yourself into something with little

144

thought to the danger.'

Did he truly think she wouldn't recognise danger if she saw it? Now he was just making her cross!

'Darling, I assure you, there's absolutely no need to worry on *that* score. I'm about as far from danger as it's possible to be. You know what it's like down here — nothing happens at the best of times and now is no exception. If it wasn't for the shortages, then half the time you wouldn't even know there was a war. It's all dreadfully dull.'

'Good to hear. I must say you do sound livelier. Keep this up and you'll be back here in no time.'

'Mm.'

'Anyway, look, sorry to have to keep this short, but I've arranged to go and dine with Father.'

'Good for you. Please be sure to give him my love.'

'Will do. Well, goodbye, then, darling. Keep at it and I'll call again in a few days.'

'Yes. Goodnight Richard.'

The receiver replaced, Esme let out a growl that owed as much to frustration as it did to despair. Concealing what she was up to — both the nature of her work and her friendship with Jack — was going to be harder than she'd thought. Even so, conceal it she must and so, the next time they spoke, she would try not to get exasperated; he did only have her best interests at heart — even if *his* idea of what constituted her best interests was rather different to her own.

Her attempt at being reasonable, though, did nothing to ease the taste left in her mouth by her guilt. In fact, it seemed only to exacerbate it. After all, by no reasonable definition could accepting an invitation to supper with a good-looking pilot really qualify as 'best interests', could it? Although . . . could it?

Reaching absently to her throat for the comfort of her locket, she wandered into the drawing room and went to stand as close to the fire as she dared in order to soak up some of the warmth. Realistically, what were the chances of Richard discovering she'd dined with Jack — that she'd had a harmless supper with a colleague? Minute. Infinitesimal, even. And as the saying went, what the eye didn't see, the heart couldn't grieve over. Besides, since it had been her husband's idea that she come here to have some company in the first place, could it not be argued that all she was really doing was following his advice . . . ?

9

Ships in the Night

'We need you to collect and deliver Cedar. First thing tomorrow.'

When, a couple of days later, Mr Mulberry had telephoned Esme with a new set of instructions, she was surprised to discover that, rather than meet the train, she was to meet an incoming flight.

'Just collect and deliver? No overnight storage?'

'That's right. Just collect the one sample from Sage and take it straight to the mill. They'll be waiting for it.'

'Anything for me to bring back . . . from the mill?' she'd thought to ask.

'No. Just drop it off and leave it. Further details within the hour.'

Not knowing what to expect, Esme had waited for a further telephone call, only to find that, barely half an hour later, a telegram arrived.

Collect 04.00. 1 x specimen Cedar for Long Luxford Mill.

After that, she'd spent ages in the study poring over Uncle Luke's map, looking for somewhere called Long Luxford Mill, and even longer trying to work out the best route to get there. Since it looked to be a considerable drive, she'd also tried to anticipate what she might need, eventually packing into the boot of

147

the Austin a can of petrol, a spade, a bottle of water and her wellingtons. On the rear seat she'd put a blanket, a thermos of Bovril and a round of corned beef sandwiches. Into the pocket of her gaberdine she slipped her torch, and into the glove box a spare, along with an extra battery. And now, despite feeling somewhat underprepared, here she was, listening to the rain beating steadily on the corrugated iron roof of the operations room while she waited for Jack to land with her cargo. Already, he was half an hour late.

With Aircraftsman Pugh slumped in a chair, a jacket draped over him as he tried to catch forty winks, she quickly came to wish she'd brought her book — or her notepaper and a pen because then she could have replied to her letter from Aunt Diana. Well, next time she had a pickup to make, she would try to remember to bring something to pass the time.

By the point at which Jack was a full hour overdue, she had started to worry.

'Is it the weather keeping them, do you think?' she asked Pugh when he opened an eye, roused himself, and offered to make some Camp.

'More than likely, miss,' he said as he swilled out a couple of mugs. 'That, or a hitch with the pickup itself.'

'It couldn't be . . . I don't really know what you would call it, but . . . something wrong with the aircraft?'

Handing her one of the mugs, its contents decidedly murky, he shook his head. 'Highly unlikely, miss. My money says he's had to divert around bad weather. There's plenty of time yet before —' With that, they heard the buzz of a propellor. 'There you go, miss. That'll be him now. Excuse me while I dash out and

148

light the flare.'

While part of her felt relief, a rather greater part of her just felt an overwhelming tiredness. Now she had a lengthy drive to make — and then an equally long one back to Woodicombe.

A few minutes later, deducing from the change in tone of the engine that the aircraft was safely down, she crossed to the row of coat pegs, lifted down her gaberdine, slipped it on and fastened the belt about her waist. With any luck, her passenger would be as worn out as she was and would want nothing more than to fall asleep. Perhaps she should even suggest he sat in the back, where he might more easily do so.

After several more minutes, during which she grew unexpectedly apprehensive, the door shot open and through it came Jack.

'Complete and utter bloody ineptitude,' he growled, slamming his goggles onto the table. 'Christ. Sorry,' he said, only then noticing that she was there.

With no clue as to the source of his frustration, Esme settled for sending him the sort of smile she hoped conveyed sympathy. Clearly, something had happened to rattle him. But, before she could enquire as to what, through the door came her passenger. Sporting a grey flannel suit and woollen overcoat, and with the insouciance only a continental could carry off, he stood looking around the hut. From one of his shoulders hung a small leather knapsack while, from the fingers of his free hand, he twirled a grey fur felt hat. Full of himself, she immediately decided.

When she started towards him, he turned to regard her more fully.

'Mademoiselle Lavande —'

'This side of the Channel,' she said, her exhaustion

making her tetchy, 'you might want to call me Lavender.'

'As you wish, *Lavender*.'

'And since we have quite a long trip ahead of us,' she went on, continuing towards the door, 'you might wish to use the facilities. You'll find them out and to the left. Here,' she said, tossing him her spare torch and watching as he made a deft catch, 'you'll need this. And then you'll find me waiting in the Austin parked directly outside.'

Having raised a single eyebrow in Jack's direction, the man Esme knew only as Cedar swivelled about, opened the door, and stepped back out into the night.

'Be on your guard with that one,' Jack lowered his voice to warn.

'I'm on guard with all of them. What do you think — is he native French or one of ours?'

'When he drops the accent, he's Home Counties through and through . . . but also a very convincing Frenchman. You can see why he's key to operations over there.'

'Right,' she said wearily. 'Well, I can't say I'm looking forward to being stuck with him for a couple of hours. I'm rather hoping he might fall asleep,'

'And he might. But truly,' he said, lowering his voice, 'just be careful.'

'Tell me,' she said, reaching into her pocket for the slip of paper she'd put there earlier, 'what do you know of this place?'

Squinting at her handwriting, he read the name of her destination. 'New one on me.' He handed it back to her. 'But then you know what they say SOE stands for, don't you?'

She grinned. 'Stately 'Omes of England? Appar-

150

ently, there's not many they haven't commandeered.'

'Go on. You'd best be going,' he said. 'Drive carefully . . . and see you Wednesday, all being well?'

'All being well,' she replied, nevertheless flushing as she turned for the door.

* * *

The rain was torrential. Barely two miles from the airfield the heavens opened, the Austin's little windscreen wipers struggling to cope with the torrents of water. Not an auspicious start, Esme thought, seeing no alternative but to slow the vehicle to a crawl.

'I think perhaps,' she said, raising her voice above the thundering of the rain on the vehicle's roof, 'I'll just pull over for a moment.'

When she turned towards her passenger for confirmation, he shrugged. 'You're in charge, Lavender.'

'It can't rain like this for much longer,' she said, leaning over the steering wheel to peer ahead. 'So, I think I'll wait for a short while and see if it passes.'

'Like I said, you're in charge.'

Pulling to the side of the narrow road, she switched off the engine. 'You know, if you'd like to try and sleep, there's a blanket in the back.'

'Thanks,' he said, shifting in his seat, 'but I don't need to. In my line, you work at night and sleep during the day.'

Thinking about it, she realised it made sense. 'How *is* the mood behind the scenes in France?' She enquired partly in the name of making conversation and partly from genuine interest. Without Richard to keep her up to date, and knowing for a fact that the newspapers rarely told the whole story, she had begun

151

to feel horribly out of touch.

'Would it help if I described affairs there as *encouraging*?'

Realising she was still gripping the steering wheel, she lowered her hands to her lap. 'Only if it's the truth.'

'You don't get a sense that big moves are afoot?'

Remembering how, some time back, Richard had mentioned there being an operation Winston Churchill was keen to see happen, she nodded. 'Perhaps.'

'Then now is not the time to lose faith.'

Coming from someone who was clearly in a position to know — for why else had the powers-that-be risked bringing him out of France? — she found his remarks reassuring.

'Oh, listen,' she said, the drumming on the roof easing. 'It's letting up. We'll get going again.'

A couple of miles further on they reached the main road and, with conditions after that improving considerably, she felt able to drive a little faster.

'So, how long have you been a part of Joint Technical?' her passenger asked.

Seeing no need for him to know she was new to this, she kept her answers deliberately vague. 'I was recruited in nineteen-forty.'

'Didn't fancy becoming an operative yourself?'

'Actually,' she said, pressing sharply on the brake pedal as a bend in the road tightened unexpectedly, 'that was their plan. But, having put me through my paces, they changed their minds, and I went into something . . . more specialist.'

'And yet now you drive.'

'Actually, now I look after other operatives.'

'Mm.'

'Could I ask you to check my directions?' she said.

'There's a sheet of paper in the glove box. And I think you still have my spare torch.'

Aided by the murky beam of light, he ferreted about and found her handwritten notes. 'What am I looking for?'

'I seem to recall something about a coaching inn opposite a cemetery. If memory serves, immediately beyond it there's a crossroads where we need to turn right. We've just been over a humpback bridge across the railway line, which was one of my other landmarks, and so I don't think it can be far now.'

'Impressive,' he said. 'Your memory for details, I mean.'

In the darkness, she grinned. 'Not much good as a driver if I can't memorise a route.'

'Bit over the top, though, don't you think — the authorities taking down *every single* road sign? It's not as though Germany didn't already have maps of the British Isles.' From the sound of it, he too was grinning. 'Or people already over here.'

'Quite,' she said. 'Anyway, what did I write down about this next village?'

'*Right turn after the cemetery opposite The Coach and Horses.*'

'And then? After that?'

'*Straight for approx. twenty miles.*'

'That's right. I remember now.'

Although, from there, the road proceeded in a straight line across open countryside, Esme quickly found her eyes growing heavy from the strain of having to concentrate so hard. At best, the beams from the Austin's shuttered headlights only illuminated the surface of the road two or three car lengths ahead, which, coupled with the fact that she didn't know

153

where she was and would therefore have no advance warning of any hazard, hardly made for a restful drive. And so, when it felt as though they must be nearing the next turn, she slowed down and pulled into what turned out to be a gateway into a field.

'Are you all right?' he enquired.

'Bit of a headache from all this staring into the darkness,' she said, switching off the engine and winding down the window to check whether it was still raining. 'If it's all right with you, I'll just stretch my legs and have some fresh air.'

'Good idea. I'll join you.' Opening his door and peering down into the darkness, he climbed out. 'Cigarette?'

'No, thank you,' she said, turning away so that he didn't see her yawning. The last thing she needed was to have him think her not up to the task.

'Look, don't take offence, but would you like me to do a spell behind the wheel? Like you said, it is jolly tiring. And I'll bet you've been up since first thing.'

His offer came as a surprise and seemed genuinely well-meant. 'That's very kind of you,' she began, 'but I'm not supposed —'

'Come on,' he said. 'Who's going to know? Out here, there's not so much as an owl to bear witness.'

Her laugh was a fatigued one. 'All right then. If you really don't mind.'

'We can swap back well ahead of getting there. And I won't tell if you don't.'

I won't tell if you don't. She was hearing that rather a lot lately.

Perhaps, earlier, she had been too quick to form an opinion about this man — not that he'd done much to endear himself to her. But he wasn't turning out to

154

be as obnoxious as she'd first feared.

'So, what's at Long Luxford Mill, then?' she asked, when, having finished his cigarette, they got underway again.

'Couldn't tell you,' he replied with a glance across at her. 'And not because it's top secret but because I genuinely don't know. I imagine it to be a covert training centre of some sort — a finishing school perhaps.'

'And when do you return to France?'

'Can't tell you that, either. But I shouldn't imagine I'll be here more than twenty-four hours. They won't want me out of action too long . . . or to risk having my absence arouse suspicion.'

'No, I suppose not. When we get to the bottom of this hill,' she said, 'you need to turn right. Not long after that, I've been given to expect a roadblock . . .' It was only then she thought to enquire about the matter of his identity card.

'The pilot handed me a British one,' he told her.

'Jack?'

'That's right. Say, you and he got a thing going on? Or am I not supposed to ask —'

'Good God no.' If her fascination with Jack was so obvious, she would have to start being more careful.

'You surprise me. Even a blind man would have seen the way he looks at you. Sure it's not a case of *The lady doth protest too much, methinks*?'

'No,' she said hotly.

'Not even close?'

'Not even anywhere *near* close.'

'Spoken for elsewhere?'

Why didn't she just tell him that she was married? 'Something like that.'

155

'Sorry. That was crass.'

'So, you have an identity card,' she directed their conversation back to safer ground. Thankfully, in the darkness, he wouldn't see just how fiercely she was still blushing.

'I have. For the purpose of this visit, I am Charles Bertram, a minor official with Joint Technical Board.'

'Good. Look, there's the turning.'

'Much further, do you think?' Changing down through the gears, he negotiated the junction.

'Through this next village and then it should be a couple of miles out the other side.'

'What about you?' he asked. 'How will you get back?'

'The same way I came,' she said drily.

'Clearly,' he was equally quick to reply. 'My enquiry was rather more concerned with the fact that you're going to be awfully tired.'

'I won't lie,' she said with a sigh. 'I'm bushed. But, thankfully, before too much longer it will be getting light. And I can always stop a couple of times for some fresh air.'

'You wouldn't rather I see if you can stop for a couple of hours? Maybe freshen up? Have a nap? Something to eat?'

'Kind of you,' she said, genuinely touched. 'But no. I really do need to get back.'

'As you wish.'

He negotiated the blacked-out village without difficulty but, as they continued out the other side, Esme kept finding herself waking up. Through sheer exhaustion, her eyes would close, her head would drop forward, and the first she would know about it was when, with a start, she came to.

156

Pulling herself more upright, she stared out through the window, noticing that the clouds had cleared to reveal stars. 'At least it's stopped raining,' she said idly.

'Here's your roadblock,' he whispered. 'Slump down and pretend to be asleep.'

'Why?' Despite asking, she did as he said.

'Trust me, it will go more smoothly. They're probably no more than Home Guard anyway.' By her side, she saw him feeling for something in the pocket of his jacket. She had a sense it was a revolver. 'Close your eyes. Unless they insist I wake you up, do nothing.'

'And if they do insist?' she asked, aware that her heart had begun to race.

Winding down his window, he started to brake. 'Then follow my lead.'

'Your business, please, sir?'

Feigning sleep, Esme listened keenly.

'Joint Technical Board. We're from Long Luxford Mill.'

'Identity card, please.'

'Of course. There you go, corporal.'

'And the lady's?'

'Look,' she heard him say, his tone conspiratorial, 'would you mind awfully if I didn't wake her up? You see, I've had a thing for her for ages and then, last night, when I finally plucked up the courage to ask her out, she agreed. But between you and me, it's been something of a disaster. First, we had to wait out a storm that had flooded the road. And then I took a wrong turn and . . . well, now we're fearfully late. So, I need to sneak us both back in, largely because Totty's father happens to be my boss.'

'Up at the mill, you say?'

'That's right. Look, it says so right there. I mean if

157

I absolutely must, I'll wake her.'

'No need, Mr Bertram,' she heard the voice say. 'Drive carefully now. We've had reports of trees brought down by the gales along that stretch to Luxford.'

'Thanks for the warning. And jolly good of you to understand.'

Feeling the car pulling away, Esme opened her eyes. '*Totty*?'

'Sorry.'

'Why all the subterfuge anyway?' she asked, pulling herself more upright. '*I'm* not even the one with the false identity card.'

'No? So, you really are Lavender somebody-or-other? And Joint Technical is an actual department of government?'

'Fair enough,' she said. 'Even so, given neither of those two would know that, why invent a story?'

'For the sheer bloody thrill of it,' he said, putting his foot down and then immediately braking hard as the road in front of them veered to the right. Her heart in her mouth, she grasped the sides of her seat. 'Because war is a bloody ghastly business, and being a covert operative is a deadly game at the best of times. So, given the chance to let off a little steam . . . amuse myself . . . well, I'm not going to pass it up. And if it wasn't for the fact that this lot are expecting me for a debriefing, I'd be driving straight past this bloody mill, stopping at the first pub we come across, begging them for a room, and hoping to convince you to take my mind off things. Because that's how it gets . . .' Detecting the jadedness in his tone, she made no comment. 'Anyway, how much further before we turn off?'

158

Rescuing the sheet of directions from where it had slid to the floor, she switched on the torch and tried to work out where they were. 'Not far,' she said softly. 'Over a river and then immediately left.'

'Over a river and then immediately left.'

'Yes.'

Less than two minutes later, having cleared the security check at the gate and pulled up on the gravel alongside an entrance to the mill, her charge switched off the engine and turned towards her. 'Sorry if I came across as maudlin back there.'

She shook her head. 'You didn't.'

'Next time they want me over here, I shall stipulate that I'll only come if it's through Pond Farm with your chap Carey.'

'Because he's the best pilot for the task?'

'Because, that way, I get *you* as my driver.'

'I barely drove at all. You did most of it.' Reflecting upon the fact, she laughed. 'Ah. And that's why.'

'Nothing to do with the driving,' he said plainly. 'Although I don't mind admitting it felt good to get behind a wheel again. No, I rather meant for the company. And because, next time, we're definitely going to find that pub.'

Despite blushing, she treated him to a calm shake of her head. 'I wouldn't get your hopes up.'

'Seriously,' he went on, 'if this game has taught me anything, it's the value of never assuming you will get another chance. If there's something you want to do, do it while you can.'

'Hm.'

'Look,' he said, making no effort to get out of the motorcar even though someone in uniform was coming across the gravel towards them, 'are you sure you

159

won't let me ask them whether you can come in for a while?'

'That's very thoughtful,' she replied. 'But no, I really do have to get back.'

'In which case, give me your word that you'll at least stop to stretch your legs.'

'I will.'

'Then this looks to be my cue,' he said, nodding towards the chap now reaching to open the door. '*A bientôt*, Mademoiselle Lavande.'

Watching as he retrieved his knapsack from the rear, and was welcomed by the waiting official, Esme slid across to the driver's seat, still warm from where he'd been occupying it. How wrong had she been about that man? And what a life he must lead: the lies; the subterfuge; the danger. It was a marvel he was still alive — that any of them were. Having unexpectedly been drawn back into SOE — albeit very much on the periphery this time — her thoughts often wandered back to her days as a decoy in Brighton, to the debonair Greg Hatton, to the sincere Marcus Latham, and to all the other newly qualified operatives she'd been tasked with putting through their paces. What had become of them? Were they still reporting back from occupied France or had they long since perished at the hands of the Gestapo? She supposed she would never know. She supposed it was better that way.

Shivering at the thought, she reached for the sheet of paper containing the directions written out in reverse order to enable her to find her way home, and poked it behind the steering wheel. Then, with a long sigh, she started the engine, found first gear, and pointed the Austin's nose back from whence they'd just come. But it wasn't until she was back on the stretch of road across open countryside that she began to appreciate how tired she was: more than once, she had to force her eyes wide to keep them open; several times she even had to wind down the window in the hope that a blast of cold air would keep her from nodding off. However, it was only when she was jolted awake in her seat to find the Austin careering onto a grassy verge, the trunk of a tree looming up out of the darkness, that the extent of her exhaustion truly registered. Narrowly managing to swerve back onto the road, she brought the vehicle to a halt and switched off the engine. Then she got out and stood, heart pounding from the shock, to draw deep breaths of the night air and recover her composure. She had told Cedar she would stop if she felt tired, and she should have done so well before now. In the darkness, she raised a wry smile: he would be disappointed with her. She was disappointed with herself.

Not bothering with her torch and thrusting her hands deep into the pockets of her coat, she took a few brisk strides along the lane. Then she turned and strode back. Already, she felt more awake, the freezing air burning the inside of her nostrils and making her cheeks tingle. Glancing up, she took in the night sky, the blackness of it absolute, the silence likewise.

Enveloped in the stillness, she found her thoughts returning to Cedar. While the two of them might have been little more than ships in the night, she had a feeling that in different circumstances they would have got on well together. *If this game has taught me anything, it's the value of never assuming you will get another chance.* An astute maxim — not just in the sphere of undercover operatives but in life generally. *If there's something you want to do, do it while you can.* How

161

many times since the start of this war had that very point been brought home to her? Life was short; she'd often said so herself. But, if she agreed with the belief that chances were there to be seized, why did Jack's invitation to supper still trouble her? When he first extended the offer, she'd accepted without qualms. So, what had changed? Why this new hesitancy? As she had reminded herself so many times over the last couple of days, all he was proposing was that they dine together at his billet — that they spend a couple of hours in each other's company. Where was the harm in that?

The harm, she thought, rubbing her hands together and stamping her feet to bring back some life to them, lay in the fact that, by rights, she shouldn't have entertained his invitation to start with. The moment he'd asked her, she should have politely declined. While she might be two hundred miles away from her husband, she was still a married woman — until recently, a happy and contented one; this wasn't like the days when she could gaily two-time a boyfriend just to be certain he was still the most handsome or desirable one out there. *For better, for worse*, that was the vow she and Richard had exchanged — a vow that wasn't supposed to be cast aside the moment it suited. And yet, viewing their situation dispassionately, in her hour of greatest need, what had Richard done? In their darkest days as a couple, he had withdrawn into his work and then, at a loss to know what to do with her, had packed her off to the countryside. Surely, then, *some* of the responsibility for her situation had to rest with him.

Deep down, though, she knew that distance wasn't the only problem; as Aunt Diana had indicated might happen, she, Esme, was struggling to know who she was. Having lost both her son and her home, the ties that had once defined her as Mrs Richard Trevannion had completely unravelled: not only was she no longer a mother but, through being apart from Richard, she was no longer even truly a wife. Her marriage, at least as she had known it, felt to have fallen apart around her — to have gradually ceased to exist in all but name. Could she and Richard somehow resurrect it, fashion something new in its place? As Aunt Diana had gone on to write, suffering loss on such a scale was bound to raise difficult questions. And the matter of her marriage was clearly one of them. But although Aunt Diana was wise, was she always right? Elsewhere in her letter, she had specifically urged against acting in haste, and yet, just now, Cedar had made an impassioned case for doing precisely the opposite. *He* advocated living for the moment. But could one *live for the moment* without acting in haste? Didn't one preclude the other?

Wrapping her arms tightly about her body, she gave an exhausted sigh. If only things were more straightforward! Still, if her circuitous deliberations told her anything, it was that she wasn't taking leave of her senses nor guilty of throwing caution to the wind. If anything, her wariness demonstrated just how lucid she really was. And no, she argued against herself, she wasn't just moulding the facts to suit her situation. If, in her hour of need, her husband had decided to send her away, then could she really be criticised for seeking company elsewhere — for accepting a colleague's invitation to supper? And yes, as colleagues went, Flight Lieutenant Carey was an exceedingly good-looking one. But he wasn't proposing that they

163

elope; as she kept telling herself, he had merely suggested they dine together. And although she might still be grief-stricken, she was no longer so wretched and despairing that she would fail to notice if things between them appeared to be getting out of control; if a situation warranted it, she would still know where to draw the line. She would still know right from wrong — still *did* know right from wrong.

By now having lost all sensation in her toes, she opened the door to the Austin and climbed back in. It seemed she had reached her decision. She would have supper with Jack. And she would do so as she imagined Cedar might in her shoes: without the need for either guilt or regret.

10

Deception

'Essie, are you busy?'

With a little sigh of frustration, Esme stuffed the pile of garments back in the drawer and gave up her search. 'What is it about gloves,' she said, 'that means they're never where they should be? I swear mine have a life of their own.'

'Maybe you left them in the Austin,' Louise offered, her demeanour as she hovered in the doorway suggesting she had something on her mind.

'No, it's not my driving gloves I'm looking for. It's my navy-blue kidskin pair from Mummy. But no matter. They'll turn up somewhere. Anyway,' she said, closing the drawer, 'in answer to your question, no, I'm not especially busy. Why? What did you want?'

Coming properly into the room, Louise turned to close the door. 'May I talk to you? About something that's bothering me?'

It was the morning after Esme's trip to Long Luxford Mill with Cedar but, despite feeling both tired and distracted, and with a feeling she knew what was coming, she affixed a smile and gestured her cousin towards the chair. 'Of course. You can always talk to me. You know that.'

Uneasily, Louise sat down. 'It's about Dad.'

At the mention of Uncle Luke, Esme tensed. But, telling herself not to panic, and continuing to smile, she moved to perch on the end of the bed. 'All right.

Go on.'

'Remember how I said I thought he might be tangled up in something?'

Just listen, Esme told herself, noticing how Louise was sat with her hands clasped tightly in her lap. *Say nothing until you know where this is going.*

'I do remember, yes.'

'Well, I've been watching him —'

'*Watching him*?' So much for just listening! 'I'm sorry, but what do you mean by watching?'

'Not watching him in a sinister way,' Louise hastened to explain. 'I haven't been spying on him or anything like that. I've just been . . . watching how he acts.'

Oh dear. Just what they didn't need. 'And...?'

'And he's definitely behaving oddly.'

'Oddly.'

'You know, quieter than usual. And sort of . . . cagey.'

Now what did she do? To whom did she owe the greatest loyalty — to her uncle, with whom she seemed to have fallen into a tacit agreement to say nothing about what had happened, or to her cousin, who had shown her nothing but kindness and compassion these last weeks? Rather unhelpfully, it seemed she owed them equally. So, what did she do? She couldn't exactly say that she was worried too — not without disclosing her reasons and, thus, what had happened that night in the lane. That said, she didn't really know for sure what *had* happened. Just because she had bumped into her uncle in the dark, in the middle of nowhere, didn't mean he was up to no good.

'All right,' she said, still with no clue how to proceed. 'Let's say it's true. Let's say it's not just your imagination and that he is behaving unusually. What

166

is it that bothers you most about that?' Perhaps, if she forced her cousin to disclose her specific concerns, she could home in on those.

'I'm concerned he's got caught up in something he shouldn't have.'

Not what she'd been hoping to hear!

'With this fellow from the pub.'

Louise nodded. 'Him, or someone *like* him.'

'Is it possible,' Esme said, trying to conceal her impatience beneath an air of encouragement, 'that you're worrying unnecessarily? I mean, you don't even know that your father *was* seen at the pub. If I'm not mistaken, the news came to you third-hand, and could have been the subject of Chinese whispers. And then there's the possibility that the person claiming to have seen him was mistaken. Or maybe even up to no good themselves and just . . . well, just trying to distract from the fact. Or was stirring up mischief.'

'I've thought about that.'

'Even if he *was* seen with someone *undesirable*,' Esme pressed on, 'it doesn't necessarily mean he's involved with anything he shouldn't be. Think about it. Your father is one of the most honest men on earth. Look at his service in the last war. Look how selfless he was, risking his life to save whole families. Look at the medals he was given for bravery. Someone as decent as that isn't suddenly swayed from the straight and narrow by some rogue they bump in to in a public house.'

'And ordinarily I'd agree with you,' Louise replied. 'But, just lately, it's as though he's hiding something.'

Into Esme's mind flashed a vision of her uncle's wrist and how the colours from the bruising stretched up his arm. 'Hiding something physically?' she asked.

167

'Or do you mean that he just seems more withdrawn?'

'Both,' Louise replied wearily. 'If I go into a room and he hasn't heard me coming, he jumps. Sometimes, he turns away when he's talking to me . . . or doesn't look at me to start with. But then, another time, he'll seem overly cheerful and jolly and . . . exaggeratedly like himself, as though trying especially hard to seem normal.'

'I see.' Clearly, Louise was too concerned just to let the matter drop. And why should she? Although she couldn't know it, she was right to be concerned. But what to do? Still undecided, Esme changed tack. 'Then all I can do is repeat the suggestion I made last time — that you talk to him. Tell him what you've just told me and ask what's happened to make him that way. But ask in a manner that sounds as though you want to help, rather than to criticise or accuse.'

Slumping deeper into the easy chair, Louise hung her head. 'I can't ask him. I just can't.'

'I think perhaps you have to,' Esme said, getting up from the end of the bed and moving to crouch in front of her cousin. Reaching for her hands, she went on, 'If you're sufficiently worried about him to come and talk to me, then you can't just do *nothing*, if only for the sake of your own nerves. With so much else to concern ourselves with lately, we shouldn't go adding yet more woes — certainly not needless ones.'

Slowly, Louise raised her head and met Esme's look. 'There is something else we could do first . . .'

We?

'And that is?'

'If Dad does go out tomorrow night, we could follow him.'

'Follow him?'

168

'Yes.'

Withdrawing her hands, Esme got to her feet. Was her cousin mad? Didn't she know how pitch black it would be? And how deathly cold? And that was without how it would look if her father caught the two of them trailing along behind him.

'Well,' she said, stuck for a way to deflect her cousin from such a hare-brained idea. While she *could* just make the excuse of having to go to the airfield — the very story she was going to have to fall back on in order to go and meet Jack for supper — she would prefer to put a rather more permanent end to Louise's plan. If she didn't, Louise would simply suggest going on another day instead. With that in mind, she said, 'Look, ignoring for a moment the myriad other reasons why the idea is foolhardy, might I ask what you propose to do if he leaves here on his bicycle?' From Louise's crestfallen look, she could tell that her cousin hadn't thought that far ahead. 'Or gets picked up by someone in a motorcar? How will you follow him then?'

'But what if he doesn't?' Louise said, her voice beginning to take on a wail. 'What if, through letting you talk me out of it, he goes on foot, and I miss my chance to see where he goes and what he does?'

'Look.' Still convinced that Louise's idea was folly, Esme opted for a firmer stance. 'I really don't think it's a good idea —'

'So, you won't come with me then?'

To such a direct question, she *could* just say no. But she would rather try to persuade Louise to abandon the idea for good.

With that in mind, she said, 'If nothing else, what will you do if it's pouring with rain? Or icy? Even if,

169

against all odds, it happens to be fine and dry, the two of us can't just go tramping about the countryside in the dead of night. Do you even know how far it is to Farracott W —'

'Farracott?'

Realising her mistake, Esme stood rigidly. 'What?'

'You said Farracott.'

Blast. Now look what she'd done!

'Because . . .' she said, searching her mind for a way out of the hole she'd just dug, 'since Uncle Luke was supposedly seen at The Black Sheep, which you told me is at Farracott, I assumed that's where you're expecting him to go.' Golly. *Close shave.* She *must* be more careful — think before speaking. 'Is that not your plan?'

'I don't know what my plan is,' Louise admitted dully. 'I suppose it rather depends on where he goes and what he does.'

'So,' Esme said, deciding to make one final attempt at getting Louise to see sense, 'let me see if I understand. Rather than overcome your reluctance to ask your father if anything is amiss, you propose to follow him in an unknown direction for an unknown length of time in the hope of finding out the very thing you could simply have asked him to start with.'

'But don't you see,' Louise said sharply, 'if he is doing something he shouldn't, he's unlikely to tell *me*.'

Weighed by sympathy and exasperation in equal measure, Esme knew that if she wasn't careful, her resolve would crumble, and she would end up agreeing to help. 'Look —'

'What about,' Louise began, 'if I agreed that we only follow him for as long as it takes for something to happen? That we just watch to see whether he goes

170

up the drive and out the front gate . . . or whether he goes through the copse and up the lane? Watch long enough to see whether he goes on his bike or, as you just said, whether someone picks him up along the road? If that's all I was going to do, would you come with me then?'

Wearily, Esme shook her head. 'You definitely won't reconsider just asking him?'

'I've already said I can't do that.'

'Or asking your mum?' Esme suggested as the thought occurred to her.

'*Mum*? I absolutely can't ask *her*. She's partly the reason I need to do this.'

'Because?'

'Because, for all I know, the reason Dad is being so secretive and slipping away at night is because he's seeing another woman.'

'*That's* your concern — that your father is having an *affair*?' Struggling to hold back laughter, Esme went on, 'Can you not see how completely unlikely that is? Uncle Luke, seeing another woman? I'm sorry, Louise, but that's the craziest thing you've ever said.'

Louise, though, clearly didn't agree. In fact, when Esme looked back at her, it was to see that she had started to cry.

'*Why* is it so crazy? M-Men d-do it all the time.'

Letting out a long sigh, Esme drew her cousin into a hug. 'It's crazy,' she said softly, 'for all the reasons I said earlier. Because your father is honest and true and loves your mother. Do you not notice how they look at one another as though they're still newly-weds?' Sensing that her cousin had stopped sobbing, Esme released her from their embrace. 'Uncle Luke would no more have an affair than he would rob a bank. And

171

I mean that. Truly.'

'So, what *am* I supposed to think? When someone starts acting secretively, it's because they have something to hide. So, if he's not having an affair, then what is he doing? If it was *your* father acting odd, wouldn't *you* want to know?'

Would she? It was a fraught question. 'Viewed in the abstract, I honestly can't say. Either way,' she went on, realising the time had come to simply refuse to have any part in this, 'I can't go tomorrow night because I have to go to the airfield.'

'But we haven't any guests,' Louise pointed out.

'I have to go and collect someone . . . and take them somewhere.' And that's how the lies start, Esme thought, suddenly seeing her cousin's point. If challenged about her own movements, in common with most people, she would stick to her story come what may. If they subsequently followed her, not only would they catch her out in a lie, but they would also find that she was actually in a pub, having supper with a pilot. Reluctantly, and against every ounce of her better judgement, she said, 'I genuinely can't go tomorrow but, if, come Friday, you're still worried, and I still haven't managed to get you to see sense, I'll reconsider.'

'All right,' Louise said miserably.

'But that's only a promise to reconsider — not a promise to go.'

'No.'

'And please, for the sake of your own health, try not to worry so. There really is no need.'

Turning for the door, Louise scoffed. 'Easy for you to say. You're not the one burdened by someone else's deception.'

172

No, Esme thought, closing the door behind her cousin and letting out a weary sigh, but she might be about to become burdened by deception of her own.

★ ★ ★

The Fleece Inn was surprisingly busy. There might only have been one other vehicle parked outside but, as Esme stepped under the porch and pushed open the door marked 'Snug', from the adjacent public bar came a rumble of laughter followed by cheering. She glanced to her wristwatch: precisely seven o'clock. Hopefully, Jack would be waiting for her.

She needn't have worried.

'Hello,' he said warmly, getting up from his chair and darting across to hold the door. 'You came.'

Partly from relief, she smiled. 'You didn't think I would?'

The way he angled his head suggested he'd considered it a real possibility.

'I wasn't entirely certain, no. Come, have a seat and I'll get some drinks. What would you like?'

'Since I have to drive back,' she said, unbuttoning her gloves and removing them, 'I should have a bitter lemon — if there is such a thing.'

At the tiny bar, Jack picked up a handbell and gave it a shake. Within seconds, the landlord appeared.

While Jack was being served, Esme glanced about. The little room was cosy: in the inglenook, logs were ablaze; on the walls, horse brasses glinted; from the chimney breast hung an oil painting of what she imagined to be a prize ram. *Snug* indeed.

'Here you are,' he said, returning to place her drink in front of her.

173

'Thank you.' It hadn't occurred to her that he wouldn't be in uniform. In grey trousers, and with the collar of a white shirt showing at the neck of a claret and grey sweater, he looked completely different: softer; younger; less sure of himself. Would it be poor form to ask him his age? Probably. Besides, there were plenty of other ways to come by the information.

'So, what brought you to this line of work?' he asked. 'And yes, I know it's not a terribly imaginative opening gambit, but I am genuinely curious.'

Much as she had the other day with Cedar — was it peculiar that they had shared confidences on that long drive without knowing each other's real names? — she relayed the bones of her recruitment into SOE.

'And then,' she said, uncertain about just how much of her personal situation to disclose, 'circumstances conspired, and I was *persuaded*, shall we say, to take over doing this.' No need for him to know that it hadn't been SOE doing the persuading but her uncle, the fact that she was involved at all coming about entirely by chance.

'Shall we take these through?' he changed tack to ask, gesturing to the table and their glasses.

'Through?'

'Sorry. Should have said. Since I'm billeted here, the landlady serves my meals in her dining room. So, shall we?'

When he held out a hand, she accepted his assistance to get to her feet. And, when he ducked beneath a low door at the back of the snug, she followed him into a tiny room that was made to feel even smaller by a towering mahogany dresser and an oversized dining table. On the dresser, an oil lamp was giving out a soft glow; in the centre of the table, a simple candelabra

174

held two lighted candles; in the hearth a log was spitting and popping. Quite by accident — at least, she assumed it to be by accident — it was breathtakingly romantic.

'You have a seat here,' he said, pulling out a ladderback chair for her, 'and I'll squeeze in around the other side.'

'Actually,' she said, looking to where he was indicating, 'might it not be better if I were to squeeze in round there?'

He grinned. 'If you're sure. It is a bit tight.'

Almost immediately after they sat down, a woman in a gingham apron appeared, in each of her hands a plate of food from which steam was rising. Accompanying the plates came the savoury aroma of onions and meat.

'Good evening,' Esme greeted the woman.

'Eve,' Jack said, and with which Esme frowned, 'may I introduce my landlady, Mrs Luscombe. Mrs Luscombe, this is Miss Eve Ward.'

Eve. Yes, of course. It was the name he'd picked to use in place of Lavender. One day she would have to tell him how close he'd come to her real name.

'Thank you for feeding me this evening, Mrs Luscombe. It smells delicious.'

'No trouble, love,' Mrs Luscombe replied, her voice friendly and warm, the wink she sent Jack hardly discreet. 'It's only sausage meat roll.'

'Which is always very good,' Jack assured her.

'Nice not to have him haring off over Woodcott the moment he's eaten. *And* for him to have some . . . company.' Lowering her voice, and addressing her remark directly to Esme, Mrs Luscombe went on, 'Seen 'im in his uniform yet, have you?'

'I have,' Esme said, looking across at Jack and smiling. If he was embarrassed, he covered it well. But then she suspected he was used to being made a fuss of.

'Bit of a catch, this one. Clean. Nicely mannered . . .'

'Yes, thank you, Mrs Luscombe,' Jack said. 'I'll take it from here.'

'Just sayin',' Mrs Luscombe defended herself as she turned to leave the room.

'Sorry,' Jack said once his landlady had left. 'She's a lovely old thing but not exactly backward in coming forward. If it's on her mind, she says it.'

'Not a bad way to be,' Esme replied, the irony of her remark not lost on her. Who was *she* to vouch for the virtue of honesty?

'Well, we should dig in while it's still hot.'

For a moment or two, they ate in silence, the sausage meat loaf proving surprisingly flavoursome, the accompaniment of boiled potatoes and carrots cooked the way she liked them — still slightly firm to the fork.

'What did Mrs Luscombe mean about Woodcott?' she asked after a while.

With a glance to the closed door, Jack leant towards her. 'Since the operation at Pond Farm is covert, she was told I'm based at RAF Woodcott. In fact, it's what just about everyone has been led to believe.'

'Even though they must all hear aircraft coming and going from Pond Farm?'

'If anyone asks, we tell them we use a field there for training flights.'

'I see. And the other pilot — Pashley,' she said, remembering the young man with fair hair, 'is he billeted here, too?'

'Pashley's at The Ring O'Bells.' When she nodded,

he went on, 'What about you?'

'I have family about twenty minutes' drive away. The house belongs to my grandfather, but it's lived in by my aunt and uncle and cousin. As a girl, I used to holiday there.' Unexpectedly recalling the summers of her youth, she sighed. 'Simpler times.' Looking up to find him watching her, she quickly went on, 'What about you? Where did you grow up?'

'Suffolk, mainly,' he said. 'Went to school near Cambridge and then later to Cambridge, but my early years were spent enjoying what, looking back now, feels to have been one long and endless summer of swimming and cycle rides . . . and cricket played under the widest and bluest of East Anglian skies. Idyllic, really.'

From there, she discovered that he'd joined the RAF because in the last war his father, desperate to learn how to fly, had been in the Royal Flying Corps; that he'd learned how to drive by taking a tractor round and round a field; that he'd graduated from Cambridge with a degree in Mathematics and no idea what to do with it. For her part, she expanded a little on her family's connection to Woodicombe; talked a little of her upbringing in Clarence Square, a little less about her recruitment into SOE and her time in Brighton. Oddly, the thing she felt the greatest desire to confide was the one from which she shied away for fear it would irretrievably change his opinion of her: that she had lost her home and her son and was only there in the first place to try to get over her grief. And of those things, it wasn't the prospect of telling him about the loss of her home or her son that held her back, but what that said about her marital status.

'Room for duff?' he asked when they'd finished

their main courses.

'Only if the portion is extremely modest,' she replied.

'I'll see that it is.' Gathering their plates, he went through to the kitchen. 'Jam sauce?' he reappeared seconds later to ask.

'With what?'

'Sorry. With Brown Betty. I recommend you say yes.'

'If it comes with your personal recommendation, then yes please.'

'Yes please,' she heard him say to Mrs Luscombe.

The Brown Betty was easily as nice as the one made by Nanny Edith or Aunt Kate — better, possibly, since cutting through the sweetness of the golden syrup was a hint of lemon. Perhaps she could suggest Aunt Kate try adding some. Although maybe not, since it would mean having to work out where to say she'd tasted it made that way.

Their puddings devoured, when Jack got to his feet, Esme did the same. 'Here, allow me,' she said, stacking their bowls and lifting them from the table. 'I should like to thank your landlady for a lovely meal.'

The kitchen, when she went through to it, was barely any larger than the dining room, beyond it a narrow scullery where she could see Mrs Luscombe scrubbing at a pan.

'Had enough to eat, maid?' Mrs Luscombe asked, apparently unsurprised that Esme should be the one to bring through their dishes.

'A little too much, if I'm honest,' Esme replied, setting the bowls and cutlery on the side and then patting her stomach. 'Thank you so much. It was delicious.'

'And what about our pilot? Had his fill, has he?'

'Would he say if he hadn't?'

'Unlikely, love,' Mrs Luscombe replied. 'Real polite, that one. You can tell he's from posh folk, can't you?'

'You can?'

''Though happen you're no working man's daughter yourself, are you?' Mrs Luscombe went on to observe.

'Well . . .'

'Anyway, I can't offer you coffee, on account of having had none for more than a month now. But happen I could make you some cocoa.'

'That's very kind. But while I can't speak for Jack, I shall have to decline. I need to be on my way before too much longer.'

''Course, dearie. Well, nice to have met you.'

Esme smiled. 'You too, Mrs Luscombe. And again, thank you for a lovely supper.'

When Esme returned to the little dining room, Jack had cleared the table of place mats and napkins.

'Since there's no one in the snug,' he said, 'how about we go through and sit by the fire?'

She really shouldn't stay much longer. He'd asked her to supper, and that was now eaten. Granted, she was enjoying his company — his attention, even — but therein lay the problem. Get too cosy and the evening was in danger of taking on the character of a date, whereas, at the moment, it could just about still pass as two colleagues keeping each other company.

'All right,' she said, nevertheless. She never had been very good at disappointing a charming and attentive man. 'But don't let me get too comfortable. I have to drive home.'

As he opened the door and gestured her ahead of him, she saw him take a surreptitious glance to his

179

watch. 'Then how about I send you on your way by nine o'clock at the latest?'

She nodded. 'That sounds about right.'

When he'd taken a poker to the fire and coaxed some life back into it, they settled into the pair of wingback chairs that stood either side of the hearth, each of them apparently content to just sit and stare at the flames licking lazily about a hefty log.

'Thank you for coming,' he eventually looked across at her to say. 'It's a long time since I've had such disarming company.'

'Disarming,' she said drily. 'I'm not sure how to take that.'

'As a compliment.'

'In which case, thank you. I've enjoyed it too. I suspect that with this particular billet, you've rather landed on your feet.'

'Is it that obvious?'

'You couldn't be more doted upon if you lived at home.'

'Hm. I'm not sure you've hit on the right comparison there . . . but I know what you mean.'

'There's something calm about this place. Tranquil.'

'Does that mean you would come again, were I to ask?'

She angled her head as though in consideration. 'I might. Were you to ask.'

'You know,' he said, hauling himself more upright in his chair, 'since I have some time on my hands for a few days, why don't we do something?'

In her chest, her heart doubled its speed. Whatever he was about to suggest, how on earth would she decline when, deep down, she had already made up her mind to say yes? But while supper at a pub was something that could be undertaken with a clear conscience, a day out with him was a different prospect altogether; a day out went far beyond something colleagues did together — especially colleagues of the opposite sex. 'I suppose it depends upon what you have in mind.' *No, no, no! Entirely the wrong answer!*

'Well, the weather's set fair for a day or two. So, how about we go for a drive?' Before she could reply, he pressed on, 'Saturday afternoon. We could . . . go to the coast.'

She gave a light laugh. 'I live on the coast. Right on the coast —'

'But not the Cornish coast.'

'I imagine it's broadly the same,' she said. 'Besides, it can't have failed to escape your notice that it's November.'

'Nothing we can do about that,' he said, undeterred. 'Just as we can't wait about for summer. Ever been to Morwenchurch or Morwen Cove?'

She shook her head. 'I can't say that I have.'

'Then let's put that right. It's quaint. Scenic. Off the beaten track. Most of the cliffs and much of the beach are out of bounds to the public by virtue of being adjacent to the RAF camp there, which is how I know about it.' When she appeared to hesitate, he went on, 'Come on, do say yes. We'll wrap up warm. Go for a bracing walk. See if the little tearoom's open. Act like a couple of out-of-season tourists trying to forget there's a war on.'

She felt like crying. What he was suggesting sounded wonderful. It also sounded wholly inappropriate and mired in danger. On the other hand, as she had recently reminded herself, it was Richard who had put two hundred miles between them.

'All right. But not if you're wrong about the weather. I have no intention of going if it's raining or blowing a gale.'

'You forget,' he said, leaning forward in his chair and grinning, 'I'm a pilot. My life depends upon me never being wrong about the weather.'

'Even so,' she said with a smile, 'my condition stands.' Was it, she wondered from beneath a surge of guilt, wrong to now pray for rain — to have the final decision taken out of her hands?

'Could you be here for midday? I'll get Mrs Luscombe to put some soup in a flask.'

'I should imagine so.'

'Good. We'll make an afternoon of it. Just make sure to wear a scarf, hat, gloves. Oh, and sturdy shoes.'

Dear God, he was lovely. 'Are you always so . . . thorough . . . so prescriptive?'

'Like I said, I'm a pilot. My continued existence is predicated upon my leaving nothing to chance.'

'All right, then,' she said, getting to her feet. 'Saturday. Midday. Dressed in pretty much every garment I own. But now, I really must head home.'

Getting to his feet beside her, she noticed how he thrust his hands in his pockets as though to prevent himself from reaching out to touch her. 'Thank you for coming. The evening was delightful. *You* were delightful.'

'Saturday,' she said, not trusting herself to say anything more.

'Saturday.'

'Oh, and by the way,' she added, turning over her shoulder to look at him. 'It's Esme.' Seeing him frown, she went on, 'My name is Esme.'

11

In Pursuit of the Truth

It had been a peculiar night. Although she had gone to bed quite early, every inch of her mind had been far too alert for her to stand any chance of falling asleep. When she had eventually nodded off, it had been to experience a peculiar dream from which she had awoken with a mixture of disappointment and relief. In it, she had been sitting in front of an old-fashioned hearth, a fire blazing, alongside her a man with his arm around the small of her back. With her head resting on his shoulder, it was a state in which she had felt warm and safe, with no doubt whatsoever that she was both loved and in love. The odd thing — that in her dream seemed not to bother her — was that every time she lifted her head to say something to her companion, his face was always just out of view, the only thing she could see with any certainty being dark hair.

While this hadn't bothered her in her sleep, once awake, it was a different matter, playing on her mind in the manner of an infuriatingly cryptic riddle. Who was he supposed to be? Richard — the vagueness of his features having to do with her continued separation from him? Or Jack, the blurring signifying his status in her life as an unknown quantity — a stranger about whom she knew next to nothing? Either way, since the dream was proving difficult to banish from her thoughts, she had been glad of the knock at the door and the appearance of Louise, whose conversation

183

she was hoping would prove a distraction.

'Did you know,' Louise said as she stood uncertainly just inside the door, 'that you'd caught the hem of this?'

Turning to find her cousin examining the bottom of the tweed skirt she'd yesterday hung on the outside of the wardrobe to air, Esme finished fastening her earrings and went over to see for herself.

'Bother,' she said, peering at the stitching. 'No, I didn't know. Thanks for pointing it out. I'll take a needle and thread to it. I should hate for it to unravel any further.'

'A stitch in time and all that,' Louise observed, straightening the skirt on its hanger.

'Mm.'

'Everything go all right last night?' Louise went on to ask.

Bending to pull a sweater from the bottom drawer of the chest, Esme tensed. Then, deliberately slowly, to allow herself time to think, she pulled it over her head. One careless answer, one throwaway remark, and she could land herself in hot water.

'Last night?' She tugged the sleeves of the sweater down around her wrists. Golly, this house was cold — and they weren't even in December yet.

'The collection you had to go and do at the airfield.'

Oh. That. 'Yes, that was fine, thank you. No hitches.' What, though, was her cousin building up to discussing? She did hope she wasn't still stewing about Uncle Luke.

'At least it was dry for you. For a change.'

Growing impatient with her cousin's continued prevarication, Esme turned to look directly at her. 'You know, there's really no need to dance about. You

184

can just say what's on your mind.'

With a little groan, Louise put down the scarf of Esme's that she'd taken to idly examining. 'Sorry. Is it that obvious?'

'Blindingly. For all your talents, I feel obligated to point out that subterfuge isn't one of them.'

Her hesitancy not lifting, Louise wandered across and sank onto the end of Esme's bed. 'Last night I followed Dad.'

Now it was Esme's turn to groan. 'For heaven's sake, Louise, I thought we agreed that was a bad idea.'

'*You* said it was. *I* didn't agree.'

With a dismayed shake of her head, Esme sat alongside her cousin. At least it explained her pre-occupation. At least she wasn't suspicious about anything else.

'So, go on, then. What happened?'

'Just before he was due to go out, I hid in the front porch. That was how I saw him go across the lawns. Then, the moment he reached the path through the rhododendrons, I set off after him. I followed him up the lane, past the church hall and over the crossroads.'

That her cousin had been able to achieve such a feat of daring without mishap was surprising. 'How on earth did you manage to cover that distance, in the dark, without being seen?' Genuinely astounded, she went on, 'You *weren't* seen, were you?'

'I can't have been. Since I know every inch of that track, it wasn't exactly hard to stay hidden. And the little pool of light from his torch meant I could see how far ahead he was.'

'Did *you* have a torch?'

'In my pocket. But I couldn't afford to use it in case he turned around and saw.'

'And he didn't hear you scrunching along?'

'I'd already thought of that and worn my old tennis shoes. Course, they got thoroughly sodden . . . and caked in mud. I'll probably have to throw them away now.'

The amount of thought her cousin had put into the venture was impressive. 'I'll admit to admiring your determination,' she said.

By way of response, Louise grinned. 'Thank you.'

'So, what happened after you reached the crossroads?'

'See, that's the thing. Somewhere along that next stretch of lane, I lost him.'

Thud. Gasp. Brake. The events of that night replaying in her mind, Esme stiffened. 'How . . . far had you gone from the crossroads before you lost him?'

Raising her gaze to the ceiling, Louise paused to think. 'If forced to guess, I'd say no more than three or four hundred yards. Why do you ask?'

Unable to answer that, Esme attempted an unconcerned shrug. 'Just trying to picture where you were. Did you see anyone else?'

'No one.'

'Did you hear anything? An engine? Movement?'

'Nothing save the wind and a couple of tawny owls.'

'So, what do you think?' Esme asked. By the sound of it, Louise had lost sight of her father in roughly the same place that she, herself, had collided with him the other night. 'Could he have gone into the woods?'

'Must have done,' Louise said flatly.

What Esme *wanted* to ask was whether the area Louise had lost him was Farracott Woods. But, having almost tripped herself up mentioning that name the other day, she decided not to.

'Any idea what he might be doing along there? Is there a short cut to that public house you mentioned?'

'Not as far as I know. Leastways, not one you'd want to use in the dark.'

'Then I'm afraid,' Esme said, getting up and going to the dressing table, 'I don't know what to say. Although I think you can probably rule out your fear that he's having an affair.' Seen in the mirror, Louise's confused expression made her laugh. 'Don't get me wrong, while I can see what might attract someone to him, what I *can't* see is any woman in her right mind agreeing to a secret assignation in the depths of a woodland!'

A cosy country pub, Esme thought, yes. But *al fresco*, at this time of year? Hardly.

Louise raised a smile. 'Me neither.'

'So, short of challenging him, I guess you'll never know why he was there.'

'Actually,' Louise said, her smile straightening, 'that's where I'm hoping . . .'

'Oh, no. No, no, no. You needn't think —'

'No, Essie, wait,' Louise begged. 'Please, hear me out.'

With a sigh of despair, Esme relented. 'Go on, then.'

'Well, as Dad's already gone out every night since Sunday, then by my reckoning, if he goes out tomorrow night, it's highly unlikely to be for Home Guard. So, I propose following him again —'

'Louise, I really don't think —'

'Because even *you'd* have to admit that from what I saw last night, Connie would seem to be right — when he's said he's been going to Home Guard, he hasn't been. And my thought is that the two of us together will have a better chance of seeing where he goes.'

'No,' Esme said with a decisive shake of her head. 'I've said already I want no part in this. Besides, don't you have to go on shift?'

'I've swapped with Polly. And anyway,' Louise went on, 'what you actually said was that if, come Friday, I was still concerned, then you would help me.' Bother. Louise was right. She'd forgotten she'd said that. Seemingly, then, she would have to do as Louise was asking. 'And,' Louise continued, 'that was before you could see that I'm right — before I had proof that he is up to something. So surely, even you can see why I can't just let the matter drop now.'

Noting that Louise seemed to be on the verge of crying, Esme took her hand and sank down next to her on the bed. 'Still no chance I can persuade you to just talk to him instead?' It was a waste of her breath, she knew that. But at least she would have tried. At least, in that regard, her conscience would be clear. If this all blew up into a ghastly mess, she could hold on to the fact that she had done her best to talk her cousin out of it.

Louise, though, shook her head. 'None.'

'Or even let *me* try to talk to him for you.'

From beside her, Louise stood up. 'Did your mum ever tell you about the time when she and my mum were living in the house in Marylebone and how, while our fathers were away fighting in France, your father's brother, Aubrey, showed up?'

What on earth was Louise talking about now? Lost to follow her, Esme shook her head. She'd heard the name Aubrey — recalled how it was only ever mentioned in hushed tones — but nothing more than that. 'Not specifically, I don't think, no.'

'Well, according to Mum, Aubrey was a bad lot but,

188

because he was your father's brother, Aunt Naomi felt obliged to take him in, which also meant having to turn a blind eye to his . . . less than desirable ways. After a while, though, *my* mum had enough of him messing the two of them about — in particular, his habit of asking your mum for money. So, one night, when he went out, she followed him.'

'And?' Esme asked, wondering why she'd never heard this story — or how she'd forgotten it if she had.

'Turns out Mum was right to be suspicious. Not only was Aubrey gambling in some seedy club and deeply in debt to some rather unpleasant people, but it also came to light that he'd deserted his regiment.'

'And so . . . ?'

'And so, the point is, it was her discovery that finally persuaded your mum to kick Aubrey out and be rid of him.'

Still Esme didn't follow. 'And you're worried that history is somehow repeating itself?'

This time it was Louise's turn to look puzzled. 'What?'

'You think your father could be involved in something similar . . . and that by doing nothing, we're all allowing him to get deeper into trouble.'

In her impatience, Louise shook her head. 'No. No, I'm not saying Dad is *gambling*. Nor am I suggesting he's as bad as this Aubrey fellow. By all accounts, he was a real cad. Sorry. Forgive my language. No, what I'm saying, is that had my mum not taken it upon herself to find out what was going on, Aunt Naomi's brother-in-law would have continued to conceal what he was up to, and the situation would have simply grown worse for all concerned. The point I'm trying to make is that sometimes, being furtive can be

189

a means of getting to the truth in a way that asking outright never can.'

'Hm.' In that respect, she could see her cousin's point. 'All right. But following him about in the hope of finding out what he's up to still isn't what I would choose to do.'

'As you make abundantly clear every time I mention it.'

'And by which I stand.'

'But you'll come with me anyway?'

'I'll come with you but only —' Squeezed in a grateful hug, Esme was unable to finish.

'Oh, Essie. Thank you. *Thank you*. Any trouble, any trouble whatsoever — which of course there won't be — I'll take full responsibility. I'll make it plain that you wanted nothing to do with it. That I dragged you along against your will. I'll say that you were only there because, having been unable to dissuade me, you had to see that I didn't come a cropper.'

'Yes, yes,' Esme said as Louise finally released her hold, 'but what I had been going to say is that I'm only coming with you if it's dry. Having committed to this driving lark for the RAF, I can't afford to go down with pneumonia — not for you nor Uncle Luke nor anyone.'

'Fair enough.'

'But be under no illusion, dearest cousin,' Esme continued as she returned to the dressing table, picked up her watch and began to fasten it about her wrist, 'I'm only doing this to prove to you that you're worrying over nothing — that there's a perfectly reasonable explanation for your father's behaviour.' Out of sight of Louise, Esme crossed her fingers. 'Your mum might have been right about this Aubrey character but, trust me, you're wrong about your dad.'

'And I hope to high heaven you're right,' Louise replied.

'Then in which case, against all my better instincts, tomorrow evening it is.'

★ ★ ★

'This was a good idea of yours.'

In the pitch black, Esme surrendered to a bone-rattling shiver. At that precise moment, she couldn't possibly have agreed less. 'To g-get ahead of him?' she whispered.

'Uh-huh.'

Earlier, when Esme had presented Louise with her idea for how they might better follow her father to Farracott Wood, she had failed to spot how her plan would require them to stand, still and quiet in the freezing cold, for an unknown amount of time. 'How long do you think we've been here?' she whispered.

Beside her, Louise stopped rubbing her gloved hands up and down her coat sleeves to peer at her wristwatch. 'Coming up on ten minutes. But it's just gone seven, so he should be here dreckly.'

'Assuming he's coming at all,' Esme whispered back. Her suggestion to Louise had been that, rather than wait to see Luke set off from home and then follow him, they should leave before he did, walk up the lane and hide themselves in the porch of the church hall. That way, she had reasoned, they wouldn't have to worry so much about him either seeing or hearing them creeping along behind him. Unlike keeping on the move, though, being forced to wait about meant they had quickly become frozen to the bone; they couldn't even risk stamping their feet in case the noise on the stone floor gave them away. 'Ridiculous,' she said, watching her breath hang like short-lived punctuation marks about her utterance.

With that, Louise grabbed her arm and pressed a finger to her lips. Nodding her understanding, Esme stood rigidly and listened: boots plodding; twigs cracking; breath blowing through pursed lips.

As one, the two women flattened themselves against the wall.

Seconds later, past the porch went the form of a man, hands in pockets, shoulders hunched, gait uneven. Feeling about, Esme caught hold of Louise's hand. Despite his features being concealed by the darkness, she had no doubt that it was Uncle Luke. But then she had known all along that it would be.

For a moment after that, neither woman moved. Then, with the sound of boots fading, Esme felt Louise let go of her hand and saw her move to peer up the lane. Seconds later, she beckoned with her hand.

Tightening her scarf about her neck, Esme stepped from the cover of the porch. But without a light to see the way ahead, her progress was halting and hesitant, the feel of every flint or a twig beneath the sole of her boot causing her to tense. How on earth had she let Louise talk her into this? It was nothing short of madness.

'Here,' Louise whispered, evidently aware of her cousin's trepidation, 'take hold. Ignore the urge to look down. Keep your eyes ahead.' Doing as instructed, Esme linked her hand through the crook of her cousin's arm and found herself being propelled swiftly along. 'Not far up here there's a grass verge. Once we're on that . . . we'll be more sure-footed . . . and able to jog to make up ground.'

Jog? In the pitch black? And gasp great gulps of this bitterly cold air? Was her cousin completely mad? Still, Esme supposed, the toe of her boot sending a dozen or more pebbles skittering ahead, if this hare-brained escapade was to count for anything, they couldn't let Uncle Luke out of their sights.

Less than a minute further on, when Louise drew her across to the side of the lane, Esme felt her boots make contact with soft turf. 'Go on,' she whispered to Louise. 'I'll be all right now.'

From there, the two women alternated spells of brisk walking with short bursts of jogging, until, just as Esme was struggling to pant without making a noise, Louise shot out an arm and brought her to a halt.

Steadying herself, Esme looked up. Overhead, a break in the trees suggested they had reached the crossroads, the accompanying smell of woodsmoke indicating habitations — in this case, the cluster of old estate workers' cottages.

'Come on,' Louise hissed. 'Look.' Further ahead, a small pool of light was roving left and right as Luke continued towards Farracott Woods.

When they set off again, it was more warily, their progress made on tiptoes, their ragged breathing muffled behind their gloved hands. Her cousin's contention that Uncle Luke was up to something appeared well-founded: this wasn't a man heading to Home Guard drill. But then she'd known as much since the moment she'd collided with him along this very same stretch of road. Had she felt able to tell Louise about that night, then this whole crazy escapade might not have been necessary. As things were turning out, though — and despite having no wish to betray the promise she'd made to her uncle about keeping quiet — she might have to tell her cousin anyway and suffer her wrath when she found out what she'd been keeping from her.

With that, up ahead, the dim beam of light swept sharply to the left and, flickering as though partly obscured by vegetation, started slowly gaining height. Seeing it doing so, the two women came to a halt.

'He must be going up the bank,' Esme leant to whisper in her cousin's ear.

'Must be what he did last time,' Louise whispered back. 'Come on, keep to the side and we'll run.' Despite Louise's instruction quickly proving easier said than done, Esme nevertheless managed to match her pace. 'Here, look,' Louise said, stopping abruptly at a break in the foliage and gasping for breath. 'He must have . . . gone up here. It's about . . . where I lost him . . . last time.'

There being no sign of the light from Uncle Luke's torch, Esme fished in her coat pocket for her own and switched it on. And while Louise doubled over, muttering about having a stitch in her side, Esme flicked the light cautiously up the bank, illuminating in its narrow beam a band of exposed rocky ledges glistening with wet. Suddenly, the events from that night made sense. At the time, she'd been baffled by his sudden appearance in front of her but now she could see what had happened: having been up the bank, he had lost his footing in the wet and, unable to help himself, had come sliding down. After all the rain they'd had, water would have been rushing down here into the lane. Indeed, she could recall seeing it happening further along this same stretch of road.

'We can't go up there,' she said quietly. 'Far too

treacherous.'

In the darkness, Louise nodded. 'You're right.'

'Do you know what's up there?'

Louise shook her head. 'As far as I know, just the woods.'

'Well, it would seem to me,' Esme said, directing the light from her torch back down to their feet, 'that all we can do now is go home before we catch our deaths. But tomorrow we could look on a map — see if we can spot where he might be heading.'

Louise's agreement was half-hearted. 'I suppose we *could* . . .'

'Better we do that,' Esme pressed on, desperate to simply get warmed up, 'and take a while to work out what to do next than jump to conclusions and act in haste.'

'Better. Yes.'

As they turned to retrace their steps, Esme withheld a sigh. Had the time come to tell Louise what she knew? Or did she still owe it to Uncle Luke to keep quiet? Back in Brighton, no level of deception or subterfuge would have troubled her. But she wasn't that person anymore; now, the idea of hiding things from people made her deeply uncomfortable — such concealment made even less palatable by the fact that, on this occasion, the people involved were her own family.

Arriving at the crossroads, she stole a glance to her cousin's face. From the little she could see of it, her expression appeared set in a deep frown. Hardly surprising — this business with Uncle Luke was turning out to be genuinely concerning. But working out what to suggest they do next would have to wait until the morning because, at this precise moment, she was simply too exhausted to think straight. On top of that, she was desperate to get some decent sleep because, tomorrow, Jack was taking her out — something else she was going to have to keep from Louise, not to mention from everyone else, as well.

12

Make-Believe

She might have known. In fact, she couldn't believe she hadn't made the connection the other evening and realised that the daring little red sportscar parked outside The Fleece belonged to Jack.

'MG Midget TA Roadster,' he said, opening the passenger door and assisting her in. 'Careful, she's a good deal lower than your Austin.'

He wasn't wrong. Lowering herself as elegantly as she could onto the red leather seat, Esme was grateful she had chosen to wear slacks, even though, when she had plucked them from her wardrobe, her decision had been based more on them suiting what Jack had described as *a bracing walk* than an open-top car.

'I see now why you were adamant that I dress warmly,' she said as he closed her door and went around to the driver's side. 'I had no idea there wouldn't be a roof!'

'She has a roof,' he said, folding his legs in beneath the steering wheel and then gesturing over his shoulder. 'But on a day like today it would be a crime to use it.'

Unsure she agreed with him, Esme nevertheless smiled. At least, in this part of the world, she was unlikely to been seen by anyone she knew: a bright red sportscar with an open top, driven by a good-looking man in RAF uniform, was going to attract attention. And she could really do without that.

'If you say so,' she said as Jack reached across to turn the key and start the engine.

'Got her in the spring of thirty-nine. The chap who'd bought her new the year before was talking about laying her up for the duration of the war — had seen which way the wind was blowing, I suppose — so, I offered to take her off his hands.'

'And do you get to drive it much?' she asked as they pulled away from the front of the pub. 'Do you even get a petrol ration?'

'I get an official allowance to get me between bases . . . and a rather less formal allowance as a perk of working where there are tanks of fuel . . .'

When he took his eyes from the road to look across at her, she raised an eyebrow. 'Naughty.'

'Although I'm told one wouldn't know it to look at me. Butter wouldn't melt, and all that . . .'

'Hm.'

'Anyway,' he said as he slowed the MG at the crossroads to turn right, 'hold tight and let's see whether we can find our way to Morwenchurch.'

'*And* back again.'

The mischievous smile returned. And as he put his foot down, he raised his voice above the sound of the engine to say, 'I don't recall saying anything about bringing you back.'

'Fine by me,' she replied, gripping her fingers discreetly around the front of the seat as they roared away.

Thankfully, he'd been right about the weather: just as he'd predicted, the day had dawned gin clear, a coating of diamanté-like dew on the lawns, the remaining few leaves on the trees illuminated in the low morning sunlight like gems of amber, citrine and agate.

'Warm enough?' he looked across at her to ask.

She nodded. 'Fine, thank you.' Ask her again in twenty minutes, though, and she might tell him differently; the sun might still have *some* warmth to it but the air rushing past had a keen edge. 'How far is it to Morwenchurch?'

'Twenty, twenty-five miles,' he said, slowing the MG and changing down through the gears to negotiate a sharp bend to the left. 'After this first stretch, the roads get better. We should be there in less than an hour.'

'Then I shall sit back and enjoy the scenery.'

Surprised by how at ease she felt, Esme found herself content to do just that —to watch Jack's hands on the steering wheel and to occasionally tilt her face towards the sun and savour the faint traces of warmth. For once, there was nothing pressing in on her, nothing clamouring to be buried or to be made sense of. There was no one to know of the events that had brought her to this point — no one to smile sympathetically or to pat her hand in commiseration. Strangely, given what she was doing and with whom, she realised she felt unburdened. *Free.* Added to that, it was enjoyable being a passenger for once; to have no concern about missing a turning or running late. Better still, it was nice to be out in a motorcar in daylight, with no need to crawl along at a tedious pace for fear of colliding with something. By that same token, it was refreshing to be able to stare out to such far horizons, not to feel hemmed in or stifled.

Savouring the unfamiliar sensation of being relaxed, she drew a long breath and turned her attention away to the left, where, behind a tractor ploughing perfectly straight furrows across a gentle slope, seagulls were flapping like starched handkerchiefs on a washing line. When she returned her eyes to the road, it was to see a stoat bound across their path, its coat a bold orangey brown in the soft autumn light. Further ahead, from out of the hedgerow strode a cock pheasant, its neck an iridescent emerald, its face wattled scarlet. Apparently disbelieving that they should be bearing down upon it, it froze in the middle of the road, leaving Jack no alternative but to stamp on the brake pedal, his left arm shooting across Esme's midriff as they skidded to a halt.

'Forgive me,' he said, returning his hand to the steering wheel. 'I didn't want you thrown against the dash.'

'It's . . . all right,' she replied, her heart racing, nonetheless. 'I was just bracing for a cloud of feathers.'

'Daftest birds on earth,' he said and started to laugh. 'Not an ounce of road sense.'

'None,' she agreed, breathing more easily.

'Onward, then.' Selecting neutral, he restarted the engine.

'To Morwenchurch,' she replied.

The remainder of their journey was uneventful, the roads free from all but a flock of sheep being herded by a land girl who, as they passed, treated Jack to a fetching smile, and an elderly farmer on a tractor who sent Esme a wink. Soon after that, they crested a steep rise to be confronted on the other side by a palette of the crispest greens and clearest of blues where the land met the sea, and the sea, the sky.

'Worth the drive already,' Jack remarked of the sight before them.

'Breathtaking,' she agreed.

Beside her, he glanced to his watch. 'Are you hungry?'

'Peckish.'

'Then we'll go down to the harbour first, have a little walk around, see if there's somewhere to get a pasty. Or a lardy cake —'

'Lardy cake?'

'A favourite of mine from school. And then we'll go on around to the cove.'

'Sounds lovely.'

When they came to a halt at a junction with a main road, Jack guided the MG straight across it and down the steep hill on the other side. Before long, the woodland around it began to thin, affording glimpses of uneven slate roofs and smoke spiralling up from teetering chimney pots.

'From back there you wouldn't know any of this existed, would you?' he said as he negotiated the pot-holed track past a terrace of tiny homes, and on down to a small harbour nestled in a natural inlet.

'You would not,' she said, instantly captivated by the scene. 'It's enchanting.'

'Even nicer at high tide, one would imagine,' he remarked, indicating the half dozen fishing boats beached on the wet sand. Just short of the quay, he brought the MG to a halt alongside a pair of houses, one of which turned out to be home to a baker's, the other, a grocer's. 'Want to come and see what they've got?'

She shook her head. 'Surprise me.'

When he rounded the front of the car and opened her door, she accepted his assistance to get out. Then, having watched him duck into the baker's, she unwound the scarf from her throat, removed her headscarf, and fluffed up the front of her hair. Dropping her scarves onto the seat, she wandered across the cobbles and stood looking out over the harbour. She'd been to places as quaint as this before, Westward Quay being a case in point. But Westward Quay was much busier and far more built up than this. Along its narrow streets were public houses; away from the centre, several hotels and even a holiday park. This little place, on the other hand, had nothing that didn't need to be there: homes; fishing boats; essential provisions. Were it not for the delivery van parked in front of the grocer's, the scene would resemble a charming turn-of-the-century watercolour.

Her thoughts interrupted by the sound of Jack's voice, she turned to see him coming out of the baker's, in his hand a couple of paper bags.

Having put them in the MG, he came towards her. 'Hard to believe there's a war on.'

She smiled. 'I was just thinking precisely the same thing. And wondering whether, when we came down that hill, we somehow travelled back in time.'

'Quaint, isn't it?'

She nodded. 'It is.'

Pointing along the harbour wall, he said, 'Shall we stroll out to the end?'

'It would seem a shame not to.'

'Be careful on these uneven cobbles, then,' he warned, offering her his arm. 'It would be easy to turn an ankle.'

The harbour wall extended around the cove like a stone arm reaching out to protect everything within against the ravages of the sea. Since it was constructed on two levels, they chose to stroll outwards along the lower, harbour side, stopping now and again to peer over the edge at the ladders and ropes stretching down towards the sand. When they reached the far end, a short flight of steps took them to the upper level, where, although sheltered on the windward side by a narrow wall, Esme felt the breeze more keenly. Nevertheless, entranced, she stood taking it all in: overhead, herring gulls offered up plaintive cries; from the beached fishing boats came the clinking of rigging against masts; at the base of the wall, seawater lapped lazily. From the lobster pots, stacked in the sunshine like a wall of wicker honeycomb, arose the pungent aroma of brine and fish; on the breeze came a tang, fresh but still salty. It was, she realised as she stood trying to commit it all to memory, about as far from war as it was possible to be.

Turning to look outwards, she sighed. 'I've often wondered what it's like to fly over the sea. From here it looks as though it would be flat and boring and all the same whichever way you look, although I suspect it isn't.'

'It can be,' Jack said, moving to gaze out in the same direction. 'On an overcast day with little variation in the colours, it can be disorienting, too. But, on an afternoon like this, especially if you're within sight of a coastline, it can be splendid. The first time I flew over it, I remember being stunned by just how many shades of blue there were, and by the patterns made by the currents. You don't get to appreciate any of that from the land.'

'No.'

'Of course, it's not often one has the chance to look about and enjoy it from the cockpit, either.'

'I suppose not,' she said, remembering that before

203

being drafted into Obsidian, he'd flown fighter air-craft.

'In a Hurricane, it's all about speed and outma-noeuvring your enemy, avoiding getting shot down yourself. In a Lysander, it's entirely different. You're still solo. You still have to be alert. But you're slower and lower. On a daylight sortie, you might get the occasional chance to take in the view.'

'Do you miss the combat?' she asked. 'Or is that a ridiculous question?'

'Not ridiculous, no. Personally, I can do without it. But some chaps live for it, thrive on a sort of blood-lust . . . say they don't feel alive without it. To my mind, there are enough thrills to be had on the ground.'

'Mm.' If he was expecting an equally flirtatious response, he was in a for a disappointment.

'Anyway.' Turning towards her, he smiled. 'You said you were peckish. So, how about we find our way around to Morwen Cove? It's just the other side of this hill. From the main road there's a track all the way down to the beach.'

'Yes,' she said. 'Let's do that.' But, although it sounded lovely, when they started back along the har-bour wall, she found herself glancing wistfully over her shoulder. And by the time they arrived back at the MG, she wished they weren't leaving.

I could live here, she thought, looking up the lane to the nearest row of cottages. *I could live there, in that lit-tle cottage with the blue door and the bulging whitewashed walls.* Granted, it was a world away from the elegant proportions of the house she and Richard had seen in Teddington, but behind its simplicity lay an honest charm: the stone steps to the front door, worn to a soft dip by the centuries of the comings and goings of its inhabitants; the jauntily tied back curtains at the little windows; the haphazard angles of the chimney pots, where, at that moment, a pair of jackdaws were sat in easy discussion — *chack-chack, chack-chack.*

If she lived there, then every winter she would fill the window boxes with daffodil bulbs so that in March, they would light up the room and dazzle passers-by with their golden-yellow. And then, in the spring, she would replant them such that, throughout the summer, they would be a riot of bright red geraniums fringed with a froth of sky-blue forget-me-nots. And her children — an entire tribe of them — would run barefoot to the baker's each morning to fetch a farmhouse loaf, still warm from the oven. Together, they would scour the beach for driftwood to make fires that filled the house with the smell of the sea. She would wear her hair loosely pinned, dress in floral frocks — and swathe herself in pastel-coloured shawls when it turned cooler in the evenings. She would grow plump and content and—

'Everything all right?' Brought sharply back, she turned to see Jack holding open the door to the MG.

Foolish woman! 'Yes. Yes, of course. Sorry, I was miles away.'

With his head, he gestured up the hill. 'Sizing up which one you'd live in, given the chance?'

'Something like that.'

'I like the look of the one with the blue door.'

Even more uncanny. Or was it? 'Me too.'

'Come on, then,' he said. 'I promised you a picnic.'

Morwen Cove, Esme quickly discovered, was a small sandy bay, at the upper edge of which had been built a little hardstanding from which, on the high tide, boats could be launched. This afternoon, with

205

the water a long way down, not only was the whole bay deserted but it was also sheltered from the breeze.

'Shall we see if the sand's dry enough to walk on?' Jack asked when he had brought the MG to a halt and was opening her door.

To Esme, it seemed more and more as though he was reading her mind. 'Let's.'

On the way down the ramp to the sand, he took her hand. Despite the tingle it sent through her — or perhaps, because of it — she made no move to take it back. Why would she when everything about being there with him felt so right?

'Perfect day for it,' he remarked, swiping off his RAF cap and tilting back his head to stare up at the sky.

'You told me it would be.'

He smiled. 'I did, didn't I? Rare thing, a day like this so late in November.'

As though it was meant to be, she thought but didn't say. 'Better, perhaps, because it *is* November,' she offered instead.

As they drew closer to the water's edge, and she felt the sand growing softer beneath her feet, she recalled a pair of blue canvas beach shoes she'd had as a girl — and how she'd cried when, after a wave had washed over them, they had dried with a salty stain that had remained until the day they had finally fallen apart.

'Perhaps we shouldn't go any further,' he said, evidently noticing her staring down at her feet.

'Perhaps not. But could we just stand for a moment and take it all in?'

'Of course we can.'

In the silence that fell between them, Esme closed

her eyes and listened. From somewhere behind on the wooded hillside, a cock robin was whistling his winter lament. A few yards in front of them, surprisingly benign waves for the time of year were folding rhythmically onto the sand. Even just standing there seemed to be slowing her breathing: gently in as the wave receded, softly out as it rolled forward to topple over. In, out. Gather, release.

How was it possible, she wondered, to feel so calm? How was it possible, to stand here hand-in-hand with a man she barely knew — while her family believed she was driving some or other official between airfields — to feel so light, so relieved of all burdens? Did it even matter? Couldn't she just enjoy the sensation?

With the notion that Jack was watching her, she opened her eyes. Unsurprised to discover that he was, she sighed. 'This is wonderful.'

He squeezed her hand. 'Isn't it? Given the chance, I'd stay here for ever.'

'Me too,' she said, before hastening to add, 'by which I mean that I should like to always feel as calm as I do at this very moment — as though I haven't a care in the world.'

'To feel how one did as an adolescent, before one became bowed by the responsibilities and expectations of adulthood?'

Her response was little more than a whisper. 'Yes.' Feeling tears welling, she directed her gaze towards the feint demarcation between sea and sky. 'When things were simpler.' *And anything seemed possible.*

When his grasp tightened about her hand, she swallowed hard.

'Are you all right? Only, you look . . .'

'Truly,' she said with a light shake of her head, 'I'm

207

fine. More than you could know.'

And it was true. Despite recognising that none of her sorrows had actually gone away, she had the sense that they had faded. Here, in this secluded little cove, she had a feeling that Esme the woman was tentatively winning out against Esme the bereaved mother and estranged wife she had recently become. Despite her momentary wobble just then, she felt a glimmer of hope. And it could only be down to the man standing beside her, and the way that, as he unwittingly drew her out from the tangle of wreckage that had lately become her life, she felt warm and safe. Fuzzy. In love. Had she ever felt this dizzy with Richard? Had she ever stood, hand in hand, picturing the rest of her life with him — imagining the fun they would have, the possibilities that awaited them? At some point, surely, she must have done. Ironic, then, if the pursuit of their shared dream had been the cause of its strangulation. Did marriage and careers and children always do that to dreams? Would it do the same to her and Jack were they to decide they couldn't bear to be apart — that they simply had to build a life together? If so, then how incredibly sad.

Realising that Jack was replacing his cap and tweaking it into position, she turned to meet his smile.

'Come on, then,' he said, refastening his hand around hers and turning about. 'Only, I don't know about you, but I'm famished.'

'Beginning to get that way,' she agreed.

Having handed her back into the MG, Jack reached behind the seat and pulled out a canvas duffel bag.

'So,' he said, extracting from within it a Thermos and a china mug, 'to start with, we have soup. I thought we might be glad of it to warm us up.' Handing her the mug, he unscrewed the metal cup from the top of the flask and put it on the dash. Then, removing the stopper, he held the flask to his nose and sniffed. 'Mushroom.'

'My favourite.'

'Hold steady.' Into each of the cups he poured some of the delicious-smelling liquid before replacing the stopper in the neck of the flask. 'I can't imagine it will be scalding but be careful just in case.'

Blowing briefly across the top of her mug before offering it to her lips, Esme took a sip. 'Just right.'

'Bread?' he asked, producing from the duffel a napkin, which he unfolded to reveal the end of a bloomer. When she nodded, he tore off a piece and handed it to her. 'Excuse fingers.'

'The soup is delicious,' she said, watching with a grin as he tried to wedge the corner of his crust into his tiny cup.

'That's because a couple of times a week, just before dawn, Mrs Luscombe goes into the field behind the pub to forage for mushrooms.'

'Since you're still alive, one imagines she knows what she's doing.'

'Living proof. Top-up?'

'Please.'

The Thermos emptied, Jack produced the two paper bags he had brought out from the baker's. 'I hope you really are hungry,' he said, 'because when it comes to pasties, they only sell one size. Here.' With that, he split open the side of one of the bags, opened it out, and was about to offer her the contents when he stopped. 'Christ. What a heathen. Would you mind — in the bottom of my duffel bag there's a couple of napkins.'

She laughed. Him? Heathen? Hardly.

Finding the pair of napkins, she opened one out, reached across, and laid it in his lap before positioning the other one on her own. 'Does Mrs Luscombe know you've taken these?'

'It was she who insisted I bring them. Left to me, you would have been covered in crumbs and have nothing on which to wipe your fingers.'

The pasties were good: the golden pastry dissolving on her tongue; the filling tasting as much of beef as it did of potato and swede. 'Excellent,' she said after a while. 'Though I'm not sure I shall manage the whole thing.'

'No matter,' he said. 'Leave what you don't want. I might have a spare corner for it.'

His turn of phrase made her smile. 'When I was little, and I wanted to get out of eating something I didn't like, I would claim to be full, to which my aunt would always coax, *Come on, now, I'm sure you've got an empty corner somewhere.* Or else, *You can't possibly have filled all your corners.* You're the only other person I've ever heard say it.'

'Really? I should like to say I remember it from Nanny . . . but I rather think I just made it up. But here, give me that and I'll just —' Opening his mouth, he demolished the remains of her pasty. 'Dispose of it for you.'

After that, he produced an apple which, with the blade from his penknife, he cut into a series of even slices and offered to her.

'Dessert, madam?'

When she took a couple of slices and popped one of them into her mouth, she was unsurprised to find it juicy and sweet.

210

'The tide's coming in,' she said, looking up and noticing how much of the sand had already disappeared.

'I seem to remember it's high at about seventeen-twenty today.'

'I should like to go down and watch it.'

He looked askance. 'The tide?'

'Yes.'

'Then you go on and I'll catch up. I'll just see to all this debris.'

Moments later, when he arrived beside her, she was staring down at the frills of bubbles which, with each little surge, reclaimed another few inches of the shore.

'When I was younger,' she said softly, 'I used to watch the tide sweeping away all traces of our activities on the sand and think that Mother Nature was tidying up for the day . . . that it was her way of letting us start again in the morning with a clean slate.'

'And now?'

'To be honest, stood here like this . . .' *Stood here like this with you.* '. . . it feels more like an ending. It feels as though once we leave here, there will be no trace that this afternoon ever existed.'

'You know . . .' Alerted by a change to his tone, she turned towards him. 'Being a pilot deepens one's appreciation of the here and now, reminds one to apply oneself a step at a time. Find the rendezvous. Land the plane. Get back up again sharpish. Make it home. And only once you've done that, and you're peeling off your goggles, do you let yourself think about anything else . . . do you think about spending time with someone who will help you to forget that tomorrow, you're going to have to do it all over again. At the end of the day, you picture finding someone you can ask

211

to go on a picnic with you, and hope that, November or not, she'll agree. And that she'll enjoy it for what it is. When you make it back from a mission, physically exhausted and mentally drained, it's the simple pleasures you crave most.' Shifting his weight, he paused for a moment before adding, 'Which is why, whatever I saw in your eyes just now, whatever it is you're not telling me, I want you to know that you don't have to explain. I don't need to know. I have no expectations of you, and I make no promises. The simpler this is — for both of us — the more we'll enjoy it. So,' he said, pulling her towards him, 'if you don't like the idea of the tide washing away all traces of us, how about we enjoy the rest of the afternoon . . . and then do as young Esme used to and simply start afresh when we next have the chance? How about we look upon each ending as a necessary precursor to there being a next time?'

A next time. The prospect sent a thrill down her spine.

'A series of distractions,' she whispered.

'Because correct me if I'm wrong, but it seems to me that's what *you're* in need of too.'

★ ★ ★

She must try not to look so happy. She must try to check the urge to keep smiling. In fact, the look for which she *should* be aiming was one approaching exhaustion.

Arriving back at Woodicombe and pulling up alongside the stables, Esme glanced to her wristwatch: not quite six o'clock. With any luck, the others would have eaten their supper early tonight, saving her the discomfort of having to sit at the table with them and lie about where she'd been all afternoon. If they hadn't, she would feign tiredness, using as her excuse a couple of hours stuck in a motorcar and the rest of the time spent standing around. Put like that, she could even convince herself it wasn't a lie.

Reaching across to the passenger seat for her handbag and her scarves, she once again started to smile, her lips curling higher and higher until she was beaming like an idiot. What a dreamy afternoon it had been. And just when she'd thought the best part was over, they'd shared that lovely drive home: the MG cosy with her roof up; the sun setting behind them; a starry twilight ahead. When he'd offered her a rug, she swathed herself in it and sat, snuggled up against him, his arm around her shoulders. For a while, to remove the need for him to reclaim his hand in order to change gear, she had tried doing it for him — moving the stick while he operated the clutch — but the crunching and grinding of the gearbox had quickly become too much for him to bear, and pretty soon she hadn't been able to see anyway for crying with laughter. Yes, his suggestion of a series of little distractions was perfect. *I have no expectations of you.* A little bit of make-believe, no questions asked.

Still grinning, she got out of the Austin, locked the door and headed across the yard to the kitchen porch where she bent to take off her boots. Everywhere seeming quiet, she pushed her feet into her shoes and, shivering in the cold, set off along the corridor. Drawing level with the scullery and noticing a light, she poked her head in. Aunt Kate was drying up. 'Hello,' she greeted her.

Turning to look over her shoulder, Kate smiled

213

warmly. 'Oh, there you are, love. You've been gone a long old while.'

'I have.'

'Hungry?'

Esme shook her head. 'What I need most is a bath and a lie down.'

'Well, there's a portion of shepherd's pie if you want it but you'll have to heat it up.'

'Thanks, Aunt Kate. But perhaps, once I've had a wash, I might just have some toast — if that's all right.'

''Course, love. There's the end of a loaf in the bin. Help yourself.'

Upstairs in her room, Esme unbuttoned her coat, gave it a shake, and was just about to slip it onto a hanger when there was a tap at the door: Louise. It had to be. Since her greatest wish was to soak in a warm bath and let her mind wander back over events from earlier, she would try to get rid of her as quickly as possible.

'Who is it?'

Don't grin too much. You're supposed to be worn out, remember?

'Me. Louise.'

Lowering her shoulders from where, to her dismay, they had already started to rise up around her ears, she called back. 'Come in.'

'I hope you don't mind but I heard you come up.'

'Of course I don't mind. Come in.'

'*You* were gone a long time this afternoon.'

'Yes,' Esme said simply, a quick glance to Louise's demeanour telling her that she looked both preoccupied and weary. 'What's up?'

'I'm thinking of telling Mum about Dad.'

Having hung her coat in the wardrobe, Esme turned

214

back. 'Tell her what?' Whatever she did, she mustn't say anything to put Louise's hackles up or get her on the defensive. Driven into a corner, her cousin was wont to become horribly stubborn.

'That Dad is up to something.'

'I see.' Crossing to the dressing table, Esme unscrewed her earrings. 'Well, ignoring for a moment the wider implications attached to such a course of action, what is it that you've decided to tell her?' With any luck, she could scupper Louise's plan before it even got off the ground. Having both his daughter and his wife on his back was something she imagined Uncle Luke could do without.

'Like I said, that Dad's up to something.'

'And when she asks you what, exactly, he's *up to*, what do you intend saying?'

Standing just inside the door, Louise shifted her weight. 'Well . . .'

'And are you thinking of telling her on her own? Or are you going to ask your father to be there as well?'

'I —'

'Only, if you're going to accuse your father of something, I'm not sure that doing so behind his back is the right way to go about it.' Just as she had hoped, Louise's conviction seemed to flounder.

'Well, what would *you* do?'

'To be honest,' Esme said, 'Unless I knew with absolute certainty that something *was* going on, I wouldn't do anything. Unless I could say more than *Dad went into a forest*, I think I'd leave well alone — avoid upsetting the apple cart.'

'Easy for you to say,' Louise complained. 'But you saw the same as I did. On a November night, with nothing more than a torch, Dad disappeared into a

215

wood. And he's done it at least twice that we know of.' *At least three times, if you included her own encounter with him*, Esme realised. 'You can't tell me that's normal behaviour for a man who's just turned fifty-one.'

Wondering briefly what Uncle Luke's age had to do with it, Esme suspected she was fighting a losing battle. When it suited her, Louise could be an immovable object. Besides, this afternoon, down in that little cove, she had experienced such calmness that, driving home, she had resolved to try to live her life differently — to follow Jack's example and live more for the moment. Moreover, in a bid to rid herself of unnecessary worries, she had determined to stay out of matters that didn't concern her. Make those two changes and she would, she hoped, live more serenely, more freely. More vividly. But, to do any of that, she had to leave Louise to take care of her own problems.

Warding off an urge to treat her cousin to a despairing sigh, she instead pictured herself back at Morwen Cove: waves lapping onto the sand; seagulls calling; her hand in Jack's and a sense that nothing else mattered. Then, drawing a light breath, she turned to meet her cousin's gaze. 'Dearest Louise, only you know what is important to you. Only you can decide which of you knows best — you or your father.'

'But Essie —'

'You asked me just now what *I'd* do, and I've told you. Since I presume you wanted honesty, I'm not sure what else to say. Now, you'll have to forgive me but I'm desperate for a bath. It's been a long day.'

'Yes. Yes, of course. I'm sorry. I'll . . . leave you to it.'

Once Louise had left, Esme felt a stab of guilt. Her cousin's concern was well-founded. But Uncle Luke was a grown man and more than capable of taking care of himself. So, now, in her regulation five inches of bath water, she was going to do the same thing — take care of herself. And reflect upon the truly astonishing and wonderful afternoon she'd just had with Jack.

13
Loyalty

'You found it, then.'

Accepting Jack's assistance out of the Austin, and submitting to a kiss on the cheek, Esme smiled. 'Thanks in no part whatsoever to your directions.'

'You know,' he said, helping her into her coat, 'sitting here waiting just now, I did begin to wonder whether, in a bid not to seem overly keen yesterday, I had failed to make clear that I was actually extending an invitation.'

'With good reason, Flight Lieutenant Carey,' Esme replied. 'Driving here this morning, *I* began to wonder whether I'd read too much into your vagueness.' *Sometimes on a Sunday morning*, he'd said as they'd arrived back at The Fleece last night, *I go for a walk along the river below Great Torrington. I start off from the bridge by the station at around ten o'clock.*

'But you came anyway,' he observed.

'Only because it wasn't raining. Although also,' she continued, accepting the arm he offered her as they headed away from their cars, 'because for the last couple of days, my cousin has been trying to drag me into a matter with which I'd rather not become involved.'

'And this was your excuse to get out of it.'

'Only where she was concerned. For my part, I didn't need an excuse.'

'Then I don't suppose I can tempt you to come back afterwards for lunch with me?' he asked as they reached a stile that gave onto a path down to the riverbank.

Once he had assisted her over it, and she was back on the ground beside him, she shook her head. 'Not today, I'm afraid. Since I wasn't entirely sure how this was going to turn out, I told my aunt I'd be back by twelve thirty.'

'In which case,' he remarked, 'we'll walk as far as the second bridge and then turn back — a little over three miles, I should imagine.'

'Sounds just right.' See, she thought, living for the moment was easy.

At the bottom of the slope, they joined a well-worn path through a wooded valley, where the river, swollen by the autumn rains, was racing its way around boulders and tumbling over fallen branches. Above them, the sky was overcast; unlike yesterday with its feeling of never-ending space and distant horizons, today felt enclosed and secretive.

'I come here to walk this particular stretch,' Jack said, reaching to take her hand, 'for the chance to see otters.'

Otters? Clearly, there was more to this man than met the eye.

'I'm not sure I've ever seen one of those.'

'Not many people have. For the most part, they only come out at dusk. But, if you're lucky, and in the right place at the right time, you can sometimes glimpse them along here.'

How odd, Esme thought as they walked along the little path, that of all the places she should come to feel at ease, it should be out in the open air. Growing up, she'd had a mild dislike for the outdoors — especially if it involved damp or cold or mud — the only real exception being summer days on the beach at Woodicombe Cove. But here she was, for the second time in two days, relishing being outside, aware of her surroundings in a way that felt new and exciting: the rushing of the water serving to blot out the clamour of her thoughts; the air that she drew down into her lungs rich with the aromas of bark and damp earth; the colours and textures drawing her eyes as though she was seeing them for the first time. The realisation made her smile; if Richard could see her tramping along a riverbank, he would be aghast — would go so far as to question the state of her mind. But then, Richard, she reminded herself, was never going to know.

Something else she discovered was that walking without feeling the need to converse could be restful. With Richard, silence signified that they were individually preoccupied. Whereas here, with Jack, it was— But why was she thinking about Richard? Hadn't she promised herself to live in the moment? And if so, then why was she spoiling the experience?

'Goodness,' she said, startled by the sight of a golden yellow mound on the trunk of a fallen tree. 'What on earth is that?'

When Jack came to a halt and bent down, she joined him.

'Yellow brain. It's a parasitic fungus. According to legend, if it appears on the door or the gate of a house, it signifies that a witch has cast a spell on the occupants. Hence its other name: witch's butter.'

'Is it poisonous?' she asked, bending lower to better examine the intricate folds of the gelatinous mass.

Getting to his feet, he pulled her up beside him. 'Wouldn't know. Never eaten it.'

'Which doesn't really answer my question,' she said with a laugh.

'Does it not?'

'No.'

From there, the path followed the sweeping bends of the river as it meandered its way back and forth across a more open stretch of land. From one of the bare fields, a flock of birds rose up, creating a patch-work blanket of black and white as, en masse, they moved away.

'Peewits,' he said of them. 'In Suffolk they're quite common. We would see them year-round. From what I can gather, here they're rather more of a winter vis-itor.'

'Striking colours,' she said, in reality less taken by the birds themselves than by his appreciation of all things natural. It was one of the things that made him so different to Richard: where her husband approached life from a start point of purpose and efficiency, Jack seemed to follow his soul. Yesterday at Morwenchurch was a case in point: when she had been stood looking at the row of cottages, Jack had felt the romance of the place. Richard, in that same situation, would have pointed out that the window frames would whistle with draughts and that the walls would have rising damp. It just made Jack seem even more unusual — certainly for someone whose con-tinued existence, as he himself admitted, necessitated precise planning and split-second decisions.

As they strolled beneath the first railway bridge to cross the meandering river, almost immediately, she saw the second. *We'll walk as far as the second bridge and then turn back.* Inwardly, she sighed. So soon! So agonisingly, horribly, soon.

221

'We can expect sorties to start up again next week,' Jack said as, in anticipation of reaching the bridge, their pace began to slow. 'So, it will be back to Pond Farm.'

'Then I'm so very glad we've done this now,' she replied.

'Me too. And we can keep doing it, you know. You can come to The Fleece — operations permitting —'

'I'd like that.'

'Still fit in the odd walk.'

'Yes.'

'Maybe even the odd drive if the weather's suitable. But only if you want to.'

'I do. You can't know how lovely these last few days have been.'

'Then *next time*, I'll issue a proper invitation and you can join me for lunch. And after that, stuffed to bursting with Mrs Luscombe's Yorkshire puddings . . . and far too drowsy to move, we'll spend the afternoon in front of the fire.'

It sounded so wonderful that she felt a deep craving to make all of this real — permanent. 'Then make sure to ask properly next time.'

'Come on, then,' he said as their ponderous progress brought them to the brick pier of the second railway bridge. 'If you're to make it back as promised, we should turn around.'

'You know,' she said as they started to retrace their steps along the bank. 'We haven't seen an otter yet.'

'Which means we'll have to come again.'

'It does, doesn't it?'

To Esme, the distance from there back to the railway station seemed cruelly short, such that, before she knew it, they were dawdling across the gravel of

222

the car park, he swinging her hand as their pace grew more and more reluctant.

'Well, here we are then,' he said as they arrived alongside the Austin.

'Do you have a date for your next mission?' she asked, desperate not to leave things between them just hanging.

'Not with any certainty. But Tuesday I have to go up to— well, let's just say I have to go for a briefing, the sort that can only be delivered in person.'

'Top secret.'

'Highly. And, since I won't be back until Wednesday, one would imagine instructions will be issued for Thursday night — Friday at the latest.'

'So, I'll see you *then*.'

'I'm rather counting on it.' Letting go of her hand, he leant to kiss her cheek. 'Drive carefully.'

When she unlocked the door to the Austin, and he held it for her to get in, she knew that if she let the opportunity pass, she would never forgive herself. And so, turning back to him, she put her arms around his neck and kissed him.

'I . . . didn't like to presume,' he said afterwards, his grin reassuring her that she hadn't misread the situation.

'Then clearly,' she said, turning to get back into her car, 'one of us is a gentleman and one of us knows no shame.'

'Go on,' he said, still grinning as he closed her door. 'Before my supposed good manners desert me once and for all.'

If only they would, she thought as she started the engine and pulled out of the car park. *If only they would*.

She couldn't stop grinning. On the drive back to Woodicombe, Esme found it impossible to contain her happiness. It kept spilling out of her in silly little giggles and childish grins. In fact, as she pulled up alongside the stables, almost skipped across the yard and went in through the kitchen porch, no amount of telling herself to adopt a straight face would bring one about. She absolutely, completely and utterly, couldn't contain herself.

Noticing from her watch that there was still plenty of time before lunch, she decided to go upstairs, get changed, and then come down and see whether she could lend a hand with anything. If she could occupy herself with a task like laying the table, she'd be less likely to draw attention to her ridiculous grin.

Detecting the aroma of pheasant roasting, she went along the corridor, intending to put her head around the door to the kitchen and volunteer her services. But, before she got that far, the sound of Luke's raised voice brought her to a halt.

'So . . . what? You're accusing me of lying?'

Her heart sank. Louise must have taken it upon herself to challenge her father about what he was up to. Stupid girl. Hadn't they agreed that wasn't a good idea?

With a dismayed shake of her head, she tiptoed closer to the door, steadied herself against the frame and listened, the person she heard speak next being Louise.

'So, you're telling me that every night last week, when you left here, you went to Home Guard.'

'Not that I have to account for my movements to

224

you, girl, but yes, that's what I'm saying.'

'In Westward Quay.'

'Well where else would I go?'

'Oh, I don't know . . . but how about Woodicombe Cross? Or even Farracott?'

'*Farracott*?' Since the person sounding incredulous now was Aunt Kate, Esme's heart sank further. 'What the dickens is at Farracott, Luke?'

'For starters, there's The Black Sheep,' Louise said. 'And Frank Hodge.'

'Frank Hodge. Dear God, tell me you're not mixed up with that . . . that crook.'

'Look,' Luke said, his voice a fraction less rattled. 'Let's all just calm down a minute. Now, Lou, tell me straight, love, what the devil's brought all this on, eh? Come on, don't stand there all stiff and disapproving. Come and sit down and tell me what this is really all about.' With that, Esme heard a chair being dragged out from beneath the table. 'Come on.'

'Some time back,' Esme heard Louise eventually begin, 'Connie said she saw you one night, coming out of The Black Sheep with Frank Hodge.'

'And did it ever occur to you that she might be wrong? Without any light to see by, everyone looks much alike, especially wrapped up against the cold. Least, to most folks, they do.'

'Yes,' Louise said, her tone shaky, 'of course it occurred to me she might be wrong. I even told her she was — said you wouldn't have anything to do with a villain like Frank Hodge.'

'There you go, then —'

'But I also happen to know . . .' Out in the corridor, Esme shivered. What to do? Did she go in, cause a distraction, and then whisk Louise out of there? Or did she leave her to get on with it? In truth, none of this had anything to do with her. Besides, even if she did manage to bring an end to his particular discussion, Louise was unlikely to just let the matter drop. Heaving a lengthy sigh, she continued to listen. '... roaming about up by Farracott Woods.'

'Whoa! You been following me, girl? Have you? And you, Kate, are you part of this, too? This . . . this witch hunt?'

From Kate there came a mumbled response too quiet for Esme to make out. But it did sound as though she was trying to distance herself.

'I don't know what to say,' Luke went on. 'I'm completely and utterly lost for words.' To Esme's mind, if he was faking dismay, he was very convincing. 'My own daughter, accusing me of . . . well, no, actually, girl, why don't you come out and say it. What is it you think I've done? No, come on, you can't backtrack now. You're the one casting aspersions. So, tell me what, precisely, you think it is I'm up to.' For what seemed to Esme to be ages, there was only silence, until eventually Luke said, 'I'm still waiting.'

'I'm worried,' Louise said, her voice faint, 'that you've got muddled up in something. That . . . that you've let Frank Hodge drag you into one of his schemes. That you're tangled up in black marketeering or some such . . .'

'*Black marketeering*? Christ, Lou. How could you even *think* that? *How*? Your *own father*?'

'Because what else am I supposed to think?' Louise wailed. 'You're seen with Frank Hodge. You prowl about in Farracott Woods. Put yourself in my shoes and tell me what *you'd* think. And *if*, as you say, I'm wrong, then put me right. Tell me what you're really

226

doing up there and I'll apologise.'

'Before we even talk about *me*,' Luke said, 'I want you to admit, here and now, that you followed me.'

Softly, 'I followed you.'

'Now tell me why.'

In the silence that followed Luke's instruction, Esme pictured Louise, her shoulders weighed by doubt, her head bowed.

'Because when Connie told me she'd seen you coming out of The Black Sheep with Frank Hodge, I wanted her to be wrong. So, I started watching what you did, to prove to myself that she was mistaken and that I had no reason to worry. But the more I watched you, the more I noticed you behaving differently . . . noticed how you've been jumpy . . . and secretive.'

'Jumpy and secretive.'

Now Esme could picture Louise forcing herself to swallow as she searched for how best to continue.

'Connie also told me that like you, her uncle and her cousin are in the Westward Quay platoon, and that they only go a few nights a week — to the drill hall on Tuesdays and then a couple of turns on patrol. But these past months, *you've* been going out almost every night . . . and saying you're off to Home Guard. So . . . surely you can see why I wonder what's going on.'

In the corridor, Esme found herself holding her breath. Were they about to find out what Uncle Luke had been up to — why he'd been in the lane on the night she'd collided with him?

'There is Home Guard on those other nights . . . just with a different platoon. A while back, I was approached about doing some extra patrols. And I agreed. And why did I? I agreed because if that invasion bell rings, I want to be ready to give my all to protect my family. That's why.'

Reflecting upon what she'd just heard, Esme frowned. *Could* that be true? Given that it *might* be, should she, in support of her uncle, go in and cause proceedings to break up — announce her arrival as though oblivious to what had gone on so far — or stay out of it? Whose side was she on anyway?

In the kitchen, the discussion continued, it being Kate who asked, 'Why can't you tell us?'

'Because there's a war on. Because careless talk costs lives. Difficult for you to accept though it must be, you're just going to have to take my word for it. Think about who I am, Kate. And you, Lou. Think about what's important to me, and then trust me when I say that I'm not doing anything I shouldn't.'

'And Frank Hodge?' Kate asked.

'Frank Hodge is a tuppenny crook who'd sell his grandmother if it'd make him a shilling. Young Connie was wrong. And now, I'm going to get cleaned up for dinner. So, let that be an end to it.'

Suddenly hearing a chair being moved, Esme straightened up. Then, with no wish to be discovered eavesdropping, she stole along the corridor, pelted up both flights of stairs and tore along the landing. Throwing open the door to her room, she shot through it and turned to close it silently behind her.

Panting for breath, she crossed to the bed and sank heavily onto it. Deep down, she had a feeling that Uncle Luke was telling the truth. The trouble was, what did she do now? Did she let him know she'd overheard and see if he would explain anything

more, or did she keep quiet? Did she, affecting

ignorance, waltz into the kitchen and enquire after Louise's morning or simply wait for her to say something?

Moving to the wardrobe to hang up her coat, she exhaled heavily. What she would do, she decided — at least for now — was nothing. She would take her cue from the mood over lunch. And if no more was said on the matter, then this afternoon she would curl up in front of the fire and imagine that rather than coming back here, she had gone to The Fleece with Jack.

Unsurprisingly, the thought of Jack brought on another smile. Wouldn't that have been the perfect way to spend the afternoon!

★ ★ ★

She might have known she wouldn't get away with it. After a lunch eaten broadly in silence, and with the clearing up afterwards complete, barely had Esme got the fire going in the drawing room and then settled herself on the sofa, when Louise came straight through the door and sat down beside her.

'Are you busy?' she asked, appearing to look about for anything to indicate one way or another.

Esme shook her head. 'Just trying to get warm. Maybe have a little snooze. Why do you ask?' Hearing movement behind her, she raised herself up to see that hovering just inside the door was Aunt Kate, her attention directed back out into the hallway. Keeping up the pretence, she asked, 'What's going on?'

'We need your help.'

'With...?'

'Dad has told us something . . . and we need to know whether or not it's true.'

229

'And you think *I* will know?'

'Not exactly. We'd like you to ask Richard.'

Briefly, Esme closed her eyes. *Richard.*

Trying to keep her tone from betraying her, she said, 'And what is it you think *he* will be able to tell you?'

At that, Louise recounted the bones of what Esme had overheard earlier, ending by saying, 'And so you see, while we *want* to believe him, neither of us will settle until we know whether or not he's telling the truth.'

At least, Esme thought, her cousin had made no reference to their joint expedition that night.

'That he really could be doing something different for the Home Guard?'

Louise nodded. 'Yes.'

'Well, I'm not sure Richard will know . . .'

'But you could ask him,' Louise persisted. 'For us.'

'Yes,' she said. It wasn't, Esme reflected, Louise's fault that she had no desire to talk to Richard at the moment. 'I'll call him. For you, of course I will.'

'Thank you, Essie,' Louise replied, wrapping her in an awkward hug. 'You don't know the weight it will be off our minds to know what's going on.'

When Louise got up from the sofa and, giving her a relieved smile, left the room, Esme let out a lengthy sigh. Well, since she had said she would do it, she might as well get it over and done with. After all, now she had *no* chance of sitting there dreaming about Jack — not with Richard on her mind, she didn't.

★ ★ ★

'Richard?

'Darling. Hello. Everything all right?'

'Fine, thank you.' With the sound of her husband's voice making her wriggle with discomfort, Esme decided to get straight to the point. 'I'm calling to ask for your help with something — something for Louise.'

'Did you say for Louise?'

'Yes. There's been a bit of a to-do. I'll spare you the details but what it boils down to is that Uncle Luke claims he's involved with what he called *other duties* —'

'I thought he was Home Guard.'

'He is. Or rather, we think he is. And Louise wants to know if he's telling the truth.'

'Can't she ask him?'

Anxious to be done with this, Esme stood tapping her foot. 'She *has* asked him. But all he'll say is that a couple of nights each week, he *does something special for the Home Guard*. Personally, I'm inclined to believe him. But Louise can't get it out of her head that he's embroiled in something shady.' Lowering her voice, she went on, 'And it would seem as though she's convinced Aunt Kate of the fact, too.'

'So, what is it you want *me* to do?'

'Find out if there's such a thing as a . . . oh, I don't know, a separate section of the Home Guard that has special duties. And whether Uncle Luke could realistically be a part of it.'

'If you ask me, this all seems a bit underhand. I'm not sure I'm comfortable snooping . . . especially with your uncle being such firm friends with Captain Colborne who is, after all, my father-in-law.'

'Look,' Esme said, her impatience deepening, 'if you don't want to get involved, just say so. I'll tell Louise you can't help, that she'll just have to trust —'

'No, no,' Richard said from the other end of the

231

line. 'Louise has been terrific to you. No, I'll see what I can find out. But, darling . . .'

'Yes?'

'Please don't make her any promises. I might be in the War Office, but that doesn't mean I have unfettered access to *everything*. No one does. For obvious reasons.'

'Don't worry, I shan't commit you.'

'And, darling . . .'

'Yes?'

'Are you *sure* you're all right?'

'Certain of it.'

'You're sleeping properly? They're not pushing you to do too much of that driving. You're not getting overtired?'

'Yes to the first, no to the rest.'

'Only you sound —'

'Truly, Richard. I'm fine.'

'All right. Well, if you insist. But *please* take care.'

'I will. I do. Thank you, Richard.'

'Goodbye, then, darling.'

With the telephone receiver back on its cradle, Esme exhaled heavily. Perhaps she could have tried to be a bit less short with the poor man. Well, when he called back to tell her what he'd found out, she would be nicer — she would summon some of that lovely warm feeling she had when she was out with Jack and make a point of telling him how grateful she was. After all, there was no sense alerting him to the real reason she was short with him, was there?

14

Out of the Blue

'Golly. Where is everyone? Am I late?'

As Esme went in through the door to the ops room and glanced about, Jack got up from the chair next to the stove and came towards her. 'No, you're perfectly on time.'

'And yet, you seem to be all on your own . . .'

'The mission's been scrubbed — couple of hours ago. I was sent orders to stand down.'

Having driven to Pond Farm expecting to collect an agent that Jack was due to bring in from France, Esme frowned. If his mission wasn't going ahead, then why was he here? Removing her gloves and tugging off her beret, she put them on the table and went towards him. 'So, having been stood down, you're here because...?'

'Because I had a feeling,' he said, stooping to kiss her. 'Well, more accurately, I had a suspicion and a hope.'

Letting him slide his hands around her waist, she kept up her frown. 'Go on.'

'My suspicion,' he said, pulling her closer, 'was that no one would remember to tell *you* it was off.'

'And your hope?'

'Was that even if they *had*, you would come anyway.'

'Then seemingly,' she said, a spike of joy shooting up through her body, 'your suspicion was right, and your hope fulfilled.'

'Of course,' he said with a wry smile, 'having walked up here on the off chance, I then had to hope I wasn't going to be left sitting here for hours not even knowing for sure that you would come.'

'Then if I may say so, Flight Lieutenant Carey, your plan was not a terribly well considered one.'

'To my chagrin, I am forced to agree.'

'Especially since the only reason I'm here so early,' Esme went on, glancing to the clock and seeing that it was only just past ten, 'is because had I stayed at home in the warm, there was a very real chance I would have fallen asleep and not made it here at all.'

'Fortuitous all round then.'

'Indeed.'

'Come on,' he said, releasing her in order to reach for his sheepskin jacket. 'Why don't we go to The Fleece? Rather easier to keep warm there.'

'Very well.' What luck, she thought as he guided her towards the door. If Mr Mulberry *had* remembered to telephone and tell her the mission was off, this particular opportunity would never have arisen!

Arriving at The Fleece, Esme followed Jack into the snug. While she unbuttoned her coat and hung it from a peg inside the door, he took a poker and stirred some life into the fire.

'There. That ought to do it. Back in two ticks.'

'All right,' she said, watching as he disappeared in the direction of Mrs Luscombe's dining room. Settling into one of the chairs at the hearth, she let out a sigh of contentment. How fortunate was this? By now, she should have been in the company of a stranger, driving through the frosty night, and yet here she was instead in the warmth of The Fleece with Jack.

'Cocoa,' he returned to announce as he handed her one of the two pottery mugs he was carrying.

'Tell me,' she said, watching him settle into the other chair, 'are there ever any customers in here? Or do they only ever frequent the public bar?'

'Interesting that you should enquire,' he said before offering his mug to his lips, 'because every Friday night, an elderly couple arrive, sit at that table over there, have a half of Mackeson's each, and then leave without having exchanged a single word. Oh, and they wear matching knitted hats.'

Glancing to where he'd indicated, Esme tried to picture the scene. 'That's either terribly romantic or else incredibly sad.' When he gave her a quizzical look, she went on, 'Either they don't need to say anything to each other because they instinctively know what the other is thinking —'

'Or they can no longer stand the sight of one another?'

'Well, *you*'ve seen them,' she said. 'So, which is it?'

He started to grin. 'Call me a romantic, but I think they come because half a pint of milk stout is sufficiently fortifying to enable them to go home and spend the rest of the night making passionate love.'

Erupting into laughter, Esme reached to place her mug on the table. Even then, she had to wait until she had stopped giggling before she could speak. 'If that's your idea . . . of romance . . .'

'Who's to say that when I'm their age, that won't be the highlight of my week.'

'The half a pint of Mackeson's,' she said, 'or the passionate love-making?'

'Would it be greedy to hope for both?'

'Do you think people of our age will live to be that

235

old?' she asked. 'Only, this war does have a habit of snatching people in their prime.' The moment she'd said it, she wished she hadn't.

'You've lost someone, haven't you? Someone close.' With her fingers going instinctively to her locket, she looked into her lap. 'It's what I saw in your eyes the other day.'

She raised her head. Since he'd guessed, there was little point denying it. 'Recently. Yes.' There was no need for him to know that the loss in question was her son.

Reaching for her hand, he grasped it tightly. 'Family?'

She nodded. 'Yes. You?'

'Colleagues by the dozen — which is rather different — but when it comes to family, no, I've been fortunate. There *was* someone, but losing her was more of my own doing, was more of an indirect consequence of —'

When he stopped mid-sentence, she turned to look at him. His expression suggested he regretted mentioning it.

'Sorry,' she said. 'I shouldn't have asked.'

By way of reassurance, he shook his head. 'It was a while ago now, actually just a week or two *before* war was declared . . . and I'd been on the verge of proposing.'

Taken aback, she inadvertently tightened her grip on his hand. 'I —'

'In fact, you might say it was a near miss,' he went on, his tone heavy with irony. 'I'd lined up the perfect opportunity, rehearsed what I was going to say. But as I stood there in front of the mirror, going over the words in my head one final time, I suddenly thought,

236

how can I ask this woman to marry me, knowing I might not be here to go through with it? How can I even contemplate putting her through the agony and the worry . . . the torture of waiting to hear whether I'd made it back each time? How could I even expect her to remain faithful when everything around us looked so uncertain . . . when we were all of us heading off into the unknown? I remember looking back at myself and knowing I couldn't do it to her.'

There was so much Esme wanted to say. And had it not been for the lump suddenly tightening her throat, she might have tried. In the event, all she could manage was a whispered apology. 'I'm so sorry.'

'Please don't be. I couldn't bear that. Anyway, now that you know, you might understand why I choose to live as I do.'

'For the moment?'

Almost imperceptibly, he nodded. 'And I shall continue to — at least until it's clear that the end is in sight. Anyway.' Letting go of her hand, he sat more upright in his chair. 'I have to stop getting mawkish or you won't want to come again.'

How wrong could he possibly be? The more she saw of this sensitive side to him, the more she wanted to get to know him. That he had resisted proposing to someone — for the wellbeing of the young woman in question — spoke volumes to his character. Was there any finer motivation on earth for doing as he had?

'And *is* there an end in sight?' she asked, desperate to steer the conversation away from such personal territory — territory that made her want to weep for his loss. 'To the war, I mean?'

'Actually,' he began, 'in the last few days, there has been the odd reason to think the tide might be starting to turn, yes. Day before yesterday, bomber command launched a massive campaign on Berlin. Reconnaissance pictures are only just now coming in, but, by all accounts, we've flattened as much as a third of the city. Early estimates suggest between thirty and forty thousand dead. Word of it hasn't made the newspapers yet — nor the radio news bulletins — but, when it does, I think it will give people reason to take heart. And we're not finished with Berlin yet, either.'

How dreadful, she thought, for anyone to be heartened by the news that thirty or forty thousand people — presumably most of them innocent citizens — had been killed. German or British, the numbers were sickening.

'Somehow, news like that manages to both comfort and appal,' she observed softly.

'It does.'

'So, you think that in the end we *will* win?' At least they had moved away from more personal matters.

'I have to. If I *didn't* believe it, what would be the point of going on? Where would be the sense of any of us continuing to put our lives on the line if we believed there was no chance of our actions affecting the outcome? If the losses we've borne so far — if *all* the losses we've *all* borne so far — are to count for anything, then we have to believe we can win this . . . we have to keep getting out of bed every morning to ensure it's the case.'

'I suppose so,' she said, reflecting for a moment upon his words. 'And I'm sorry if I've cast gloom upon the evening.'

His expression, when he turned to her, was one of surprise. '*You* didn't cast gloom on *anything*. I did that all on my own. Besides, it's only natural that you

238

should seek reassurance. We all need some of that from time to time — to know there's a point to all the suffering, to know that we're not being deluded to hope that life will one day return to normal . . . to know that we're not being foolish to look forward and to hope for better.'

'No.'

With that, from the adjacent public bar came the sound of the landlord calling time, prompting Jack to get to his feet, go to the door to the porch, turn the key in the lock and then draw the bolt. On his return, he continued past her to the bar, where he leant over and called out. 'All locked up through here, sir.'

'Thanks, son,' a voice called back.

'Son?' she whispered when he returned.

Unbuttoning his jacket, he grinned. 'To Mr Luscombe, I'm only ever *son* or *lad*, which I'd take any day over *Flight Lieutenant*.' Hanging his jacket on the back of an adjacent chair, he removed his cufflinks, slipped them into his trouser pocket, rolled up his shirtsleeves and then removed his tie.

When he then moved aside the chair he'd been occupying, she watched, intrigued, as he manoeuvred the small sofa from nearby to stand in its place. With it positioned to his satisfaction in front of the fire, he extended a hand. 'Now that we have the room to ourselves, we might as well be comfortable.' Realising what he meant, she took his hand and let him pull her to her feet. And when he pointed to the end of the sofa furthest from the fire, she kicked off her shoes, sat down, and folded her legs beneath her. As she nestled against him and felt his arm slip around her waist, she gave the tiniest of sighs.

'There,' he said.

239

Through her blouse she could feel the beat of his heart. From his skin she could smell traces of cologne: faint, earthy aromas of sandalwood, cedar and moss. This close to him, she felt warm and relaxed. And it was no wonder, really. How desperately, she realised in that moment, had she been missing the touch of another person: a guiding hand in the small of her back; fingers brushing lightly against her cheek; the sloppy kiss of a toddler saying goodnight. Since the day she'd lost Kit, next to no one had touched her. Richard had held her at the funeral, of course. But, with his grief as jagged as her own, he had done so purely to prevent her from crumpling to her knees under the pain. After the unbearable rawness of that morning, they had both gradually withdrawn into themselves, separated, rather than united, by their common grief. More recently, Louise had hugged her, Aunt Kate, too. But it wasn't the same. It couldn't be. But now, here was Jack, who apparently wanted to hold her as much as she, herself, needed to be held.

'This is lovely,' she risked whispering after a while.

'Comfortable?'

'Perfectly.'

She had no idea how long they stayed like it; with neither of them speaking, and her attention given to idly watching the shapes suggested by the flames, she soon lost all track of time.

Eventually, though, beside her, Jack stirred.

'The fire's dying,' he said. 'And I don't want you to get cold.'

She pulled herself upright. 'It just needs the poker.'

'Or,' he said, grasping the tips of her fingers as she sat up, 'we *could* go upstairs.' Rising to his feet, he reached for her other hand, his fingers closing softly

240

about her wrist. 'Say you'll stay.'

In that moment, Esme thought she was going to cry. Letting him lead her up to his room would be the most natural thing in the world. The problem was, not only was she married but, since for the purposes of her missions she had taken to leaving off her wedding ring, he didn't know that. And, if he was going to take her upstairs, didn't he have the right to? Shouldn't they do this from a start point that didn't involve deceit? More importantly still, though *he* might not know she had a husband, *she* did. And *live for the moment or not*, to go with him would be to take an enormous step — a step down a path from which there could be no going back. In reality, what seemed like the most natural thing in the world was anything but.

'I think perhaps I need to be more . . . sure,' she whispered, unable to bring herself to decline completely, to deny the possibility that she might not always feel so torn.

'Of course,' he whispered back. 'Consider the invitation open-ended. *No expectations.*'

Struggling against tears, she somehow managed a smile. '*No promises.*'

'Come on, then,' he said. 'If you're going to go home, you shouldn't leave it too much longer. I'll see you to your car.'

When he had helped her into her coat, she turned to face him. 'I'm sorry.'

'Don't be,' he said, pulling her collar up around her neck. 'When I said no expectations, I meant it.'

'Maybe next time.'

'Only if that's what you want.'

'You still think it will be Friday for the next mission? Or will this one from tonight be rescheduled?'

241

'No, tonight's is cancelled. So, yes, most likely Friday or Saturday. Early hours.'

'I'll see you then.'

'As our American colleagues say, you can count on it.'

Despite every inch of her body urging her to change her mind about staying, she went with him to the door. There was no need to act in haste. There would be other opportunities. *Consider the invitation open-ended*, he'd said. And when another chance did arise, she would remember how she felt at this very moment and take it from there.

Driving back to Woodicombe, though, the only word Esme could think of to describe how she felt was *torn*. While part of her was proud of the way she had managed to resist Jack's invitation — of the control she had shown when she had put on her coat, got into the Austin, and pulled away — another part of her was incredulous: a warm and wonderful man had asked her to spend the night with him — and everything about their situation in that moment had made it possible. But for the stabbing of her conscience, she would be there with him now, rather than returning to a cold house and an empty bed.

Getting out of the Austin in the stable yard, still unable to believe she'd let slip such a tempting opportunity, she crept in through the kitchen porch, went silently along the servants' corridor and started up the staircase to the ground floor. Perhaps the depth of her regret told her all she needed to know. Perhaps, next time the chance arose, she would ignore her qualms and seize the moment. In fact, she was already sure of it: let tonight's regret be a lesson about chances not taken! *If there's something you want to do*, Cedar had

242

said, *do it while you can.*

Reaching the top of the stairs, she succumbed to an almighty shiver; should she fetch her hot water bottle and fill it? Common sense said yes. But could she be bothered? At the door to the hallway, she reached for the handle and let out a weary sigh. No, it was too late, and she was too tired; she would just go straight up and— Dazzled, she stopped dead. Why were all the hall lights burning? Narrowing her eyes against the brightness, she cast about. Was someone still up? At this hour? Unlikely. More probably, the last person to go to bed had simply forgotten to put them out. Crossing towards the switch, she flicked it off, only to turn back and notice light coming from the drawing room as well. Perhaps Louise had just come in from her shift up at the beacon and was trying to get warm.

Creeping across on tiptoes, she called softly towards the doors. 'Lou? Is that you?'

'Esme. Thank the Lord! Where the devil have you been?'

Richard?

She stopped dead. What on earth was *he* doing here? With her mind darting all over the place, she fought to summon a response.

'Richard . . .' *Come on,* she urged her woolly brain, *think!* 'Darling,' she said, moving to pick her way between the furniture to embrace him. 'You startled me.'

In comparison to being held in Jack's arm's, her husband's clasp as he returned her embrace felt perfunctory.

'Do you have *any* idea what time it is?'

'I . . . Richard, what are you *doing* here? Please tell me there's not bad news. Tell me it's not Great Aunt

243

Diana? Or Grandpa Hugh?'

When he lowered his arms, she stepped back to study his expression. It was a cross between exhaustion and displeasure. But predominantly displeasure.

'I've been worried sick.'

'About me?' Hearing the astonishment in her tone, she cursed under her breath. Of course he meant about her. For Christ's sake *buck up*, a distant corner of her brain warned, unless you *want* to make him suspicious.

'*Of course about you.*'

'So concerned that you came all the way down here?'

Why did so much about this feel *off*? What had someone told him?

'When we spoke on the telephone the other day, you sounded worryingly . . . odd. And now Louise tells me —'

'You've spoken to *Louise* again?' Feeling her fingers curling into fists, she forced them straight. Louise might at least have told her!

'Only a few words . . . and only when she came in just now.'

That it had only just happened did nothing to ease her concerns. 'I do wish you wouldn't talk to her behind my back. I'm not simple. Grief hasn't robbed me of my ability to know my own mind.' Feeling the onset of a yawn, she tensed her jaw in a bid to ward it off.

'No one's saying it has,' Richard replied. To Esme, his tone was out of keeping with his demeanour; his voice might have softened but his stance was still rigid — as were the muscles in his face. There was even a tic pulsing beneath his left eye. 'But when you

244

weren't here, and neither your aunt nor your uncle could tell me when you would be back, well, I'm sure you appreciate my concern. Not for one moment did I expect to arrive and find my wife still out at gone midnight.'

With every nerve in her body on full alert, she tried to think what to do. If nothing else, it was far too late for a conversation of this nature — of any nature, really. On the other hand, she couldn't just say that she was going to bed. Supposedly, her husband had travelled all the way from London because he was worried about her. And, so far, she had done nothing to demonstrate to him that his concern was unfounded.

'Look,' she said, still trying to work out what to do for the best, 'why don't you sit down. Let me pour you a whisky. There's still some of that single malt you like.'

As she turned towards the drinks cabinet, and his fingers closed upon precisely the same spot on her wrist as Jack's had done not half an hour previously, she stiffened.

'Thank you, but I've had one.'

On the lamp table she spotted the decanter, alongside it the stopper and an empty whisky tumbler. Clearly, he'd been here a while — which perhaps went some way to explaining why he was being so short with her. That, and the fact that despite all her sudden fussing, she probably didn't seem terribly pleased to see him.

She looked back up. Still, he hadn't sat down.

'Oh. Well, good for you,' she said. 'So, what time did you get here? Have you eaten?'

'I left work early to catch the four fifteen and ate in

245

the restaurant car. Got here just after ten.'

So narrowly. So narrowly before he'd arrived had she set off for Pond Farm.

'And how long are you staying?' *Friday — Jack had said the next mission would probably be Friday.* She held her breath.

'I have to go back Thursday afternoon. In return for taking a meagre two days' leave, I shall have to work over the weekend.'

She exhaled. *Narrow escape!*

'I see.'

'For Christ's sake, Esme, you still haven't told me where you've been so late.'

Withholding the instinct to sigh with frustration, she reminded herself not to sound defensive. 'Driving, of course. I had to collect someone and take them . . . somewhere.'

'For the RAF.'

'RAF. SOE,' she said with a shrug. 'The line's a somewhat blurry one.'

'At *this* time of night?'

'Covert flights don't keep office hours.'

'Covert.' His tone when he said it made her realise her mistake. 'Christ, Esme, when you told me what you were going to be doing, you omitted to mention *that* detail, didn't you?'

'Look, Richard,' she said, suddenly so drained that she felt light-headed, 'could we sit down? Better still, could we finish this conversation in the morning?'

Without waiting for him to respond, she dropped heavily to the sofa and then watched as he lowered himself to perch rather woodenly opposite. His expression, she noticed, hadn't really changed from when she'd first come through the door.

246

'So, let me get this straight. This driving job — when you told me about it, you said you were taking over from your uncle.'

She nodded. 'That's right.'

'Who was already carrying it out.'

'He had agreed to do it,' she said, fearing where this might be heading, 'but only managed to make the one run before realising the work would mostly involve evenings, when he was already committed to the Home Guard. He said that had he known, he wouldn't have taken it on. But Aunt Kate likes the little bit of money she gets from having people billeted here, which was why, when he realised he wasn't going to be able to do it himself, he was eager to find a replacement. He thought of me because he knew I was looking for something to do.' Meeting his look, she went on, 'But you already know all that.'

'Apparently I didn't,' Richard replied. 'Apparently, you were economical with the truth.'

Now he was just making her cross. And she wasn't sure she had the stamina to conceal the fact. 'No I wasn't.'

'So, what time did you leave here this evening?'

'Richard, must we really do this *now*?'

'I am merely trying to ascertain what sort of duties could possibly have kept my wife out, on her own, until one o'clock in the morning.'

'For what good it will do you to know,' she said wearily, 'I left here at around nine thirty.'

'To go where?'

'You know I can't tell you that.'

'For heaven's sake, Esme, I'm in the War Office. My clearance exceeds yours by some leagues.'

It wasn't the matter of his status that made her

decide to relent; she relented in the hope that she would then be able to go to bed. Even so, she knew to speak in only the most general of terms — no sense hanging herself on unnecessary details.

'I drive to an airfield. I collect a passenger from an incoming aircraft. I take him — *or her* — wherever I'm told. I drive home. That's really all there is to it. I'm a driver. Plain and simple. What else can I say?'

'So, what was going on when we spoke on Sunday?'

Now she genuinely didn't know what he was talking about. 'Sunday?'

'When you telephoned and asked me to see what I could find out about special units of the Home Guard, you sounded distinctly off.'

Special units of the Home Guard? So, there was such a thing?

'I'm sorry,' she said, 'but I really don't recall. I can only think that if I sounded *off* in some way, it was because I had just failed to convince Louise to let go of her idea that her father has become mixed up in something untoward. Truly, Richard, she's obsessed with it. She even confronted him and brought on a huge argument. Before I stepped in, she was in danger of —'

'And how often do you make these trips?'

She sighed. Back to this again.

'On average? Twice a week. There isn't really a pattern to it. Which I suppose is rather the point.'

'So, twice a week you are out, alone, until all hours. And that doesn't bother you?'

Unless she wanted this to turn into a full-blown argument, it might be time to soften her stance, to act a little more conciliatory.

'I will admit that at first, I was quite nervous. But I

needed something to do. Up until Uncle Luke thought to suggest it, everything I'd tried, everything people kept suggesting to me, was of no help whatsoever.'

'But being out in the middle of the night is.'

Reigning in the urge to growl with frustration, she shook her head. 'Not by itself, no, especially not in the middle of winter. You know me — too fond of my creature comforts. But, unlike knitting gloves, or sorting out donated clothing, this job does at least require my full attention, does serve to distract me from my grief —'

'And remarkably successfully, it would appear.'

In her state of exhaustion, his remark was a red rag to a bull. 'And what, might I ask, do you mean by *that*?'

'Merely that having spent the last few days worrying that you might be slipping back into depression, I arrive to find a woman remarkably in control —'

'So how would you *prefer* to have found me?' she demanded. 'In full mourning, withering away in a darkened room?'

'Now you're just being ridiculous —'

'Probably because I'm exhausted. Probably because *you're* exhausted.'

'I merely meant —'

'*Merely*. That's twice you've used that word in the last sixty seconds. But I assure you, Richard, there's nothing *mere* about any of this. When I arrived here, I was a sobbing mess. Inconsolable. A drain on everyone around me. But, thanks to the encouragement of my aunt and my cousin, and to an inspired idea on the part of my uncle, I've turned a corner. I don't know how it's been for you — I suspect having your work to occupy you has been of enormous help — but if the

249

germ of *my* recovery offends you, then you might want to remember it was *you* who insisted I came here — to have the company of people who would help me get over our loss.'

'Which you would seem to have done just fine.'

Conciliatory, she reminded herself. Don't make him even more angry. With that in mind, she moderated her tone. 'I haven't. Not yet. But the well of a person's grief only runs so deep. And once you reach the bottom, it seems to me you have two choices: stay there and wallow . . . or accept that being continually sad is exhausting. I still have grief. I doubt I shall ever be completely free of it. And nor should I be. But, as you yourself told me, ceasing to feel acute pain doesn't have to mean forgetting.'

If she had thought that speaking her mind would help, she was disappointed to find she was wrong: she just felt even more drained and even more irritated.

'Look, Esme, let's not argue.'

'I didn't realise that's what we were doing.'

'Well, it feels like it to me.'

'Hm.'

'Perhaps just try seeing it from my side,' Richard went on. 'Just lately, every time we speak on the telephone, I feel as though all I'm getting is a veneer. Without being able to see your face — to read your expression — I can't tell whether you really are getting better or whether you're putting on an act, trying to save me from concern. I simply have no idea. So, when I speak to you one day and your mood is different, what am I supposed to think? Surely you can understand why I would be concerned.'

'I've already explained. If I sounded *off*, it was down to Louise.'

'So you said.'

'You don't believe me?'

'What I'm saying, Esme,' Richard began, his voice determinedly even, 'is that I have no idea *what's* going on. Which is why I think it's time you came home.'

'Home? Home *where I belong*?' Esme rounded on him. 'Is that what you mean?' How dare he!

'I didn't say that. But we *are* married. We're *supposed* to support one another through thick and thin.'

'What you seem to forget, Richard,' she said, all thoughts of conciliation gone as she sat glowering at him, 'is that we *have* no home. So, where, exactly, do you propose we try to support one another? Where do you propose we rekindle our perfect lives? In some damp little hole of a place that you find for us to rent until . . . well, until I don't know what. Until this war is over? And please don't say there's Windsor because rather than face travelling into town from *there* every day, you'd pretty soon be back to staying in Whitehall. And don't say Clarence Square, either. Shut up like that, it's hardly a home. Even were we somehow to give it the semblance of one, what would I find to do there all day? I *need* to be busy. At least here, not only do I have the company that *you* — yes, *you* — maintained I needed, I also have purpose.'

'And that's another thing I've been thinking about,' Richard said, getting to his feet and pacing away from her. She knew, of course, what was coming next. But she wanted to hear him say it. 'While I don't mind you volunteering, I find I'm not altogether happy with what you've chosen to take on.'

'Of course you aren't. *You'd* rather I sat and knitted scarves or . . . or strolled up to the church hall with Louise a couple of times a week to sit and address

251

parcels for sailors. If you could think of me doing something mind-numbing like that, you'd be happy. But this isn't about *your* need not to worry . . . this isn't about *your* comfort. It's about me giving my life some meaning while . . . while all the more usual avenues to achieving that are denied to me.'

'Esme —'

'Would I rather wake up each morning and be a mother to Kit? Of course I would. Would I rather we lived in our apartment in Anstruther Court and you came home every night? What do you think? But this war has seen to it that I can't do either of those things. I'm not the only woman to suffer such hardship, I know that. I also know that you lost Kit too. But, as you said to me before I came here, you have the luxury of going into an office every day and doing something that not only takes every ounce of your attention but that has real meaning.'

Feeling her throat tightening, and knowing that she was about to cry, she forced herself to draw a long breath. She would not dissolve into tears — especially not tears that stemmed from frustration and anger. Crumpling into a wailing heap would only reinforce her husband's view that she was overwrought and needed to lighten her load whereas, actually, the truth of the matter was quite the reverse.

'Look,' Richard said, 'I know how much it means to you to feel purposeful. I've seen what happens to your expression when you talk about your time in Brighton. You come alive, even now, after all this time. But I also know that *you* were the one who gave it up, who did do so that we might be married, and who spelled out to me precisely what it would mean you having to forgo in order to bring that about. And while I shall

252

be forever grateful that you did, and while I don't for a moment regret that we did marry, I do think it rather unfair of you to now suggest that by being concerned for your welfare, I am trying to clip your wings. Every day, I remind myself that you lost your son in one of the cruellest manners imaginable. I lost him, too, remember? And while I'm not saying that we should all manage our grief in the same way — that we should all bury our feelings in the manner of the Trevann-ions — I do think it wouldn't harm you to remember that while you are still grieving, you're not thinking as clearly as you might believe you are —'

'Now you're questioning my judgement?' Having listened passively up to that point, Esme couldn't contain herself. 'Is that it? I'm too grief-ridden to know what I'm doing?'

'I didn't say that!' Despair and frustration seeming to suddenly get the better of him, Richard threw up his hands. Since he abhorred displays of emotion, it was a gesture that made Esme back away in surprise. 'Look,' he picked up again, 'I'm not saying that throwing yourself into something purposeful is wrong — far from it. Nor do I blame you for seeking something to fill the emptiness. But I *am* concerned about you putting yourself at risk. From what I've seen in the past, grief can cause a person to become reckless, to act impulsively, without regard for the consequences, to think *why not? What does it matter? What the hell,* as the Americans seem so fond of saying.'

Briefly, Esme bowed her head. She couldn't let him see that he'd struck a nerve. 'And you think that's what I'm doing? Acting recklessly?'

'I have no idea *how* you're acting. I'm not here to observe. But, based on what I've seen tonight, I'm

253

concerned that you're not necessarily weighing the risks.'

She looked up. 'You think I'm unstable.'

'I didn't say that either. But I do know that if, by now, I had been able to sort out somewhere for us to live, then tomorrow morning I would be taking you home with me.'

'That rather assumes,' Esme said, her hands screwed into fists and her jaw tense, 'that I was willing to go.'

With a dismissive scoff, Richard gave a stiff shake of his head. 'Can't you, just for one minute, stop being so bull-headed and consider that I might be right?'

'Why did you really come here, Richard?'

Her question seemed to baffle him.

'Why did I *come* here?'

'Yes. Why now? What made you leave work in the middle of the week, get on a train and, without saying a word beforehand, just turn up?'

'I told you why. When we spoke on the telephone you seemed odd.'

'And that's the only reason.' While part of her knew to tread carefully, another part of her wanted to get to the bottom of what was increasingly beginning to feel like an ambush. *Was* it possible someone had spoken to him — specifically, Louise or Aunt Kate — and told him that she was behaving without due regard to consequences? Of the two people who might conceivably do that, it was unlikely to be her aunt: before involving Richard, she would come and talk to her directly. But this wouldn't be the first time *Louise* had spoken to him and aired her concerns. 'You weren't hoping to catch me out in some sort of a lie?'

'What? What the devil are you talking about? I *came* because I was worried that my wife wasn't faring as

254

well as she had led me to believe. I came because I wanted to see her, to know that she was all right. Had I known *this* was how I'd be received, I might not have gone to all the effort.'

'Huh.'

'Look,' Richard said, his voice weary, 'you and I can bandy recriminations like this all night, but it won't get us anywhere. So, to prevent one of us saying something that can't be taken back, I'm going to bed.'

'Oh, yes, that's it —'

'No, it's not *it*,' Richard rounded on her. 'Quite the contrary if you would but let yourself see it. No, what I'm prepared to do is attribute your behaviour tonight to overtiredness — give you the benefit of the doubt — and hope that perhaps, tomorrow, having had some sleep and some time to reflect, you'll find it within yourself to be a little less confrontational and a little more open to the idea that all I want is what's best for you . . . what's best for us.'

'Hm.' Golly, he could be sanctimonious!

'But now, since your Aunt Kate mentioned there being a room made up on the bachelors' corridor that I could use if I didn't wish to disturb you, I shall go and find it and leave you to get what is clearly some much-needed rest.'

'But Richard —'

'No, Esme. I can't do this anymore. Clearly, we're both immensely tired. So please, just stop and think about what I've said, and perhaps, in the morning, we'll be able to have a more civilised discussion. But until then, I'll say goodnight.'

Left to stand in disbelief, Esme watched her husband leave the room. *Did* he have a point? *Was* he right to maintain that she was being reckless? One

255

thing he definitely *was* right about, she realised as she got wearily to her feet and then bent to switch off the lamps, was that she had changed. Where the unbearable loss of Kit felt as if it had closed off a part of her, through doing something useful — and, through meeting Jack — a different and forgotten part of her had been reawakened. And while it might not be the answer in the long term, right now, that sense of purpose and excitement was the sole thing getting her out of bed in the morning. And although she couldn't explain any of that to Richard, one thing she knew for sure was that nothing and no one was going to persuade her to give it up. Not even her husband.

15

Decisions

'Good morning, Aunt Kate.'

'Hello there, love. Late in again last night, were you?'

In response to her aunt's enquiry, Esme raised a smile. 'I'm afraid so.'

'Keep you out all hours, don't they?'

'They do.'

'Just yesterday, your Uncle Luke said had he known just how much driving there would be, he would have thought twice about suggesting you take it on.'

Esme held her smile. 'As I said to you a while ago, I don't mind being kept busy.'

'Still,' Kate said, standing back to admire the bowl of late-flowering chrysanthemums she'd just placed in the centre of the hall table, 'must have been a nice surprise for you, coming back last night to find Richard waiting.'

'It was certainly a surprise, yes. Is he about yet?'

It was the morning after Esme's argument with Richard and, to her dismay, after tossing and turning for hours, she had eventually awoken to find that it was almost nine thirty, her immediate concern being to wonder what had been going on in her absence. Was Richard still cross with her? Probably. Had he told anyone what had happened? Probably not, he couldn't abide people who spouted their private business to anyone who would listen.

'He went out for a walk, love,' Kate replied to her enquiry. 'Said he needed to clear his head. But he's just this minute come back in and gone into the study with your uncle.'

Gone into the study with Uncle Luke? Damn.

Galvanised by the prospect of missing the chance to find out what her uncle had been up to, Esme swivelled away from her aunt and darted across the hall to the study where, without bothering to knock, she opened the door and breezed in. For now, talking to her husband about last night would have to wait.

'Sorry,' she said, stopping Richard mid-sentence and bringing both men to look at her. 'But I felt I should join you . . . this being a family matter.' In her favour, Esme realised, was the fact that, in front of Uncle Luke, Richard wouldn't want to appear unreasonable.

'Forgive me, Luke,' Richard said, 'but I need a word with my wife.' Drawing level, he took her arm and ushered her back out into the hall. 'Family matter or not,' he said, his voice lowered to a cross whisper as he closed the door behind them and glanced about, 'this is a thoroughly sensitive business, and allowing you to be present would be highly irregular.'

'Irregular or not,' she replied, 'I have grounds for wanting to know what's going on. You see —'

'Grounds?'

'Yes,' she said calmly. 'You see, what I haven't had the chance to tell you yet is that even before Louise asked me to telephone you, something had already raised my own suspicions.' When, to her surprise, Richard didn't interrupt, she went on, 'One night, driving back from the airfield, I came across Uncle Luke in a remote lane. More precisely, he came out

258

of nowhere to land right in front of me. With no time to stop, I clipped him with the Austin's wing. Thinking I'd hit a deer, I got out to check for any damage. When I realised who I'd *actually hit*, I couldn't believe it. And neither, I think, could he because we had a truly bizarre exchange, followed by him refusing to let me bring him home. That's why, when Louise told me she was worried about him, alarm bells rang.'

'And during this *bizarre exchange*,' Richard said, 'he didn't explain what he was doing there.'

Esme shook her head. 'He didn't.'

'Well thank the Lord for *that* at least.'

'In fact,' Esme went on, 'the moment he spotted the Austin, he did everything he could to conceal himself from me. Of course, by then, it was too late — I'd recognised his voice. And he knew that.'

Having heard her out, Richard frowned. 'And that was *before* Louise approached you with *her* concerns.'

'Yes. So, please, may I come in and listen?'

From his expression, she sensed he was close to yielding.

'Look,' he said, 'I'm not trying to be difficult but the operation with which your uncle is involved is classified top secret.'

She shrugged. 'Isn't everything these days?'

'What I mean,' Richard picked up again, 'is that no matter what you learn, you won't be able to tell Louise anyway. And nor will your uncle.'

'And there's no possibility of you giving him clearance to tell her?' Even while she was asking, she knew what he would say.

'I don't have anything like the level of authority necessary to do *that*. What we're talking about here is guerrilla fighting units and so you can probably —'

259

'*Guerrilla fighting units*?' What on earth had Uncle Luke got caught up in?

Glancing about the hallway, Richard lowered his voice. 'In this instance, small groups of men trained to disrupt the operations of an occupying force.'

'Then surely you see why I need to be in there with you,' she said, her voice trembling. 'Since I'm still bound by the Official Secrets Act not to relay details of anything to anyone, could you not allow me to just listen in — if for no other reason than to help you work out what Uncle Luke's going to tell Louise? He's going to have to placate her somehow.'

'Look,' Richard said. To Esme, the careful respect in his tone suggested he was trying not to raise his voice. 'Operationally, this business is more sensitive than anything I've come across in a long time.'

She sighed wearily. 'I smell an excuse coming.'

'Actually, what I was going to say is that while, ordinarily, I am privy to plans known only to a few dozen people, until the other day even *I* knew nothing about this set up. I've only been able to gather the sketchiest of details, even now.'

She wondered for a moment whether to believe him; if he was minded to exclude her, hiding behind the Official Secrets Act would be the obvious means. Either way, she resolved not to give up. Someone had to tell Louise and Aunt Kate something to reassure them.

Carefully, she said, 'I understand what you're saying. And I appreciate you even agreeing to get involved. I'm well aware that you needn't have. But had you seen the worry in Louise's eyes when she came to me, you would also understand that for the safety of Uncle Luke's operation, she has to be told

260

something. Clearly, she can't know the truth, or anything close to it. But, if we're to protect Uncle Luke's need for secrecy, then someone . . .' With that, she glanced over her shoulder. '. . . needs to keep Louise and Aunt Kate well away from it. And if, as I suspect, that's going to fall to *me*, then at the very least I need to know the bones of what he's engaged in. Are you aware that Louise followed him one night? And intended to keep doing so until she found out what he was up to?' There was no need, she decided, to mention that Louise had subsequently roped *her* into trailing after him as well.

Digesting the fact, Richard looked mildly alarmed. 'Dear God.'

'Exactly. Look, Richard,' she said, her voice lowered, 'all I want to do is put her mind at rest while safeguarding Uncle Luke and his activities.'

'Very well, then. But you're to just sit there and listen.'

When he reached for the door handle to go back in, Esme nodded. 'Fair enough.'

In the study, they found Luke stood at the window. 'So, what's all this about then?' he turned to ask as they went in. 'Not in trouble, am I?'

'Not as far as I know,' Richard replied, gesturing Esme towards the armchair in the corner. 'But Esme tells me you've attracted some unwanted attention surrounding your duties with the Home Guard — a specific unit of the Home Guard, if my research is to be believed.'

'Although not through anything *I've* done,' Esme ignored Richard's instruction to remain quiet in order to point out.

'I know, maid,' Luke said. 'Sorry about what

261

happened that night. Must have frightened the living daylights out of you.'

Feeling as though her presence there had just been vindicated, Esme smiled. 'It did rather.'

Turning back to Richard, Luke continued, 'I came sliding down the bank and landed right in front of her. Hurt like hell where I caught the front wing.' Looking back at Esme, he went on, 'I felt terrible not being able to tell you why I was there. But I'm grateful to you for not making a fuss — then or later.'

'*I* still maintain I hit a deer,' Esme said, offering her uncle a wry smile.

'Anyway,' Richard said. 'The thing is —'

Remembering her word to Richard, from then on Esme sat quietly, astonished to learn how, on account of her uncle's service in the last war, his appointment as sergeant to the local platoon of the Home Guard, and his detailed knowledge of the local countryside, he had been recruited into what was correctly called an Auxiliary Unit, known in some quarters as the *British Resistance*, its activities referred to by its members as *scallywagging*. By piecing together what she went on to hear, it became clear that these units — situated throughout the British countryside but completely unknown to one another — consisted of groups of up to seven men who, in the event of Britain being invaded by the Germans, would work in secret to sabotage the occupying forces' attempts at government. Each unit, she discovered, had an underground operations bunker stocked with supplies of not only food and water, but of weapons such as sub-machine guns and Sten guns, and a supply of explosives that her uncle referred to as *Nobel 808*. They also had maps they had marked with sites such as bridges, railway

262

lines and fuel depots, all targets they had identified for speedy destruction in the event of an invasion.

The discovery was sufficiently chilling to make Esme shiver: not only was her uncle prepared to take extraordinary risks — the digesting of which somewhat contrarily engendered in her an enormous pride — but called into question everything she had been recently given to understand, namely, that the threat of invasion had receded. Indeed, only yesterday, Jack had reassured her on that very point. Given what she'd just learned, though, she was no longer so sure it was true.

'So,' Luke went on, and with which Esme had to push a picture of Jack from her mind, 'in my unit's case, to serve as our base, we've fortified an old mine working. And so as to keep it good and ready, we meet there twice a week.'

'But Louise and Aunt Kate,' Esme said, 'believe — or *did* believe — that you're on patrol with the Home Guard.'

'It's all I could come up with . . . you know, to avoid arousing their suspicions.'

'And that's where you were the night Esme saw you,' Richard chipped in, 'about your auxiliary business.'

Luke nodded. 'I was. But you're the only folk to know that. When we were recruited, we were instructed never to speak of it to anyone at all. But I know you two are . . . well, you know what I mean . . .'

'Then what I think we should do,' Richard said, 'is expand just enough on your Home Guard story to satisfy Louise that she was right — that you have been withholding something.'

'We can develop the story you've already told them,'

Esme agreed, getting up and going towards her uncle. 'With a little thought, we can keep it sufficiently distant from the truth while at the same time making it sound dull enough for them to lose interest.'

'And how do we do that?' Luke asked, glancing between their faces.

Having discussed several possibilities, the three of them eventually settled upon a version of events they felt would do the trick. Luke would say that, given his service in the last war, he had been selected to train several members of his Home Guard platoon to use new weapons. He would hint that, since practising with them had to be done in secret, the platoon members in question were forbidden to tell even their families what they had been selected to do.

'No matter what they ask you after that,' Richard stressed, 'don't be tempted to embellish the details. Stick to the story.'

'In fact,' Esme said as the thought occurred to her, 'the more you maintain that you are bound to secrecy, the more likely they are to accept what you say.'

'You can always say that I reminded you about the consequences of disclosing anything,' Richard suggested. Turning to Esme he went on, 'Presumably I'm right to think they don't know what I do in Whitehall?'

'All they know is that you're in the War Office.'

'Then I suggest,' Richard went on, 'you say something to the effect that since Louise has unwittingly put you in a difficult position by demanding to know what you're doing, you've spoken to me and I've pointed out that if you are even *suspected* of breathing a word more than you've already told them, you face being sent to jail as a traitor.'

'That ought to do the trick,' Luke said. 'Neither of

them would want to risk that.'

Richard nodded. 'Good, because, as you were no doubt warned when you were recruited, it's true.'

'Leave it to me. I'll speak to them.'

'I'm sorry you can't tell them more,' Richard said. 'Deceiving those close to you is a sordid business.'

His words made Esme wince.

'It's war, son,' Luke observed with a shrug. 'No one speaks about what they do in times of war, especially not to family, if for no other reason than you know what they don't — that ignorance is bliss.'

'Ignorance *is* bliss,' Richard replied.

Yes, Esme thought, hoping that signalled an end to the matter, sometimes, actions taken in time of war were best kept quiet — no matter how much one's nearest and dearest thought they wanted to know.

When Luke shook Richard's hand and thanked him for his help, Esme went to stand at the window and stare out across the gardens. In the last few days, gales from the Atlantic had ravaged the remaining few embers of autumn to expose the stark skeletons of winter. In any normal year, she reflected as she studied the vista, this would be a time of bracing walks through Regent's Park for Kit to kick through fallen leaves and feed the ducks; of nursery teas in front of the fire to get warmed through afterwards; of the first turning of thoughts to Christmas. This year, though, the part of her mind that should be considering that felt as empty and inhospitable as the view from this window: she had no son to take for walks, no home to return to, and not the least inclination to contemplate feigning bonhomie with one or other of their two families.

And now she had Richard to face. In front of Uncle

Luke, they had maintained a semblance of harmony, which meant she had yet to discover her husband's true mood.

'Thank you for your help with that,' she said when he came back in and closed the door.

'Singular circumstances.'

'Indeed.'

When he said nothing further, she supposed that he was waiting to see whether she would apologise. Part of her certainly felt as though she should — if only for the way she had spoken to him. But another part of her was adamant that he was the one who had been in the wrong: she hadn't taken on too much, nor was she guilty of poor judgement — on the contrary, given events at The Fleece last night, she considered her judgement thus far had been exemplary. Neither was she putting herself in harm's way. But how to convince *her husband* of that?

'Richard —'

'First thing this morning, I went for a walk.'

'Yes,' she said when he paused. 'Aunt Kate told me you'd been out.'

'I hoped some fresh air would bring a new perspective.'

'In relation to . . . ?'

'In relation to our situation. To your recovery . . . to mine. To where we go from here.'

Conscious of the speed with which her heart was suddenly beating, Esme tried to breathe more slowly. 'And what did you decide?'

The wait for his answer was an agonisingly long one.

'I realised that this is my fault. No matter how clouded your judgement —'

'*My judgement?*'

'Please, Esme, hear me out. By not keeping a close enough eye on your wellbeing, I've fallen short in my duty as your husband. That has to change. You're my wife. It's my job to look after you.'

Was he about to insist that she went back to London with him? 'Only up to a point,' she said, at great pains to sound reasonable despite rapidly rising panic.

'So, I've decided that next week, you're coming back to London.'

'But Richard —'

'This weekend, I shall speak to Mrs Colborne and ask her permission to engage a daily woman for Clarence Square — someone to take care of the laundry and the cleaning, to prepare meals and so on.'

'But what about air raids?' In that moment, it was the only grounds she could summon for challenging his proposal. 'You said I shouldn't be there because of the risk of air raids.'

'*Should* there be air raids,' he said, 'the wine cellar is as good a shelter as any, coupled with which, I shall make it my point to be home every night. We'll sit them out together.'

The prospect sounded so stifling that her vow to remain calm completely deserted her. 'But I thought you said you didn't want to clip my wings? I thought you said —'

'I *don't* want to. And that's not my intention — far from it. There will be plenty of opportunities for you to keep busy in Clarence Square — to volunteer your services, to see your mother from time to time, to reacquaint with friends.'

The more he painted the picture, the more appalling the prospect became. 'If you think my doing *any* of that is going to help me, you're mistaken. If you truly have my wellbeing at heart, you wouldn't force me to do any of those things.'

'I shan't force you into anything, you know that. You are your own woman. But all the while you're not thinking clearly, then it falls to me to —'

'*Not thinking clearly*?' In her increasing agitation, she was finding it hard not to take him by the shoulders and shake him — to *make* him listen. When would he understand that there was nothing wrong with her! She knew what she was doing. Her missions gave her reason to get up in the mornings — gave her Jack.

'Well, I will only countenance you staying here, if you agree to give up this driving business. And yes,' he said, raising a hand to silence any potential interruption from her, 'I understand you want something to do. But there are plenty of good causes that would welcome your services without requiring you to be out at night, in a motorcar, with strangers. I will not stand by and let you continue to put yourself at risk. It's simply not on.'

'Risk? What risk?' All she knew in that moment was that she mustn't give in. Either she had to talk him round, or else she would have to disobey him. 'I know what I'm doing.'

'Proof, if proof were needed,' Richard said firmly, 'that you do not see the dangers, that you're not thinking clearly. So, what's it to be? Are you coming back to London? Or are you going to stay here and inform your contact that you must withdraw your services? Since you're adamant that you know your own mind, I shall leave you to choose. But you need to do so in . . .' Pushing back the cuff of his jacket, he checked his wristwatch. '. . .the next thirty minutes.'

Thirty minutes? *Now* who was being unreasonable?

'The significance being?'

'The significance being that in thirty minutes' time I shall be leaving. Since it's clear you would rather I wasn't here, I shall take the afternoon train back to Waterloo. So, be ready by then to let me know what you've decided to do.'

When he turned to open the door, she very nearly reached out and stopped him. In the event, she let him go. If he was so entrenched, why bother even *trying* to reason with him? If he'd got it into his head that she was unstable, nothing she said was going to change his mind. In fact, by continuing to try to persuade him otherwise, she was in danger of simply confirming his opinion that her judgement was still clouded by her grief. So, since he'd left it to *her* to decide, that was precisely what she would do.

16

Doubts and Dilemmas

'Oh, there you are. I've been looking for you.'

At the sight of her cousin coming along the landing, Esme withheld a sigh. Having so far managed to avoid an inquisition from Aunt Kate about why Richard had left early, she would rather not now become mired in an explanation to Louise.

'Yes, here I am,' she said, her tone deliberately bright.

'Good, because I want to ask you something. But first, I'm looking for Richard.'

'Richard.' *Bother.*

'Dad just had a long chat with me and Mum, something I think was Richard's doing. I know the two of them were having a confab earlier. Anyway, since I'm certain you'll want to know, it turns out that Dad's been drafted into a different platoon of the Home Guard — a platoon that trains other men. Honestly, you've no idea what a relief it is to know he's not involved in something shady — that it's all above board. Now that he's explained, I feel foolish for having got so het up.'

Hoping that would be an end to the matter, Esme made to continue on along the corridor. 'It's natural to worry about our nearest and dearest, even under normal circumstances. But this war, well . . . it's turning everyone into nervous wrecks. Nice to see you smiling again, though.'

Louise agreed. 'It's a huge load off my mind. Anyway, thanks for your forbearance when I was in a such tizzy. And thanks for tramping up the lane with me that night in the freezing cold.'

To Esme, Louise's relief was clear. 'That's all right. Compared to how you've put up with me, it was nothing.'

'But I must thank Richard, too. So, do you know where he is?'

Oh well, her cousin would find out soon anyway. 'He had to go back to town.'

'*He had to go back?* But he's only just got here!'

'I know. Blame the War Office. Anyway, when I speak to him, I'll make sure to pass on your thanks.'

Seeing no reason to say any more than that, and hoping to deflect her cousin from further enquiries, Esme went to start down the stairs only for Louise to grab hold of her arm.

'Essie, stop a minute and look at me.'

Softening her expression, Esme complied. 'Yes?'

'What happened?'

'I don't understand. What happened with what?'

'You know very well,' Louise said, her grip on Esme's arm tightening. 'What happened *with Richard?* He arrived last night and now he's gone back? Mum said he was staying until tomorrow afternoon.'

Disclose as little as possible, Esme reminded herself. 'He *was* going to.'

'So, what happened? What did you do?'

Shaking off her cousin's hand, Esme glowered. 'What did *I* do?'

'Mum says she heard raised voices —'

'So?'

'And so she asked me if I thought everything was

271

all right between the two of you.'

In her dismay, Esme sighed. What had she thought was going to happen: Richard disappeared a whole day early and she didn't think anyone would be curious? Sadly, even though the matter was none of Louise's concern, once she thought she was onto something, she rarely let it drop — the business with her father being a case in point. But what on earth did she say that wouldn't make it sound as though she was concealing something?

'Everything is fine,' she said, largely to give herself time to think.

'I don't believe you. You might have been a spy . . . or whatever you were . . . but you don't fool *me*. So, what did you do?'

'I told you,' Esme said. 'I didn't *do* anything. Richard and I talked. He told me he was going back early. He asked me if I wanted to go with him. I declined. He left on the twelve fifteen to Waterloo.' Nothing there, Esme thought, that wasn't true.

'So, was Mum right? *Did* she hear raised voices? Were you and Richard shouting at one another?'

With a shoulder-deflating sigh, Esme shook her head. 'Louise, what if we were? What if we *did* have a disagreement? To be honest, it's none of your business. Besides, it's what married couples do. From time to time, they disagree.'

'And shout at each other?'

Plainly, Louise wasn't going to give up. But that didn't mean that she, Esme, had to disclose more than she wanted to. The matter between her and Richard was, after all, private.

'Sometimes, yes, they shout at one another. On occasion, one, or indeed both of the parties, gets frus-

272

trated at the other's intransigence.'

'Hm. Well *I* suspect that it was you who upset him. These last few days, you've been real short with everyone. You've been how people get when they're hiding something . . . when they're struggling with their conscience. And don't say I don't know what I'm talking about because I saw it in Dad, didn't I? And I was right about him. I could tell —'

'For Christ's sake, Louise, Richard and I had a disagreement. So what? When did you become the expert on marriage? What would you know about it? You're barely even married —'

'What I *know*,' Louise said firmly, 'is that when one spouse feels the need to raise their voice to the other, it's over more than a chipped teacup or one of them having walked dirt across a clean floor. And since the two of you aren't even living under the same roof at the moment, you can hardly have been disagreeing over something as trivial as that anyway. And, yes, I know it's none of my business. But that doesn't mean I can't be concerned —'

'Well, don't be. There's no need.'

'You know, sometimes, Esme Trevannion, I don't think you realise how lucky you are.'

Lucky? By whose definition could Louise possibly think her lucky? 'In case you've forgotten,' she said pointedly, 'I lost my son. And my home. My *whole life*.'

'Yes. You did. And every time I see you staring wistfully off into the distance, my heart goes out to you. I simply can't imagine the depth of your pain. But you're lucky because you do still have Richard, who cares about you so deeply. You're lucky, because, if you choose, you can see him every day. You can touch him, kiss him, know that's he's safe. I can do none of

273

that with Douglas. Nor do I know how long it will be before I can. Already, it's been three years. Three years of being Mrs Douglas Ross without actually being a wife. Three years of being back at home with my parents, trying not to think about what might be happening to him . . . wondering when I might see him, month after month of my life slipping through my fingers with nothing changing, with no hope of becoming a mother, of being unable to make even the smallest of plans or look forward with any certainty. Three years of talking about one day going to Canada, of wondering what it will be like, when, to all intents and purposes, it might as well all be make-believe. You can't imagine what it's like — three years of only half living. So, yes, while you've had some of the worst luck imaginable, you also continue to have some of the best. But, if you carry on like this, it will run out. You'll drive Richard away. *He's* grieving too, remember? Perhaps stop for a moment and think about *that*.'

The trouble was, Esme thought as she stood pressing her fingertips into the bannister rail, Louise wasn't wrong; the words she'd flung at Richard were already haunting her. He did only have her wellbeing — and her safety — at heart. But therein lay the problem: she didn't want to be kept safe. She didn't want to be swaddled and cosseted and sympathised with. She wanted to feel alive. She wanted — no, she *needed* — to feel the way she did with Jack, to feel the sheer, uncomplicated, warmth and joy he brought her. He might not be able to bring back her son, but he could distract her from her loss in a way that no one else seemed able to.

'And *I* just wish,' she said, guilt twisting at her

insides as she turned back along the landing towards her room, 'that you wouldn't constantly meddle.'

★ ★ ★

'Thought I'd find you in here, love. Everything all right?'

It was after supper that same day and, largely in the name of keeping warm, Esme had retreated to the drawing room to sit in front of the fire, her feet curled up beneath her, a travel rug thrown over her lap.

'Fine, thank you, aunt. Just keeping off the chill.'

'Good for you.' Pausing to shift her weight, Kate went on, 'Foul out there tonight. I said to Louise before she went off up that draughty beacon, I hope you've got your long johns on.'

The picture of Louise in long johns made Esme smile. 'I think we could all do with some of those.'

'Finished your book, have you?'

Noticing her aunt glance to the side table, Esme realised she was referring to *Candleford Green*. 'Oh, yes. Quite a while back, actually.'

'Then you could do worse than try the WVS Christmas Fayre next week. There's usually any number of donations on the book stall. Never know, you might find something of interest.'

'Yes,' Esme replied lightly. 'I might.'

'Look, love,' Kate began, lowering herself onto the other end of the sofa, 'tell me it's none of my business if you like, but these last few days you seem all over the place. One minute you're all bright and chirpy, the next, you're either down in the dumps or else scowling as though someone's got your back up. You still not sleeping any better?'

275

Feeling tears forming, Esme swallowed hard. Aunt Kate showing concern almost always started her off; it must be her kindly tone. 'Oh, you know,' she said, gesturing airily. 'Some nights I sleep quite soundly. Others, I barely close my eyes.'

'Aye, I recall all too well what that's like.'

Remembering afresh what had happened to Arthur, Esme nodded. 'Yes, of course.'

'I daresay being out into the small hours doesn't help much in that regard either,' Kate observed mildly.

Had Aunt Kate been discussing her with Louise, Esme wondered? Was this the second stab of a two-pronged attack? 'It's the way of the job,' she said evenly.

'Wouldn't do for me. But young Lou don't seem hardly affected by keeping such odd hours. Coming up on three years now since she started with the corps. Settled into the routine, I suppose.'

'Yes.' While she was grateful for the company, for the distraction it afforded her from the tumult of her thoughts, Esme had to wonder at the real reason behind her aunt's arrival.

'Listen, child, did Louise come to you today? Did she come and ask you what you thought about something? Only, I'm minded something's troubling *her* again, too, though this time I've a feeling it has to do with Douglas. I asked her what was on her mind, you know, now she's no need to fret over her father anymore, but you seen how she is — makes light of everything, even though, deep down, she's stewing away. And I just thought, well, if the two of you'd had a chat, then happen she's all right again . . . at the very least that she'd confided in you.'

Looking up from where she'd been staring into the

fire, Esme regarded her aunt's expression. 'To do with Douglas? No.' Thinking about it now, though, when Louise had met her on the landing — before they'd got into that needless argument —her approach had started out with something along the lines of *Good, because I want to ask you something.*

'Worries about everything, that one,' Kate went on. 'I know it's hard on her — not knowing when the two of them will see one another. I had it just as bad with Luke when the two of us were first wed — and your Mum and Captain Colborne had it the same.'

'Yes, I remember Mummy telling me.'

'Don't know whether it's better or worse these days — what with constantly hearing the news. And what about your Richard, then? Get called back, did he?'

Had this just been polite conversation, Esme wondered, or had it only ever been a cautious build up to a rather poorly aimed stab of that second prong?

'Unfortunately, yes, he had to go back.'

'Must be a terrible burden on him — being in the War Office. Poor fellow can't hardly get a moment's respite.'

'He doesn't.'

'For which we should all be grateful, I suppose . . . grateful there's chaps like him plotting how to defeat Hitler and get this thing over and done with.'

'Grateful. Yes.' If her aunt had set out to prick her conscience, she was doing an admirable job; at this precise moment, she didn't feel very proud of herself. *Was* Richard right? *Was* she guilty of poor judgement? *Was* she taking needless risks? She didn't think she was. After all, half the time when she led the family to believe she was driving about in the dark on a mis-

277

sion, she was actually with Jack, there being no risk attaching whatsoever. Well, not unless you counted the risk that, in a moment of weakness, she would give in to longing.

In truth, to be sitting there discussing Richard at all made the thought of letting another man take her up to his room bring her out in a cold sweat. But when she was actually *with* Jack, it was a different story. When she was there, nothing else mattered. Was that a sign that she wasn't thinking clearly — or that she was? So often she'd asked herself that question in the last twenty-four hours and yet still she had no idea. The only thing she knew for certain was that tomorrow night, she would be on her way to await Jack's return from France with his special cargo. That the two of them would barely have the chance to say hello was frustrating. But he'd led her to understand that, from this week, ordinary missions would resume, which would provide her with legitimate reason to be at the airfield — to arrive pleasingly early with her passengers, thus enabling the two of them to sit and talk.

And therein, she realised, spotting with relief that her aunt's attention was now given over to the fire, was her answer. That she was excited by the prospect of seeing him told her all she needed to know — for right or for wrong, she wasn't ready to give him up. When *would* she be? That was a bridge she could only cross when she came to it. In the meantime, she would enjoy the serenity, the warmth and the sense of escape that came from spending time with him. And, as far as Richard was concerned, she would simply look upon it as a case of *what the eye didn't see, the heart couldn't grieve over.*

Hearing the clatter of the letterbox, Esme looked along the hallway: stooping to pick up an envelope from the mat was Louise — the very individual she had been trying to avoid. But, since she couldn't do that forever, and since she really did need to go down-stairs and clean her shoes, she continued on her way, pausing at the door to the staircase to wait for her.

'Letter from Douglas?' she enquired as her cousin approached. When Louise made no move to reply, Esme turned to look directly at her, surprised to notice she had tears in her eyes. A glance to the enve-lope she was carrying told her that since she hadn't opened it yet, it wasn't because she'd had bad news. So, what had happened? 'Is everything all right?'

Her enquiry simply brought more tears. 'N-No. I m-mean, I don't kn-know.'

Unable to help herself, Esme sighed. 'Look,' she said, 'why don't we go along to the drawing room, and you can tell me what's wrong.'

Apparently in two minds, Louise eventually nod-ded. 'All . . . right. Th-Thank you.'

In the drawing room, Louise sat on the sofa. And when she reached to put the envelope on the table, and Esme could see from the stamp that it hadn't come from Canada, she recalled something her aunt had said last night: *I'm minded something's troubling her again . . . I've a feeling it has to do with Douglas.* If Aunt Kate was right — and when wasn't she? — then she owed it to her cousin to try and help. Despite their falling out yesterday, Louise being upset was a state of affairs she couldn't ignore, especially since, on the day of their weddings, she had promised Douglas that

279

while he was away, she would keep an eye on her for him. So far, she wasn't doing a very good job.

'Now,' she said in a bid to remedy the situation, 'why don't you tell me what's upset you?'

Still, Louise hesitated. 'Y-You'll probably think I'm stupid.'

'So what if I do? *You* think *me* selfish and inconsiderate. It doesn't stop us looking out for one another.'

Louise responded with a weak smile. 'That's true.'

'On top of that, despite our differing views on certain . . . matters, I think we both agree that if something is bothering one of us enough to cause tears, then it behoves the other to find out why. A worry on that scale probably shouldn't be kept bottled up.'

'I'm worried about Douglas. There. I've said it.'

'Worried that's he's come to harm?' Esme asked, striving to come up with an alternative explanation. 'Because if that's the case, then I'm sure it would be easy enough to —'

'No . . .' When Louise shook her head, it was with such conviction that tears flew from her cheeks. 'No, I'm worried that . . . well, I'm worried because it's three weeks since he's written.'

'And he normally writes every week.'

'Without fail. And sends telegrams for birthdays and Christmas and our anniversary.'

Reflecting upon what her cousin had just said, Esme weighed the possibilities. 'Well,' she began after a moment's consideration, 'before I say something trite like you have to remember there's a war on, maybe you should tell me what, precisely, it is that worries you about his silence? What is it that you fear has happened?'

'That he's gone off me, of course.'

280

'*Gone off you?*' That was her cousin's concern?

'Please don't belittle my worry —'

'I wasn't. I just —'

'You asked my worst fear. Well, that's it. I worry about how long we've been apart and what that must be like for a man . . . you know, not being a proper husband . . . and how it would be entirely understandable if he went off with someone else. Or at the very least, that he wants to go off with someone else but can't because he married me. I worry that after all this time on his own, he regrets that we got married so quick.'

Esme hadn't a clue what to say. She certainly couldn't blurt what was on the tip of her tongue, which was something to the effect of *Why on earth would you think such a thing? Douglas is madly in love with you!* After all, how did either of them know for sure that he still *was?* Three years was a long time. A dreadfully long time — especially after what had been something of a whirlwind romance. No, far better than telling Louise she was wrong would surely be to try and understand what — other than the lack of correspondence — could have put the idea into her cousin's head.

'All right,' she said, conscious of the need to choose her words carefully and not make matters worse, 'do you remember his last letter?'

Louise shrugged. 'I suppose so. Since there's not much he can tell me about what he's doing, they're all a bit the same.'

'But the last one he sent was no different to the rest,' Esme pressed on. 'It didn't say anything to alarm you. The tone of it wasn't any different.'

Louise gave a heavy sigh. 'I remember thinking it

was shorter than usual. Barely one side of a piece of paper.'

Hm. A detail perhaps best glossed over.

'Maybe on that particular day,' Esme said evenly, 'he was in a hurry, and would rather that you had a few short lines from him than nothing. Perhaps he's been moved to a different base . . . or posted overseas . . . or is now part of an operation where he can't easily get word to you.' Unsure how many of those were genuine possibilities, she wracked her brain for other ideas. 'Perhaps he *has* written to you but there's a delay in his letters getting here. We're forever hearing about difficulties in the Atlantic.'

'That's what I've been telling myself,' Louise said wearily. 'That he has been writing to me but that his letters are all stuck somewhere . . . and that they'll all turn up at once.'

Meeting her cousin's look, Esme raised an encouraging smile. 'There's certainly a good chance of that.'

'But then, last week, I got a letter from Winnie.' When Esme frowned, Louise went on, 'One of the girls at Jubilee Street.'

'Ah, yes. I thought I knew the name.'

'Anyway, mainly, she wrote to say that Jess is getting married. Not sure if I told you but there's only the two of them at the dockyard now. Queenie left to look after her mother. Jean was dismissed. And Nora and Liddy and Mrs H were all lost when that bomb fell . . .' Not wishing her cousin to become side-tracked, Esme kept quiet. She remembered hearing that Plymouth had been badly bombed, and how grateful she'd been that Louise was safely back at Woodicombe. 'I still think sometimes what a close shave that was . . . how that could have been me, perished alongside them.'

'Yes. I can see how that would play on your mind.'

'Anyway,' Louise picked up again, 'Winnie wrote about a girl from the dockyard called Sally who, back in the summer, got engaged to an American she met at a dance. Flash fellow, apparently. The thing is, a few weeks back, this Sally got an anonymous letter, suggesting she ask her fiancé about some girls back home. What she actually did was ask one of his pals, only to find out that her fiancé had already been engaged several times before . . . and that one of the girls had got pregnant and had his son. Word was, that's why he'd joined up — to get away from the mess, I suppose.'

Esme had a feeling she knew what was coming next. 'All right. But what does this have to do with —'

'With Douglas?' Louise asked, her eyes once again filling with tears.

'Well, yes.'

'When I read about this Sally and her chap, it got me to thinking just how much I don't actually know about Douglas. I mean, he told me about his family — showed me some photographs of them and their home. But I don't know anything about the girls he went out with before me. I mean, there must have been some, mustn't there?'

'Without a doubt. But that would have been a long time ago — four years or more now, maybe even longer.'

'In one of the photographs,' Louise said, picking up where she'd left off, 'there was a girl. A pretty one. I remember her because while everyone else was on the lawn, she was standing on her own under the porch. I thought perhaps it might be one of his sisters-in-law. But when I pointed her out, he said she was the neighbour's daughter. Amy, he called her.'

'And so?'

'And so . . . and so . . .'

When Louise started crying again, Esme reached for her hand and held it tightly. 'Dearest Louise, think about it. Very few people marry the first person they meet. In this day and age, pretty much everyone has dated at least a couple of people before stumbling upon the one. But that doesn't mean they're like this chap Winnie wrote about. *I* had boyfriends before I met Richard. *You* went out with Harry.' At the mention of Harry, Esme felt her cousin stiffen. 'Few people over the age of twenty-one come into a marriage entirely . . . chaste. I might not know Douglas very well, but I am an excellent judge of character — I was trained by the best to see through assumed identities. And I can tell you, hand on heart, that if it came to it, I would trust Douglas with my life. And so would Richard. Surely you remember how the two of them got on. Like a house on fire, they were.'

'*I know that*,' Louise wailed. 'I know *all* of that. But *three years*, Essie. *Three years* is enough to test the patience of a saint.'

'Has it tested *yours*?' Esme asked. Despite her question being designed to get Louise to see things differently, asking it caused her a ripple of unease. Who was she to lecture on fidelity?

Louise hung her head. '*Of course* it's tested me . . .'

'But has it made you look around for someone else?' *Someone like Jack?*

'Never! Not for a single second. I ache real bad to be proper married, but when I do, I comfort myself with the knowledge that all I have to do is wait.'

'And so why would it be any different for Douglas?'

'Because . . .'

284

'No,' Esme said softly. *'Because nothing.'*

'Then why has he stopped writing?' Louise demanded. 'How can you be certain that after all this time of being patient, someone from his past hasn't appeared . . . or even someone new? And when he claps eyes on her, he thinks, well, my wife's on the other side of an ocean. She'll never know. And maybe, that first time, he really only meant for it to be a drink . . . or a bite to eat . . .'

Listening to Louise describing the possibility made Esme cringe. As she knew all too well, married or not, people did find themselves in such situations. Things like that *did* just happen.

Flushing hot, she squeezed her cousin's hand even tighter. 'Listen to me —'

'But then there's a second time and a third and . . . for heaven's sake, Esme, it's even what happened with me and Douglas in the first place. I went out with him while I was still seeing Harry.'

'That wasn't the same —'

'And then before he knows it, he's thinking to himself, why was I so quick to marry some girl in England? Some girl I hardly even know . . . who can't even come to Canada until the war's over . . . and only then not without a lot of fuss and bother. And because his heart's no longer really in it, or perhaps because he feels guilty, he stops writing. I mean, why else would he give up, other than because he wants to leave me for someone else and is trying to work out how to go about it?'

'For all manner of reasons,' Esme rushed to point out. 'He might have been ill. Or had a family emergency. Or, as we said just now, maybe he *has* written but his letters are stuck somewhere between here and

285

Canada. Maybe the boat bringing them across the Atlantic was torpedoed.'

But Louise wasn't listening. 'After all, if something *terrible* had happened to him, I would have been told by now. Before he went, he put me down as his next of kin. He told me so.'

'Look, how about . . .' But with Louise now sobbing noisily, all Esme could think to do was hold her.

'I . . . can't . . . bear . . . not knowing.'

'No.'

'It . . . hurts . . . so . . . much.'

'I know.' Even as she was saying it, Esme recognised that nothing she could say would ease her cousin's pain; at best, she could only suppose what had happened to cause Douglas to stop writing. On top of that, the poor girl had exhausted herself with worry. She worried for everyone. First there was the business with her father, then she'd worried for Richard. And throughout all of that she'd been waiting every day for letters from Douglas that never came. No wonder she was so upset. With two of the people closest to Louise acting oddly because they were concealing things, it was no wonder she was so quick to jump to conclusions over her husband's silence. But of all the people Louise needn't worry about, Esme felt pretty certain one of them was Douglas.

With Louise continuing to sob, Esme sat staring ahead. If no one ever told lies, then family, friends and lovers would have fewer reasons to doubt: fewer would worry; fewer would get hurt. But, faced with an urge to fulfil some or other need, not many people stopped to consider the consequences. And yes, she was thinking about her own situation right now — a situation that, if she didn't heed the signs, could so easily tumble out of control. Not that this was the moment to be thinking about herself.

Fishing about in her pocket for a handkerchief, Louise dabbed at her eyes and blew her nose. 'I'm so sorry,' she looked up to say.

'It's all right —'

'And I'm sorry I had a go at you about Richard. You were right to tell me not to interfere. Just because I have an opinion doesn't give me the right to air it. Apart from the two people concerned, no one can ever truly know what's going on inside a marriage.'

'Look,' Esme said, anxious to steer her cousin away from that particular subject. 'Am I right to think that Douglas gave you an address for his parents?'

Louise nodded. 'He did. He said I should have it in case of emergency.'

'So, why not write to his mother? All you need say is that it's a while since you've heard from him, and can she tell you whether he's been posted away. There's no need to mention being worried about anything more specific than that.'

For a moment Louise seemed to consider the idea. 'I suppose I *could*.'

'If you worded your letter carefully so as not to alarm her, I'm sure she would write back. It's more than possible she's even spoken to him. He might not be able to telephone *you* but that doesn't mean he hasn't been able to speak to *her* from time to time. Maybe she's even seen him.'

Heaving a long sigh, Louise eventually nodded. 'All right. But I might wait one more week first. As you say, there's no need to alarm her.'

'If that's what you want.'

'I think it is. And thanks, Essie. Given the things I

said to you yesterday, you've been very kind. A true friend.'

Engulfed by yet another wave of unease, Esme shook her head. 'Nonsense. If friends can't have a disagreement now and again, then they're not worthy of the name friends, are they?'

With a weary sigh, Louise screwed up her handkerchief and stuffed it back in her pocket. 'I suppose not.'

When her cousin got up and walked away, Esme remained where she was. Tonight, she was going to the airfield. Tonight, she would see Jack. But rather than just feeling her usual excitement at the prospect, she also felt a degree of hesitancy. Could they just pick up where they'd left off before Jack asked her to stay the night, or were they now unavoidably heading in a different direction? Could their relationship even carry on if it had to be on a platonic basis? Having this morning seen what doubt and suspicion was doing to Louise, did she really wish the same for Richard? She'd made a vow to forsake all others, after all. Wasn't she bound to do the right thing?

So many times she had tried to picture what her future might look like if she followed her heart and chose Jack. But could she bring such humiliation upon Richard? Could she bear the shame of what would become a very public divorce, sully the name of the Colbornes and the Trevannions in the process, become *persona non grata* just about everywhere? So many things to consider. So many risks.

No expectations, Jack had said, which was all well and good for him but left her, a married woman, facing all manner of quandaries. Her experience of losing everything — well, *almost* everything — seemed, as

Aunt Diana had so accurately pointed out, to have thrown focus upon her whole existence: with no home and no son, who was she? Where did her future lie? Did she want to return to what she'd known previously, or go forwards, into the unknown?

Rising slowly from the sofa, she exhaled heavily and then stood for a moment before crossing to the door. Perhaps, when she was actually with Jack, the way ahead would become clear. Perhaps she would just know, one way or the other, what she should do. She could only hope so because, at this precise moment, other than wishing that things were different, the only thing she knew with any certainty was that she couldn't bear the thought of just letting him go.

17

Standing Down

It wasn't the sort of night one would choose for a drive to the edge of Dartmoor to find an isolated country house. Although not particularly cold, there was a blustery wind that kept bringing squally showers. And if it wasn't for the prospect that, despite her earlier crisis of conscience, she was hugely excited about seeing Jack, Esme knew she would far rather be at home.

'Sage has a sample of Walnut,' Mr Mulberry had said on the telephone earlier. 'They're waiting for it at High Moor House. Be a dear and drop it down to them, would you? It should be ready for collection by three o'clock tomorrow morning. Jolly good.'

And so, now, here she was, pulling up alongside the ops room at Pond Farm to await the arrival of Walnut. In the Austin she had a couple of blankets, a flask of coffee — or what passed for it — a spare torch, a map and her handwritten list of waymarkers-cum-directions. She'd estimated the distance to High Moor House as about twelve miles, which, if she met with no mishaps, meant a drive of about three-quarters of an hour. With a fair wind, she should be back home and asleep before anyone else was up, certainly well before daybreak.

Stepping inside the Nissen hut she found Aircraftsman Pugh, who got to his feet to greet her. Glancing to the blackboard to see Jack's details chalked along the top line, she asked, 'Are we still on schedule?'

'He departed here in good time, ma'am. There's heavy weather going down, but it does also mean he'll be blown home.'

She smiled. 'Thank you.'

'Can I pour you some cocoa?'

About to decline, she changed her mind. 'Yes please.'

The good thing, she acknowledged as she pulled a chair from under the table, was that she didn't have to come to a decision about Jack tonight. Since all they would get to do when he landed was exchange a few words, she could wait and see how she felt in a day or two, which was just as well because, tonight, she had to concentrate on getting her passenger to High Moor House. From the little Jack had told her, this particular agent was a key member of the French Resistance and was being brought here to brief officials from the British government ahead of a forthcoming operation. More than that, he'd said with a wink, he couldn't disclose. More than that, she remembered thinking at the time, he didn't know. Only the people at High Moor House and a select few in SOE would know what this was really all about.

'There you go, ma'am.'

Cupping her hands around the mug of cocoa Aircraftsman Pugh brought her, Esme glanced to the clock: ten minutes to three. Jack should be within sight of the coastline by now. Not long to wait.

When she had drained the last of her drink, she once again checked the clock: ten past. With the way the wind was gusting and rattling the fabric of the building, they probably wouldn't hear his approach until he was pretty much overhead. And since she

291

wouldn't be able to hang around once he was, perhaps now was a good time to use the lavatory.

'Back in a minute,' she said to Aircraftsman Pugh
as she thrust her arms into the sleeves of her gabardine and turned up the collar.

Moments later, about to return inside, she paused
with her fingers around the doorknob to listen. Apart
from the clattering of branches behind the hut, and
the buffeting of the wind, there was nothing to suggest an aircraft coming in. But then operations such
as these didn't run like clockwork; zero three-hun-
dred hours had only ever been an estimate of the time
he would be back.

'Shouldn't be long now,' Aircraftsman Pugh looked
up from his game of patience to say when she returned
inside.

'Good.'

'Far to go tonight?'

She shook her head. 'Not too bad, no.'

After that they fell silent, and Esme had to force
herself not to hold her breath as she waited for each
subsequent click of the minute hand on the clock.
A watched pot never boils. It was an expression she
remembered hearing as a little girl; one of Aunt Kate's,
presumably. Tonight, it seemed painfully appropriate.
But what else could she do to pass the time other than
sit and wait?

Soon after that, the shrill peal of the telephone
made her leap to her feet.

'Pond Farm,' Aircraftsman Pugh answered calmly.
'No, sir. Not yet, sir, no. Very well, sir.' Replacing the
receiver, he turned to her to explain. 'Group Captain
Hall wanting to confirm they were back.'

'Ah.'

'Wants someone to call the minute they're down.'

'Yes.'

'Don't know who we're expecting,' Pugh continued in a conversational tone, 'but everyone seems real jumpy about him.'

'Yes.'

For Esme, the silence after that grew steadily more unbearable. Rather than being grateful for the time to sit and consider what she was going to do about Jack, she found that she couldn't concentrate at all. The decision she had to make was an impossible one. She really ought to stop seeing him. This wasn't like her time in Brighton, when she'd been single and the odd week spent flirting with a charming agent had been perfectly harmless — indeed, expected of her. She had a husband now; she'd had a son, for heaven's sake. And Jack wasn't just passing through, either: every time there was a mission, their paths would cross; unavoidably, she would keep bumping into him. Well, she would . . . unless she went back to London. If she really did decide to stop seeing him, then for her own sanity she would have to. But could she do that? If nothing else, didn't she owe it to Obsidian, to SOE — even to Uncle Luke and Aunt Kate — to keep going? Did she even have the strength to make the decision to go home to London, let alone see it through?

When the telephone rang for a second time, she shot a glance to the clock. Just gone four.

'No, sir. Yes, sir.'

'Group Captain Hall again?' she asked.

'Yes, ma'am. Said he'll try to see whether there's any word from our man at the other end. If there's bad weather across the Channel, they might be waiting it out.'

'Is that usual?' she asked. She was pretty sure she remembered Jack telling her that the aim was not to get stuck on the ground for more than three minutes.

'It wouldn't be ideal, ma'am.'

'But it happens.'

'If there's no other choice.'

'But if that has happened, the group captain will be able to find out.'

'He'd hope to.'

'Yes.'

From there, the minute hand on the clock continued its steady descent towards the half hour before proceeding to climb back up the other side. Five o'clock came. Then five fifteen, five thirty. Still no aircraft.

But then, shortly after that, the telephone rang.

Anxious to learn what was going on, Esme got to her feet and, in a bid to calm her nerves, stretched her arms above her head.

'Understood, sir. Standing down, sir. Yes, sir. Goodnight, sir.'

'What is it?' she asked before Aircraftsman Pugh had even hung up the receiver.

'We've been instructed to stand down. Whatever the reason for the delay, Flight Lieutenant Carey won't risk coming back now, not with dawn breaking.'

She didn't understand. 'So . . . he's still in France?' At least, she supposed, if someone knew that much then it meant he was safe.

'Unknown. No one has been able to get through to France.'

'But he'll be back after dark this evening?'

'That would be the plan,' Pugh replied as he set

294

about damping down the stove. 'Wait out the daylight and then set off as soon as it's dark tonight.'

To Esme, it all seemed rather casual — too casual. 'Should I just go home and wait?'

The aircraftsman shrugged. 'It's what *I* would do.'

'Yes,' she said, his answer doing nothing to still her fears. 'Well, then I'll say goodnight and see you this evening.'

'Yes, ma'am. 'Night, ma'am. Mind how you go.'

Despite having to concentrate on negotiating the country lanes, Esme found her thoughts continually wandering, only realising the fact when she had to brake sharply to make it safely around a bend. Not knowing what had happened to Jack was agonising. Where was he? He must have made it to France in the first place or else word would have reached them by now. Was it possible his landing had been tricky — as he had hinted they sometimes were — and that damage to the Lysander had meant he couldn't take off again? Had he been shot at, sustaining damage in that way? Was there a mechanical problem with his plane? Or was it, as Aircraftsman Pugh had suggested, simply a case of bad weather? Any and all of those were preferable to the picture of him being picked up by the Germans. Unfortunately, the only way she would find out was when she returned to the airfield tonight — after a whole excruciating day's wait. Equally unfortunately, she understood now why Jack had chosen not to propose to that young woman: when he'd said that the waiting around, not knowing, would be torture for her, he'd been right.

Bringing the Austin to a halt in the stable yard, she sat for a moment trying to gather her thoughts. Noticing from her wristwatch that it was a few minutes after

295

six, she supposed she should try to sleep, even if it was unlikely that she would succeed. After all, when Jack returned this evening, she would still be required to drive this French agent to his meeting on Dartmoor. So, yes, she would go to bed.

Stepping in through the back porch, and seeing light in the passageway, she realised that someone was already up, the chinking of china telling her they were in the kitchen. Poking her head around the door, she saw Louise filling the kettle. 'Any chance you're making tea?'

'I am.'

'Coming in or going out?' she asked, crossing to the dresser to fetch another cup and saucer, and nodding to the fact that Louise was in uniform.

'Just back from the midnight shift. Turned out to be quite an eventful night.'

In her exhaustion, Esme yawned. 'Really?'

'Well, when I say *eventful*, I mean dreadful. But then perhaps you've already heard.'

With no idea what her cousin was talking about, Esme frowned. 'Heard what?'

'About the aircraft that was shot down.'

Realising what her cousin had just said, Esme thrust a hand to the edge of the sink. 'What sort of aircraft?'

'That's the thing. Down the coast, the post who were first to spot it couldn't pick out any identifying marks. So, they telephoned through to Control. Next thing we know —'

With the sound of her heart pounding in her ears, all Esme caught after that was fragments. *Scrambled . . . shot down . . . lost in the sea . . .*

'When . . . was this?'

'A little after three.'

'But it was . . . German. The aircraft shot down was German.'

'German? No, that's why there's such a to-do,' Louise said. 'Turns out it was one of ours. Unmarked, if you can believe that.'

'I . . . have to go.' Swivelling blindly about, Esme thrust her hand into the pocket of her gaberdine and fastened her fingers around her keys.

'Golly, Esme, are you all right? You're as white as a —'

'Sorry but I have to —'

Please don't let it be Jack, Esme willed as she tore along the corridor, darted out through the porch and dashed straight across the yard. *I'll give up seeing him, anything, just please don't let it be Jack.*

Fumbling the key into the Austin's ignition, she started the engine, reversed across the gravel, engaged first gear and accelerated up the drive and out through the gates. When she reached Woodicombe Cross she drove straight over the junction without even slowing down. *Please let this just be a coincidence. Please!* Frustrated at having to keep her speed down in the dark, she gripped the steering wheel hard and stared fixedly out through the windscreen, each turn along the way made without even noticing.

Eventually arriving at Pond Farm, she swung the Austin in through the gate and came to a stop alongside an expensive-looking saloon. Hurrying around the front of it towards the hut, she noticed the leaping jaguar ornament on the bonnet. Somebody important was here. It didn't bode well.

Taking no more than a second to steel herself first, she opened the door. Inside, Group Captain Hall was talking on the telephone while another officer, who appeared from the amount of braid on his cuffs to be more senior, was staring at the wall map of the English coast.

'Well I certainly don't envy the poor sod who has to tell Air Vice Marshall Carey-Soames,' Group Captain Hall shouted into the telephone.

From where he had been standing in the far corner, Aircraftsman Pugh came towards her. As he did so, she glanced to the blackboard. Just as she'd expected, there was still only one name on it: no one else had set off from here in the last few hours.

'Sorry, ma'am,' Aircraftsman Pugh said. Putting a hand under her arm, he drew her into the corner. 'Group Captain Hall is just trying to find out what happened.'

To Esme's surprise, all she felt was a kind of numbness. 'It was definitely him, then.'

'It will be a while yet before we know for certain . . . but no other pilot from any base in this sector is overdue or unaccounted for.'

Still, she felt nothing. 'What happened?'

'Unclear,' Aircraftsman Pugh lowered his voice to say. 'Since no one knows this squadron exists, the group captain is having difficulty establishing the details. But it seems that in the absence of any markings, the Lysander was taken to be enemy. And one of our own fighters was scrambled to intercept.'

Intercept. What a cold and mechanical word for the taking of another life — for the taking of *two* other lives.

'It couldn't be that they survived?' Despite knowing it unlikely, she had to ask. If there was any hope whatsoever that Jack was alive, she had to know.

Slowly, Pugh shook his head. 'Direct hit. Went down

298

in the sea. Even if he was still alive when he went in, at this time of year it would have taken less than five minutes for the cold to get him.'

Across the room, Group Captain Hall was on the telephone again. 'Mistake or not, I wouldn't want to be in the shoes of whoever scrambled that ruddy Mosquito. Not only have you shot down my best pilot, but you've cost us the French Resistance agent he was bringing in as well. And this wasn't just any old agent, either. He was a member of this new Réseau Écarlate lot. By all accounts, Churchill considered his knowledge critical to a forthcoming operation. Absolute mess, the whole bloody thing.'

'I think,' Esme whispered to Aircraftsman Pugh, 'I had better go.'

'All right, ma'am. But take it easy going home.'

Despite nodding, Esme had no intention of returning to Woodicombe. So far, she'd managed to keep her composure — although she guessed that was largely down to being in shock. Once the news sank in, it would be a different story. Either way, she knew that for some time yet, she wouldn't be able to face Louise — nor Aunt Kate, both of whom seemed to possess an uncanny knack for reading her mind.

Instead, nosing the Austin out of the gate, she pointed it in the opposite direction. Less than a mile on, she pulled up in front of The Fleece. Even at the sight of Jack's MG parked outside, she remained dry-eyed.

Shunning the front entrance on the basis that it would probably be locked, she went down the side path and around the back. Arriving at a door that she hoped led into the scullery, she tried the handle. And when it opened, she stepped inside.

'Hello?' she called out.

Bustling through from the narrow hallway came Mrs Luscombe. 'Oh, hello there, love.'

'I'm terribly sorry to barge in like this . . . at such an ungodly hour, but would you mind if I just . . .' She gestured along the hallway.

''Course not, dear. But I don't think he's back yet. Said he was on late duty last night.'

'You don't mind?'

Mrs Luscombe chuckled. 'I seen the way he looks at you, love, so no, you go right on up and wait, if that's what you're minded to do. Pop back down if you want a cuppa.'

At the top of the creaky flight of stairs, Esme arrived at a tiny landing to find just three doors. Since one of them stood partly open, she could see that it was a bathroom. From one of the others came the drone of the BBC Home Service. Tiptoeing to the third door, she reached out and turned the knob. Beyond it, the room was in darkness. Leaving the door slightly ajar, she stepped inside, waited for her eyes to grow accustomed, and then gingerly felt her way further in. When her hand met the edge of what she imagined to be a table, she extended her fingers and groped about. When they then found the base of a lamp, she felt for the switch. In the resulting yellowy glow, she crept back and closed the door.

A quick look about the room revealed that it was compact but comfortable: double bedstead covered with a patchwork quilt; washstand; tallboy, one of the doors to which stood partly open to reveal a row of air force blue shirts. But it was the small bureau she'd initially thought to be a table that drew her attention, its lowered flap home to an assortment of personal

300

items. Spotting among them Jack's driver's licence, she flicked open the dog-eared cover. *Suffolk County Council.* Yes, she remembered him mentioning growing up there. Struggling to read the name written underneath, she held it to the light. John Mortimer Carey-Soames. *Well I don't envy the poor sod who has to tell Air Vice Marshall Carey-Soames.* Recalling the group captain's words, she frowned. Coincidence? Unlikely. Staring down at the driver's licence, she read the address: Long Farley Hall, Long Farley, Suffolk. Carey-Soames. And yet Jack was entirely without airs or graces. Indeed, he'd told her more than once how he'd upset the top brass by turning down promotions because all he wanted to do was fly. Now his comments made sense. Included within that *top brass* was his father.

Replacing the driver's licence, she picked up a signet ring. It was clearly a family heirloom, the gold of the band worn perilously thin at the back, the crest on the front barely still discernible. Perhaps it had belonged to a grandfather. Had Jack worn it when they'd been together? That she couldn't recall unsettled her; if her memory of him was already fading, for how long would she remember him at all?

Idly, she lifted a fountain pen and then replaced it. Then she aligned a pair of cufflinks. These few items — personal, and yet at the same time anonymous — might be all that remained of this warm and wonderful man. How cruel. How wasteful. How utterly, utterly avoidable.

With that, she finally started to cry. And, unable to think of anywhere she could go for comfort, or of anything she could do to lessen the pain suddenly tearing her in two, she kicked off her shoes, folded back the

301

quilt covering his bed, and climbed in. Flight Lieutenant Jack Carey had flown his last mission. He was never coming back. She would never know how they might have loved. Her chance to choose whether to go forwards with him into the unknown, rather than back to the familiar, had been taken out of her hands.

18

Above All Else

'Oh, *there* you are! Thank heavens. I was just about to send out a search party.'

Climbing out of the Austin back at Woodicombe, Esme buried an urge to sigh in dismay. She'd been hoping to go straight in through the house and up to her room without anyone seeing her. Now she would be forced to explain to Louise why she had been gone for the best part of seven hours. And why, despite trying to tidy herself up before creeping out of The Fleece, she looked as though she had spent most of that time crying, even though she'd actually spent it in an exhausted and unrefreshing sleep.

'No need for that,' she said, locking the car door and slipping the keys into her pocket.

From where she had been on her way to the porch, Louise waited for her to catch up. 'Essie, are you all right?'

Holding herself rigidly, Esme shook her head. 'Not really.'

'Oh dear. The pilot. He was one of yours. You knew him.'

At the feel of Louise's hand on her arm, Esme struggled to hold back tears. 'Rather well, actually.'

'Tell you what, you go on upstairs, and I'll bring us some tea.'

Unable to summon the wherewithal to refuse, Esme nodded. Waking up in Jack's bed barely an hour previously, she'd had no idea what to do, knowing only that she would prefer not to go back to Woodicombe, where there would be little chance of being left alone. Eventually, realising that she would have to return at some point, she had got up, done her best to pull herself together and crept out. She'd felt mean leaving without telling the Luscombes what had happened to Jack but had chosen to spare herself the agony of having to relive the details.

And now here she was, back in her own room, desperate to confess to the extent of her latest loss but unable to breathe a word of it to anyone. Since it was going to be nigh on impossible to hide her distress, she would have to say something. But what? She couldn't tell the truth or even anything close to it. Besides, what was the truth? It wasn't as though she had committed adultery: *thinking* about being unfaithful to one's husband was a world away from actually going through with it. Cruel irony that Jack's death should spare her the agony of having to decide whether or not to spend the night with him. *Spare her the agony.* Huh. She would far rather endure that agony than this.

With that, Louise arrived. Carrying a tray of tea things, she set them down on the table.

'I ummed and aahed about bringing you a bowl of soup — Nanny Edith has made some celery.'

Unable to recall when she had last eaten, Esme shrugged.

'But I thought you might prefer tea first.' With that, from the pocket of her skirt, Louise produced a hip flask. 'Though perhaps with a little drop of something for the shock.'

'On this occasion,' Esme said, 'don't be too sparing.'

The tea poured and, in Esme's case, liberally fortified with whisky, Louise crossed to the easy chair and sat down. 'Do you want to tell me about him? Your pilot who was lost?'

Trying not to flinch at the way Louise said *your* pilot, Esme wondered how much her cousin already suspected and, therefore, how much she would need to admit. Deep inside, she longed to bare her soul — if for no other reason than to be shown some sympathy and understanding. That she couldn't do so was the price of her deceit; duplicity always exacted a cost and seemingly this was to be hers.

Looking up from her teacup, she drew a breath. 'His name was Jack, and he was a flight lieutenant. Apparently, as a pilot, he was one of a kind, handpicked to do a tremendously difficult job. Only the other day I learned that he could just as easily have been squadron leader by now, or even wing commander . . . but because all he wanted to do was fly, he repeatedly turned down promotions. I don't know how old he was . . . about my age, I suppose. And although given the nature of what he did means I probably shouldn't be telling you, his family home is— was somewhere in Suffolk, and this morning I discovered that his father is Air Vice Marshall Carey-Soames.'

'Dearest Esme,' Louise whispered. 'I'm so sorry. What a terrible waste.'

'A *needless* waste. Entirely needless. It would have been bad enough had he been shot down by the Germans — a possibility he would have been alert to. But to be so close to home, and to be shot down by one of his own, is just so utterly cruel.'

'What *we* heard,' Louise began carefully, 'was that his aircraft was unmarked. And that no one at

305

Control had been alerted to his flight.'

'They wouldn't have been,' Esme slowly replied. 'He flew what they call black operations. Scarcely half a dozen people in the whole country know about them.'

'Then sadly,' Louise said softly, 'that explains how it happened, doesn't it?'

Feeling how tightly her fingers were gripping her teacup, Esme replaced it on its saucer and met her cousin's look. 'And that's supposed to make me feel better? Being able to see how it happened makes it *all right*?'

'No, no of course not,' Louise hurried to say. Putting down her own teacup, she went on, 'That isn't what I meant.'

'*Then why say it?*'

Silently, Louise moved to sit alongside Esme on the bed and put an arm across her shoulders. 'Esme . . . is there something you're not telling me?'

'Such as?'

'Such as just how well you knew this man.'

Unclenching her jaw, Esme raised her head but, to avoid meeting her cousin's eyes, fixed her gaze across the room. 'I saw him often. We would sit together and . . . talk.'

'*Just* sit and talk?'

'If you're trying to establish whether there was anything between us, there wasn't. Jack Carey was a gentleman.'

'Forgive me,' Louise said. 'I'm not suggesting he wasn't. Nor do I mean to pry. I'm just trying to understand. Only, for someone you apparently just chatted to, you seem . . . tremendously upset.'

'*Of course I'm upset*,' Esme snapped. 'He was considerate . . . thoughtful . . . in the prime of his life.'

'You know,' Louise began more tentatively, 'if there was something more, I wouldn't condemn you. In your situation I can quite see how —'

'You wouldn't condemn me? For heaven's sake, Louise, how many times must I say it? *Nothing happened* between me and Jack. I wish dearly that it had done . . . but it didn't. There. Happy now?'

'No, of course I'm not happy. But I do understand. You've been through a lot. Scarcely four months back you lost almost everything —'

'And now I've lost even more. I've lost a friend. A warm and . . . and generous friend. Still, what was I expecting? Everyone I get close to dies.' Despite part of her feeling ashamed of her spite, flinging words without stopping to think brought her a perverse sort of satisfaction — made her feel as though not only was she was shedding some of her pain, but that she was casting it upon Louise.

'My dearest, dearest cousin,' Louise began, her tone no less tender, 'that's really not true. You're in shock. You're angry. What happened to your friend is terrible. A cruel waste. But you haven't lost *everyone*. It's an unfortunate and awful fact of war that pretty much no one gets through it without losing someone. You lost Kit. We lost Arthur. You lost dear friends in Brighton. I lost friends in Plymouth. It hurts. The unjustness of it makes you want to shout and rail. But you haven't lost everyone. You still have us, and you still have the Colbornes and the Trevannions. But most of all, you have Richard. And if he could see how hurt you are right now, I think he would be here like a shot —'

'Don't . . . you . . . dare!' Leaping to her feet, Esme

pointed her finger in Louise's face. 'Do not . . . get on that telephone . . . and tell him I need him. Because *I do not.*'

Although Louise didn't flinch, her tone stiffened. 'Well I beg to differ. I think it's precisely what you need. You need to be reminded how lucky you are —'

'*Lucky? For the life of me I can't see why you keep telling me I'm lucky!*'

'You're lucky, Esme,' Louise continued evenly, 'because not only does Richard happen to be in the safest place in the whole of London — as opposed to doing God-only-knows-what thousands of miles away across an ocean like Douglas — but also because he's a wonderful man who thinks the world of you, despite the way that, the other day, you did everything you could to drive him away.'

When Louise paused for breath, Esme cringed. Clearly, she had underestimated her cousin's powers of perception. 'I really don't think —'

'Don't bother denying it. We all saw how you behaved towards him. Even so, as I keep trying to reassure you, *I understand.* You lost your son. You've been trying to wrestle with your grief, trying to battle on alone. But with that very grief can come a sort of . . . recklessness. Not just in your case but for everyone going through the same thing. It's a fact. Which is why, whatever comfort you drew from being in Jack's company, I understand. But now, with the way things have turned out, it seems to me that perhaps the time has come for you to pause and . . . and to reflect . . . to look elsewhere for the understanding you need. Last week, when Richard was here, you weren't far short of evil to him. To my eyes — and to Mum and Dad's, you should know — you seemed hellbent on doing everything you could to make him feel so unwelcome and so unwanted that he left.'

'I . . .'

Seemingly from frustration, Louise got to her feet. And when she resumed talking, her manner was even more direct. 'But just think about this. If, when you emerge from this current bout of grief — and emerge from it you will — you still hope to have a husband, then I suggest you telephone him and beg his forgiveness for the way you treated him. If you need an excuse for the way you carried on, you might blame it upon your exhaustion. Either way, tell him you're sorry and that you'd like to see him. But before you do that,' Louise picked up again, evidently spotting that Esme was opening her mouth to interrupt, 'I strongly urge you to have a bath, get into bed and get some sleep.' Glancing to Esme's travel alarm, she went on, 'At five o'clock, I'll come and wake you so that you can come down for supper. That way, when you do decide to telephone Richard, you won't be doing it from a point of hunger and exhaustion. And then, from tomorrow, we need to get you back into some sort of routine. You need to start sleeping sensible hours and eating regular meals. All the while you're weak from tiredness, then *of* course your mind will struggle. And don't try and tell me otherwise. Now, having got that off my chest, do you want me to go and run the water for your bath or will you do that yourself?'

Too ashamed to meet Louise's look, Esme gestured indifference. But then, reflecting upon her cousin's words, she turned to face her. 'Thank you, but no,' she said, 'I'll see to it myself.'

'Then just make sure that you do. And I'll come and get you later.'

'Five o'clock. Yes. Thank you.'

With Louise gathering their tea things onto her tray, Esme went to the door, held it wide for her cousin to leave and then closed it quietly behind her. Finally alone, she went back across the room and sank heavily onto the bed.

How had she thought she would get away with it? How had she imagined, even for one moment, that Louise would fail to spot what was going on — that she wouldn't notice the strange hours she'd taken to keeping, and what she realised now must have been her wildly unpredictable moods? In truth, she hadn't thought she would get away with it: she hadn't stopped to think about it at all. So swept up had she become with Jack and the prospect of seeing him each time that everything else had ceased to matter. The only truly surprising thing in all of this was that Louise had waited so long to challenge her about it. More alarmingly, if Louise had noticed, then Richard couldn't fail to have done so either. *You're not thinking as clearly as you might believe you are*, wasn't that the accusation he'd levelled at her?

With the sentiments of both her husband and her cousin washing about in her head, she was forced to wonder how she'd got into this situation to start with. Was it, as Louise had suggested — as Richard had also implied — down to her grief over Kit, or had something else previously been awry? Had she already been craving more, even before she'd lost Kit? Looking back upon it now, her daily routine at Anstruther Court had become rather pedestrian — but then with this war on, whose hadn't? Hadn't everyone, everywhere, been battling on, hungry, worn out and utterly fed up?

310

Exhaling a lengthy sigh, she spotted her reflection in the dressing table mirror, her eyes drawn to where her locket lay nestled in the open collar of her blouse. Reaching to undo the fastener, she took it off and opened the tiny clasp. Dearest Kit. How perfect he was. And how fiercely she had loved him! Until he had come into her world — in fact, from the moment she had left The Aurelian — she had been restless, her days bereft of purpose. No matter the activities into which she had thrown herself, nothing had given her anywhere near the fulfilment she'd got from her work in Brighton. But then Kit had come along, and not for one single moment had she regretted having him. She had loved him more than she'd thought possible. Hardly surprising, then, that in the wake of his death, the things to rouse her again had been those that had previously made her feel alive — those that not only presented her with a sense of purpose, but that hinted at secrecy and subterfuge.

Smiling down at the face of her son, she exhaled heavily. The unfortunate reality was that, without those very elements of intrigue, working for Obsidian might have turned out very differently. Had her role been purely about driving — as it would have been had Uncle Luke kept it up — she might, with Richard's full knowledge and approval, still be doing it. Had she done solely what was asked of her, had she never got carried away and decided to delve into what was really going on at Pond Farm — certainly, had she never allowed herself to become entangled with Jack — then she probably wouldn't be in this mess now. Moreover, had she done as Aunt Kate had repeatedly entreated, and joined the WVS, *none of this* would have happened *at all*. Without Obsidian, she would gradually have emerged from her suffering rested and ready to go home, all set to resume her life as Richard's wife. Instead, too grief-stricken to realise that it was even happening — too bewildered to stop and ask herself why, with all that was going on, she was being drawn to another man — she had fallen for Jack and the distraction he offered, had become almost addicted to the way that even just thinking about him made her feel breathless and giddy.

She didn't blame *him*. His proposal had been plain enough: *no promises, no expectations*. No, the mess in which she had ended up was entirely of her own making. In her anguish over Kit, she had clung to the fantasy Jack had woven about them, fixing upon it as her path to salvation. Indeed, had she not chosen to conceal from him that not only was she married but also a newly bereaved mother, he would almost certainly have kept his distance, which was, of course, the very reason she hadn't told him. With the shroud of her grief blurring her judgement, she had seized upon the chance to escape into a world of fantasy, where there was no need to confront the enormity of her loss.

Continuing to stare down at the photograph, she heaved yet another sigh. She'd often heard it said that hindsight was a powerful tool, but how foolish must she have been to think that she could simply bury such an all-consuming grief? Her son — the little boy whom she had loved to the ends of the earth — had been ripped from her life, and so, of course she was grief-stricken! And the natural route through her grief ought to have involved mourning — for however long it took. If nothing else, trying to avoid the sorrow she felt had been selfish, and disloyal to Kit. Faced

312

with grief, some people chose to adopt a stiff upper lip or maintain that it was a case of *least said, soonest mended*. But that didn't mean that for her, wallowing and wailing and feeling lost would have been wrong. Belatedly, that much was now plain.

Carefully closing the locket, she turned it over and stared down at the inscription on the back. *With grateful thanks on the birth of our son.* But when she folded her fingers so tightly over the words that her fingernails dug into her palm, she was struck by a realisation. It wasn't too late. It wasn't too late to mourn for Kit. Nor was it too late to make amends with Richard. It almost had been. Indeed, were it not for Jack's death, it more than likely *would* have been. But thankfully, it wasn't. Thankfully, she could still do as Louise had said. She could apologise to Richard for the way she had behaved; more importantly, she could ask for his help in mourning their loss and making a proper recovery. Avoiding him, and avoiding her grief, had to stop. And it had to stop now. The person to help her through this was her husband, as it should have been throughout. It was time to let him back into her heart.

Getting up from the bed and taking in the crumpled state of her blouse, she realised that Louise was right about something else, too: she was in desperate need of a bath, some sleep and something to eat. With those immediate needs addressed, and with her memories of Jack respectfully consigned to a safe but distant corner of her heart, she would telephone Richard and set about repairing their marriage . . . always assuming, of course, that was what he still wanted, too.

* * *

313

'Richard? Hello? Are you there?'

'Esme. Yes, I'm here. What's the matter now?'

'The matter?' It was after dinner that evening and, true to her resolve, and from the privacy of the study, Esme had dialled the number for her husband. Unfortunately, now that he was on the line, his manner was rather cooler than she had anticipated. Although, given the way she'd left things with him, should she really be surprised?

'These days you only seem to telephone when you want something.'

Having been tracing her forefinger idly across the leather desk blotter, she froze. The rebuke was well deserved.

'I'm sorry,' she said. 'I should have asked, is this a bad time? Have I caught you in the middle of something? Only, if I have —'

'No. No, I was just on my way to the canteen for something to eat.'

'Oh. Yes. Well, I won't keep you.'

'It's all right. Go on. What do you want?'

Despite squirming at the brusqueness of his tone, Esme determined not to beat about the bush. 'I'm hoping you can find your way to forgive me.' Pausing just long enough to draw breath, she hastened on, 'When you came to visit, I behaved appallingly. While I didn't want to hear it at the time, you were right — I haven't been thinking clearly.' Despite pausing for slightly longer this time, at the other end of the line there remained only silence, leaving her no choice but to plough on. 'I was so desperately sad . . . felt such a powerful need to fill the hours in order to stop dwelling on what had happened to Kit, that I jumped at anything seeming to offer relief. I haven't done anything I regret, nor did I truly put myself in harm's way . . . but I see now that I could have done.' Feeling as though the hardest part of her confession was out of the way, she kept going. 'You were also right when you pointed out that I was tired. Through no fault of yours, you arrived at the very moment where my . . . where my exhaustion was beginning to overwhelm me, another thing of which I wasn't aware at the time. That being so, I didn't want to hear what you had to say — nor did I listen to Louise. In short, I accused you of some terrible things, for which I apologise unreservedly.'

This time when she stopped speaking, Richard broke the silence.

'That was a very gracious apology, which of course I accept. Looking back, we could both have conducted ourselves differently. *I'm* not proud of how *I* behaved, either. I, too, was exhausted. Still am. Perpetually drained. Add to that the shock of discovering you were out, alone, at past midnight and well . . .'

Listening to him talking, Esme still didn't truly believe, even now, that being out at night was, by itself, unreasonable. However, if her husband believed it, and if she wanted their marriage to have any sort of a future, it behoved her to pay heed. She had to do whatever it took to put this right. 'Do you think . . . we can put it all behind us?'

'Bury the hatchet?'

'Learn from it and move on was rather more what I was hoping.'

'If that's what we want, then absolutely we can.'

'In which case,' she said, surprised by how nervous she suddenly felt, 'is there any chance you could take a couple of days' leave and come down for Christmas?

315

There will only be a few of us, and it won't be grand, but I'd really like it if you could . . .'

'I'd love to.'

'You would?'

'Silly, there's nothing I'd like more.'

'And you think you'll be able to swing it? After all, Christmas Eve is next Friday.'

'I'll grant you it's rather short notice. But yes, I'll be there. If necessary, I shall simply go ahead and do it. To hell with the lot of them.'

'Oh, darling, that's wonderful.'

'It is rather, isn't it? Now, do let me know if there's anything you want brought down. I have no idea what that might be . . . or whether I stand the least chance of getting it, but if I can find it in time, I will.'

She smiled warmly. This was more like it. 'Bring anything you can think of to jolly things up.'

'Right-o. Will do.'

'Thank you so much, Richard. And goodnight.'

'Goodnight, darling. Try to get lots of sleep and I'll see you soon.'

The telephone receiver replaced, Esme resumed tracing her finger across the surface of the desk. It wasn't going to be plain sailing, she knew that. Ahead of them lay all manner of decisions, including how and where they were going to live. For some long time to come, they were bound to face hardships and disruptions. But, while she couldn't undo the last few months, she could resolve to start over and face it all head-on. When it came to Richard, it was clear that she hadn't fallen out of love with him, nor he with her. Her little dalliance had caused no permanent damage to their marriage. And with that reassurance came the recognition that everything was once again back within her grasp. Together, they could rebuild their lives — howsoever they might look.

More immediately, though, since she had just invited Richard to stay without first asking Aunt Kate, perhaps she really ought to go and tell her he was coming!

19
Glad Tidings

'I'm so glad I thought to invite your folks.'

Casting an eye over the hastily dug up spruce tree Uncle Luke had just manoeuvred in through the French doors and positioned adjacent to the grand piano, Esme nodded her agreement. 'Yes. It feels like fun, doesn't it?'

'You know what?' Kate replied. 'It does. Although I must say I don't envy your mum and poor old Aunt Diana having to spend the best part of Christmas Eve squashed cheek-by-jowl into a railway carriage.'

'Oh, they'll be all right,' Esme replied, her aunt overlooking the fact that they would be travelling first class. 'Get some mulled wine inside them the moment they arrive, and their ordeal will soon be forgotten.'

'Which reminds me,' Kate went on, 'I must fetch out them proper little mugs for it. Your mum's a bit of a stickler for that sort of thing.'

Esme laughed. 'Trust me, Aunt Kate, Mummy will just be grateful to be getting away from Grandmamma Pamela for a few days!'

'Found a hotel to go to, has she, your grandmother?'

'Apparently, she's taken up a long-standing invitation from some old friends near Ascot.'

'Good for her. Anyway,' Kate said, 'handy you still having the motorcar to be able to run to the station and fetch them.'

'Even better that it still has a full tank of petrol.'

When, the other morning, Esme had answered the telephone to Mr Mulberry, she had assumed he was calling with details of another mission and had been preparing to explain that, since she would shortly be returning to London, this would have to be her final run. As it turned out, what he'd actually been calling to say had rendered her news moot.

'Just to let you know,' he'd said, 'Obsidian's been suspended, indefinitely, the upshot being that your services are unlikely to be required again any time soon.'

'As a result of what happened?' she'd asked, the degree of her relief taking her by surprise.

'If you want the official answer to that,' Mulberry had lowered his voice to reply, 'there's to be a review of procedures. But if you want my opinion, now that the cat's out of the bag, and the squadron's activities are known to more than just a handful of people, its very premise as a covert unit becomes untenable. *My* guess is that the operation will be stood down permanently, and the airfield given over to another purpose.'

Then at least *something* good would have come from Jack's death, Esme had thought as she'd stood listening to him explaining; at least no other pilot need lose his life in such wasteful fashion. 'And the motorcar?' she'd thought to ask. 'What will happen to that?'

'Not my department, I'm afraid. But until someone says otherwise, I should hang on to it. Just try not to prang it in the meantime, there's a good girl.'

'—you'll miss doing it, though, won't you? Being out and about.'

Realising that her aunt was still talking to her, Esme frowned. 'Sorry,' she said, returning her thoughts to the present. 'I was miles away.'

'Going out and about. You'll miss it.'

Deducing that her aunt was referring to the chauffeuring, Esme kept her tone light. 'I suppose I will. Although I don't imagine I could have kept going indefinitely. Driving at night was extraordinarily tiring.' Given that everyone already assumed her exhaustion to be down to the steadily increasing hours demanded of her, she saw no reason to disabuse them. 'But I will miss having the Austin.'

'We'll *all* miss you having *that*!' Kate remarked. 'Real little bonus, that's been. Anyway, just so I'm clear, your mum and Aunt Diana arrive on the two forty-five . . .'

'That's right.'

'. . . and Richard's in at?'

'Two hours after that. Not that either of their trains will be on time.'

''Course they won't be. You fancy the government having the cheek to tell people not to travel again this Christmas — to leave the trains free for servicemen. As if anyone was going to heed that instruction after the year we've had! No, we might have another wartime Christmas on our hands, but folk want to be with their families all the same.'

'It's a pity Victor couldn't be here,' Esme said, recalling Louise mentioning that her brother had been unable to get leave.

'Pity about Douglas, too.'

With a quick check towards the door, Esme lowered her voice. 'Still no word from him?'

Kate's sigh was a weary one. 'None.'

'It is becoming rather worrying now, isn't it? Not that I'd ever say so to Louise.'

'Me neither, even though, the longer it goes on, the

320

more I fear for what's happened. If he'd always been unreliable at writing to her, we'd none of us think anything of it. But his letters have always come like clockwork. Still, like I said to the poor girl just yesterday, since there's been no word from his mother either, then you got to think there's a problem with the post.'

'I said the same. Not that it's of any comfort for her to keep hearing that.'

'It's not, no,' Kate agreed. 'But these next few days, we'll make a point of keeping her busy. We'll find her things to do and try to keep her mind off it. Now, what do we think of where my husband's put that tree?'

From where he'd been standing patiently throughout, Luke treated his wife to a despairing shake of his head. 'For all the good it'll do me, I say it looks fine where it is. But if you're not happy with it . . .'

'No, no,' Kate hastened to reassure him. 'Happen you're right. You know, I had thought to wait until everyone arrived so that we could all hang the decorations on it together. But, looking at it now, I'm wondering if it mightn't be nicer to have it done beforehand.'

'Beforehand. Definitely,' Esme said. 'I've promised Louise I'll go with her to the rectory when she takes Nanny Edith's mince pies to the orphans, but the two of us could do it after that.'

'That's that settled then. Tell you what, when you come back along the lane, how about the two of you cut the greenery for the table centre and whatnot? We didn't go to the bother last year but, since we've guests this time, I'm minded to polish up the candelabra and make a bit more of an effort, make a decent show of it. Lou knows where to look for decent holly . . . and

321

where to find mistletoe. Take the handcart from the stables, and Grandpa Channer's old loppers. Bring a few sprigs to poke behind the mirrors, too. Oh, and plenty for the mantels.'

'Will do,' Esme said, turning to head off in search of Louise.

'And borrow my old coat from the porch,' Aunt Kate called after her. 'You don't want to go snagging your nice one.'

On her way down to the kitchen, Esme smiled. She was looking forward to this. A nice little family gathering and some low-key festivities was just what she needed. What she and Richard both needed. What *they all* needed, come to that.

* * *

'I'm sorry you still haven't heard from Douglas.'

It was later that morning and, having been to the rectory to deliver the mince pies and then cut armfuls of greenery from along the lane, the two women were on their way home.

'You know the worst part?' Louise said, trundling the little handcart along behind her.

Fixing an expression of sympathy, Esme shook her head. 'I wouldn't even presume to.'

'It's not having the least idea what's going on.'

'Entirely understandable.'

'It's not knowing whether he's met someone else —'

'As I've said to you so many times, he won't have.'

'—whether he's lying injured in a hospital somewhere —'

'In which case, you would have heard by now.'

'Maybe. Or maybe not.'

'I'm pretty certain you would have,' Esme said, trying to keep from sounding patronising. 'Bad news has a habit of travelling faster than good.'

'That's what Mum keeps telling me,' Louise said flatly. 'She said that when Dad was in France during the last war, word that he was dead came real quick. The subsequent discovery that he wasn't took weeks and weeks. And then it took even longer for him to actually come home.'

'There you go then. I rest my case.'

'But when Arthur's ship was sunk,' Louise continued regardless, 'despite knowing well enough what had happened, it was weeks before they pronounced him lost. And it would have been even longer had Dad not thought to ask Captain Colborne to intervene.'

'For what it's worth,' Esme hastened to point out, her aim being to steer her cousin from drawing the obvious parallel, 'I still choose to believe there's a problem with the post. Either that or else there's a genuine operational reason preventing him from putting pen to paper.'

'Hm.'

With Esme stuck for anything more reassuring, the two women continued on in silence, eventually arriving home to find preparations well in hand: alongside the stables, Luke was splitting logs; in the yard, Kate was beating a pair of rugs. And in the kitchen, Nanny Edith was stood, hands on hips, staring down at two fat geese and a bowl of giblets.

'Good Lord,' Esme whispered as they hurried on past, 'wherever did Uncle Luke get *those* at short notice?'

'I hesitate to suggest Frank Hodge,' Louise replied. 'But if not him, then almost certainly one of his cro-

323

nies.'

'Well, since it is Christmas,' Esme said, wary of courting a lecture on principles, 'perhaps, just this once, we could turn a blind eye?'

For the first time in a while, Louise laughed. 'A saviour is born — scruples be damned.'

From there, having been set to work by Aunt Kate, Esme found herself with no time to think. In the dining room, where Louise insisted on raising all the sash windows *to let in some fresh air*, she grew steadily colder as the two of them worked together to clean the insides of the window glass, dust the skirting boards and dado rails, and then, finally, to remove all the covers from the furniture. From the foot of a step ladder, she directed Uncle Luke in the hanging of hastily put together swags of laurel, pine and ivy. She drew satisfaction from fashioning fragrant and surprisingly respectable table centres from holly, box and bay. And, while Kate and Louise polished silverware and washed glasses, Esme unpacked the best dinner service from the crates in which, for a decade at least, it had lain, unused, in the cellar. That done, she sat down with the others for a late but welcome luncheon of Jerusalem artichoke soup and crusty bread.

The clearing up afterwards taken care of, a glance to the clock told her she had just twenty minutes to get to the railway station. Ripping off the headscarf she'd fashioned into a turban over her hair, and removing the housecoat she'd borrowed from Aunt Kate, she paused in front of the hall mirror just long enough to check her appearance. Yes, she looked dishevelled, but it couldn't be helped. It was only her mother and her great-aunt she was collecting — not royalty. Nor was it, thank the Lord, the Trevannions.

Thrusting her arms into the sleeves of her gabardine and positioning her beret on her head, Esme trotted along the corridor, slowing as she passed the kitchen to call to the others. 'Off to fetch Mum and Aunt Diana!'

'Drive carefully,' two voices called back.

Barely an hour later — the train from Exeter having been delayed by a mere ten minutes — she was back, bringing the Austin to a halt alongside the front porch and helping her passengers out onto the gravel.

'Thank you so much for inviting us,' Naomi Colborne said as Kate came across the hallway to greet them. 'Already, this feels just like old times — you and I here with family. And don't you look well. Must be all this sea air keeping you looking so fresh. But then your complexion always was better than mine.'

Embracing her half-sister warmly, Kate laughed. 'Stuff and nonsense, woman. These days, my face looks more like a slept-in bed than starched linen. But hey-ho. Can't none of us halt the march of time.'

'Sadly not,' Naomi agreed.

Escorting Diana Lloyd on her arm, Esme smiled at the sight of Aunt Kate looking so happy. On the surface, her mother and her aunt couldn't be more different and yet, looking at the pair of them together now, it was plain that their bond, forged during the privations of war three decades previously, was as strong as ever.

'Darlings!' Relinquishing Esme's support to sweep on ahead, Great Aunt Diana held open her arms. 'So lovely to see you after all this time. Dreadful how this war's scattering families to the four corners, isn't it?'

'So nice you could come, Aunt Diana,' Kate replied, submitting to an embrace.

'Aunt Diana,' Louise greeted her.

'Now, listen,' Diana began, grasping Kate's arm and leaning closer, 'in my Gladstone, you'll find a couple of bottles of gin. Fetch me a glass and then put me to work. My eyesight might be going, and my fingers might not be as dexterous as they once were, but I can still remember how to set a table and turn out an immaculately folded napkin.'

'Yes,' Naomi agreed, 'find me an apron and let's set to. I'm sure you'd rather we got stuck straight in than fiddled about with unpacking!'

Watching the scene unfold, Esme experienced the flicker of a recollection: she was standing in the hallway of the house in Hartland Street — the home in Marylebone where they had lived when she was tiny — waiting for Aunt Kate to come home from her volunteering and, as was her habit, scoop her up and swing her around in a circle. In that same memory, looking on from the side was Naomi, smiling serenely, much as she was doing now. Almost four years Mum and Aunt Kate had spent without their husbands during the last war and yet, eventually, despite their continual worries and their worst fears, and the terrible things that had happened to their soldier husbands while serving in France, they'd come through it together and lived contentedly ever since. In fact, they were, Esme thought, watching the pair of them move away, the perfect example not only of wives who, despite everything, were still as committed to their marriages as they had been more than thirty years previously, but a lesson about counting one's blessings.

From there, finding herself charged with putting the finishing touches to the bedrooms — spare blankets, carafes of water, candles and matches in case of power cuts — Esme's eyes kept returning to her watch: twenty to four; four o'clock; ten past. Finally, at four-twenty, it was time for her to head back to the railway station to meet Richard. But when she then had to steady her hand to even get the key in the Austin's ignition, she couldn't believe how nervous she felt — especially since she couldn't wait to see him.

Arriving at the station and parking the Austin directly in front of the entrance, she went straight through to the barrier, where she showed the platform ticket she'd purchased earlier. Far too fidgety to sit still, she shunned the relative warmth of the ladies' waiting room in favour of walking from one end of the platform to the other and back again. Her greatest hope was that she and Richard could find a way to pick up again without needing to rake over recent events, nor to reignite subsequent arguments. Of course, in the long run, it would be better for her conscience if she could just come clean: if she could simply confess to having briefly entertained a dalliance with another man; if she could receive Richard's forgiveness and start over. But she knew from experience that confessions of that nature were only ever self-serving. And so, in the same way that she'd never told her husband how taken she'd been with Greg Hatton, or how, once she'd thought she'd lost Richard to another woman she had rushed back to Brighton to accept a proposal of marriage from Marcus Latham, she would never be able to confess to how captivated she'd been by Flight Lieutenant Jack Carey. Admitting to her infidelity, even if it had only existed in her thoughts, was something she would never be able to do. What she *could* do, though, was remember what those brief moments with Jack had shown her: that she *could* be happy again; that she needn't be defined by her grief for Kit. That she could get on with her life.

'Next train to arrive —' Her thoughts interrupted by the station master calling along the platform, Esme looked up. '. . . from Exeter St David's.'

Turning about and realising how far she'd wandered, she retraced her steps, spotting in the distance the plume of smoke from the approaching locomotive. Any minute now he would be here. And golly, she was nervous! Lowering her hunched shoulders and uncurling her fingers, she drew a long breath of the sharp evening air and told herself not to be daft. Then, catching a glimpse of her reflection in the window of the station buffet, she yanked off her beret, stuffed it in her pocket and ran her fingers through her hair.

With the locomotive rumbling and hissing steam as it lumbered to a halt, the squeal of its brakes setting her teeth on edge, she scanned its length for the first-class carriages and started towards them. And then, there he was, stepping down onto the platform, over one shoulder his weekend bag, in the opposite hand his briefcase, clutched to his midriff a box bearing the insignia of Fortnum & Mason. Exhaling a mixture of excitement and relief, she ran towards him.

'Richard!'

'Darling,' he returned her greeting, his part in their embrace restricted by his luggage. 'Careful, this one's fragile.'

Ignoring his instruction, she kissed him warmly. 'I'm so glad to see you.'

From his face, she read a mixture of amusement and delight.

'So I see.'

'Here, let me take this,' she said, relieving him of the box. 'The Austin's right outside. I collected Mummy and Aunt Diana a couple of hours ago and they certainly haven't wasted any time getting stuck in. Such a pity Daddy couldn't make it —'

'Actually,' Richard said, shifting his briefcase to his other hand, 'we can't go just yet because there's someone coming in on the next train and I said we'd wait for them.'

Someone on the next train? Frustrated not to be going straight home, Esme frowned.

'Who?'

'Shall we see if there's room to wait in the buffet? See if there's any tea to be had? Or maybe a nip of something stronger to keep out the cold while we wait?'

When he started along the platform, Esme had no choice but to follow. 'Richard, wait, *who's* coming in? And how long will they be?'

'Hopefully,' Richard said, manoeuvring the door wide and gesturing her into the crowded buffet, 'no more than half an hour. Look, over there. Far wall.'

Realising that he was indicating a free table, she went towards it. 'Is it Papa?' Pulling out a chair, she sat down.

'No. I did try calling him last night to see if he would change his mind, but no one answered.'

'One of your lot then?'

'No, the Trevannions are all in Bath.'

Small mercies. 'Well, I know it's not Uncle Ned. And I highly doubt it's my grandparents — not with Grandpa Hugh having been unwell again.'

'Correct on both counts,' Richard said, putting

329

down his bags. 'Tea?'

'Please. Or even the *something stronger* you mentioned if we're to be here a while.'

When Richard went to queue at the counter, Esme puzzled over who he might have invited all the way down to Woodicombe without telling her first — and why he was being so secretive about it. Had he, for instance, even told Aunt Kate?

Returning to the table, Richard set down two teas. 'I'm afraid they don't look terribly inviting.'

Peering into one of the cups, Esme was forced to agree. 'You're not wrong.'

When he returned from the counter the second time, it was with two brandy balloons. 'I asked to see the label,' he said, placing one of them in front of her, 'so I know it's not *completely* gut-rot.' Sitting down opposite, he raised his glass. 'To us.'

'To us,' she echoed, and braced herself for a sip of the brandy. About the best she could say of it, as it burned down her throat, was that it immediately warmed her insides. 'So, tell me, then,' she said, 'for whom do we wait?'

'I promised I wouldn't say anything. And so, I shan't.'

'Male or female?' she pressed. If she could narrow it down a bit, perhaps she could guess.

'Not telling you.'

'At least tell me whether I know them.'

'You know them as well as I do. But that's all I'm saying.' Now he was just torturing her. Not that she minded. It was just a relief to have him there at all, and for the two of them not to be at each other's throats. 'So, how's everyone at Woodicombe?'

Crammed into the steamy little buffet, seated

beneath garlands of handmade paper chains strung between the grimy globes of the ceiling lights, Esme explained about her driving coming to an end — but not precisely why — and about Louise's concerns for Douglas. She described her part in preparing the house for the festivities, and the magnificent hamper of provisions Uncle Ned had sent in response to her request for ingredients to make a plum pudding.

In return, Richard told her about life in the dormitory and how, in the War Office, all hopes were now being pinned upon Churchill's latest plans.

Eventually, hearing the station master announcing the next train, they got to their feet.

'Come on, then,' Richard said. 'Come and help me look for them. It's rather a long time since we've seen one another.'

Could he *be* any more cryptic, Esme wondered as she followed him out?

By the time they had threaded their way onto the platform, exhausted-looking passengers were already spilling from carriages and thronging the exit. But, somehow, despite there being barely any light, she saw him immediately and, squealing in recognition, pressed her way through the mass of overcoated bodies to greet him.

'Oh, my goodness,' she exclaimed, grinning broadly as she threw her arms around him. 'You are the icing on the cake! This is perfect, just perfect.'

★ ★ ★

'Right, both of you, please wait here.'

'Esme, darling, couldn't we at least just —'

'Seriously, Richard, please don't spoil this.'

331

In a gesture of defeat, Richard held up his hands.
'As you wish.'

Back at Woodicombe, her instructions issued, Esme
crossed the hall and went downstairs. But part way
along the passage, she had to stop and straighten her
expression; if she was going to keep grinning, she was
in danger of ruining the surprise! 'Louise? Are you
down here?'

'In here.'

Fixing her expression, Esme went into the house-
keeper's parlour. 'I'm glad I've found you. You're
needed in the hall.'

Without looking up from where she was rummaging
through the drawer of her mother's desk, Louise tut-
ted. 'Can it wait a moment? I'm trying to find the —'

'No, it can't. Quickly.' Seeing Louise's frown, Esme
reached for her cousin's arm. 'Come on,' she urged.
'I promise you, this is something you'll want to see.
Although . . . I suggest you take off your pinny.'

Heaving a vexed sigh, Louise untied her apron.
'For goodness' sake,' she muttered, dumping it on the
chair and rounding the end of the desk, 'this had better be important. Anyway, where's Richard?'

'Don't worry about Richard. Just come with me.'
Grasping Louise's hand, Esme dragged her cousin
along the passage and then, at the bottom of the staircase, gave her a push.

'Where am I going?'

'Front porch.'

'Why?'

'Well if you just keep going, you'll find out, won't
you?'

Still grumbling under her breath when she arrived
at the top of the stairs, Louise opened the door and

332

stepped out into the hall. But then, with a gasp, she stopped dead.

'*Douglas? Oh, my goodness. Douglas!*'

Needing less than half a dozen strides to reach her, Commander Douglas Ross swept his wife into his arms. 'Hello, you!'

When Louise started sobbing uncontrollably, dabbing at tears of her own, Esme crept away to re-join Richard. 'Did he really just telephone you out of the blue?' she asked, reaching for her husband's hand.

'He did. He'd hung onto my telephone number, and when he found out he was being posted back here, he decided to get in touch.'

'And when did he arrive?'

'Docked in Portsmouth the day before yesterday. He was due in more than two weeks back, but his vessel had to make all manner of diversions — some to avoid skirmishing with U-boats and once to pick up the crew of a torpedoed cargo vessel.'

'Heavens. Then no wonder Louise hasn't heard from him for so long.'

'Just before he left his old base, he put in a request for a few days' leave to come and see her for Christmas. But with the way things were going, he was beginning to think he wasn't going to make it. Even when he did come ashore, he was whisked straight off for briefings.'

'And is he staying? In England, I mean? Will the two of them have a chance to spend some time together?'

Evidently considering the possibility, Richard pressed his lips together. 'Well, he's been made up to commander and been given charge of a vital operation. So, one would imagine he's set to be here for a while, yes.'

Looking across and seeing that her cousin was now laughing, Esme gave a contented sigh.

'Why didn't you *tell* me you were coming?' Louise was demanding of her husband.

To Douglas, it seemed obvious. 'Because then it wouldn't have been a surprise. Although had I known how long I was going to be stuck at sea, I might have gone about things differently.'

'Come on,' Louise said, 'let's go down and see Mum and Dad. They're going to be so thrilled you're here.'

'Look, darling, I don't suppose —' Having watched Louise drawing Douglas away, Esme turned her attention to Richard. '—there's any chance of a freshen up? I know I should really go and say hello to your parents first, but I feel absolutely filthy.'

Still smiling with joy, Esme nodded. 'Of course. Come on up.'

'You know,' Richard said as he followed her into her room and closed the door, 'these last few days I've been doing a lot of thinking.'

From where she'd gone to fix the blackout, Esme turned to look at him. Something about his tone as he put down his bags made her think she knew what he was going to say. 'A lot of thinking about...?'

'About how we might rebuild our lives — about what we might do from hereon. And whether it might still involve —'

'A certain house in Teddington?'

As he stood unknotting his tie, his countenance gave nothing away. 'Teddington? Why would you say that?'

Convinced she was right, she went towards him. 'Oh, I don't know . . . call it intuition.'

'Intuition or not, one would imagine that particular

house has been sold.'

It was a fair point; they couldn't have been the only people to fall in love with it. 'Perhaps.'

'In fact, I happen to know that it has.'

'Then why,' she said, taking his tie from him and draping it over the end of the bed, 'do you suddenly have a silly grin on your face?'

Catching hold of her hand, Richard pulled her towards him. 'Seriously, if it was available, would you still like to make it our home?'

In her throat, Esme felt a lump form. 'More than almost anything.'

'Which is, rather fortuitously, what I thought you'd say . . . and just as well really because, yesterday, I made the owner an offer . . .'

'*And?*' Now he was just teasing her! 'Richard! Don't be mean!'

'And . . . he accepted.'

The way her whole body chose that moment to soften told Esme that as much as she was overjoyed, she was also relieved. This was going even better than she had dared hope. 'Oh, but that's marvellous!' she breathed. 'Truly wonderful.'

Lowering himself to sit on the edge of the bed, Richard pulled her down onto his lap. 'Seriously, darling,' he picked up again, 'a couple of the things you said when I was here before made me stop and think. Walking along the Embankment the other day, looking at the ruins standing out against the skyline, I found myself reflecting upon the tens of thousands of other families bombed out of their homes — many of them, like us, robbed of loved ones — and I realised how few of them would have anywhere near the same means to start over as we do. It made me realise that

335

by comparison to them, and despite our own loss and everything we've been through, we still have much to be thankful for. But every time I tried to picture how we might move forward, my thoughts just kept returning to Teddington. So, when I made enquiries and found that it was still for sale, I knew I had to seize the moment.'

Esme's tears, when they finally came, flowed with relief. It was going to be all right. She hadn't ruined everything. Richard still loved her, and she still loved him. And, yes, rebuilding their lives was unlikely to be as simple as he was making it sound; it could be years before this wretched war was finally over, before all thoughts of it could be consigned to history, and the forging of their future could be undertaken without the need to wait and hope. But no matter the trials that still lay ahead of them, she knew that together, they would find a way to overcome them.

Until then, she thought, her fingers going instinctively to her locket, she would just be grateful that unlike thousands of other families this Christmas, she and Richard, and Douglas and Louise, were going to be celebrating it with family, in an atmosphere of warmth and happiness and love. And in the depths of such a terrible war, that really was the best gift she could have.

Epilogue

Clarence Square, London
10 August 1945

'Goodness, what a commotion out there! All that noise is making my ears ring.'

'Mine too! But isn't it wonderful to see such high spirits after all we've been through? The whole of London must be out on the street. It's like VE Day all over again —'

'VJ Day, the papers are calling it.'

'Hard to believe it really is over . . . that the whole world is finally at peace.'

Shifting the weight of her daughter in her arms as she followed her parents in through the front door of their home in Clarence Square, Esme Trevannion stared down at the headline on the copy of the Evening News lying on the hall table. *Japan Surrenders*. Even now, it seemed impossible to imagine life without rationing and queues; without hardship and loss; to imagine daring to look to the future and make definite plans.

'Something of a coincidence that we should all be in town on the very day it's announced,' she replied to her mother's observation.

Naomi Colborne smiled warmly. 'It is, yes, and a true shame Papa didn't last just that little bit longer to see it. He would have been rubbing his hands with glee at the prospect of an imminent end to shortages.'

'Good for business?' Esme remarked with a sly grin.

337

'My dear girl, I don't know what you mean! Seriously, though,' her mother went on, 'as Ned put it earlier, Papa had a good innings, especially given how unwell he'd been of late.'

'And did we do him justice?' Esme asked. 'Was that a fitting way to remember him? Eating ourselves full in his memory?'

'It was perfect. It symbolised everything he loved in life — good food, plenty of drink and convivial company in which to enjoy it.'

Or, as Esme thought but knew better than to say, wine, women and song. 'Yes indeed.'

'Besides, it was *his* instruction that his memorial be held in a restaurant rather than a church. If you don't believe me, ask your grandmother.'

Esme returned her mother's smile. 'Oh, I believe you. He was very much a man to walk his own path through life.'

'You're not wrong there!' Arriving alongside them to voice her agreement was Kate. 'I mean to say, who would have thought it? Hugh Russell and I pass my entire life without exchanging so much as a dozen words . . . and then he goes and leaves me Woodicombe? Never in all my born days did I see *that* coming!'

'Have you thought any more about what you're going do with it?' Esme enquired. In her arms, her daughter was starting to wriggle, thrusting out her hands and kicking her feet. 'Poor darling,' she looked down at her to say. 'You need a nap, don't you?'

'To be honest,' Kate replied, 'it still hasn't really sunk in. Although, having said that, last night, me an' Luke explained to Vic about an idea we've had to turn it into a little hotel — you know, now that people will

338

be starting to think about holidaying again. Nothing grand or stuffy, more a sort of home from home.'

With a smile, Esme reached to Kate's arm. It sounded just the sort of thing her aunt and uncle would do brilliantly. 'What a lovely idea.'

'Luke's been totting up everything we'd need to do to get the place up together, and he reckons the sum your grandfather left me to go with it would cover a decent part of the costs. So, who knows? It would certainly be a way to make the old place earn its keep.'

'*I* said I think it's a brilliant idea,' Louise arrived to join them and remark. In her arms, she, too, had an infant. 'I've even told Mum we'll be her first guests — a sort of dummy run, if you will.'

'You and your husband aren't interested in staying on to help run it then?' Naomi enquired.

But before Louise could even open her mouth to reply, Kate had an observation of her own. '*Douglas* seems quite taken with the idea. Fair to say he's grown real fond of the place, ain't he, Lou?'

Raising her eyebrows and giving her mother a dismayed shake of her head, Louise directed her reply to Naomi. 'He might have grown *fond* of it, Aunt Naomi, but while it's one thing to enjoy a stay there with family, it's quite another to rely upon it for your living.'

'So, you never know,' Kate continued unabashed as she sent Naomi a wink, 'it might yet become a family affair.'

'No word yet on when you'll be leaving for Canada?' Naomi went on to enquire of Louise.

'Douglas says a couple more weeks. He lodged all our forms with the authorities in Canada ages ago and so it's just a matter of time.' Her attention turning to her son, Louise proceeded to make soothing noises. 'Yes, I know, lovey, you're tired, aren't you?'

'Perhaps it's time we put them both down for a nap,' Esme looked across at her to suggest, her own child growing increasingly restive. 'And yes, Mummy,' she went on, reading her mother's disapproving look, 'I do know it's rather late.'

'Good idea,' Louise agreed. To Esme, her cousin's eagerness suggested that, more than anything, she would welcome the excuse to escape talk of Wood-icombe. 'Eugene's fighting sleep. And he definitely needs changing.'

'Well don't be too long, the pair of you,' Naomi cautioned them as they left. 'Cocktails at five thirty.'

'Yes, Mummy.'

'Yes, Aunt Naomi.' Following Esme up the stairs, Louise lowered her voice. 'I don't know about you, but I don't reckon I could force another morsel past my lips.'

'Me neither. There was a moment part way through lunch when I thought it was never going to end. Given all the shortages we still have, I simply can't imagine how Uncle Ned and the hotel pulled off such a meal.'

'Neither can I.'

Going ahead of her cousin into the nursery, Esme switched on the light. 'Clean nappies in the basket. Everything else on the shelf by the basin. Help your-self.'

'Thank you.'

'You know,' Esme picked up again, 'I suspect that my most vivid memories of Hugh Russell will always be those where he's sitting at a table, eating. Or at the very least where he has a glass in his hand.'

'Mm. Have you thought what you're going to do with the money he left you?'

Seeing her cousin looking about the room, Esme gestured towards the door. 'Soiled nappies go in the pail.'

'Oh, yes. Thanks.'

Attending to her daughter, Esme nodded. The inheritance she'd been left had been as generous as it was unexpected.

'Just last night,' she said, securing her daughter's fresh nappy with a safety pin, 'I suggested to Richard that once things get back to normal, we look for a little place in the south of France. Perhaps near Biarritz — you know, skiing in winter, beaches in summer.'

'Sounds lovely.'

'It was Mummy who put the idea into my head. She was wondering how long it would be before things there got up and running again. And I suddenly thought what a great place it would be to take the children — see to it they learn to speak French.'

At her use of the word children, Louise turned, wide-eyed, to regard her. 'Did you just say…?'

Realising what she'd just let slip, Esme flushed. 'Oops! We weren't going to announce that just yet.'

'*You're expecting again?*'

Unable to help it, Esme grinned. Deep down, she'd been itching to tell her cousin all day. 'Doctor Cranston says I'm due in the new year.'

'Golly, Essie.' Louise's expression was one of incredulity. 'You're going to have your hands full!'

Esme's grin didn't waver. 'I know. We didn't exactly plan for another one *quite* so soon. But, by the time it's born, this little madam will be eighteen months. And as I said to Richard, if you still want four, then we've got to get stuck in.' When Louise erupted into laughter, sending into the air a plume of talcum powder,

Esme went on, 'Personally, I don't think we'll make it to four. I'm getting too old —'

'Nonsense.'

'— although one more after this next one would be nice.' Staring down at her daughter and tickling her little feet, she said, 'What do you think, darling Eve? Two siblings or three? How many would *you* like?'

'Too many more and your lovely house will be too small,' Louise pointed out.

'Richard said much the same. You know, I'm so glad we bought it in the end. I'll admit that initially, I did have reservations about moving so far from town. We both did. But now, well, we love it. And yes, before you say anything, I *do* know how lucky I am.'

'*I should hope you do*,' Louise replied. 'It's a beautiful house. And thank you again for letting us stay with you.'

'It's a delight to have you. I suppose you'd like *your* next one to be born in Canada.'

'Douglas would,' Louise said, refastening her son's romper suit.

'But he still has no idea what he's going to do once he leaves the navy?'

'Not yet.' Lifting Eugene into her arms, Louise kissed the top of his head. 'There. Don't *you* smell better now. Oh, yes you do.'

'At least I know that Richard will be staying in Whitehall,' Esme said with a light sigh.

'Something to be said for certainty.'

'After these last six years, there is.'

'And now your Mum's got this place,' Louise went on, gesturing with her free hand to indicate the house, 'that's another thing secured for the future.'

'It is. Although of course, she's known her whole

342

life that it would come to her eventually.'

'Grandpa Hugh did right by everyone in the end, didn't he?'

Lifting her daughter into her arms, Esme nodded. Louise was right: no matter his misdemeanours over the years, in the end, Hugh Russell had been scrupulously fair, even bucking convention by recognising his illegitimate offspring. 'Mummy's got Clarence Square — even if she does have to put up with Grandmamma Pamela for as long as she lasts!'

'And my mum's got Woodicombe, with Nanny Edith for as long as *she* lasts!'

'Uncle Ned got the businesses.'

'And *you* got the share that would have been due to your real mother.'

'As you say,' Esme remarked calmly, her own line of descent from Hugh Russell something with which she had long since made peace, 'in the end, he did his best by everyone. Which just goes to show that no matter how hard we might try to . . . well, how hard we might try to strike out on our own . . . to shake off the shackles and the expectations of our upbringings . . . in the end, it's actually our ties to our families that endure the longest, that keep drawing us back.'

'They're the ties that bind us.'

'They are. You know, on our way to lunch, Mummy said something that made me stop and think.'

From where she was settling Eugene into one of a pair of cots, Louise looked over her shoulder. 'Oh yes? What was that?'

'She said that coming as it has at the end of the war, Grandpa Hugh's death feels like the end of an era.'

Her son settled, Louise straightened up. 'I suppose it does rather.'

'But, to *my* mind,' Esme went on, her voice lowered to a whisper, 'standing here now, looking down at Eve and Eugene, and talking about what comes next, I prefer to think of it not as the end of an era . . . but as the start of a whole new one.'

'You should propose that as a toast,' Louise whispered back as, with their children settled into the adjacent cots, the two women crept from the room to go and re-join the family.

Linking her arm through her cousin's, Esme smiled warmly. 'That's a good idea.'

'To the start of a whole new era . . .'

'. . . and whatever it might bring.'

Acknowledgements

Having guided my characters through the *Woodi-combe House* and *On the Home Front* series of novels to their happy endings, this would seem a good time to acknowledge the help and assistance I've had in writing these six books.

Firstly, for her patience, her guidance, and her ongoing support generally, I must thank my agent, Kiran Kataria.

When it comes to the team at Canelo, I should like to express my gratitude to Louise Cullen, who took a chance on my writing in the first place, to Laura McCallen, who, with her editing hat on, exhorted me to 'dig deep' — advice that remains with me to this day — and, for her help with the three books in the *On the Home Front* series, I must say thank you to Emily Bedford.

Finally, to my husband, I say thank you for everything, but especially for your timely reminders that moaning and gnashing my teeth in despair is just part of the process and that it always works out all right in the end.